Love

Pau

CW00493290

BROWN SAUCE

Pauline Lagan

BOOKS

Brown Sauce

Published by Razur Cuts Books (2022), a subsidiary of Nameless Town

razurcuts.com
razurcuts@gmail.com

ISBN: 978-1-914400-72-8

Edited by Dickson Telfer and Gordon Robertson
Proofed by Gillian Gardner
Typeset by Dickson Telfer

Jacket design by stonedart and Dickson Telfer
Door image obtained from iStock

Author photograph by Katie White

Printed and bound by Martins the Printers, Berwick-upon-Tweed

BOOKS

For oor Mary

CHAPTER 1

BROWN SAUCE

Davina Brown was used to being woken in the morning by pricks: noisy bin men; whistling postmen; clinking milkmen. This particular prick, however, was ramrod hard and pressing into the small of her back. It also happened to be attached to the ramrod hard body of Logan McIntyre.

Logan was an old family friend, a friend with delicious benefits. Twenty years ago, his family had moved in a few doors down from the Browns in Gibson Street, in the west end of Glasgow when he and Davina were both ten. Not known for his shy, retiring qualities, even at a young age, he'd promptly introduced himself to the Brown family, impressing them with his football skills, his quick-wittedness, and by letting them play *Super Mario Bros.* on his Nintendo. The fact he had a whole bedroom to himself kitted out with all mod cons had all the Brown siblings green with envy.

The Browns lived in a three-bedroomed tenement. Davina and her younger sister, Marge, shared one room while their parents and two brothers occupied the other two. Their granda, who "needed somewhere to stay for a few days," had become a permanent fixture on the living room couch. There was only one TV in their house, which, as far as the siblings could work out, was there mostly to put ornaments on. Logan, being an only child, always preferred the rabble in the Brown household to the tranquil atmosphere of his own, and he and the Brown brothers soon became inseparable.

Logan, Hector – the eldest of the Brown clan – and Hector's brother Joshua, soon became known as The Three Amigos, and it was universally known that if you take on one, you take on all. With the Brown brothers insisting that their ma always made too much food, Logan appeared more and more frequently at the family table for tea, much to the delight of the Brown sisters. "The more the merrier," Da would say. As if to reiterate this fact, he later added another four to the Brown clan.

As they grew, Davina and Marge vied for Logan's attention. And while Davina used her keepy-uppy ability (her record was 62) and her footballing knowledge to catch Logan's attention, Marge depended solely on her cheery personality, having absolutely no interest in anything boyish apart from boys themselves. Neither sister, however, even if threatened with having their pocket money denied, would ever admit to their attraction to him. Logan, for his part, was apparently oblivious to their attempts anyway.

As the years progressed, Marge's interest in him waned, whilst Davina's blossomed into a full-blown obsession, despite her conviction that Logan never noticed the frumpy, shy tomboy sister, i.e. *her*, yet always had time for the confident, gorgeous, well dressed (but not so bright) sister, i.e. Marge. But Davina had noticed lately that Marge was none of these things; well, apart from the not so bright part. She made a mental note to arrange a liquid lunch with her sometime this week, without the ever-present Robert Clarke. She didn't want to think about her little sister and her obsessive boyfriend right at that moment; she had another pressing matter to attend to. Reaching behind her, she fondled Logan playfully.

'Ah, just what I need,' she said. 'My very own early morning alarm cock.'

'Yip, and it's set to go off at any minute.' Slowly, Logan ran the tips of his fingers down the side of Davina's body. She quivered at his touch, but didn't try to stop him. His hand ventured further down and stroked her bum. 'I could do this all day,' he said.

'What! And not touch the same bit twice?' She never could pass up on the chance to berate herself.

'Aw, very funny.' He pulled her so that her back was flat on the bed, and then straddled her. Shuffling his shoulders to the groove, he hummed 'Baby Got Back' by Sir Mix-a-Lot, the song that opens with a reference to big butts.

Davina recognised the song. 'Well, that'll be the two of us that are into big arseholes,' she said, trying to look serious, but couldn't hide the smile in her eyes. She leaned over and picked up the packet of mints that were always strategically placed on her bedside cabinet and took one out for both of them. Logan, being all too familiar with Davina's morning mouth phobia, took his mint, no questions asked. He looked down at her and a huge smile crept across his face.

'What's so funny?' Davina asked. His smile was infectious and she found herself unable to contain hers.

'Oh, I was just wondering why we can't possibly kiss in the morning until we've either brushed our teeth or chewed one of these mints, and yet my dick seems to taste just fine at any given time.'

When she was younger, Davina used to blush at the drop of a hat, but over the years she'd grown more confident and hardly anything embarrassed her now.

Right at this moment, though, even her ears were burning. *Bloody McIntyre.* His vibrating stomach felt so hot against hers that she couldn't help but be turned on. She stuck her well-manicured nails deep into his back, and dragged them downwards at a ridiculously slow pace. Leaning up on his hands, Logan stretched his head and shoulders as far back as he could.

'Aaaaaaah!' he grimaced, looking down at her. The sound of his laughter had stopped, but it was still there in his gorgeous blue-green eyes. The smile that spread across his face had Davina involuntarily spreading her legs. The now familiar look that passed between them spoke volumes, and when he finally kissed her, it was slow and caressing with just a hint of tongue. His hand was travelling at a leisurely pace down her now taught, curvy body until he reached her pubic hair. Giving it a gentle tug, he then explored her wetness, first with one, then two fingers, teasing her mercilessly. Replacing them with the tip of his dick, he taunted her with slow circular motions that had her, unashamedly, pushing herself down the bed and down onto him. *Jeezo, McIntyre, this is torture.* Grinning, he removed his weapon of torment and reached above her, feeling for the silk scarves they had used to tie him to the bedposts the night before. Realizing what he was planning, Davina tried to wriggle free.

'Oh no, you don't,' said Logan. 'What's good for the goose . . .'

As he was securing her hands, she rubbed her knee against his erection whilst biting his nipple.

'Ouch! Holy shit, Davina!'

She'd been so focused on his dick, she'd never noticed how hard she'd bitten him. As he pulled away from her, she noted the small red patch on his nipple. She tried reaching for him, but the restraints dug into her wrists.

'I'm so, so sorry,' she implored. *Oh my God, I must remember he's not one of my clients.* She could feel the heat rising up through her neck again.

'Don't you dare be embarrassed,' Logan reassured her. 'That was one of the hottest things I've ever felt. However, I do feel a little retribution is in order.' The look Logan gave her was criminal in its intensity, causing the heat in her body to change direction and make her even hornier. Rubbing her legs together at the top to try and alleviate some of the frustration she was feeling, she realised he was watching her and her embarrassment returned. *Shit.*

'Could you scratch my thigh please?' she asked with a smile. 'It's a bit itchy.'

'Oh, I know you've an itch that needs some attention, Davina. Don't worry, I'll take care of it.' His dick was between her legs again, pressing into her just a little, then pulling out, torturing her all over again. 'Is this where it's itchy?'

He kissed his way down to her erect nipple, looked up at her and smiled, then bit his teeth together with a loud clicking sound. She inhaled sharply, his intent obvious. His bite was sharp, and the impact hit her right between the legs. Logan chose that precise moment to ram into her, thrusting before she'd had a chance to exhale. The top half of her body jerked up and the restraints stung her wrists a second time. The suddenness and harshness of his actions were new and she couldn't believe how wet she had become. The noises that were coming from both of them were throaty and loud. This, too, was totally out of character for him. With his tongue, he flicked the nipple that had been the object of his attack a

11

moment before, the sensation again feeling hot-wired to her crotch. She was at his mercy, but didn't want him dictating all the play, so she thrust her hips up with the same force he was using to thrust his down. *This should definitely be an exercise programme they have on at six in the morning instead of all that aerobics shit. And to think the family believe my new found figure is down to hillwalking.*

'God, Davina! I'm going to come if you don't stop that.'

But she didn't. She was enjoying herself too much, watching him come apart so quickly. Applying more pressure to her thrusts spurred him to go faster, and he pressed his mouth to hers. There was nothing delicate about his tongue this time; licking her open lips, he thrust his tongue in and out her mouth like a man possessed. Moaning, she could feel her orgasm building at a rate of knots.

'Logan . . . Oh my God . . .' Before she could finish her sentence, Logan let out a loud, guttural moan and then stilled. Hungry to experience the same ecstasy, she writhed below him . . . 'Oh my God! Ohhhh myyyy Gaaaawd!'

He pumped into her again, the sensation wracking her body, pleasing every last drop out of her. Slouching forward, his damp forehead fell on her chest.

'Sorry, Davina. I couldn't hold back any longer.' Logan's breathing was as labored as her own.

'Are you joking?' she said, incredulously. 'That was amazing. Plus, you've got a train to catch, so we'd no time for a leisurely fuck.'

'Leisurely fuck?' he muttered, defensively.

'You know exactly what I mean.'

The grin that was plastered on his face was all the proof she needed to know she was right. He undid the ties, kissed her sweetly – lips closed, no tongue, just the way she liked it – then collapsed next to her.

It took a good few minutes before they got their breath back. Davina stretched out lazily, then faced Logan, following his gaze around her cream and purple bedroom. She'd chosen those colours because they reminded her of the reason she could afford to buy her parents' holiday bungalow near the River Ness in the first place.

The bungalow had belonged to Davina's great-granma, Bessie Simpson, a great advocate of the suffragette movement. With her strong belief in women's rights, Bessie, in her infinite wisdom, had decided that the bungalow was to be handed down to the eldest daughter of every future generation. Apparently this had caused a huge rift in Ma's family, but Davina's da had stood firm on his wife's behalf and the holiday home had been handed down to its rightful owner. The upkeep for both this place and the family home in Glasgow had proven too much for her parents though. The leaky roof and lack of central heating caused serious problems in the winter, and since Scotland's summer was basically winter-like anyway, they had problems all year round.

When Davina had first approached Ma with what she'd thought was a solution to everyone's problems, she'd been greeted with suspicion. How could she possibly afford to buy it and pay for all the work that needed done? Davina also had to overcome her ma's sense of guilt at offloading the problem of the bungalow onto her daughter. Davina assured her that that wasn't the case, and that with her savings and a loan from the bank, instead of a mortgage, she'd be able to afford it no problem. Little did Ma know that Davina actually bought the bungalow outright with her well-earned "hospitality" money.

Davina had also pointed out that, like all the generations before, the bungalow would belong to the eldest daughter in the family, although Ma was quick to point out that no money had ever changed hands in this agreement. Davina gently reminded her that she'd only come into possession of the bungalow after the death of her own ma, and that since she was going to live forever the bungalow would eventually become a mound of rubble with no use to anyone. This had at least made Ma smile. Then Davina assured her that if they did it this way, she and the rest of the family would still be able to enjoy the bungalow without the worry and stress it was obviously causing her and Da. After eventually talking Ma round, they'd had a family meeting where Davina had promised them that once she'd finished refurbishing they'd all be more than welcome to come for as many visits as they liked. This excited the four youngest Browns and appeased everyone else, except Da. He soon changed his tune, however, when the money from the sale came through and they were able to buy the tenement house they'd stayed in all their married life for a fraction of the price it was worth, due to the Government's Right to Buy scheme. They refurbished, redecorated, and still had a tidy wee sum left in the bank, which went a long way in paying for Da's horses, and for nights (and days) in the pub.

Davina's bedroom in the bungalow was minimally decorated, with two of her favourite paintings hanging on the wall. Davina loved her family life and loved children, hoping one day to be a mother to maybe two or three kids herself, so it was no surprise that the paintings that hung on her wall portrayed children having fun. Her

14

favourite of the two showed a boy of about four standing on the top ledge of a chute, scanning the horizon, and a girl behind him looking down, annoyed at a boy in dungarees pushing her up the steps, while a third boy behind them patiently waited his turn. Davina loved this painting and the feelings of happiness it stirred in her, but what she loved most was its title, *Social Climbers*, and while that's probably what they'd become in later life, their interest in climbing only the chute's ladder was perpetual in the permanence of the painting.

The rest of the walls were bare apart from the small window she'd needed to replace. Now, no matter how windy it was outside, she was protected from its screech and its cold. The cupboard in the corner of the room housed books, CDs, a couple of board games, and mementos from her family's childhood. Hidden at the back was the most important item: a suitcase with a combination lock, the contents of which helped her pay for the bungalow, her little slice of heaven.

Logan interrupted Davina's daydreaming. 'I've always liked coming up here. It's so peaceful, and the scenery's amazing. You've done well for yourself, buying this place off your ma and da. I bet it wasn't cheap! You've got it fair braw.' Davina knew he wasn't prying, it wasn't in his nature, but she feigned a surprised look anyway.

'Holy shit. That's shocking. Why not just say "How the hell can you afford this?"' Caught off guard by Davina's response, Logan looked genuinely mortified, stammering out a response of his own.

'I . . . didn't mean to imply–' He stopped mid-sentence when he saw the smile Davina was trying to suppress, and shook his head. 'That's not funny,' he said, his smile contradicting him.

15

'Not even a wee bit?' *My God, an embarrassed Logan. That's new.*

'No.' He pushed her playfully. 'Not even a wee bit.'

'It wasn't that pricey,' she said. 'The weather had taken its toll on the outside and the damp had got inside. It was the perfect solution. I needed a place of my own anyway. Home is still too crowded, even with a few of us gone. And it's helped Ma and Da. They were struggling with the upkeep of two places. It's good it's been kept in the family. I've got to do all the things Ma always wanted to with it. I got a firm that our Hector had used for some building work on his flat. Well, they're not going to mess with a policeman's sister, are they? They built on the extension Da always wanted but couldn't afford.' *Because he wouldn't drag his lazy arse out of bed and get a job.* 'And before you can say Bob's your uncle, I'm a homeowner in sunny Inverness. I can burp, fart, scratch my arse, walk about in the scud, and even entertain gentleman friends at my leisure without someone tutting, shaking their head, or saying "That's not very girly-like."'

She said that last part like her six-year-old sister, Lucy. Davina had a soft spot for Lucy, or The Wean as she was affectionately known. She smiled to herself, remembering her brother Joshua saying "We should call her The Ball Breaker," because when their ma found out at the ripe old age of 45 that she was pregnant with her eighth child, their da was sent for the snip. Not that her parents had told any of them in any way, shape or form. Such things were never discussed in the Brown household. Their da, however, had confided in their granda, and the night their parents had gathered all the family in the living room to tell them of the new addition, all hell had broken out. Davina and Hector had reacted furiously to the news, much to everyone's

16

amazement. Granda, trying to calm things back down, had lowered his newspaper, a sure sign of the seriousness of the situation.

'Stop all this shouting,' he'd said. 'And don't worry, there'll be no more weans.' Shaking his head, he'd shot their da an exasperated look through narrowed eyes, which had earned him a crimson-coloured glower in return.

Davina was pulled back from her reverie with a tweak to her nipple.

'Ouch!' she yelped, slapping his hand gently.

'And are you planning on entertaining a lot of gentleman friends here, Miss Brown?' Logan asked.

'Why would that concern you, Mr McIntyre?' she said, getting off the bed. She never took her eyes from his, hoping for a glimmer of jealousy. It annoyed her to find herself thinking like that. What they had was fun, uncomplicated and extremely enjoyable sex, but she couldn't help hoping that her strong feelings for him were reciprocated.

'It doesn't concern me,' he said. *Shit, there's that smile again.* 'Just want to know if I need to book my bonking buddy in advance.'

'Hmph.' There was a smile playing on her lips. *If only you knew, McIntyre.* 'Just don't turn up at my door unannounced. I'd hate to have to turn you away.'

'Oh, I know you would.' He winked at her and left the room, wiggling his sexy as fuck arse as he went, knowing only too well she'd be watching.

They showered, dressed, then ate breakfast together. The only sound other than the crunching of toast and slurping of tea was the radio at a low volume in the background, Liam Ó Maonlaí of Hothouse Flowers

17

pleading "Don't Go!" over a bed of bright acoustic guitars and piano.

'Don't worry, I'll be back within the month.' Logan didn't even lift his head from *The Press and Journal*. Davina slapped his arm playfully.

'Come on,' she said. 'Time you stopped taking advantage of my hospitality and eating me out of house and home. You've a train to catch.'

With a piece of toast hanging from his mouth, Logan threw his suitcase onto the back seat of Davina's white Audi, her pride and joy.

'Swallow that before you get in my car!' Davina insisted.

'Said the bishop to the actress,' Logan snorted.

She watched him over the top of the car as he stood facing her, stuffing the remaining toast in his mouth. He then licked each of his fingers loudly and suggestively.

'Okay, Your Eminence,' she conceded. 'You may get in now.' *Or we could go back in the house and put your gorgeous mouth to much better use.*

'You're thinking dirty thoughts, Davina. I can tell.' *How come the two main men in my life always know when I'm thinking of sex?*

Inside the car, before she'd even put her seat belt on, Logan pulled her towards him and kissed her. 'Thanks for putting up with me again.'

'It's a hard job, but someone's got to do it.' They were eye to eye now and she had a contented smile on her face. 'As long as I'm not entertaining any gentleman friends, that is.' *Like that would ever happen in my bungalow with anyone but you, McIntyre.*

He smiled at her, then relaxed back in his seat. Looking out the window, he asked: 'Is that why you had the extension built . . . to house all your male friends?'

'Very funny, smart arse. No, I did that so when my family come to visit, there's not three to a bed like there used to be.'

'Oh, a threesome! Now we're talking!' *Over my dead body, McIntyre. I'm not the sharing type.*

She punched his arm then drove to the station, the 20-minute journey passing quickly thanks to a mixture of singing and shouting out answers to *Pop Master* on Radio 2. As they pulled into the car park, Davina turned the radio down. Logan breathed out a satisfied sigh.

'Well, I think I whipped your arse there,' he said with a smile. *God, if only.*

'I think I'd have wrapped the car around a tree if that had been the case,' she replied.

Logan's eyebrows shot up in surprise. Then he leant over and, to quote her sister, sucked the face off her. They were slightly breathless when he eventually pulled away. He couldn't let her go though, continuing to hold her face in his hands as he rested his forehead on hers.

'Well . . . as usual, Miss Brown, it was amazing. I don't know what happened to the smart-arsed tomboy I grew up with, but I like this Davina a lot better.' He looked at her solemnly. 'We really should have done this years ago.' *You're telling me.*

Logan's happy-go-lucky look returned and he kissed her quickly this time, reaching over and grabbing his suitcase off the back seat before jumping out the car.

'I'll think of you when I'm in *freezing* Saudi,' he said, not hiding his sarcasm. 'Thanks for the bed, I owe you one. See you later, pal.' *Could've sworn you did just give me one, or was it four? Who's counting?*

She watched him cross the road and take out his mobile. The moment was gone and so was he. She knew exactly what had happened to the smart-arsed tomboy he remembered, and promised herself that, along with her family, he'd be the last person on earth to ever find out.

By the time Davina was back in the comfort of her small kitchen, Logan was safely on his way to Glasgow, and a flight to freezing Saudi Arabia. Lucky sod. She took out her phone. There was a message from Hamish Hamilton.

> Hi gorgeous long time no see!
> Are we still on for tonight.
> Mind and bring my "wee pal"

CHAPTER 2

BROWN SAUCE

Davina first met Hamish Hamilton in Glasgow's swanky Rouge Monte hotel, having landed the receptionist's job there on the glowing recommendation of Mrs Butcher, one of the college lecturers she'd impressed on her way to attaining her HNC in Hospitality.

'You'll be running the place before they know it,' Mrs Butcher had gushed, when told that Davina had been accepted for the position.

Why couldn't her teachers at school have been as generous with their praise? "You've got a great face for radio" was just one of the more helpful pieces of advice – not – that had been passed on to her. Her mother always told her how proud of her she was; that she was great at everything she did, but Davina longed to be told that by someone who didn't feel obliged to, who said it because it was truth. Mrs Butcher fell into that category, although she also gave her, and about twenty-six other people in her class, the best piece of advice she'd ever heard. Near the end of their exams, Mrs Butcher had stood at the front of the class and addressed them all.

'Looking around me today,' she'd said, 'I see lots of young men and women of all shapes and sizes, from all walks of life, and from many different nationalities, but all with one goal: to make something of themselves and their lives. All of you have a history. Most come from

21

humble backgrounds. Do not, however, let that define you; let it *refine* you. This is not a dress rehearsal; this is your life. Make the most of it, and be all you can be. There are no do-overs.'

Okay, so it wasn't up there with Martin Luther King's 'I Have a Dream' or any of William Wallace's speeches, but it definitely struck a chord with Davina. She promised herself she would do everything in her power and use all the skills at her disposal to achieve her goal in life: to own her own property, and maybe run a small Bed and Breakfast somewhere in the west of Scotland. When she'd made this promise to herself, she could never have envisaged the skills she was now using.

Mrs Butcher also taught her to be more assertive and had helped her with her speech and accent. This in turn had helped her with her shy awkwardness, but there was still no denying her Glasgow roots, not that she ever wanted to.

Ever eager to impress and be accepted by anyone and everyone, Davina visited a beautician the day before she started at the Rouge Monte. Her long dark hair was tinted with a few discrete red streaks, her eyebrows plucked within an inch of their lives, and her moustache, legs and bikini line – the latter only after a significant amount of coaxing from Marge – were waxed.

'It was fecking agony,' she said, wincing, as she relayed the experience to Marge and their ma that night as they made dinner together.

Ma was the rock of the family. She stood six foot two inches tall and had a no-nonsense attitude to anything that would disrupt her perfect family life. She'd always been a proud woman, never looking for handouts even when money was scarce. Soup was cheap, filling, and lasted two days, so it was on the Brown menu frequently while Davina was growing up, not that anyone ever complained. A steaming hot bowl of soup and at least four slices of homemade bread meant no-one ever went to bed hungry. All her children loved and respected her, and knew – even though she wasn't a gushy, lovey-dovey parent who smothered her children with kisses and cuddles – that they were her pride and joy. She always gave their da his place, though, and insisted her children do the same. They'd met when Ma was seventeen and Da a 24-year-old welder. It was never discussed openly, but it was well known that Ma's da didn't approve of the attention she was receiving from the much older boy. Davina often wondered how her granda had reacted to the fact his daughter was in the early stages of pregnancy when she'd gotten married.

After her da was laid off from the shipbuilders ten years ago, his less than enthusiastic attempts at trying to find new work seemed to go unnoticed by their ma. She believed his bad moods and ill temper were because, as Da put it, "All the good jobs have been taken by bloody foreigners." So, at the ripe old age of 47, he'd more or less declared himself retired. Over the next couple of years, the bulk of his redundancy money was donated, pretty much evenly, to the local bookies and the local pub, The Black Bull. Still, Ma thought the sun rose and fell with him.

Many an argument in the Brown household would end with Hector, the eldest Brown, storming out after trying to get their da to see that what he was doing was wrong. At 21, Hector had moved to Tulliallan to train at the police college. Davina, 20 at the time, and Marge, 18, were both at City of Glasgow College, studying Hospitality and Hair & Beauty respectively. Joshua, at 19, had stunned them all by joining the Army. Then there was the latest, but apparently not unplanned, addition to the family. Henry Stuart Brown was three years old. Having loved them all as kids, their da – in his infinite wisdom – had decided that, even though he could hardly support his family as it was, "It was time for another wean."

With Joshua posted in Germany, and Marge sharing the same blinkered view of their da as Ma, Davina and Hector often spoken in private, at great length, as to their da's reasons for adding another three weans to the family after Henry. Granted, even he couldn't have predicted Ma having the twins, Derek and Kenneth, but he acted like the cat that got the cream on hearing the news. Then, when the twins were three and their ma fell pregnant with The Wean, Davina thought Hector was going to kill their da. The anger and resentment they shared concluded with their unproven accusation that he was using Ma to produce more kids just to get more family allowance money to piss against the pub urinals or place on a three-legged donkey. This was still a sore point with both of them to this day. Ma was adamant they show their da respect, as he was still the head of the house. As far as Davina could remember, Da had never lifted a finger to help around the house in his life. Playing on the fact that Ma would never hear of such a thing, Da was more than content to sit in his chair and watch her skivvy about after him and the four younger kids.

Still sharing a room with her sister Marge, and loving the bond she had with all her siblings, Davina had bit her tongue, studied hard, and hoped against hope to have a place of her own soon. Then she could visit when, and if, she wanted, and not have to witness her da's moods and undisguised selfishness.

24

Ma was at the kitchen sink, peeling veg for the dinner, when Davina told her about her escapades at the beautician's.

'Leave your hair longer down there, they get more of your roots that way,' Davina mocked, mimicking Marge in a conversation they'd had the previous night after Davina had suggested a trim down below might make things less embarrassing for her on the day. 'Honestly, Ma, it was that sore, I thought she was pulling on the roots of my teeth, never mind the roots of my hair.'

Ma was in stitches, as was Marge, who was standing by the kitchen door – but it had only topped up the laughter they'd shared when they saw Davina hobbling up the lobby into the bedroom she shared with Marge. Looking back, Davina realised they probably thought she'd shit herself.

Through her ma and sister's laughter, Davina continued with the story, this time mimicking Betty the beautician's squeaky voice. '"Go behind the screen and strip from the waist down, hen, then lie on the bed behind it. I'll be back soon." Yeah, right, act like this is nothing; a walk in the park. I'll take off my big Evans knickers that two of you could fit into and lie there and pretend I've never been so embarrassed in all my life. Even my fandango was burning with embarrassment, and she hadn't even started yet. When she came back in, I kid you not, she was whistling *The Bare Necessities*. What the hell!'

Marge was doubled over with laughter by this point, while Ma's potato peeling had clearly been impacted by an inability to grip anything properly. Although she was the butt of the joke, Davina carried on, reintroducing the incredulous, high-pitched voice she used to mimic the beautician. '"Let me know if this is too hot, hen." Then she spread some hot gunk on me and– as if we'd known each other for years – asked me "Are you going any holidays this year?" But before I could answer, whateesh! She'd pulled a strip of hair right off my fandango. "Holy shit!" I shouted, and sat bolt upright. The poor girl got the fright of her life and jolted backwards, knocking the wax off the table and whacking her elbow on the wall. What a mess! The wax ran right down the wall and all over my good Evans pants and my shoes. What a red face!'

'Don't tell me anymore, I've peed my pants,' Marge said, running down the lobby to the bathroom. Davina looked at Ma, who had stopped peeling potatoes and had tears in her eyes.

'I'm not joking, Ma. I know I've never experienced it before, but I bet getting your bikini line waxed is sorer than having a wean.'

Ma looked at her. 'Well, Davina,' she said through her laughter, 'it'll be you who'll need to make that comparison one day, because as enjoyable as you've made it sound, I won't be getting my bikini, or any other line for that matter, waxed any time soon.' Then, quite suddenly, she adopted a poker face that stopped Davina in her tracks. 'Promise me that won't happen any time soon, though,' she said, seriously. 'There's more to life than marriage and weans. Enjoy yourself, and see some of this world before you settle down.' *Wow, where did that come from?*

'Like that's going to happen, Ma. Who's going to even look at me, never mind want to have kids with me?'

'Listen to me, Davina Roseanne Brown.' *Uh-oh, she's used my middle name; this is serious.* 'You're a beautiful person inside and out. There's somebody for everybody

26

in this world, and I bet they're a lot closer than you think.' *Like Logan McIntyre?*

Marge burst back into the kitchen, lightening the mood again. 'I've been to the loo and changed my pants, so we're good to go. What happened next?'

As Ma went back to her potatoes, Davina went back to her story. 'Well, another girl came in, took one look at me and Betty, then ran away and came back with the manageress.'

'Aw, God, Davina,' said Marge. 'I know her. I've been asking her for ages for a job. What an embarrassment! I can't go back there now!' With a scowl, Marge folded her arms over her chest. *My fandango's throbbing, but hey, let's make this about you. Selfish bitch.*

'Yeah, right,' Davina scoffed, 'it's not as if they've made me an honorary member. I don't think my face or my fandango will be welcome in there again.'

'But you did get done?' Ma asked, no denying the protective edge to her question.

'Oh yes, and I've got the scars to prove it.' Ignoring Marge's huff, Davina carried on. 'Once Betty had explained what had happened, I was asked if I wanted to continue and I said yes. I was actually excited about looking a bit different with my tache, eyebrows and hair all done for tomorrow. My bikini line was all her idea,' Davina said, nodding towards Marge.

'Sorry, Davina,' Ma said. 'We've been too busy laughing, I forgot to say that you look lovely. The red streaks in your hair are a lot nicer than I thought they'd be. And your nails are really smart too; the red really suits you.' Ma stopped what she was doing and gave Davina a rib-crushing cuddle. 'Never forget . . .'

'There's nobody better than you.' They said this in unison, although Davina never truly believed it.

'Correct! You'll be fighting all those posh businessmen off with a stick,' Ma said.

'Thanks, Ma,' said Davina.

Ma wasn't one to overly show affection, but cuddles were her speciality. After a minute or two, she broke off and went back to the sink.

Marge had stopped scowling at Davina by now, lifting her sister's well-manicured hands and stroking her polished nails. 'Your nails are amazing,' she said. 'I'd love to learn to do that.' *Praise indeed.* Marge was looking at Davina's nails as though for the first time. *Yes, Davina Brown, you've come a long way.* "So what happened next?" Marge dropped Davina's hands, all smiles again.

'Well,' said Davina, 'I got a towel to cover myself, and a complementary hot chocolate, while The Three Stooges tidied up. I told them to leave my clothes though. After all, the whole of Aphrodite's Apex – Jeez, somebody should have been shot for coming up with that name – didn't have to know I was a svelte size 14 slash 16. Then, once the tidying up was done and I'd finished my hot chocolate, I lay down and said to Betty, "No." She stopped stirring the hot gunk, gave me a really befuddled look, and in a gormless voice said, "What?" And I said, "No, I'm not going any holidays this year!"' Marge and Ma buckled up with laughter again, Davina joining them this time. Although it wasn't exactly the best experience of her life, it was still one she'd repeat. She felt like a new woman, not to mention a little lighter with all her body hair gone.

The next day, when the good-looking, tousled, dark-haired, robust gentleman in the Armani suit – *Christ, you could play second row for Scotland* – with the most welcoming green eyes she'd ever seen, approached her with his Gucci holdall, Davina was feeling quietly confident.

'Morning, sir, and welcome to the Rouge Monte Hotel. How can I help you?'

'Morning to you, too . . .' He leaned over the reception desk, the smell of his aftershave like an aphrodisiac. *Christ almighty, do they sell sex in a bottle now?* He read the name on her badge. 'Davina Brown. I have a reservation booked under Hamish Hamilton.'

'Okay, sir. Let me just check we're ready for you.' As she clicked away on the computer, she could feel him watching her. She could also feel some of her confidence slipping away. *Keep it together, Brown.*

'You're new here, Davina.' This wasn't a question, but she answered anyway.

'Yes, I am.'

'Well, can I just say, you're a lovely addition to the place.' *Oh no.* She could feel the heat rising from her chest. *Shit, shit, buggery shit.*

'Thank you. Here we are, sir, room 556.' She took his details, finished checking him in, and gave him the key card to his room.

'What time do you finish, Davina Brown?' *Oh my God, are you actually flirting with me?* She'd never experienced this before and it was a couple of seconds before her brain engaged her tongue, and when it did she promptly bit it. Her hand automatically covered her mouth. *Holy shit, that was sore.* She looked up. Mr Alliteration was stifling a laugh. *Smarmy git.*

'Are you okay?' he managed to spurt out.

'Glad you found that amusing,' Davina replied through a tight smile. *Don't offend anyone on your first day.*

'It would amuse me more if I could kiss it better.' Their eyes locked and the heat Davina felt in her face headed south for the winter. *Jeezo, what are you trying to do to me?*

'It feels better already, thank you,' she said, finding herself unable – or should that be unwilling? – to look away from him.

'Pity,' he said. There was something in his green eyes she'd never seen before.

'Enjoy your stay at the Rouge Monte, Mr Hamilton.' Thankfully, some of Davina's composure had returned.

'Hamish,' he corrected her.

'Okay, have it your way. Enjoy your stay at the Rouge Monte, Mr Hamish.' To her surprise, Davina found herself enjoying this exchange with this amusing hulk of a man, and unless she was totally out of touch with men, he was enjoying it too. His eyebrows lifted and the hint of a smile played on his lips.

'Good looking *and* a sense of humour!' *Did you really just say that?*

She couldn't get her head around this. This handsome, well-dressed, well-spoken man – even his aftershave was doing things to her! – was definitely complimenting . . . no, *flirting* with her. It didn't help that the heat from her confusion that would normally spread from her chest to the top of her head had emigrated south to her nether regions, and was getting hotter by the minute. She squirmed a little, cleared her throat, contained the stupid grin she could feel building and, in the most professional voice she could muster, said: 'If there's anything else you need, don't hesitate to ask.' She lifted some papers and organised them in a neat pile to indicate the end of their business.

'Just the one thing that you have eluded to answer,' he said. 'What time do you finish, Davina Brown?' *Are you winding me up?* Davina straightened her shoulders, smiled, and looked him square in the eye.

'Staff are requested to be polite, well-mannered, and attentive whilst maintaining a profession distance with hotel guests. Sir.' Just as she thought she'd pulled it off, the stupid grin she'd managed to control earlier escaped.

'Hear, hear, very good advice. So, in order for me to decrease the . . .' – he made air quotes. *Bugger, just when I was beginning to like you as well* – '"professional distance" between us, I should book into . . .' Pausing, he looked upwards, tapping his chin with his index finger, and when he lowered his head, there was a wicked look in his eyes. 'The Hilton . . . and I'll leave you to explain to management why one of their most valued patrons has taken his custom elsewhere.'

There was a cross between a smile and a smirk on Hamish's lips. Davina, on the other hand, looked like a rabbit caught in the headlights. *Holy shit! What am I supposed to say to that? This scenario definitely never came up in training.*

She swallowed loudly, then opened her mouth to speak, unsure of what words were going to come out. He saved her the trouble by putting his index finger in it. His finger tasted of aftershave. *Could've been worse.*

'You'll catch flies like that, Miss Brown.' With that, he turned and headed for the lift. Davina's eyes never left his sturdy, athletic frame. He entered the lift, turned, and shot her the most mischievous smile she'd ever seen. The doors closed and it took her a second to realise where she was, and what a gormless expression she was wearing.

'Way to go, Davina. Aw, shucks.' This was said in her best hillbilly accent. 'Us country bumpkins just don't know how to act in front of y'all city folks.'

After she'd done chiding herself, she noticed Hamish's business card on the counter, which said

"Hamish Hamilton, Glenshee Whisky Distilleries Ltd." followed by his email address and mobile number.

Davina stared at the card, wondering why it was there. Maybe it'd fallen out when he'd given her his credit card.

'Uhh,' she inhaled loudly. *Was it possible he left it for me intentionally?* She ran a finger over the gold embossed name on it, not daring to pick it up. The butterflies in her stomach were doing a merry dance as she ran the whole incident through her head, over and over, from the moment he walked up to the desk to the agony of the lift doors closing. Could he possibly be interested in her? *Dafty Brown, Dafty Brown, she looks like a big fat clown.* How reassuring. If ever there was even a hint of self-belief crawling through her, the old school ditty that had stayed with her throughout her life would raise its ugly head and bring her back to earth with an almighty thump. How ironic was it that being bullied about her size had driven her to comfort eat even more? And even though she'd lost a lot of weight, toned up, and was now a lot more accepting of her size, in her mind there was always room for Dafty Brown to improve. She lifted Hamish's card and threw it in the bin.

Compared with the morning, the rest of the day was uneventful. She informed Elaine, the skinny, gorgeous, overly made-up night receptionist, of a couple of guests who'd cancelled and another who'd be checking in late as their flight from London was delayed.

'So, how was your first day?' Elaine enthused, her huge lips done in the reddest lipstick Davina had ever seen. 'Anything exciting happen?' *What, like one of the most handsome guys I've ever seen ripping the piss out of me?*

'No, just people coming and going.'

'Wait till you do a night shift,' said Elaine. 'You see all sorts. When I get fed up doing this, I might just write a book about it.' She laughed, but it was more like a snort. *Bugger. Just when I was starting to like you too.*

Davina got her personal belongings from her locker and was heading towards the door when she felt a firm grip on her elbow. Birling around, she came face to face with Hamish Hamilton. He led her firmly and wordlessly to one of the large, luxurious mauve-coloured secluded seats at the window in the bar area. She'd noticed those seats when she'd been shown around at her induction and wondered if they were as comfy as they looked. She practically sank into the thing, but told herself this was more to do with the design and material than her petite frame. Once Hamish had settled in next to her, he fixed her with a perplexed look.

'Maybe I didn't make my intentions clear when I flirted with you and then left my card at reception,' he said. His face softened. *Shit, he looks offended.*

'I thought it had fallen out your wallet by mistake.' Never before had she experienced the emotions and feelings that were running through her mind and body at this moment in time. *What do you want from me? Yes, we've enjoyed a bit of playful banter, end of. Why are you acting like we had some kind of unspoken agreement?*

'Seriously?' The surprise in his voice was genuine. 'A businessman has never given you his card before?'

How could she tell this handsome, rugged stranger she'd never been given the time of day, never mind a business card, from any man she'd ever met? For some inexplicable reason, though, right at that moment, she felt she could tell him anything. Fortunately, her sensible side kicked in.

'No,' was all she could muster.

'Well, their loss.'

Davina couldn't detect any sarcasm and Hamish's smile seemed genuine.

'I'm sorry, Mr . . .' His eyes narrowed before she corrected herself. 'Hamish.'. He smiled hearing her say his name. 'It's not that I don't appreciate the attention.' *In fact, let me take a picture to show my best pal, Grace.*

'But?' he frowned.

'But . . . I don't understand what you want from me, and I really shouldn't be sitting here in my uniform.'

'Well, in that case, if it would help put you at ease, it would give me great pleasure to remove it.' The tone in which he said this was new to her ears, but sounded sexy as hell. Her face turned beetroot. Hamish licked his index finger and touched her cheek. 'Tsss,' he said.

She didn't think it was possible, but that small gesture made Davina burn even more.

'How hot, if you'll pardon the pun,' Hamish continued. 'I thought in this day and age that blushing girls were well and truly a thing of the past.' He kissed her lips so softly and gently, she wasn't sure it had actually happened. *Wow! What the . . .* 'And seeing you like this makes me horny as hell.'

He sat back and, if she didn't know better, which she didn't, she'd have thought he was trying to compose himself. He rubbed his impressive thighs with his equally impressive hands, lifted his head, and gazed into her wide open eyes. There was a fleeting moment of awkwardness before he dazzled her with his smile.

'You're right to think I want something,' said Hamish. 'You!' *Holy shit!* Before Davina had the chance to react, he took her hands in his. 'Don't look so scared,' he laughed. 'I'm not going to eat you. Well, not just now anyway.' *What the hell does he mean by that?* Taking a deep breath, he carried on. 'In my line of work, I find myself at a lot of boring but necessary events, and I find they're a lot more enjoyable and less annoying if I have a lovely lady escorting me. No strings attached; purely business. I have two such evenings coming up, and if you would do me the honour of accompanying me, I would make it worth your while.' She snatched her hands back. Her whole face was screwed up in disgust.

'Sorry! Let me get this straight. You want me to go out with you, and you'll pay me?' She couldn't keep the disdain from her voice. She tried pushing up off the seat with her hands, but was stopped with the pressure of his on her knees. He looked surprised by her reaction.

'I'm very sorry if I've offended you. It certainly wasn't my intention. Let me buy you a drink by way of an apology.' What the hell was going on? A guy I fancied the pants off was not only asking me out, but was willing to pay me for the privilege? There must've been something I was missing. Did my name badge say Receptionist/Prostitute?

Suddenly a light bulb lit above Davina's head and her self-destruct, low self-esteem barriers shot up. Unable to hide her rage, she leaned towards him, her voice low but clear. 'Very good, Havering Hamish,' she spat. 'You nearly had me there. But you can tell our Hector and Joshua that if they thought they were going to pull off this charade, they should've come up with a better name for their accomplice than fucking Hamish Hamilton. It's laughable, and this . . .' – she gestured erratically with her hands – 'whatever the fuck *this* is, isn't funny.'

Tears threatened, but there was no way she was going to give any of them the satisfaction of making her cry. She'd been on the receiving end of gentle ribbing from her brothers all her life, but this . . . this was different. This really hurt. She didn't handle confrontations very well, and the anger she'd felt earlier was now replaced with embarrassment. She tried in vain, against the pressure of his hands on her thighs, to stand up. 'Please,' she muttered, 'let me up. I've a bus to catch.'

Despite the strange look on his face, Hamish's words were clear and deliberate. 'I know I probably didn't handle the situation very well. Just propositioning you out of the blue was,' he shrugged, 'in hindsight, a bit odd; to you, at any rate. So, again, I apologise, but for me that's just how I operate. I'm 29 and had a shitty experience when I was younger, so I prefer the company of ladies with no strings attached, and I don't mind paying for that privilege. It might surprise you, Miss Brown, but there are hundreds – no, I'd go so far as to say thousands – of men in the world who think like me. Obviously you have issues of your own, but I had no intention of embarrassing or hurting you, far from it. I don't know any Hector or . . . Joshua, was it? And I don't understand why you find it so difficult to believe that I'd want to spend time with you. You're gorgeous, witty, and I was going to say smart, but I'm not so sure now. The credit card I booked in with has H Hamilton printed on it and regardless of how laughable you may find it, I'm quite proud to be a Hamish.' *Holy crap, could this be any more embarrassing? I've ridiculed his name and accused him of being in cahoots with my brothers. Shit. How do I get out of here?*

Davina felt as though she was red from the feet up. She fixed her eyes firmly on her thighs. 'I'm sorry,' she uttered.

'Can we start again . . . please?' He put out his hand. 'Hi, I'm fucking Hamish Hamilton.' His smile was warm, emphasising just how gorgeous he was, but Davina was still mortified with herself. *Mrs Butcher would be so disappointed in the way you've handled this. Is it too late to rectify the situation? Maybe not. He's still speaking to you after all, and he does seem genuinely interested.* She shook his hand. *I wish I was fucking Hamish Hamilton.*

'Unusual name. I bet that's an icebreaker.' She was smiling again at last.

'There you go. There's the girl I met earlier. Now, let me buy you a drink.'

'I can't,' said Davina. 'I really do have a bus to catch. Plus, we're not allowed to drink in the hotel.'

He stood. towering above her. 'Let me give you a lift. It's the least I can do.'

'No, you're okay. It's a bit far.'

'Not the way I drive.' Hamish flung his hands up in a mock defensive pose. 'Joking, joking. And I promise not to get fresh.'

'Pity.' She threw his word from earlier back at him with a smirk on her still red face. *Where did that come from, Brown?*

'Touché, Miss Brown.' He stood, took her hand, and led her to the lifts. 'I need to get my car keys first.' He pulled her inside. The doors closed before she could object.

'I really shouldn't.' The rest of Davina's protest was forgotten. Wordless, he pinned her by the arms to the back of the lift, his gorgeous eyes searching hers for consent. The rush of adrenaline she felt brought a smile to her eyes and mouth. Taking his cue, he excited her further with hard, sensual kisses, his tongue coaxing hers to come out and play, which it did, with gusto. His hands stroked up and down her sides. A ping alerted them that they'd arrived at his floor, but still he carried on with his sweet torment. She was breathless when they finally pulled apart, the look that passed between them igniting

37

something inside her. The plush carpet made her feel as though she'd floated to his room. He opened his door and stood to the side, letting her enter first. *Holy crap, this is really happening. Car keys my arse. You've waited a long time for this, Brown! You ready for it? It's shit or bust.* Inhaling through her nose, she entered the room gracefully, shoulders back, chest out, juices flowing.

Looking back on this moment, as she often did, she was reminded of a poem she'd studied at school, 'The Road Not Taken' by Robert Frost. For once in her life she'd taken what was, for her, definitely "the one less travelled by" and had never looked back since. The room wasn't one of the presidential suites, but was an impressive size nonetheless. Taking off her coat, she placed it on a chair along with her bag.

'Let me show you what I've done with the place,' he joked. He took her hand and gave it a reassuring squeeze, relaxing her immediately. *Holy crap, Brown. Even Grace won't believe this.* 'This is the seating area where I entertain guests,' gushed Hamish. 'Well, I say "entertain", but my juggling skills aren't what they used to be.' Davina giggled and shook her head. *You sound like my granda.* They walked through the room. 'And this is the bar area.'

The dark oak-paneled bar was about five feet across by four high, had two wooden bar stools of the same finish in front of it, and was polished to an exceptionally high standard. Davina ran her fingers over the top. She loved things made from natural wood. She'd wanted to take Standard Grade Craft and Design at school, but it had been in the same column as Home Economics, so with one eye on running her own Bed and Breakfast when she was older, it was a no-brainer. She went on to take Higher Home Economics, passing it with flying colours, as she had Mathematics, English, Secretarial Studies and Chemistry.

'Would madam care for a drink now?' Hamish's French accent sucked, but it made Davina smile.

'But Monsieur hasn't shown me all of his apartment yet,' she said, surprising herself with her boldness. Grinning, he pulled her into him and kissed her again. 'Your wish is my command.'

The bathroom was almost the same size as Davina and Marge's bedroom back home. She noticed he kept his toiletries lined up neatly, a bottle of top end aftershave sitting at the end with its top loose. *So that's the stuff that turns women on in an instant.* The towels looked about six inches thick.

'How the other half live,' she whispered.

'Expenses, Miss Brown,' said Hamish. 'And like L'Oréal say, "I'm worth it."' It embarrassed her slightly that he'd heard her. *Well, at least he made a joke of it.*

'I'll take your word for it,' she replied.

'You should,' he smiled. He opened the door to the bedroom with a flourish. 'And last, but by no means least . . .' Hamish stood aside to let Davina enter first, which she did, and with more conviction than she felt. She'd seen these rooms before, but the sight that greeted her still held her in awe. The rich cream décor with hints of purple here and there was breathtaking. The bed was covered with a plush cream-coloured silk throw upon which sat three silk, embroidered, purple scatter cushions. It all looked luxuriously welcoming.

'Beautiful,' she said, barely audible.

'You took the words right out of my mouth,' said Hamish. She turned to find him gaping at her. *Holy shit!* The heat in his look took her breath away, while the kiss that followed took all her inhibitions with it.

'Come on, the bar's open. And I won't take no for an answer.' He took Davina's hand and led her to a bar stool, lifting her effortlessly onto it. Walking behind the bar, he clapped then rubbed his hands together. 'Right . . . what can I get for the lady? We have a well-stocked bar and an impressive cocktail list.'

Davina watched him with a furtive look. *God, he's stunning.* Hamish's Ralph Lauren top clung to every inch of his torso, the outline of his muscles easily traced. *Lucky top.* He lifted a napkin from a shelf Davina couldn't see, opened it, and held it like a menu.

'Hmm.' He cleared his throat. 'Let me see,' he said, looking at the empty napkin. 'Could I interest the lady in a Long Slow Screw?' *Probably.* The smile was splitting his face, and the laugh that jumped out of her mouth was entirely unforced. *Maybe later.*

'No? Okay, let's see.' He ran his finger down the napkin. 'A-ha, here's one. What about Sex on the Beach?'

The atmosphere between them was comfortable, yet charged. She shook her head in mock irritation. *Never mind the beach, this bar will do fine.*

'A fussy customer, eh? Ah, here's the one. The all-time classic, Penis and Abba.' He announced this in a triumphant voice, making her laugh.

'Wh-wh-what?' she stammered.

He slapped his forehead. 'Sorry, my mistake. I read it wrong. Pina Colada.'

'Thank God for that, I'm not really into Abba.' They were both laughing now.

Enjoying Hamish's company and wit, Davina was keen to prolong the experience. 'Just a glass of wine please,' she said.

'Well, okay, but you don't know what you're missing.' Rolling the makeshift cocktail list into a ball, Hamish tossed it over his shoulder and poured them both a glass of Pinot Grigio. Looking her in the eyes, he gracefully walked back round to her, lifting his glass in a toast and announcing, 'Here's to new acquaintances.'

Davina clinked her glass to his. 'Hear, hear.'

The wine was chilled to perfection. The effect hit her empty stomach immediately, reminding her that she hadn't eaten since lunch and, according to her watch, it was now almost nine. *So it's true, time really does fly when you're enjoying yourself.* Sitting his, then her, glass down on the bar, Hamish opened her legs and stood between them. *Fuck.* Placing his strong arms around her back he pulled her into him, angled his head, and gently licked her lips, before kissing her with a tenderness that contradicted his size. After all, as Granda would say, he was "Built like a brick shit-house." His kisses grew stronger, and although it wasn't as frenzied as it had been in the lift, it was definitely having the same effect on her. She felt herself melting into him.

Their sensual embrace was broken by her mobile phone playing 'Amarillo' by Tony Christie. She pulled away from him, jumped off the stool, retrieved her phone from her bag, and gawked at it. *Shit, shit, buggery shit, not now!*

'Are you going to answer it?' he asked, but as soon the question had left his lips, it stopped.

'It was my ma,' Davina said. Hamish smiled at her turn of phrase. 'She'll be wondering where I am.'

'So?'

'So?' Davina's voice was incredulous. 'Right then, how would this sound to you? "Hi, Ma. Just met a complete stranger who's absolutely gorgeous,"' – *Shit, did I just say that out loud?* The smile on his face told her he appreciated the quip – "'and I'm now in his hotel room drinking a lovely Pinot Grigio.'" As she heard herself say this, she couldn't believe that was exactly what she'd done, and rather than make her run for the door, the revelation made the sensation between her legs build even more and she actually felt proud of herself. He was standing next to her now. Taking her hands in his, he pressed them to the bulge in his trousers. *Holy shit and fuck.*

'Tell her something's come up at work.' He kissed her hard this time. *Sorry, Ma.* She knew, for the first time in her life, that she was going to tell her ma a serious lie. Reluctantly, she pulled back from him. He carried on kissing her neck and ear and was stroking her arms so gently, she had goose pimples. Her whole body tingled. Her fingers shook as she texted her ma.

> The night shift girl isnt able to com into work for some personal reason and Im having stay on until they can get cover. The company will pay for m taxi home. I cant phone as Im not allowed to mak personal calls at work

The last part, at least, she knew Ma would believe, as she'd shown her the extensive list of dos and don'ts she'd been given before starting work here. Exhaling loudly, she pressed Send. Impatient, Hamish grabbed the phone from her and threw it back in her bag.

His relentless kisses and touches had her burning with the need to do something, but she wasn't sure what. He kissed his way back to her lips and spoke into her mouth. 'Are you okay?' *Am I okay? My heart's racing, there's a pulse*

42

in my pants I've never experienced before, and right now there's no other place in the whole wide world I'd rather be.

With trembling hands, she reached for his. 'Yes,' she said.

He pressed her hands to his chest. 'You are allowed to touch me, you know. In fact, I'm kind of counting on it.'

'Sorry.' She was staring at the floor because his oh-so-sexy gaze was doing weird and wonderful things to her. But now that she could feel his rock hard pecs beneath his top, her barriers started to rise again. *What would he say when we're naked? – which is inevitable if we carry on this way. Maybe he wouldn't say anything; just point and laugh like the bitches in the changing rooms after P.E., led by that super-bitch, Jennifer Caldwell. No! Better to leave now with your clothes and dignity intact.* Gently, he lifted her face with his index finger.

'Hey.' He said this so gently, she thought she'd melt. 'Talk to me.' The warmth in his face reassured her. She felt she'd known him for years. She took a deep breath, then exhaled.

'I'm not that used to being intimate with men.' *Well, it's non-existent actually.* There. She'd said it. 'Or women, for that matter,' she added, as an afterthought. He was holding her hands again.

'And which do you prefer?' The smile on his face, his easiness and tenderness, had her entirely at his mercy.

'Definitely men,' Davina replied with a nod and a close-lipped smile.

'Glad to hear it.' He led her back to their drinks. They gauged each other, smiling over the tops of their glasses as they drank.

'You really are beautiful,' he said. *You're not so bad looking yourself, AND you've got me twitching in places I didn't even know existed.*

'Thank you. No-one's ever said that to me before.' The heat was rising from her neck again. He raised his eyebrows and moved closer. Although not touching, she could feel the warmth exude from his body, his aftershave intoxicating.

'Nothing's going to happen that you don't want to. Just say the words and I'll take you home.' She couldn't remember ever wanting something or someone as badly before. *Except Logan, but you're not even on his radar. It's now or never, Brown.*

She downed her wine, took his from him and sat it next to her empty glass, then grabbed his hand and almost dragged him over to the inviting super-king bed. At the edge of it, and before her bravado abandoned her, she pulled him to her with two fistfuls of his top. Now her hands were in his hair, tugging him even closer. She devoured him with open, inexperienced kisses. He cupped her breasts, kneading them gently. It was as if someone had sounded the reveille. Her nipples had jumped to attention and were ready for action. He made light work of her buttoned blouse, kissing her neck as he removed it, then letting it fall to the floor. Davina sucked in her stomach. *Thank God I wore matching bra and knickers today.* She pulled his top over his head and it joined her blouse on the floor. He was perfect. She stroked and admired his hairless chest and hadn't even noticed him undo her bra until he pulled the straps across her arms. He drew her close and the sensation of skin on skin was exhilarating. She explored every inch of his back with eager hands. His lips and tongue teased her nipple and the sensation made her mad for more. The slight breeze she felt around her legs drew attention to the fact that her trousers were now round her ankles. She returned the favour. With shaky hands, she undid his buckle,

44

button, and zip. The whole time, she could feel his hardness against the edge of her hands. His size intimidated her. Swallowing nervously, she looked into his eyes, her anxiety obvious.

'Don't worry,' he reassured her, 'it'll be okay. I'll be gentle, and if you want to stop, just say.' He kissed her tenderly. Less awkwardly than she expected, they slipped out of their shoes and trousers, and then he lifted her onto the bed. They lay on their sides, exploring each other's bodies with their eyes, kisses and hands. Rolling onto his back, he lifted his hips and removed his snug-fitting boxers. As he sprang free of the restraints, she was mesmerised. *No fecking way, that's massive!* Taking her hand, he folded it around him and dragged it up and down his impressive length at a slow pace. His skin was so soft and yet he was solid. She couldn't take her eyes off it.

'That feels amazing,' he breathed in a low voice. *You're telling me!* Then he gently forced her onto her back and freed her of the last boundary between them. As he pulled her pants down, he kissed and nipped her skin with his teeth. This sent tiny shockwaves through her whole body. Crawling back up, he was right above her now. He reached up and flicked a switch. The main light went off and the bedside lamp came on. Finally, she let her stomach muscles relax. His eyes found hers and the look was so comforting, she pulled him down and kissed him hard. She was so charged, her entire body tingled. He pulled away, then removed something from the drawer. Holding a condom in his fingers, he looked at her for approval. She smiled and nodded. Hamish bit open the packet and removed its slippery contents, rolling it on with expert fingers. Kissing his way to her chest, he stopped at the nipple, took it in his mouth, sucking leisurely at first, then nipping it gently with his teeth.

'Ahhhh,' Davina moaned. Slowly, he prised her legs open with his and, moving down, kissed his way to the top of her pubic hair.

'Very nice.' Stroking what remained of her modesty, he gently blew on her. Her breathing became ragged, then stopped completely when he thrust his tongue inside her. *Holy shit!* His tongue darted in and out frantically whilst his fingers flicked and rubbed her clitoris vigorously. He was driving her mad and she squirmed like an eel beneath him. From somewhere in her body she couldn't place, she could feel a sensation growing and growing. She knew something had to give, and it did. The spasms that took over her bottom half had her whole body jerking.

'Oh my God, oh my God!' She had to cover her mouth with her hand to control her screaming. Wave after wave of orgasm coursed through her, her heart pounding ten to the dozen, and she wasn't sure if, at one point, she'd actually passed out. Finally, he slowed his movements and Davina caught her breath. *Holy fuck, so that's what all the fuss is about.* He edged his way back up the bed, still above her, and removed the arm that was now covering her eyes. He gazed down at her, his smile dazzling. He'd done all the work, yet she felt exhausted.

'Thank you,' she said.

'Anytime.' His kiss was slow and seductive. She could taste herself on his lips and, much to her surprise, didn't mind it one bit. Gradually, his kisses became more vehement and his breath quickened.

'Are you still okay with this?' he murmured, then nibbled her earlobe. *Jeezo, is every part of a woman's anatomy hot-wired to her crotch? Surely after that I can't be feeling horny*

46

again? However, when his stubbly chin grazed the curve of her neck, she knew that's exactly what she was feeling. Shuddering, she lifted her shoulders to her neck to try to stem this relentless attack on her senses, but to no avail. He pushed her head up gently and carried on with his assault, causing goose-pimples to break out all over her.

'Tell me, Davina.' His voice was hoarse this time.

'Yes. God, yes.' The eagerness in her voice was unmistakable, and slightly embarrassing.

'Thank you,' he said.

Those two words were her undoing. All her anxieties and trepidations melted away. He was thanking *her* for this mind-blowing encounter. She kissed him, greedily, with a new-found confidence. Her tongue challenged his this time, and he didn't disappoint. Unsure of what to do, she pulled his hair, scratched his back, and tweaked his nipples. The moaning sounds he made told her she was doing something right. He ran his hand down the length of her sweating body.

'What a figure.' The admiration in Hamish's voice had Davina blushing again, but before she'd had time to absorb his compliment, he was kissing her and had eased a finger into her wet fandango.

'Oh, Hamish, I'm . . .' Taking this as a sign, he pulled his finger out and thrust two back in, teasing her mercilessly. Her head was flung back into the pillow, and her body went into convulsions again. Her enjoyment was shameless. 'Yes! . . . Yes! . . . Yes!'

Just as she was floating back to some kind of normality, she felt something that was most definitely not a finger being forced slowly into her. Her breathing stopped and so did he. *Holy shit, this is it.* With all his weight on his hands at either side of her arms, his face was inches from hers. He ran his thumb across her

47

cheek, wiping away a solitary tear. Taking hold of his hand she kissed his palm, reassuringly. He put his hand back on the bed, kissing her slowly and gently, whilst using the same pace with his dick. She found that her body was a lot more accommodating than she thought it would be. *But then, if two mind-blowing orgasms couldn't relax you, Brown, what the hell could?* The sting she felt when he'd filled her completely was more uncomfortable than sore. He kissed her harder now and picked up the pace of his thrusts. Unsure what to do, she ran her nails along his back until, using one hand, he lifted her hips to meet his. She understood his unspoken instruction, grabbed his shoulders, and pushed up on his downward thrusts.

'Christ, Davina, you feel amazing.' His breathing was short and shallow, their bodies working in perfect sync, the sweat between them lubricating where they met. The noises they were making made her even wetter, and the fullness she felt physically was matched emotionally. If only her tormentors could see her now. The smile on her face was unadulterated arrogance. She let his shoulders go and twisted his nipples softly.

'Oh, Davina, I'm . . . Oh, yes!' The obvious pleasure he was experiencing rapidly brought the now familiar signs of an orgasm flooding through her body. She dug her nails into his shoulders and pumped him as if her life depended on it.

'Aaaaahh!' Hamish trembled to a stop. Beneath him, Davina carried on, pushing both of them over the edge, until he collapsed on top of her. He kissed her, breathing heavily into her mouth. 'That was amazing.' He rolled off her and onto the pillow next to her.

'Amazing?' yelled Davina. 'Are you kidding? That was *the* most intense, phenomenal, mind-blowing thing that has ever happened to me, and if I never experience it again, I'd still die happy.'

Hamish's laugh vibrated through the bed. 'Well, thank you very much. We aim to please, and if you give me time to get my breath back and it's okay with you, Miss Brown, I'll gladly let you experience it again.'

***

That had been what Davina could only describe as the start of her life. For the first few months, she'd kept her job at the Rouge Monte, until her diary had become crammed full of "dates". She was in turmoil, however, because she'd told her family she was being sent on managerial courses all over the country and they'd been so proud of her, Ma especially, even though she was concerned about her spending so much time away from home.

'But that's a small price to pay for getting on in the world,' she'd said.

The alternative to lying to her family didn't bear thinking about, and there was no way Davina was going back to being Dafty Brown. She was enjoying herself too much to give it all up.

Hamish Hamilton had become a mainstay in her new-found vocation, teaching her how to deal with the opposite sex on a personal level as well as a sexual one. He somehow managed to introduce her to more clients without it feeling weird. She often laughed that it should be her paying *him*, not the other way around. Her quick, dry humour had sometimes embarrassed her at the start of their endeavour, but Hamish was quick to reassure her that he loved a woman with a sense of humour. Most men did. He encouraged her in all things, never more so than learning to drive. He told her she could do anything she put her mind to, and she believed him. Davina believed every word that came out of this handsome, gentle giant's mouth. He was honest enough to admit that his suggestion wasn't exactly unselfish. Enjoying her company as much as he did, he wanted her to accompany him whenever he was in Scotland. It therefore made sense for her to be able to drive.

Whatever his motive may have been, Davina couldn't believe how much confidence and self-belief both Hamish and driving gave her. They'd often meet hours before the function they were attending together, taking in movies, museums, and galleries that appealed to both of them. Davina suspected, by the way Hamish dressed and the hotel rooms he utilised, that he was a man of means. Whenever they were out and about, however, if an item or object caught his eye, he could haggle with the best of them, and Davina was yet to see him pay full price for anything he really wanted. His work as a sales rep took him all over the world, although he and his family were well-rooted in Ballater, not far from his employer, Glenshee Distillery, which was actually owned by his family.

Over the years, they'd both divulged various titbits about themselves and their families to each other without getting overly intimate. Davina learned that Hamish was the youngest of three. His sister, Kirsty, was the eldest, and the apple of their dad's eye. His brother, Rodrick, had vied in vain, all his life it seemed, for his father's approval and attention, often taking his frustrations out on his younger brother. This backfired later in life when Hamish, taking after his father's side of the family, grew a foot taller and a whole lot broader than his older brother. His father, Jamie, who Hamish was apparently named after, insisted that Rodrick and Hamish work their way through the ranks at his distillery, on the same wages as the rest of his staff. Although Hamish thrived on the challenges they faced, the experience only made Rodrick bitter. Kirsty had worked in the offices next to their father from the minute she left school. The fact she was on the same wages as her brothers did little to appease Rodrick. Hamish hated the politics that went along with working for family, so when he realised there was a lot of travelling involved in being a sales rep, that was as far up the business ladder as he was willing to go, despite numerous conversations/ lectures from his parents.

Davina had never confessed it to him, but she was really glad hers wasn't the only screwed-up family on the planet. They might never have met otherwise. She knew with an unwavering certainty that her life would've been a very dull place without fucking Hamish Hamilton in it.

CHAPTER 3

BROWN SAUCE

Now back in her cosy bungalow, Davina poured herself a cup of tea and took it into the bedroom. Remembering Hamish's text message, she lay the cup down on the bedside table and pulled the locked suitcase from the cupboard, placing it gently on the freshly-made bed. She turned the digits on the lock. The number would always remind her of one of the best nights of her life: 556, Hamish's room number in the Rouge Monte Hotel the first time she'd met him, and the first time she'd ever had sex. She opened the padded case and removed the ball gag, vibrators, handcuffs, eye-masks and other assorted goodies until she finally found Hamish's "wee pal". Placing all the unrequired toys back in the case, she returned it to its hidey-hole. Now happily organised, sitting at the top of her bed, tea safely back in hand, Davina gave her sister Marge a call.

When they were pre-teens, Marge was everything Davina had wanted to be: tall, beautiful, skinny, and popular. Her delicate, feminine face was surrounded by soft, straight, shoulder-length blonde hair. Her eyes were a dazzling blue, her lips red and plump. The perfect ensemble, in Davina's opinion. Lately, however, Davina thought she looked more God-awful than Goddess. After several rings, a flat, lifeless voice answered.

'Hiya.'

52

'You okay? You sound rubbish.' Davina hated hearing her sister like this.

'Probably just getting that bug that's going about. And I'm not sleeping too great.' She tried to sound more enthusiastic, but she wasn't fooling anyone.

'Maybe,' said Davina. 'But if you're not feeling right, go to the doctor.'

'I'm fine, just a bit tired. I'll be better after a good night's sleep.' She had perked up a bit, but Davina wasn't convinced. She knew from Ma that Marge was working every shift going in the salon, but never had anything to show for it. She also knew every penny was a prisoner with Robert Clarke, Marge's partner.

Robert Clarke had chased Marge for years, but no-one ever thought she'd actually go out with him, let alone move into his flat. There was something about him that Davina didn't like but couldn't quite put her finger on. He was the epitome of good manners and kindness any time he was around the family, always buying their da a drink at The Black Bull, on the rare occasion that they left their flat. "You're a fine lad" Da would gush, but the way Robert looked at Marge sent shivers down Davina's spine. If any of the regulars in The Black Bull approached Marge, Robert was right there. If anyone asked her to play pool, he'd suggest they make it a doubles game. Whenever Davina even tried to broach the subject, her sister laughed it off or spoke about something else.

'Why don't you come and stay with me for a couple of days?' Davina asked. 'The fresh air will help you sleep and we could catch up.' There was a sharp intake of breath on the other end of the phone. Davina knew the answer before she heard it.

'Eh! I better say no. We're heaving at the salon and Robert would worry.' Marge tried to sound flippant, but the terseness in her voice was undeniable.

'Surely they could both spare you for two days. You've been working non-stop lately.' Davina couldn't keep the irritation out of her voice. She was getting annoyed listening to her sister make one excuse after another about why she couldn't possibly go to or do anything that was even remotely enjoyable.

'Sorry Davina, but we're not all big fancy manageresses.' It was Marge's turn to be annoyed. 'Some of us have to work all the hours going just to get by.' *Well, thank God. At least this proves that the old Marge hasn't completely disappeared. There's hope yet.* Knowing that arguing with her sister wasn't going to solve anything, Davina changed tack.

'Maybe you're right. But you're going to work yourself into an early grave. I just worry about you, that's all. I'm in Glasgow on Saturday. Why don't we say to the boys and go to Merchant Pride? Pauline should be singing. Surely you can drag yourself away from work and Robert for one afternoon?' She was calm again and she really wanted to spend time with her sister. *Maybe I'll have a word with Hector and Joshua, and between us we can sort our sister out.*

'Okay, I'll see what I can do, but I'm not promising.' The change in Marge was heartening. 'You're right. Barbara Bryceland's an amazing singer, and maybe our Joshua will get a lumber.' The laugh they shared was like a throwback to when they were young and carefree. 'Okay. I'll try my best. And Davina . . . sorry for shouting at you, I'm just jealous.' *There's the sister I know and love.*

'Hey, what are big sisters for if not to shout at now and again? I'll see you Saturday. It'll be a laugh.'

Davina drove into the underground car park of The Edward Hotel in Aberdeen and quickly found a space. She liked the Granite City, and The Edward Hotel had become one of the more frequent places she and Hamish would meet. She was wearing a dark grey pencil skirt, white blouse, and fitted jacket. She really pulled off the confident businesswoman look, and that's exactly how she felt walking in to the hotel's Jacobean Bar, clutching her overnight suit bag.

Davina spotted Hamish first. At just over six foot, he was a fair bit taller than her, but the perseverance of Marge to persuade her to wear high-heels meant the gap between them was a lot less comical. Hamish held himself well and walked with the fluidity of a man confident with himself and his looks. He was a big man all over, as Davina could testify, without an ounce of flab. His tousled dark brown hair had no identifiable style, but it suited him to a tee. His good looks turned heads everywhere he went, and his green eyes had a hardness to them. Recently, however, Davina thought they had taken on a slightly softer glow.

Davina nudged Hamish's arm and he turned to face her. His dazzling smile still did things to her, especially when he wore it with his tailor-made suit and expensive aftershave, which made him smell amazingly hot.

'You look gorgeous as ever, Davina, but what have I told you about losing too much weight?' His tone was rebuking, but he was smiling as he said it. He kissed her, tight-lipped and scowling, then in a mocking voice said, 'You remember Gavin, don't you?' She gave him a dig in the ribs and set her bag over a chair, turning her attention to the handsome man to Hamish's left. Gavin Anderson was 31 years old, and the same height as Hamish. He was well-dressed, well-mannered, and a long-term friend of Hamish's. He was also well groomed. In contrast to Hamish, however, there wasn't a hair on his head out of place. Davina would have loved to take him home to meet Ma. She would definitely do something about his painfully thin frame. His dark brown eyes looked so empty and lost sometimes, Davina just wanted to give him a cuddle and tell him everything would be okay. Two years ago, through Hamish, he had become one of Davina's acquaintances. There were only three of her clients who knew her real name, and he was one. All the others knew her as Katy Miller. He, too, was in the whisky business, and had asked Davina to accompany him tonight, but Hamish had gotten hold of her first. Even though they were both in the same business, it was rare for them to attend the same event.

Davina really enjoyed her liaisons with Gavin. They were purely for the company. His wife had been killed in a car crash five years ago and he still missed her. Never sharing the same hotel room, let alone bed, they would talk for hours, and he'd shown genuine interest when she'd spoke of growing up in Glasgow. She loved the way Gavin spoke fondly of his wife, the short time they'd had together, and the plans they'd made. Her heart really went out to him. He'd thanked her for being a great listener, joking that she'd saved him a small fortune on a therapist. His wife still came up in conversation, even now, but she no longer monopolised it.

'Hi, Gavin, how've you been? Can't believe I got the short straw tonight.' Davina nodded cheekily in Hamish's direction, then kissed Gavin on the cheek. There was no awkwardness between them. Neither of the men had been informed of the other's "habits" by her, and she liked to think that they were true gentlemen on that count, although she knew it definitely wasn't the case with the rest of her clientele.

'I'm great, thanks,' said Gavin. 'I'll get in quicker next time. You look lovely, by the way.' He gave her a soft peck on the cheek. 'Well, I'll see you both tonight. Things to do.' He nodded and left.

'See you later,' Davina and Hamish said in unison. When Davina turned back to Hamish, he had a weird look on his face that she couldn't quite fathom.

'Poor Gavin,' he said. 'He needs someone in his life to take care of him.' The statement really surprised Davina.

'I thought you were totally anti-marriage?' she said.

'Oh, I am!' Hamish conceded. 'But he's the sort of man who functions better with a woman to guide him.'

'Well, if he does settle down again, she'll be a lucky girl, whoever she is. He's a great guy.' *Wow, there's that look again.* 'Anyway! Enough about Gavin. What's a girl got to do to get a drink around here?'

Hamish lifted his open bottle of wine and his glass. 'We'll finish this in the room,' he said, handing the bottle and glass to Davina and lifting up her things. They didn't speak again until they were in the lift.

'How was the drive up?' he asked. *What, no passionate tit-squeezing, pants-exploding kiss?*

'Fine. The usual couple of caravans and lorries. Apart from that, it was okay. I had my country CD on. You wouldn't believe the amount of times they get the words wrong on those things.'

'That always seems to happen with you,' he chuckled.

The doors opened and they walked the short distance to Hamish's room, again in silence. Inside, he flung Davina's suit bag over a chair. His own things were sitting neatly around the room.

'I take it wine's okay for you?' he asked. *Wow, what's eating your arse tonight, Hamilton?*

'Fine, thanks. So how's the whisky work treating you?' She took the glass from him and they both sat on the comfy double chair.

'Well, if Scotland ever becomes independent, it won't be the oil that keeps us afloat, it'll be our national drink. And I don't mean Irn-Bru. Anyway, enough shop talk. You said no more diets, and look at you. If I'd wanted a bag of bones to keep me company I'd have gone to the butcher's.' His hands were skimming over her belly, which to her was still a fair size.

'I'm hardly a bag of bones, Hamish. I yo-yo between a 12 and a 14, and I've got to keep the customers satisfied.'

'Well, this customer's definitely not satisfied, and I should have priority.' *Wow! Something's definitely eating your delectable arse tonight.*

'Sorry. No favouritism in this line of work,' she said. 'I'm only here for the money.' *How d'you like them apples?*

A deep frown appeared on Hamish's brow. 'Correct,' he replied. 'And I'm the one paying, so you'll definitely earn it today. Did you bring my wee pal?'

'Yes, sir.' *We don't do bad moods, Hamilton.* In an attempt to lighten things up, she sauntered with an exaggerated wiggle over to her suit bag, opened a zip, and pulled out a small vanity case. 'Here we are.' She lifted out a four-inch long, inch thick butt plug and rolled her tongue around it. There was no concealing his arousal. 'Have you missed us?'

'I don't know why I ever let you talk me into trying one of those things,' he said, 'but it's been one of my finer mergers.' The grin on his face was outrageous and his eyes were smouldering. Normally she'd have jumped

58

him there and then, but there was something about the atmosphere between them tonight that stopped her.

When she'd embarked on this voyage of discovery, Davina had reasoned that not all men would find her as sexy and attractive as Hamish had, therefore they might not be so easily pleased in the bedroom department. Taking matters into her own hands, at the age of 22, for the first time in her young inexperienced life, Davina visited an Ann Summers shop. Standing outside the branch in Sauchiehall Street, she pulled her scarf up to her face – nothing at all suspicious about that in mid-July – and her hood down over her head. She'd considered wearing glasses, a false nose and a moustache, but that would be going too far, even for her. She scanned the street warily, because as sure as there's shit in a midden, the minute Davina Roseanne Brown enters such a den of iniquity, the nosey battle-axe that has been their next-door neighbour forever, Mrs Parker – how apt – will tap her on the shoulder. Convinced she hadn't been followed, far less seen, Davina entered the shop.

'Have you been to the dentist, hen?' The confused look on Davina's face prompted the assistant to explain. 'The scarf. I hate the dentist.' She shuddered at the thought. Deciding that was a great cover story, Davina played along.

'Yeah, but the anesthetic's wearing off now,' she said, 'so hopefully I'll not bite my lip.' She pulled down her hood and unwound her scarf, before examining some of the products nearby. Running her hands over the silk and lace garments, Davina quickly realised that the less material there was, the more the bloody thing cost.

She remembered her best friend, Grace Steele, who was the same build as her, telling her, in her most serious voice, that she'd come in here once for a nice Basque.

'Do you have anything in my size?' she'd asked. With her arms folded over her chest, Grace had mimicked the assistant. 'The stuck-up bitch looked me up and down and said "If we do, someone's getting fired."' They had laughed until they were sore at that one. 'Had you going for a minute there, Davina,' Grace had said.

'No you didn't,' Davina had replied. 'Because, a) no way either of us would have the nerve to show our face in a place like that, and b) what would you be doing with a Basque?'

'Not what . . . who!' The tears had been running down their cheeks by this point.

Davina made a beeline for the older of the two shop assistants. It had been hard enough plucking up the courage to come into the shop; there was no way on earth she could explain to someone of similar age, but skinnier and better looking, what she wanted.

'Is it something in particular you're after today?' The assistant's smile and tone made it sound like this was the most natural thing in the world, and Davina felt neither uncomfortable nor unwanted.

'I don't suppose these outfits cater for the . . . larger lady, do they?' Davina said, pointing at a nearby rack.

'Out of stock at the moment I'm afraid,' replied the assistant, 'but we are expecting a delivery in the next few days.' Then, with a genuine smile: 'Our rabbits are one size fits all, though.' *I appreciate you're trying to soften the blow, pal, but you're being a bit too condescending for my liking. Of course bunny ears fit all. It's not head gear I've got trouble fitting into.*

Davina smiled back and made for the door. 'Thanks anyway.'

'Why don't you have a look at our toys?' the assistant suggested.

Intrigued, Davina nodded and was then led to the back of the shop where, hidden from view by a wall of nurses' uniforms, French maid costumes and other skimpy outfits, was an Aladdin's cave of goodies. Of course, she'd heard of such things before, but had never in her life seen anything like them. This was to become, along with Oddbins, Davina's favourite shop.

'I'm going in the shower; why don't you join me?' Hamish was oozing sex now.

'That sounded more like a command than a question,' Davina replied.

'Correct.' Hamish walked to the bathroom, discarding his clothes as he went. His huge, robust frame always amazed her. *How could such a huge guy not have an ounce of flab on him?* She followed suit, undressing en route, whilst admiring his tight arse.

Hamish placed his iPod on the large sink and Lily Allen started singing 'Who'd Have Known?' He turned the shower on, took Davina in his arms, and started dancing. *Katy Perry's 'Hot and Cold' would be more apt.* He kissed her passionately as she reached for his dick and, with slow, purposeful strokes, made him even harder.

'Oh no you don't.' He stilled her hand. 'You're not getting off that easy, Miss Skin and Bones. I'm not happy with you, so you need to make it up to me – and I'm not going to make it easy for you.' His eyes were glinting wickedly, but there was something in his tone. *Bring it on.* She squeezed his balls playfully.

'Well, you're the customer. What would sir like?'

'Well, maybe I should feed you this.' Both their eyes fell on his immense dick. In this moment, he was arrogance personified, which was really out of character for him.

'I did eat before I got here, but I'm sure I could squeeze another morsel in.' Sniggering, she stepped into the far end of the bath and sat the butt plug on the rim. He climbed in with his face to her, hot water running down his back. He pushed her back against the wall and they kissed. She could feel the cold tiles against her spine, but his embrace was heating her up all over. She reached for the shower gel and squeezed some out for both of them. They washed and fondled each other's chests. Sliding their hands downwards in unison, they teased each other with eager, slippery fingers.

'Hamish, I'm . . .' Sensing her orgasm, Hamish quickly withdrew his hand and stepped backwards into the cascading water, winking at her. The implications of his actions were obvious. The longing between her legs made her unsteady.

'I'm the customer, remember.' He was smiling, but serious at the same time. *Seriously, you can't leave me in this state.* She glowered at him and rubbed vigorously at the origin of her discomfort, never taking her eyes off him. Hamish reached her in a single stride and pinned her arms to the wall above her head.

'No-no-no,' he said, putting a halt to her attempt at relief. 'I could have sworn the customer comes first, or something like that, if you'll pardon the pun.' He lowered his head, taking her nipple in his mouth, and tormented her some more. Gripping it between his teeth, he flicked it mercilessly with his tongue. She'd never experienced an orgasm without some kind of contact to her fandango before, but right now that's exactly where she was heading. Trying not to show any emotions, but failing miserably, she straddled his thigh seeking sexual refuge, rubbing herself up and down him. *That's it, right there.* She was so close, she thought she was capable of killing if he didn't stop this torment. He opened his legs and pinned hers between them.

'I know your game, Miss Brown, and I won't let you use and abuse my leg like that. It has feelings, you know.' There was no humour in this statement and his face was serious.

'What the hell is your problem tonight?' She was all for prolonged gratification, but there was something different tonight in his mood and in his attitude. He was being a complete shit.

He looked down at her through narrowed eyes. 'Nothing. Just reinstating some boundaries. You did, after all, remind me that ours is purely a business relationship.' *Ouch.* The words stung, but the tone in which he'd said them was like a slap in the face. Pulling back, there was nowhere for her to go. Tears built up behind her eyes. He was still holding her arms above her head, his face full of torment. Suddenly he let her arms fall, turned off the shower, and got out of the bath. Snatching one of the fluffy towels from the heated towel rail, he strode out of the bathroom. *What the hell just happened?*

Davina was suddenly cold, unsure if it was the atmosphere or because she was naked and wet, and not in a good way. She wrapped one of the extravagant towels tightly around her, put the toilet seat down and sat on it, contemplating her next move. Her demons from long ago began circling inside her, but this time she wouldn't entertain them. *Did I do something wrong? The money quip was meant as a joke.*

Grace had often told her, "If you think or say a thing often enough it will happen, good or bad, whether you want it to or not." Now, sitting on the toilet, Davina couldn't remember telling herself she needed a pee, but somewhere along the line the power of thought persuasion must have kicked in. Lifting the lid and sitting back down with the towel still covering most of her, she was about to let loose when the bathroom door opened.

'Sorry.' A forlorn Hamish handed her a glass of white wine. *Are you kidding me? There are nine people on this planet I can pee in front of, and even then the majority of them need to have their back to me, and as far as I'm aware they're all in Glasgow right now.* 'I'm being an arsehole.' *You can say that again, but we can't have this conversation now.* He sipped from his own glass, which had an adverse effect on Davina. Funny, a minute ago she probably could have held on for a good wee while, but now that he was standing watching her, she was bursting to pee. She pretended to take a drink from her glass.

'It's alright. Please just go.' He hadn't taken his cue and her bladder had sent a Clydesdale horse to open the flood gates. *When we speak later, I'll point out that when I said "It's alright," what I actually meant to say was "You're an arsehole." Shit, why didn't I practise my pelvic floor exercises more?*

'It's not alright, I'm being a wanker.' He looked her in the eye for the first time since he'd come back into the bathroom. 'You can't even stand up and look at me.'

The disappointment in his voice cut her to the quick, but the annoyance she felt right now far out-weighed that. She threw her wine over him, holding back her pee with all her might. 'You're right. You are being a wanker. Maybe we did screw up by getting too friendly, but don't treat me like some junky slag you just picked up off the street and can say what the hell you like to, then throw your money about and toss me out like I'm a nobody. You don't get to come in here with your expensive glasses of wine, apologising, and expect everything to be hunky-dory. Now piss off and leave me alone.'

64

The hurt in Davina's voice was matched by that in Hamish's eyes. She didn't have a clue what the hell was going on, but right now she was hurting badly, and needed to pee. Still sitting, she leaned over and closed the door, forcing him backwards, just as the gush between her legs let loose. The relief she felt was instantaneous.

'Aaaaahhh.' She couldn't care less if he'd heard that, as long as he hadn't heard her pee.

Washing her hands, Davina looked at herself in the mirror and ran over the scenario that had just unfolded. *He stormed out raging at something, but what? Came back, tried to apologise, and you threw your wine over him – which he might have deserved, but it was also a waste of wine. What the hell was going on?* Standing at the door, she took a deep breath and slowly opened it. Sitting on the couch, Hamish had his jeans and top back on. Davina gathered up her clothes and crossed the room to where he was sitting. She felt the anger and hurt grow inside her again. *Who the fuck are you to make me feel so cheap?* Once she'd found every item of clothing and had pulled her bra back on, she turned to look at him.

'Have I done something to offend you?' she asked. For the first time since meeting him, her lack of clothes had her feeling vulnerable. The amber liquid in his tumbler was definitely not wine and she'd never known him to drink anything else.

Memories of Nosey Parker, the Browns' long-standing neighbour, sporting a black eye and banging their door late at night, desperate to get away from her abusive husband because he'd been "drinking whisky and wasn't himself" came flooding back to Davina. Hamish stood up and walked over to her. She only had her bra and panties on, and she stiffened, uneasy, hoping he didn't notice. *Don't give him anything else to be angry about.*

'I really am sorry,' he said. 'I know you deserve an explanation and if I had one, believe me I'd give it.' She could smell the apple juice on his breathe and the relief she felt was audible. He looked tormented. 'I've never had these feelings since . . . well, since Donna.' He spat the name out. Davina could tell this was difficult for him, but she still wasn't sure what it was he was saying exactly.

'Who's Donna?' Baby steps were needed here, but there was no point letting him carry on if she wasn't keeping up with him.

'The bitch I fell in love with, who took me for everything I had then ran off with a tosser, who in turn did the same to her and went back to his wife.' He smiled at this last remark, despite his obvious agitation. *That explained a few things he's said before, but not his behaviour tonight. Shit. Had she somehow hurt him as badly as this Donna?* A shiver ran through Davina and she picked up her blouse. Gently, he took it from her.

'Don't go. Please. Let me finish.' He walked purposely into the bathroom, bringing back a robe that he wrapped tenderly around her. *Why didn't I think of that?* He sat back down on the couch and pulled her into him. Staring into his gorgeous green eyes, she could see the turmoil he was going through. The thought that it was she who'd brought it about cut her to the quick. She took his hands in hers.

'Tell me what I've done and we'll fix it. Your friendship means the world to me, Hamish.' His brows knitted together and he looked more confused than angry.

'What *you've* done?' he asked.

'Obviously I've pissed you off, stirring up feelings that remind you of your ex.' Her worried expression dissipated when he threw his head back and laughed.

'No, no, no. That's not what I meant.' His laughter subsided and he looked her in the eye. 'I think I'm in love with you.'

Her heart was suddenly in her mouth and she'd stopped breathing. *Holy shit, noooooo!* 'I never wanted this to happen, Davina. Never thought I'd let it happen again. I was devastated when Donna left me. I built a nice wee wall around myself,' – *I know what that's like* – 'to prevent it from ever happening again. But I think it has.' He pushed her hair behind her ear. 'Seeing how comfortable you were with Gavin literally brought out the green-eyed monster in me. It opened old wounds I thought I'd sealed forever and I retaliated in the worst possible way. I hurt and offended the nicest, sweetest, most gentle person I know.'

Davina's brain was scrambled. She imagined lying naked with Logan in front of her coal fire and him finally making all her dreams come true by telling her he loved her. But those images were quashed with ones of a raging Hamish, lambasting her with words of hate-filled bile after learning she was in love with someone else. Her eyes were dampening and she was lost for words. *Love wasn't on the menu. We both knew that. FUCK! Of course I love you, Hamilton, but I'm not in love with you.*

'What do we do now, Hamish?' Her flat voice mirrored the way she was feeling. It was as if someone, or something, had sucked the life out of her.

'Honestly?' He shrugged. 'I don't know.' He squirmed and cleared his throat. 'How do you feel about what I said?' *Shit, shit, buggery shit. How do I tell you how I feel without hurting you?*

She took a deep breath. 'You were always the one saying love was for losers. You hate seeing people falling all over each other, holding hands and, I quote, "Making an arse of themselves in public." I like the way things are: no strings, no complications.'

Hamish inhaled deeply. 'I know, you're right. I should've kept my stupid mouth shut and let you roger me with that butt plug.'

His weak smile did nothing to lighten the mood, as a tear dropped into her mouth. Lifting his towel, he gently wiped her face. His voice was etched with pain. 'Don't cry, Davina.'

'I'm sorry,' she said. 'It's just I feel I owe you so much, but I never expected this and I feel bad that I can't give you a better answer.' He stopped wiping her face and pulled her into him. Being embraced by this mountain of a man usually made her feel safe and secure, but not today. Her guilt at not being honest with him was ripping her apart.

'Sorry, Davina. I've ruined everything. Why do fucking feelings have to get in the way of great sex?' They both smiled weakly at this. He pulled her away from his chest and kissed her so gently that it took her breath away. She held him tight, wanting to feel the closeness they'd always shared, unsure if they'd ever feel that way again. Undoing the belt around her robe, he pushed it off her shoulders and wrapped his arms around her waist, pulling her closer. Slowly, their kisses became harder and he sat back and discarded first his top and then her bra, wanting no barriers between them. He pulled her down the length of the couch and lay on top of her, supporting his weight with his hands. Kissing his hairless chest, she slowly began to relax. She giggled.

'What's so funny?' Finally, a genuine smile from him.

'After I threw that wine over you, I thought *what a waste*, but now that I'm getting to lick it off you, I've changed my mind.'

A sly smile crossed Hamish's face. 'You've missed a bit.' His finger circled his nipple. *This is what we're all about, Hamilton. Sex, sex and more sex. None of this lovey-dovey complicated crap.* 'Would I be pushing it if I suggested we take this to the bedroom and retrieve my wee pal along the way?'

The glint in Hamish's eye made Davina's fandango clench. 'Whatever you want. You're paying, so you're saying.' She smiled, but Hamish's look was sombre.

'I'm really sorry about that.' He stood and helped her up.

'Why, Hamish Hamilton! I do believe you're blushing,' she teased. His infectious smile split his face.

'It's the lighting in here, it's terrible.' They'd reached the bathroom. Eliza Doolittle's 'Skinny Jeans' was playing on Hamish's iPod. He walked over and picked up the butt plug. Davina followed him in and turned on the shower.

'Let's get clean and dirty at the same time,' she said. 'I've a dinner date later and he's the jealous type.' She grinned at him. 'So I better not be late or smelling of sex.'

She removed her pants, then set her sights on his jeans, licking him across his flawless, hairless chest as she undid the buttons all the way down, his dick impatient for attention, making the task a little more awkward. Once undone, she pushed them down to the floor using her foot and he stepped out of them. He hadn't bothered to put his boxers back on. She slid her tongue down his abdomen and she cupped his balls with her hand. Stroking him with slow deliberate caresses, she bent and gently kissed the tip of his dick, before standing back up and leading him to the same position he was in earlier, this time with the warm water running down his face. She only put shower gel on her own hands this time, lathering his smooth, muscular shoulders and back. The conversation they'd just had popped into her head. *Where do we go from here? Could this be our last time together?* She decided that if it was, he deserved it to be memorable. He'd shown and taught her so much, not just about sex, life and culture; more importantly, he'd taught her to accept and be proud of who she was. Pushing these thoughts to the back of her mind momentarily, she relaxed and started to enjoy the task at hand. He was clenching then releasing his impressive bum muscles, and the effect had her crotch twitching like mad. Rubbing the hollows of his arse cheeks in a circular motion, she lifted her right hand and brought it back with such force that he stumbled forward.

'Sorry,' she laughed. 'I don't know my own strength.'

'Are you sure that's not just payback for earlier?' He spoke over his shoulder, his eyes glinting wickedly. 'And rightly so. I deserve a few more for my shocking behaviour.' He placed his hands on the wall under the shower and bent over invitingly. Her eyebrows rose in amusement. *Who am I to deny him this?* The red handprint on his buttock was like a target. With no warning, it was joined by another, then another.

'Phewww!' He blew out harshly and flinched at the same time. Her hand stung, but she was enjoying this. Turning sideways, she took up position for an assault on his left cheek. With three slow but powerful strikes, both cheeks were soon a satisfying pink.

'There we are. Rosy cheeks, or is it just the light in here?' she teased.

'Smart arse.' He started to straighten up, but she stopped him.

'Not so quick, big man.' By pushing his shoulders further down, she forced his arse upwards. She squeezed more gel onto her hands and eased a thumb into his star anise bud. He clenched tightly again, but it wasn't for her gratification this time. Working the shower gel in a circular motion, he was thoroughly lathered and she breeched his defenses easily. She picked up the butt plug and rubbed soapy liquid along its length, placing the tip at his entrance. She rubbed her other hand soothingly across then up and down his back. With the gentlest of kisses, she caressed his taut arse, then slowly but forcefully pushed the plug all the way in, up to its hilt. *I don't know about you, Hamilton, but that certainly did something for me.* She heard a faint hum as she switched it on. The vibration was strong. Turning him to face her, she was rewarded with one of his pants-splitting grins. He lifted her easily, kissed her hard, and set her down again.

'No need to thank me . . . yet.' Sounding sultry wasn't her strong point, but she thought she'd pulled it off. She twisted his nipples and kissed her way down to his abdomen, his soft moans music to her ears, her torment intensifying. Releasing him slowly, she scratched her way down his sides, feeling him squirm. She smiled. Ticklish men were rare in her experience. Nipping with her teeth and lowering herself at the same time, she was positioned right in line with his impressive dick. She slid her hands around his bum and made sure his "wee pal" hadn't slipped out. She then pulled his hips forward, forcing his dick into her waiting mouth. Circling his tip with her tongue, she teased him for a while, feeling his hips rock back and forth, listening to his moans, harsh and loud. With a full hand caressing the bottom of his shaft, she slipped her mouth as far down as was possible without gagging. He held her head in place, his hips picking up the pace. Elvis was singing 'Viva Las Vegas' in the background, which he set his tempo to. Her lips, tongue and breathing were working in overdrive and her knees were starting to get sore. *Must concentrate on the blow job at hand, Brown.* She smiled at her own crude joke. Hamish's breathing was erratic now, as she squeezed his balls firmly with her left hand. Her right hand travelled around his tight arse and found the plug. With rapid movement, she pushed and pulled it in and out. He was grunting now and she knew he was close. His fingers were really digging into her scalp. She sensed the urgency in him and picked up her pace.

'Oh my God, oh my Gaaaawwdd!' Just as she felt the first gush of fluid hit her tongue, she quickly pulled out the butt plug. 'Holy fuck!' He collapsed onto her shoulders, barely able to stand. Her head was still bobbing, taking everything he had to give. She felt small tremors in his thighs, and only when he straightened back up did she stop. His fingers massaged her head. 'That was the best one yet, Davina.' He helped her to her feet, cuddling her into him. She could feel his heart racing. The warm water was a Godsend. His impressive frame had blocked most of it from hitting her, but now she basked in its warmth. They washed each other again and sang along to Prince's 'Purple Rain'. Stepping out the bath, he took the remaining robe from the back of the door and wrapped it around Davina's shoulders.

'That's quite a varied selection you've got on there,' she said, nodding to his iPod. 'Usually I find love songs work best in a situation like this. Maybe a bit of Norah Jones, or even Michael Bublé.'

'Well, they worked for me,' said Hamish, winking at her. Finally, his usual light-hearted self was back. 'And as you so rightly pointed out, I am the customer.' He retrieved the other robe from the couch and poured them both a glass of wine.

They headed into the bedroom, where Davina wrapped a towel around her wet hair. They both sat with their backs against the headboard, catching their breath, lost in their own thoughts and feelings. The wine, as usual, was dry, crisp, and chilled to perfection.

'I think we need to talk about the elephant in the room,' said Hamish. 'And if you say anything derogatory about your size, I swear I'll put you over my knee.' They were facing each other now. Davina clamped her lips closed in an over-exaggerated manner. *Am I that obvious? And you know being put over your knee isn't a deterrent for me, but right now we do need to talk*. She kept her dirty thoughts to herself.

'Okay,' she said. 'You start.' She hoped this would buy her some time as she still didn't know how to respond to his revelation without hurting him.

'It's just . . .' She could see he was struggling to find the right words, but was powerless to help him. She didn't know how or what he was feeling and hated seeing him like this. She stroked his face with her free hand. *Christ's sake, Hamilton, you're breaking my heart here*. He took her hand and kissed her fingertips. 'This is exactly what I'm talking about. People in our situation have an understanding. They meet up, make small talk, go to whatever boring function requires their presence, make more small talk and, depending on their arrangement, go their separate ways, or fuck and then go their separate ways. They do not carry on like this. Sitting relaxed on a bed, drinking wine, stroking your face while looking at you with a fuck-me-fuck-me look. And they definitely do not kiss the other person's soft, tantalising fingertips, because it makes them want to fuck them again.'

He'd placed her hand on the bulge in his robe. His face was a picture of confusion and hers mirrored it. She knew what he was saying made sense. What he'd described, to start with, was exactly what she had with all her other clients: meet, go out, fuck, then go their separate ways, and she liked it that way. What they had was different. Looking back, to her, it always had been. He took her to the theatre, concerts, the pictures, even museums, before and sometimes after they'd been to whatever function demanded his presence. They'd shared more than numerous beds and numerous conversations. Now that was about to be blown apart because they'd gotten too close. *You're the experienced one, Hamilton. You should've noticed how things were going; should've kept it businesslike between us.*

'Do you think about me when we're apart, Davina? Do you want to phone just to hear my voice? I do.' *That's exactly how I feel, just not about you. I know we talk and text a lot, unlike me and Logan, but he works abroad a lot. But then again so do you and you manage to find the time. AWWWW . . . Shit, shit, buggery shit! Stop fucking complicating things, Hamilton.* Still holding his hand, she gently removed it from his crotch and kissed his knuckles.

'Any other woman would take this as a declaration of love, Hamish. But it's killing you saying that to me and I know it's not what you're looking for. I don't know how to act or react. You're right. The way I am with you is different to my other clients, of course it is.' He winced at her words. Her tone took on a harder edge. 'Don't look at me like that. You introduced me to some of them

74

and to this way of life. I thought we were okay the way we were.'

'I didn't know seeing you with another man would get to me like this and I acted like an arse. I've been telling myself for ages to stop being stupid.' *Ages? Shit!* 'We're great together the way things are, but all of a sudden . . . I don't know! I want something more and it scares me shitless.' They both took a drink at the same time. He looked a little more at ease now. Maybe getting it off his chest was what he needed, but she was sure it wasn't what she needed to hear.

'Maybe it would've been better for us if you'd had this wee chat with a friend,' she said. He took her wine from her and sat both glasses down. Turning back to her, he took her wrists in his hands, restraining her.

'I've thought about that, Davina.' There was a glint in his eye and a smile on his lips now. 'But you're fucking them all.' They both laughed loudly, even though she was trying to act angry. She half-heartedly tried to pull her wrists free.

'Unbelievable, Hamish. One minute you're pouring your heart out to me, the next I'm the slapper who's humping all your pals.' Still laughing, he rolled onto his back and pulled her on top of him.

'Tell me about it!' he said. 'Every time I phone them to go for a pint, they're out drinking with you.'

'Well, get used to it,' she replied, 'because I'll be more available to them now. You're too clingy for my liking.' He licked her face coarsely with his wet tongue.

'Mm, mm, mm, oh yeah baby, you can't get rid of me. You'd miss this too much.' He let go of her and she punched him playfully in the stomach. Wiping her face with her robe, she got off the bed.

'That was the slobberiest kiss I've ever had. Oh, and FYI, that wasn't my fuck-me-fuck-me look earlier, that was my 'I'm about to chuck your pitiful arse' look. Now, are we going to this . . .' – screwing up her face, she made air quotes and used his words from earlier – '"boring function that requires your presence" tonight, or not?'

As usual, it was a grand affair. Bouffants, flashy jewellery and swanky dresses were the order of the day. Davina wore a simple plunge-necked orange sleeveless chiffon dress, her ample breasts taking the weight of the necklace with the single diamond-encrusted jet pendant that hung around her neck. With her hair up off her face, the matching earrings looked amazing. The ring on her finger completed the set that Hamish had given her. Hamish had his very own Hamilton tartan kilt ensemble on. Gavin, with his kilt and all its regalia, stood up as they approached the table.

'My God, Davina, you look stunning.' Holding her by the arms, he kissed her cheek as he always did. *Whatever you're thinking, Hamilton, I don't care. I've waited all my life for men to look at me like this.* 'This is my sister, Isobel.' He moved to the side, and Davina caught sight of a female version of Gavin: blonde hair, brown eyes and the same nose. They shook hands and introduced themselves properly. Davina learned that Isobel was a police sergeant in Aberdeen, that she hated fancy dos like this one, and that she was only here as a favour to her brother.

'Apparently, the friend that normally escorts him had another engagement.' *Friend, Hamilton, did you hear that? Friend.* Obviously, Isobel had a great fondness for her brother. The tenderness with which she told Davina she wished he could get over his wife's death and move on was heartfelt. Hamish, never known to be a wallflower, helped Isobel out of her seat. 'You look ravishing as usual,' he gushed, planting a noisy kiss on her lips.

'And you're full of it as usual.' Isobel smiled and playfully slapped Hamish's chest. Letting her sit back down, he turned and winked at Davina. *Was that show for my benefit? To make me jealous?*

He pulled Davina's seat out for her. As she moved in front of it she could feel his hot breath on her neck. He bent in and lightly kissed her cheek, his hands gently rubbing her goose-pimpled arms. His voice was thick and sensual. 'She could never be as ravishing as you, Davina,' he said.

When they'd started their arrangement, Hamish had made two very specific rules: no getting romantically involved with each other, and no public shows of affection or emotion. Right then, however, Davina felt as though he was letting everyone know, especially Gavin, that she was off-limits.

The evening was a great success, the four of them laughing at, and with, each other most of the night. Hamish and Gavin occasionally talked shop with the other three men around the table, but the majority of the night was spent dancing, which Davina loved as much as singing karaoke. Gavin received an award for his charity work for victims of drunk-drivers on behalf of Glenmuir Whisky, the company he worked for.

'These are the sort of things he should be celebrating with a wife or partner, not his sister.' Even over the din coming from their table, Davina heard the choke in Isobel's voice and concurred. Gavin was too nice a person not to have someone in his life.

Towards the end of the night, Davina and Hamish stood up from the table somewhat unsteadily, both feeling more than slightly drunk, and said their goodbyes. Davina and Isobel swapped phone numbers and promised to keep in touch. With a slight swagger, they entered the lift with two other couples and stood at the back. While everyone else faced the front, a drunken Davina tried to fondle Hamish's dick. This wasn't as easy as she'd thought it would be. Standing side by side, she had to push his sporran to the side and then try to grab his dick through the thick tweed. She gave up, frustrated, but he grabbed her hand back and forced it under his kilt. She hadn't seen him dress and didn't know if he was a true Scotsman or not. She got her answer when her soft hand met hard flesh. The lift stopped and they were the first out, barging past the other couples. Davina walked down the corridor with an air of mock disgust, her hand on her chest.

'That, sir, is gruesome,' she said.

Hamish held a pretend cigar up to his mouth, and in his best Groucho Marx voice, replied, 'Put your hand back up, it's *grue-some* more.' They fell into the room laughing, she unceremoniously kicking her shoes off on the way to the mini bar; he collapsing, knackered, onto a comfy chair.

'Great idea,' he said. 'I'll have a brandy.' Davina handed him a bottle of cold water. 'Or maybe not,' he added, giving her his petted lip look.

'We're both driving tomorrow,' she said.

Hamish took the water grudgingly as Davina walked to the bedroom, shimmied out of her dress, put it back on its hanger and hung it on the outside of the wardrobe door. In the bathroom, she peed, took her make-up off, moisturised, and brushed her teeth. Returning to the bedroom, she collapsed onto the bed, falling asleep immediately.

She woke soon after, or so it felt, disorientated and cold. Sitting up, she slowly remembered where she was. There was a half-empty bottle of water lying next to her, but no Hamish. If the clock next to the bed was to be believed, it was 20 past four in the morning. With the room spinning a little and a head like mush, she retrieved two paracetamol from her bag, used the lukewarm water to swallow them down, and then forced herself up to find out where Hamish had got to. She found him slouched in the same chair she'd left him in earlier, a full, unopened bottle of water on the floor next to him. She put a cover over him, removed her underwear and jewellery, and plodded back to bed. *Holy shit, we never even had sex last night.* An uneasy feeling passed through her and it seemed to take her forever to fall back asleep.

She was woken by the smell of fresh coffee. Opening her eyes tentatively, she assessed how groggy she was feeling. The two bottles of water and the paracetamol had done their job. Hangover-wise, it was only a four out of ten, but there was a dull feeling deep down in her stomach. Hamish was sitting next to her on the bed, wrapped in a fluffy robe. He'd just showered and looked a hell of a lot better than she felt.

'Morning. I've made coffee.' He gestured to the cup on her bedside table.

'Thanks.' *Did something crawl into my mouth and die?* She got up and went to the bathroom, where she closed the door, peed, and brushed her teeth. He smiled at her as she walked back to the bed.

'Does your morning mouth taste better now?' he asked. She poked her tongue out at him, got back under the cover, and slurped her coffee.

'Remind me never to piss you off again. Leaving a man sleeping on an uncomfortable chair . . .' – he rubbed his neck – 'just so you can have the bed to yourself.'

'Maybe if you hadn't got us so drunk, we wouldn't have passed out the minute we got in the door,' Davina countered.

They spent the rest of the morning blaming each other for the amount of drink they'd had the night before. As they showered, got dressed and packed, they talked about what a great night it had been, how well Gavin had done, and how nice his sister was. The only thing they didn't discuss was the white elephant again. They were standing beside Davina's Audi, having just checked out. Hamish looked at the ground and kicked an imaginary pebble.

'Well, here we are.' He looked at her, uncertain what to do or say next. Davina laughed at his choice of words, the atmosphere between them slightly strained all of a sudden.

'Hamish Hamilton feeling awkward. Let me take a picture.' His smile was uneasy and his eyes drifted in the direction of his own car. *No way you're getting away from me that easily.* She pulled him into her and kissed him. Pressing her fob, her car beeped sharply.

'Oh, need to go, there's my phone.' They both laughed. Both the atmosphere and Hamish's intense look eased slightly. She yanked him by the lapels. 'Phone me any time, Hamish, even if it is just to hear my manly voice.' He looked slightly embarrassed and stuck for words again. She pecked him on the cheek, rubbed his arms, winked at him, and then got in her car and drove away.

She'd only just put her phone in its hands-free cradle when it rang. 'Hello,' Davina said, brightly.

'Bye.' Hamish's short response, uncharacteristically awkward, made her smile.

Then he was gone.

CHAPTER 4

BROWN SAUCE

Looking around her brothers' luxury two-bedroom flat, even though she'd been in it many times before, she still couldn't believe how organised and tidy it was. *I suppose that's the forces' influence for you. You certainly weren't this neat or clean growing up.* It was carpeted with the same beige and brown fleck design all the way through. The walls were magnolia, the new white, colourful abstract prints hanging on most of them. *Each to their own.* On the main wall in the living room was a huge bronze-framed mirror. The kitchen was off the living room, separated by a long breakfast bar. Gleaming silver pots and utensils hung from the gantry. Some kind of incense stick was burning somewhere. Davina couldn't see it, but was nauseated by it all the same. She didn't complain, though. It was a damn sight better than the pungent smells that used to emanate from their bedroom back home. Even the smoke from their da's pipe couldn't mask that smell sometimes. Joshua, the younger of the two brothers, came back into the living room with three cups.

'Here we go. Do you want a piece, or a biscuit, Davina?' Having served in the Army for eight years, Joshua seemed to stand taller than his five foot seven frame. His hair was only slightly longer now than army regulation, even though he'd been out almost three years.

82

You can take the boy out of the army, but you can't take the army out of the boy.

Their granda, being ex-army himself, always said this whenever Ma gave Joshua a row for sitting poker straight on the couch. He was a strapping, handsome man. Davina often thought he could have had any girl he wanted growing up, and that's exactly what he seemed to do.

What a change this well-mannered, confident man in front of her was to the awkward, moody boy she'd grown up with. Back then, if he wasn't having a hissy fit about his school clothes not fitting properly, he was bemoaning the lack of toothpaste or some other obscure thing. He'd storm down the length of the lobby and slam his and Hector's bedroom door shut. The noise would reverberate throughout the house like a submarine in the wake of a depth-charge. Being as helpful as ever, their da would shout, "Must be the time of the month again," which no-one understood until much later in life.

Had it really only been six months since he'd sat across from Davina and Marge in that pretentious Merchant City wine bar, with its pretentious Merchant City prices? Davina remembered thinking it was a strange place for him to choose, but everything soon fell into place when Hector got up from his seat next to Joshua, squeezed him reassuringly on the shoulder. 'I'll get a round in,' he said.

Once Hector had left, Joshua had become agitated and nervous. *Don't say you've got cancer, don't say you've got cancer. Fuck's sake, Davina. Why did that even come into your head?* She leaned over the table and took his hand in hers, trying to take some of his anxiety from him. Marge frowned over at both of them.

'What's going on?' Davina asked.

A tense smile formed on Joshua's lips as he squeezed Davina's hand. *Christ's sake, Joshua, just tell us what it is, but don't say cancer.*

Still holding Davina's hand tight, Joshua turned to face a perplexed Marge. 'Remember the other day when I came in to your boutique and got my hair done and you talked me into getting a manicure and my eyebrows done.' *Where the hell are you going with this?* The smile plastered on Marge's face was one of pride.

'Of course, and all the girls fancied you,' Marge replied.

Joshua cleared his throat again. 'Well, anyway, do you remember you said to me, "You look like a new man"?'

'That's right,' said Marge, 'and you did. You looked amazing.' His grip on Davina's hand had gotten uncomfortable and his eyes flitted between hers and Marge's. He took a huge, unsteady breath.

'Well, to be honest, I did feel like a new man, so I went out and got one.' *Holy fuck.* Davina managed to pull her hand free from Joshua's and slapped it over her mouth. She looked at him incredulously. He looked back at her, watery eyes beseeching her. *Shit, shit, buggery shit. Well, at least it's not cancer.* They sat like that, not moving, not speaking.

'Went out and got one what?' Marge asked. Davina's hand fell slowly from her mouth and she held Joshua's again as tears fell slowly down her face. She raised her eyebrows questioningly for confirmation. Joshua's own eyes were moist. He swallowed hard and gave an apologetic nod.

Brusquely, Davina wiped her face with the back of her hand and laughed. 'Well, thank fuck. I thought for a minute you had cancer.'

'Davina!' yelled Marge. 'That's shocking language. Will somebody tell me what he went out and got?'

Laughing through his tears, Joshua mouthed a thank-you to Davina, then turned his attention to their not-so-quick-on-the-uptake sister.

'I went and got myself a new man,' he said.

Marge's face contorted in confusion. 'You what?'

'I'm gay, Marge.'

'Aaaahhhhh!' Marge's ear-piercing screech had quite a few pretentious heads turning. She leapt out her chair and ran around the table, cuddling and rocking Joshua excitedly. 'Oh my God, this is amazing. Wait till I tell them all at work.'

Joshua pulled away from her, his eyes and mouth smiling. 'I wouldn't say it was amazing, Marge,' he said.

'Wanna bet? That bitch Gail at work's brother's gay and she's always going on about how well-dressed he is. Oh my God, do you know what I always say to her? I say, well our Joshua's always dressed smart . . . and now I know why.'

'Just because a man dresses well doesn't mean he's gay, Marge.' Joshua rubbed his chin and winced. 'As I've found out to my detriment.' Davina guffawed.

'What does that mean?' Marge asked.

'It means,' said Davina, 'that you and Joshua shouldn't judge a book by its cover.'

'And what the hell does that mean?'

Davina looked at her sister as though looking at an infant. 'Seriously, Marge, are you really that thick? It means Joshua's made the same mistake as you and got a sore face for his troubles.'

'Aw.' Finally, the penny dropped, which led her to ask Joshua lots of cringeworthy questions that mostly went unanswered.

Now, here they were, her wee brother more relaxed, more open, and happier than she'd ever remembered him being. He handed Davina a cup of tea.

'You got any plain biscuits?' she asked.

Just then, Hector entered the room. At a walloping six foot five, he had to duck the door frame to avoid scalping himself.

'Watching your figure, Davina?' he asked. 'You've lost a lot of weight, have you not?' Built like a runner bean, Hector had the opposite problem from Davina: he could never put weight on. His gangly physique meant he was also on the receiving end of a lot of ridicule at school. He was, however, as he took great delight in telling them in the mimicking tones of the recruitment officer, "Just what the police force were looking for."

'I have indeed,' replied Davina proudly. 'It's all that hill-walking I do around by the bungalow.' *And sex, of course*.

Joshua handed her a biscuit. 'There you are, pal. You can't beat a suggestive digestive.' Hearing her wee brother use the phrase their da always used made Davina smile. Chocolate biscuits had only featured at Christmas time in the Brown household, and even then they were rationed out by their da.

'Is Marge coming along?' Joshua had aimed his question at Hector, but Davina spoke without thinking.

'She'll need written permission from his lordship first.' The bitterness in her voice was blatant enough to stop both her brothers' cups in mid-air, their eyebrows rising in surprise. *Well, you've said it now*. 'Come on,' she said. 'You're bound to have noticed she can't even fart without his permission.' Their blank expressions told her she was on her own with this line of thought.

86

'Hiya!' The front door opened and their sister breezed in. Even Davina had to admit that she sounded good. Marge had no make-up on, and the jumper she wore went right up her neck. Even though she was gorgeous, Marge usually insisted on caking her make-up on, so much so that the family had taunted her rotten about it for years.

'What have I missed?' Marge had a knack of lighting up every room she entered.

'Where's the tits 'n' slap?' Hector asked, unable to hide his surprise at his sister's appearance. 'Not that I don't approve, but normally your top's so low you can see your breakfast, and you've usually got more make-up on than Katie Price.'

'Leave her alone,' said Joshua, ruffling her hair as he passed. 'She looks great.' He smiled at his sister. 'Wait and I'll get you a cup of tea and you can wrestle the biscuits from Davina.'

'Cheeky shit! Did you say to Robert about coming out with us on Saturday?' Davina asked Marge.

'Yes,' said Marge. 'Text me the details. It'll be a laugh.' Her smile was infectious and Davina wondered if she was wrong about her sister's situation.

'Right, Operation Tell Ma and Da I'm Gay can commence,' said Joshua. He sat Marge's tea on the table next to her as Hector threw her a coaster. The sisters looked at each other and laughed.

'What?' said Hector. 'Do you know how much that table cost me?'

'Christ, Hector, you're gayer than me.' All four of them were laughing now. Davina missed the time they all spent together; missed the banter between them. They talked about going out to Merchant Pride on Saturday. The pub was cheap and cheerful on a Saturday afternoon, and had singers on. The fact it was a gay bar was a bonus as far as Joshua was concerned. They discussed what time they should be there as the show started at five. It was well known in Glasgow that Barbara Bryceland was the best singer around. When she was singing there, the seats went fast. Davina had a shindig at The Admiral Hotel in Glasgow on the Friday night, but had made sure her calendar was clear for the Saturday. The girls discussed whether it was a heels or flats event, while the men were thinking about which football match was on at the same time and if it was worth watching it in the pub next door first before going in.

'Well, we're not keeping seats again,' said Davina. 'Mind the last time, Marge? Desperate Dan in a pink dress and an old slapper with an *Oor Wullie* hairstyle asked us if we . . .' – Davina put on a deep voice – 'wouldn't mind the company of two queers with beers.' They all laughed at the memory.

'Turns out they were brother and sister,' Joshua said incredulously. 'What are the chances?'

Without looking at each other, Davina and Marge replied in unison. 'None!'

'Oh, I don't know, Davina,' teased Hector. 'You used to have the same haircut back in the day.'

'Don't remind me.' Davina shuddered at the memory.

Laughing, they finished their tea and biscuits and Joshua cleared everything away. The real reason for them getting together couldn't be put off any longer. The thought made Joshua a little apprehensive, and it showed.

'Don't worry about it,' Marge reassured him. 'Da'll be fine. He'll probably need time to get his head around it, that's all.'

'Easy for you to say, Marge. You were always his favourite.'

It was a well-known fact in the Brown household that Marge was indeed Da's favourite. 'It was bad enough when I told him I was leaving the Army,' said Joshua. Puffing on an invisible pipe, he adopted Da's voice. '"What will I tell them down the pub? They all came to your going away party." I couldn't give a shit what he told them. I'd been in for eight years. Let him go over and watch his pals get blown to bits.' He was angry now. Joshua had never told any of them his reasons for leaving the Army. They didn't care, as long as he was back in one piece.

'Aw, come on,' said Marge. 'He's not that bad. He was really proud when you joined and just a bit disappointed when you left, that's all.' Marge couldn't help herself. She wouldn't hear a word against their da. Noting Joshua's irritation, Hector stood up.

'I think you should get Ma to invite us round for dinner tomorrow night. We'll come with you into the kitchen and tell Ma, then we can tackle Da in the living room. Divide and conquer, as it were.'

'You're not going to hit him, are you?' Marge's idiocy never ceased to amaze.

'No,' replied Davina. 'They're not going to hit him, although we might give you a slap.'

Undaunted by her sister's remark, Marge carried on. 'It could've been worse. You could've been thrown out of the army for, you know . . .' Her eyes and finger were pointing at Joshua's crotch. 'That would've been really embarrassing for you and Da.' Three perplexed faces stared back at Marge, exasperating her. 'Like Tam Webster!' she added. She paused, as if this explained everything. It was well known that Tam Webster had been thrown out of the Navy because of his drinking, but what that had to do with Joshua and his crotch God only knew. Davina and Hector were still nonplussed, but Joshua had a huge grin on his face and was struggling not to laugh.

Still getting no reaction, Marge's face turned scarlet. 'Premature ejaculation!' she blurted out.

'What the hell are you talking about?' Davina was as puzzled as Hector, but when she looked across at Joshua she couldn't help but smile. *What did you tell her?*

'His wife was in the salon,' Marge continued, 'and told us he'd gotten a dishonorable discharge from the Navy. Joshua told me that's just a fancy name in the forces for premature ejaculation.' As the three of them laughed hysterically it was Marge's turn to look perplexed. 'Did I say it wrong?'

Wiping the tears from her face, Davina shook her head. 'Un . . . believable.' She was shaking her head but grinning ridiculously. 'Right, it's sorted. Joshua's going to get Ma to invite us all to dinner tomorrow night and we'll do this once and for all.' Turning to Joshua, she smiled. 'You're shocking! You know how gullible she is.' Joshua shrugged his shoulders apologetically.

Marge's face was serious now. 'I can't go tomorrow night. Robert wouldn't like to be in by himself two nights in a row.' Davina turned to her brothers, wearing her "told you so" expression.

'But, Marge,' said Hector, 'if you're there, Da won't lose the plot.' Her brother's tone told Davina that, like her, he wasn't exactly looking forward to this either. Standing up and putting her coat on, Marge looked at them regretfully.

'Sorry, Joshua, I can't. Let me know how it goes.' She turned to Davina. 'Mind and text me about Saturday. See you all later.' She gave them a quick wave then made a hasty exit. Joshua slumped into his chair.

'That'll be that then,' he said. 'She was my secret weapon.' *Christ's sake, Marge, this is going to be a nightmare without you.*

'Listen,' said Davina, 'we'll be fine without her. Phone Ma right now and get the ball rolling.' Davina's heart went out to her brother, but this couldn't be postponed any longer. He needed to deal with it and get on with his life. She squeezed the tops of his shoulders. 'It'll be fine, honest.'

Hector had been in the kitchen, listening, and came back in holding up a half-empty black bin bag. 'I'll get you out, Davina. This needs emptied. Joshua, I'll be back in a minute. Phone Ma.' Once they were outside the flat, Hector turned to Davina. 'So what's going on with Marge?'

'I'm not sure,' said Davina, 'but she's changed. Even you noticed that today. She hardly does her make-up or goes out, and when she does, that tube she stays with is always with her. I've got to phone or text *her*, it's never the other way about anymore. I'm worried she's going to end up like our old neighbour, Nosey Parker.'

Hector grabbed Davina's arm and spun her around. 'Robert's hitting her?' The anger and shock was etched across his face. 'I'll kill him. I see this sort of thing day in, day out. Women phoning us up, scared shitless of their men, but when we arrive it's all "It was a mistake, Officer, he didn't mean it, he loves me, it won't happen again." To tell the truth, Davina, I feel like giving them a shake for putting up with it, but if you're telling me this is what's going on with Marge, I can't stand by and do nothing.'

'I know,' said Davina. 'I feel the same way. I don't know if he physically abuses her, but he certainly calls all the shots. He tells her when she can and can't go out, what she's to wear, when she's to be home. She can't fart without his say so and she won't hear a word said against him.' Looking pensive, she carried on. 'It's easier to go with a bully than against them. I should know.' She sighed and her brother gave her arm a squeeze. A smile appeared on her face, but quickly dissolved. 'I just never imagined our Marge would be in this situation. I don't get it. So, on Saturday, if she does go out with us, I'm planning on getting her drunk and getting to the bottom of it.'

Hector ran his fingers through his greased-back hair. 'I could do a background check on him at work, but I've got this promotion coming up. I wouldn't want to jeopardise my chances.'

Davina knew how hard he'd worked at trying to become a Detective Inspector, and didn't want the likes of Robert Clarke threatening that. 'No, no, don't do that. He's not worth the risk and, anyway, people like him always fly under the radar. I'll talk to her on Saturday.'

Their phones beeped at the same time. It was the same message.

'Well,' said Davina, 'Joshua's done his bit. Ma's making lasagne. Magic. Let's get Joshua sorted then we can work on Marge, okay? I'll see you tomorrow night.'

Davina walked the short distance from her brothers' flat to her parents' house. Ma always made her welcome when she came back home. When she wasn't "socialising" with a client, there was nowhere she'd rather stay, but her thoughts were all over the place. She knew Ma would be fine about Joshua after the initial shock wore off. She just wished the same could be said about Da. He was old school, and that worried her. At five foot five and 12 stone something, he wasn't the most intimidating man to the average punter, but to the Brown clan he definitely was. His tongue could do more damage than his fists ever could. He was never one to raise his voice though, because he'd never had to.

Davina couldn't remember there ever being a big drama in the Brown household, but this one – Joshua's coming out – had the possibility of causing a massive upset. Then there was the Hamish issue. Pulling her mobile out, she changed her mind about staying over and called her best pal. Fuck, who was she kidding? Grace was her *only* pal. *Don't be at work, don't be at work.* Just when she thought the phone was going to ring out, a breathy voice answered.

'Hello, stranger. Long time no speak. How you doing?'

'Shite, but thanks for asking. What you up to? Have I interrupted anything?'

'Chance would be a fine thing. No, I was in the shower – alone, may I add. After all, we've not all got men on tap, like some I could mention.'

'Cool. I'll be over in ten.'

CHAPTER 5

BROWN SAUCE

Having left her car at Ma and Da's, Davina walked the short distance to the local taxi rank and was soon sitting in the back of a black cab. She gave the driver Grace's address and sat back, thinking about the first time she'd told Grace about her new life:

Davina had never looked so good. Down to a size 12, her cheekbones were well defined and her complexion was glowing. When she caught her reflection in the mirror or a shop window, she had to do a double take. Yes, she looked amazing, even if she did say so herself, but she felt lousy; her double life was taking its toll. She hardly ate or slept and kept conversations and socialising with her family to a minimum for fear of tripping herself up. Sir Walter Scott had summed it up perfectly, it *is* a tangled web we weave. She positively thrived being known as Katy Miller and rubbing shoulders with Scotland's rich and sometimes famous, wearing stunning dresses, jewellery to die for – donated mostly by Hamish – and being complimented by all who met her. *That* Davina Brown, she discovered, was well-versed, well-dressed, well-liked and, by this point, well and truly fucked. It was like a dream; someone else's life. The flipside, though, was making her ill. Whenever she was in any of her family's company, her hands sweated, her throat dried up, and her stomach did cartwheels. The stress was killing her. After almost ten months of delirious hell, she decided enough was enough.

Armed with three bottles of wine, she pressed the buzzer to Grace's door, hoping against hope that her friend wouldn't be working tonight. With Davina's new-found employment, and Grace working shifts at Churchman's Care Home, there was a severe dent in the amount of time they could spend together. Grace had a bathrobe on and a towel wrapped round her long auburn hair when she opened the door. She smiled at Davina, her eyes widening at the sight of the wine.

'Oh ya beauty, what's the occasion?' she asked. Davina ignored her and barged past into the hallway. Both girls were the height of nonsense, as Ma would often say. They shared the same buxom figure and their looks were often referred to as pretty as opposed to beautiful, but in each other's company, looks and appearance never came in to the equation. They never judged each other, or anyone else for that matter. Davina hadn't planned anything more than getting pissed, but after drinking the lion's share of two bottles of the corner shop's finest Pinot Grigio, she turned to her friend and said, as nonchalantly as possible, 'Do you think you'll get a male roommate?'

'Oh, definitely.' Grace's reply oozed sarcasm. 'And pigs'll fly.' She shuffled around on the couch, trying to get more comfortable. 'Let's face it, Davina. It's not going to happen for us. We'll die virgins.'

'Don't be so negative,' replied Davina. 'We'll have plenty men in our lives . . . and our beds.'

Grace raised her eyebrows. 'Now you're virgin on the ridiculous. Girls like us don't get Prince Charming on his mighty steed coming to rescue us from our ordinary lives, shagging our brains out, and living happily ever after.'

Davina smiled at her friend's personal take on bliss. 'Why not? We deserve happiness the same as everyone else. There's nobody better than us.'

'Spoken like a true Brown.' Grace clinked her glass with Davina's.

Davina braced herself. 'What would you say if I told you I'd already slept with someone?'

Grace sat bolt upright, sloshing her drink over both of them. 'Are you shitting me?' She suddenly looked sober. 'Who? When? Seriously? Are you kidding?'

The mixture of Grace's disbelief and shock made Davina feel quite pleased, possibly even proud. They'd gone through a lot together. Neither of them had been that good-looking when they were younger, and as a consequence they'd been bullied or ignored by their peers most of their lives. Sharing a lack of confidence in speaking up for themselves, a bond had soon formed between them, one that had grown strong over the years. Davina wasn't sure it would withstand her revelation tonight, though. She wasn't ashamed of what she'd become, but she wasn't ready to shout about it from the rooftops either. She just needed someone to confide in. *Who better than the one person in life I'd hate to lose the most?*

With much trepidation she carried on. 'More than one person actually, there's been a few.' Grace's mouth fell open, eyes wide. It was the next admission, however, that had Davina almost choking with fear at how Grace would take it. 'And . . . they pay me.'

'Holy fuck! Holyyyy fuck!' While Grace struggled to digest what she'd just heard, tears fell from Davina's eyes.

Say something.

'You're serious.' Grace's voice was so soft, the loving look in her eyes so tender, it brought a fresh wave of tears down Davina's cheeks. Grace reached up and stroked her friend's face, crying herself now. Sitting both wine glasses on the floor, Grace folded Davina up in her arms, holding her tight. Even if they never spoke again, the relief Davina felt was instantaneous. The huge weight she'd been carrying around, which had been mental rather than physical for once, fell away.

Grace took Davina's hands in hers. 'Why didn't you come to me? I'm not loaded, but I could've got a hold of some money for you.'

The pity and concern in Grace's eyes was unbearable, yet the laughter rising in Davina was unstoppable. She threw her head back and let loose the most heartfelt, relaxed laugh she'd had in ages. Bringing her head forward again, she saw confusion mixed with sadness on Grace's face.

'It's not like that.' Davina said, handing Grace her glass back. She took a big gulp of her own and started from the beginning: how she'd met Hamish, how he'd become so instrumental in her transformation from the frumpy, quiet, unimposing, well-to-do, girl from next door, to the charismatic, thinner, confident, bubbly woman sitting beside her now. It hadn't been the money or extravagant gifts Hamish had lavished on her that had brought about such a dramatic change. It had been the enthusiasm with which he'd complimented her, and all of his words of encouragement, not to mention his ability to laugh with, and at, her without her feeling self-conscious. The furtive, sometimes lecherous, looks he often shot in her direction hadn't hurt either. She explained how he'd introduced her to safe businessmen, and had encouraged her to get her own business cards, which she discretely left on the tables of men who were on their own at the various functions she attended. She admitted to an initial awkwardness with these men when they realised that the intelligent, sharp-witted voice on the end of the phone wasn't quite matched in the looks department when they met in the flesh, but that the awkwardness soon dissolved once they got talking.

A couple of times during her confession, Davina had to close Grace's mouth, which kept gaping. When Grace sat their drinks down again and squeezed the life from her, Davina finally relaxed. Letting Davina back up for air, Grace smiled incredulously and shook her head slowly from side to side.

'Bitch, I'm so jealous,' she said. 'Can you throw any of them my way? Just the two will do, I'm not greedy.' *That's the Grace I know and love.* Suddenly, Grace turned serious, brows knitted together. 'What's it like, Davina? You know . . . actual sex. Is it really sore the first time?'

'Not really, but then I was really relaxed and really, really wanted to do it.' Her eyes were smiling, reliving how caring Hamish had been. She was starting to feel horny just thinking about it. Grace was still looking at her, beseechingly. Davina squirmed uncomfortably and cleared her throat. 'Well, anyway, remember when we were young and your ma and da used to take us to the beach at the weekend in their car?'

'Uh-huh,' Grace said, her expression quizzical.

'Well, mind the windy roads with the bumps that made our stomachs flip and go berserk?'

'Yip, and we'd scream and sometimes pee ourselves.' Grace laughed at the memory.

'Well,' said Davina. 'Imagine that feeling times a million . . . but between your legs. That's what sex is like.'

The rest of the evening was practically an interrogation, but instead of a bright light being used to loosen Davina's tongue, it was white wine. Neither were necessary; she loved finally being able to tell someone of her new status as a high class escort.

Now, seven years later, sitting next to Grace in her girly – she hated that word – flat, Davina felt herself unwind. Grace didn't always have the answers, or say what Davina wanted to hear, but she was a good listener and never bullshitted her. She handed Davina a mug of hot chocolate.

'Let me get this straight. Hamish declared his undying "maybe" love for you five days ago and you haven't heard from him since. And you,' – she shrugged her shoulders – 'miss him? Don't miss him? What?'

'I'm missing him like mad,' admitted Davina, 'but am I missing him this badly because of what he said? Or did I always feel like this about him and not realise? Fuck, what a mess. I just don't know, I've never had to think about it before. We've never not spoken or texted for this length of time since . . .' – Davina stared into space – 'well, since forever! Then there's Logan. I've always loved him, you know that, but to him we're just fuck buddies. My place is just a place to crash when he's here.'

Grace looked at Davina sceptically. 'I wouldn't be so sure about that, Davina. If you're in Inverness, he flies into Aberdeen then heads to you. If you're down here, he gets a flight to Glasgow and you meet up. The boy's besotted with you.'

It took Davina a couple of seconds to comprehend that what Grace had said was true. *How could I have missed that? It was right in front of you, Brown. No, it's just convenient for him to stay at mine, even though he does have a great flat right here in Glasgow. Granted, there's hardly anything of his in it, but . . . besotted? No, that wasn't right; wasn't possible.*

'You could enter Britain's funniest face competition; it's contorted about a million times.' Grace was laughing now. 'I can just see you on that programme, with your head through a toilet seat pulling faces. The one you're wearing right now would be the winner.' Not biting, Davina threw Grace what she hoped was one of her best shady looks. *Great, I've come here for answers and advice and all I've got is more headache and ridicule.*

'It's not like that with Logan.'

'Says who? You! Have you asked him how he feels?'

'Are you joking? Ask Logan how he feels about me and jeopardise everything we have? No thank you. I just know we're fuck buddies, end of. I mean, it's not like we text each other that often. We don't even go out in public together.' *Not like me and Hamish.*

'Are you trying to convince me or yourself?' asked Grace. 'When's he back in the country?'

'God knows,' Davina shrugged. 'See, we haven't even discussed that yet! We're just . . .'

'Fuck buddies, yes, I heard you the first ten times. How about the next time he's here, you suggest going for a meal or the pictures, something normal outside the bedroom?' Grace's smile covered her face. 'However, I can understand why you'd be reluctant to leave the bedroom with a man like him at your beck and call.' Davina grinned like a Cheshire cat as she remembered the last night and morning she'd shared with Logan. The cushion that hit her square in the face brought her back from her delicious daydream and had her spilling some of her hot chocolate. 'Lucky bitch,' Grace growled. They laughed, finished their drinks and took their cups into the kitchen.

'So, seriously though,' asked Davina. 'What do you think I should do? Things can never be the same again for me and Hamish. We can't go back to the way it was, but I don't want to lose him as a friend, or, if I'm completely honest, a lover either. I talk to him about almost everything. He's always made me feel special and that anything's possible. With Logan, though, it feels different. In some ways it's a lot more complicated, but in others it's more natural. But I can't confide in him as much, for obvious reasons.'

'It seems to me the only time you meet up with both of them is to have mind blowing sex. Your words, bitch. So the only way to find out how you really feel about them, and vice versa, is to have a normal relationship. You know, go on proper dates, maybe even eventually introduce them to your parents and family. Obviously they already know Logan, but not as your boyfriend. No sex involved, just like normal people. You know, like the rest of us mere mortals that aren't getting any.' Grace put on her sad face and stuck out her bottom lip.

'Right then,' nodded Davina sarcastically. 'I can just picture it. Hi, Ma and Da, this is Hamish. He's been paying me to have sex with him for eight years but, to be honest, I'd have done it free of charge. And you know Logan of course. Well, he's my fuck buddy, and we've been shagging each other senseless up at the bungalow every opportunity we can get.' Grace giggled childishly, no doubt picturing Davina's ma and da's faces receiving such news. 'A normal relationship?' Davina went on 'I don't even know what that means, or what that's actually like. Somewhere along the line I missed out the middle man.' She leaned against the worktop looking pensive. 'That was the part I'd always dreamt of: holding hands in the street with someone who wasn't embarrassed to be seen with me, kissing and laughing in public like normal people.' She realised that although her life had turned out better than she could have wished for, there was still something missing; still a void that she hoped to fill. 'You're right, though,' Davina said, serious now. 'I don't regret the way things have gone, but I've done things arse for elbow. Although I've been having great fun, most of the time, I've missed out on a lot of the things having a boyfriend brings, before getting down to the nitty gritty part. Obviously I've never looked at my clients as boyfriends, but you know what I mean.'

'Ew, yuck! I'd hope not,' said Grace. 'Especially not the one that likes you to fold the hotel towels around him like a nappy and breastfeed him. Can you imagine taking him home to meet your parents? A big nappy on his arse, a baby's bonnet on his head, and a big tit in his mouth. And I don't mean the dummy type.' Grace was buckled up as she played out the scenario in her head.

'And you think my life's all glitz and glamour,' said Davina. 'I had to go all the way to fecking Coventry for that particular pleasure. It makes me shudder thinking of some of the things I've done. I've definitely earned my stripes, as Granda would say.' She stood up. 'Right!' she said. 'I think you've slagged me more than enough for one night. I'm off. Thanks for the chinwag. I'd like to say you've helped immensely, but you haven't!' She grinned down at Grace.

Grace laughed and stood up, linking arms with Davina. 'Just telling it as I see it. Why don't you stay the night? We can reminisce about more of your extreme endeavours and I'll drive you home tomorrow.'

'Okay,' said Davina. 'I'll text Ma, but I'm not cheap, mind.'

'And I'm not that easy, Grace laughed. 'Get over yourself.'

CHAPTER 6

BROWN SAUCE

Grace, having been talked into coming out on Saturday, dropped Davina off at the town centre for a shopping spree. She wanted to buy gifts for Ma, Da, Granda, Henry, the twins, and Lucy. She smiled to herself as she traipsed through John Lewis. *It wasn't that long ago you could walk the length and breadth of Glasgow without anyone noticing you, Brown. Yet already this morning you've been on the receiving end of more than a few admiring glances . . . Yes, I could definitely get used to this.*

An hour or so later, Davina was back home, cheerfully doling out her presents.

'What's the occasion?' Da asked, holding his new jumper to his chest. 'I like that. I'll wear it the next time I go to the pub. Thanks, Davina.' *Hopefully he'll be in a good mood tonight as well.* Ma and Granda were just as pleased with their new perfume and tobacco respectively.

'Come on, Davina, you can help me dress my dollies with their new stuff.' Taking her hand, Lucy pulled Davina down the lobby to the bedroom she shared with Henry. They stayed there most of the morning, changing, feeding, then putting the dolls to bed. Davina had detested playing with dolls when she was a kid, but watching how seriously Lucy took what they were doing, she had to smile, even if it was just on the inside. When the twins got in from school, they were delighted with their gift. They gave their big sister an awkward hug, then ran into their room to play Fifa on their Xbox, shouting, 'Thanks, Davina!'

When Davina had arrived two days earlier, the four kids and Granda had been seated around the dining table in the living room. A chorus of 'Hiya, Davina!' had gone up and she'd taken the seat next to Lucy, smiling across at her granda, whose twinkling eyes had beamed back at her. This grey haired, 77-year-old version of her da was, to her, the man of the house. Having become a widower at the age of 30, he'd brought his son up on his own. Apparently, there wasn't a woman on God's green earth that could hold a candle to his beloved Marjorie and so he'd never married again. He'd stayed with the family for as long as Davina could remember, sleeping on the couch. Having served in the army as a young man, he was regimented in everything he did. The clothes he took off at night were folded neatly beside the couch and the shelf he had in the bathroom had his toiletries lined up in an orderly fashion. He was always up at the crack of dawn, tidying away his bedding long before anyone else had risen. Ma had told him umpteen times that there was no need for him to get up so early and do this. They'd manage breakfast at the table – a mere six feet away from his makeshift bed – just fine without him troubling himself. But Granda wouldn't hear of it. As far as he was concerned, he was already taking advantage of her good nature by adding to her extensive family, so there was no way he was going to be a hindrance to her hectic mornings as well. Unlike Da, he was more than happy to muck in, as he put it, helping the weans get ready for school, tidying up after they were gone, and then helping them with their homework when they got back. And if the contented look on his face was anything to go by, he loved every minute of it.

Even now, sitting with his captive audience, his smile spoke volumes.

'Did you know, Granda,' Henry said, reading from a book on deaths, burials and reincarnation, 'that they tied tags to the dead person's big toe with their name, sex and date of birth on it, and if their feet were missing, they put it on their wrist?' Henry was quite matter of fact with his statement.

'Yes, but did you also know . . .' – Granda winked at Davina – 'that before tags, they used to write their details on the soles of their feet, because that's the most sensitive part of the body, and if by any chance they were still alive, they'd move or wake up? And when that happened, the mortician had lollipops steeping in a strong tranquiliser, which he'd make the person sook on until they fell back asleep. Then he'd arrange for them to go back home, and when they woke up, they were none the wiser as to where they had been. And to this day, some doctors still give out lollipops to their patients.'

The three youngest sets of eyes were drawn as far back in their heads as was humanly possible, their chins almost hitting the table. Henry, however, lifted his book, and the rest of his dinner, shook his head despairingly, and left the living room. Lucy shimmied off her seat and ran into the kitchen.

'Me no like the lollies Doctor Jenkins has,' she whined at Ma. The twins looked at each other, turned back to Granda, and in an incredulous high-pitch tone, with the uncanniness they'd all gotten used to, asked in unison: 'Did that ever happen to you, Granda?'

Even their da, who was as deaf as a door-post, heard the awe in their voices and sat in his armchair, laughing.

'It sure did,' said Granda, 'but that's a story for another day, lads. Let me talk to my favourite girl.'

Now, two days later, handing Henry the book on deaths, rituals, ceremonies and beliefs she'd bought him, Davina knew by the expression on his face it was the right choice.

'Thank you, Davina.' He kissed her and gave her a cuddle. 'Wait till I show Gordon this, he's coming over later to do maths homework. He'll love it.'

Sitting on the ancient couch next to Davina, Granda lifted her hands, squeezed them tight, and gave her a genuine smile.

'How's things, pal? You get prettier every time I see you.' She squeezed his hands in return and smiled back. His capacity for spinning a yarn was legendary in this part of Glasgow, but when it came to family, his feelings were 100 percent genuine.

'I'm great, Granda. Remember, you can visit me anytime. I've got the bungalow looking good and there's always a bed there for you. You should come up for a few days. Put your feet up and relax.'

'Yeah, because we run him ragged here.' Da spoke without lifting his head from his paper. 'It's a hard life he's got!'

'Don't listen to him,' said Granda. 'He's just jealous you didn't ask him.' *Like that would ever happen.* 'I might just do that, pal,' he said to Davina. 'Can I bring a friend? We could do some fishing while we're there.'

'Of course you can,' said Davina. 'As long as they're not too rowdy.' She winked at him and got up. 'I better see if Ma needs a hand.' She kissed Granda's cheek and went into the kitchen.

Ma was where she'd seemed to spend most of Davina's childhood: humming away to herself at the kitchen sink, wearing the same pinny she'd worn for years. As usual, the radio was on in the background. Music had always played a huge part in the Brown household.

When they were young, money had been scarce, so the radio had been on more often than the TV. It was one of three items in the house that had a "special bank" attached to it that "did wonderful things when you put 50 pence pieces in them," as Granda had informed them. This encouraged family members to part with their savings and make a deposit just before the highlights of an Old Firm match were about to come on, or if the gas fire hadn't been on for a while. The electricity's "special bank" got priority, though. It was never allowed to run out because of the food in the freezer. Granda was right though: wonderful things did happen if they put 50 pence in them. When the nice men from Granada, and the gas and electricity boards, came and emptied the boxes with their special keys, they counted the money for Ma, then took some away – which didn't make sense until later on in life – and gave her the rest back. For every 50 pence of their savings they'd put in, they got 55 pence back from their ma. "It pays to invest" she'd always say.

Davina was standing in the small kitchen now, watching her ma. 'Do you want a hand, Ma?' she asked.

'You could make a cup of tea,' said Ma, without lifting her head from the mushrooms she was cleaning. 'How's our Marge not coming tonight?' she added. 'She'll be the only one missing. D'ye think I should phone her?' Davina got the impression that, if Ma did phone, it would only make things more difficult for Marge. Unlike sharing her fears with Hector, this was a no-no. Taking the mugs from the cupboard, Davina tried to sound as flippant as possible.

'If she can tear herself away from Robert, she will. They're love's young dream at the moment.'

Ma looked at her sceptically. 'If you say so, Davina . . . How's your love life going? Anyone special I should know about?'

'No-one serious, I'm too busy,' said Davina, purposely avoiding making eye contact.

'You always were a terrible liar, Davina Brown. Just remember, I'm here if you ever want to talk.'

'I know that. It's just a bit complicated at the minute.' Davina both loved and hated these conversations with her ma. She desperately hoped that, one day in the future, when she was in a so-called normal relationship, she could share her problems with her.

'Men aren't complicated creatures,' said Ma. 'As long as they're fed and watered, they're happy. And sometimes, if you're lucky, they'll show you just how happy they are.' She turned and gave Davina a knowing smile and a wink. *Holy shit, you're not going to talk to me about sex, are you?* Davina's was appalled. In contrast, Ma's expression was one of bewilderment. 'I meant they'll share their wages, before they go to the pub,' she explained, as Davina let out a small gasp of relief. 'What did you think I meant?'

Davina lifted her cup and beat a hasty retreat out of the kitchen. 'I'll set the table,' she said, without turning round.

Henry's pal, Gordon, arrived, armed with maths books, at the same time as Hector and a pensive-looking Joshua.

'Ma, can I get my dinner in my room please?' asked Henry. 'I'm going to show Gordon my new book.'

'Okay,' said Ma. 'I'll shout you when it's ready.'

'Can we get ours in our room as well?' asked the twins, surprising no-one by spouting out in unison. 'We're playing Fifa.'

'I suppose so,' said Ma. 'But no mess, mind!'

The twins stood up from the table and frowned at each other. 'You never said that to Henry,' Derek griped.

'That's because I don't *have* to say that to Henry,' Ma replied, firmly.

The twins shrugged identical shrugs and traipsed off to their room.

'Hope you've made plenty, Ma,' said Hector, kissing her cheek as she returned to the kitchen. 'I could eat a horse.' He squeezed past and plopped himself down on the living room couch next to Granda.

'Well,' said Da, his nose in his paper as usual, 'if we're to believe the news, there's a good chance that's exactly what we have been eating.'

Granda took his unlit pipe out of his mouth. 'It won't kill us. We've been eating stuff for years without knowing exactly what's in it and it hasn't done us any harm. When we were in the army, me and Tam Colson used to hunt, kill, and cook zebra for the whole regiment, and it went down a treat. Jawbreaker Johnston, our sarge, used to roar at us. "Brown and Colson, that's the only way you'll get your stripes!" Then he'd laugh, and if you didn't laugh with him, you soon found out why he was called Jawbreaker.' Rubbing his cheek, Granda looked thoughtful. 'Christ, he had some punch on him.' He stuck his pipe back in his mouth and the room was left, not for the first time, wondering if there was any end to the bullshit this man could spin.

'Zebras!' sneered Hector, shaking his head. 'That would mean you were fighting in *Africa* – over 100 years ago!'

'So, you think the only place you find zebras is Africa?' asked Granda.

'Oh, sorry,' said Hector. 'I forgot about the great war that broke out in Edinburgh Zoo.'

Granda let a little smile escape. 'Well, I'm sure you've aw seen the film,' he said.

Hector frowned. 'What film?'

'Zulu.'

'Ahhh, I can't believe I fell for that!' Hector laughed, pushing Granda playfully.

'Joshua!' Hearing Ma shout his name snapped Joshua out of his daze. His head zipped between Davina and Hector as he walked into the kitchen with a look of dread on his face. Five minutes later, he came back with two plates of lasagne and sat them on the table. He bent down and whispered to Davina, who was sitting at the table next to The Wean.

'She thinks there's something up. I'm awfully quiet.'

'No shit, Sherlock,' said Davina. 'You're a bag of nerves and it shows. Calm down, it'll be fine.' She hoped her smile hid her own nervousness.

'Fuck, Davina, I hope you're right.' Straightening up as if he was back in the army, Joshua took a deep breath, smiled, and walked back into the kitchen. The rest of the plates were brought through with less tension in his shoulders, although his eyes gave his anxiety away. The boys collected theirs and returned to their rooms. Davina couldn't remember a quieter meal around the Brown dinner table. Even Granda was stuck for something to say.

'Is somefing a matter?' asked The Wean. 'Nobody's speaking.' Lucy's observation had everyone suddenly talking about the weather, the news, and any other mundane subject they could think of. Davina stood and started clearing away the plates.

'You've hardly touched that, Davina,' said Da. 'No wonder you're getting as skinny as Marge.'

'I wish,' said Davina. 'I'm just not that hungry tonight. I had a Burger King up the town this afternoon and I still feel full. Sorry, Ma.' She could feel the lasagne she'd eaten doing a merry dance in her stomach and knew it wouldn't remain there much longer. It was taking a great deal of effort and coaxing of her sphincter not to let it escape. The fact that her ma was looking at her through narrowed eyes wasn't helping her cause one little bit. 'Here,' Davina said to Hector, 'you can finish mine.' She pushed the plate towards her brother and ran the short distance to the bathroom. *Well done, Davina. Joshua's bound to be a lot more relaxed after that performance.* When she was done, she stood up then had to sit back down twice before her body gave her the all clear.

After her hands were well and truly scrubbed, her hair well and truly fixed, and she was well and truly sure she didn't need to do the toilet again, Davina left the bathroom.

'Do you want a play dollies again?' The Wean was waiting on her to come out, her eyes imploring, her smile huge.

'Can I play after my cup of tea?' Davina asked.

'Okay.' Lucy skipped along the lobby to the room she shared with Henry.

Ma was back at her usual posting by the sink when Davina entered the cramped kitchen. This time, though, she had her back to it and was looking alternately at her two sons, who were both looking at the floor. Closing the door behind her, Davina walked over to Joshua and gave his hand a reassuring squeeze. You could have cut the atmosphere with a blunt butter knife.

'Would somebody please tell me what's going on?' Ma's voice was etched with fear and Davina thought she heard a sob in it too. 'Is it our Marge? Has he done something to her?' There was no denying the sobs that time. Davina and Hector's heads snapped up. The anguish in Ma's face was heartbreaking. Davina turned to her brother, her eyes encouraging him to speak. Still staring at the floor, Joshua took a deep breath.

'I'm gay, Ma,' he said, in an almost apologetic voice. His tears fell freely now. Within a split second, Ma had him in her arms, swaying him side to side like he was five again.

'Shhh, shhh, shhh.' As she stroked his hair, Davina knew everything would be okay. It always was when Ma did this.

All four of them were crying now. Joshua's huge frame, engulfed by Ma's, was wracked with sobs. No-one spoke. After what seemed like an eternity, Joshua pulled himself together, cleared his throat, wiped his face with the backs of his hands and, for the first time since Davina had entered the kitchen, looked Ma in the eye. With her hands holding his face, she tenderly wiped the wetness away with her thumbs. Davina watched her shake her head slowly from side to side. Her smile was so sad looking Davina thought her heart would burst from her chest. She could practically feel the love oozing from her.

'You're a daft bugger,' said Ma. 'Why didn't you come to me earlier? And without Hoddit and Doddit here.' She nodded in Hector and Davina's direction. 'Am I that

113

bad?' Joshua shook his head, his lips clasped together, holding back the flood. Ma pressed her lips to his forehead and his shoulders jerked, years of pent-up emotion finally being released. 'Come on, son.' This was a heart-felt plea. The sight of this huge man, still her wee boy, in such distress was tearing Ma apart. She wrapped her arms around his shoulders and pulled him into her formidable chest. 'We'll be fine,' she said, rubbing her hands reassuringly up and down his back. 'And let's face it, it's not as if you're the only gay in Glasgow.' Joshua let out a little laugh. 'There's my boy,' said Ma, her smile matching his. She kissed his forehead again.

'Thanks, Ma. I love you more than you'll ever know,' he managed to say between sobs.

'I know, son, I know.' While the two of them were cuddling and swaying in the middle of the kitchen, Hector had put the kettle on and was getting the cups from the cupboard. Davina got the milk out the fridge and, taking a page from the twins' book, brother and sister smiled and winked at each other, wiping mock sweat from their brows and laughing. Ma and Joshua pulled away from one another and looked over at Davina and Hector.

'You had to be there,' said Hector, and laughed again.

Ma sat on the only chair in the kitchen, cup of tea in hand, as the others found whatever space they could on the floor to sit on. 'So now I suppose you'll need to tell the walrus in the living room, or do you want me to do it? I don't mind, but I think it'd be better coming from you.'

'I'll tell him, Ma,' said Joshua. 'Just let me get my second wind.'

'Before you do,' said Ma, 'make sure you're okay with everybody knowing your business, because as my granny

114

Bessie used to say, "For three men to keep a secret, two of them would have to be dead!"' The three siblings looked at each other and burst out laughing.

'Right, Ma,' said Hector, struggling to stand up in the confined space, 'that's worse than Granda's patter.'

'Now I understand why giraffes sleep standing up,' Davina said, having stood up with ease, and now trying to help Hector.

'Aw, very funny,' said Hector. 'If you all go out, I'll be able to get up.'

'For God's sake.' Joshua moved behind Hector and, with his arms under his brother's pits, hauled him up. 'There you go.'

'Cheers,' said Hector. 'You're pretty strong for a gay boy.' Hector hadn't seen Ma's palm come up and slap him, but he'd certainly felt the impact. 'Holy shit!' he cried, his hands automatically flying to his face to protect himself from any further attack.

'Don't – you – ever – EVER! – let me hear you – speak to – your brother – like – that – again.' Ma's rage was unbounding, each word delivered with such force that it was Hector's turn to be five again. She glowered at him as he skulked out of the kitchen with his head bowed.

'Sorry, Ma. Sorry, Joshua,' he muttered, rubbing his face.

Davina wasn't sure if the embarrassment in Hector's voice was because of what he'd said or the fact that, at the age of 31, he still wasn't too big to get a slap off his ma. Either way, she felt a wee bit sorry for him as she followed him out. Glancing at Joshua, she noticed him casting a smug look at his big brother. There was no doubt in her mind that he'd heard a lot worse from him. *Oh well, at least that's one down.* Davina padded down the hall to The Wean's bedroom. *Playing with Lucy will be . . . well, child's play after that.*

It wasn't. Ma had to rescue her, and just in the nick of time. The Wean was playing at being Ma, with Davina taking on the role of The Wean.

'It's cheeky to speak when adults are talking!' said The Wean/Ma to Davina/The Wean. 'You need your bum skelped!'

'Okay, bath time, Lucy,' interrupted Ma, saving Davina from a certain thrashing. 'You can take one of your dollies in.' Forgetting Davina's punishment, The Wean undressed Molly, her favourite dolly, in anticipation of a shared bath. Tidying up after her, Ma and Davina shared a smile.

'I spoke to Joshua,' whispered Ma, so The Wean wouldn't overhear. 'I told him your da'll be alright, but that it'll take a wee while. He's away to speak to him just now. Maybe once we've sorted out our Joshua, we can see what's going on with our Marge.' She fixed Davina a knowing look, one that didn't invite argument.

Back in the living room, Davina settled herself on the floor between Joshua and Hector's legs.

'Mind you'll need to speak up when you talk to Da,' Hector told Joshua. 'Watch this. Hey, Da? Idiots say what?'

'What?' Da lowered his paper and turned his so-called good ear towards a grinning Hector.

'I'm saying, Ma's lost the plot.' All three siblings were struggling to suppress their laughter.

'You're right there,' said Da, flicking his paper back up.

'Da?' Hector was enjoying himself now. 'Joshua likes the cock.' For this, he received a swift dig in the ribs from his brother.

'That's a great idea,' said Da, folding his paper. Leaning over, he gently shook Granda, who was asleep on the couch next to Hector. 'The lads are wanting to go for a walk. Do you fancy it?' Muffled laughter came from the couch. Da got out his seat and headed to the door. 'I'll wear my new jumper Davina bought me, and we could get a pint.'

'Thank God for that,' said Granda, opening one eye and looking at Hector. 'For a minute there, I thought you'd said that Joshua likes the cock!' *Holy shit!* The laughing stopped abruptly and three mouths fell open. 'Think I'll give this one a miss, son!' Granda shouted towards the door.

Da walked back in with his new jumper on, jacket in hand, pipe in mouth. 'Suit yourself. I'll have one for you.'

'Think you better have ten.' Granda had closed his eyes and folded his arms over his chest.

'What's that you're saying, Da?'

'I said, say hiya to Len.' With that, Granda snuggled further into the couch and began making the noises Davina, Hector, and Joshua normally associated with him sleeping. After today, however, they vowed never to assume he was sleeping again.

'Will do,' said Da. He kicked at the soles of Hector's shoes. 'Come on then, this was your idea.' He grinned. 'You should see your faces. Have you never heard Granda refuse a drink before?'

Still open-mouthed, the siblings slowly they got to their feet. Searching each other's faces for some kind of inspiration as to what to do next, all they found was the same dumbfounded expression looking back at them. They put their jackets on in silence and headed out the door.

'Good luck!' Ma shouted from the kitchen. The only thing she got back was silence.

Davina walked arm-in-arm with Da. Behind her, she could hear Joshua remonstrating with Hector.

'You fucking idiot. Now Granda knows.' There was more annoyance than anger in Joshua's voice.

'I'm sorry,' Hector said, holding up his hands. 'I genuinely thought he was sleeping. How many times have we spoken about . . .' – he shrugged – 'well, everything in front of him, thinking he was asleep? The fly old bugger's been listening to us for years.'

'I was just thinking,' said Joshua. 'It's a good job you never went into much detail that time you told me about the slapper you picked up with the false leg.' For the first time that night, Joshua really laughed. 'Thankfully, you kept the gory bits until we were in our room!'

'God's sake,' said Hector. 'I forgot about her. When she told me to throw her leg over my shoulder, I didn't think she meant literally.' Both men fell about in hysterics.

'Then she told you to sook her big toe, and you said . . .' Joshua couldn't finish the sentence. He was holding his stomach and laughing too hard. Hector had to finish it for him.

'"Why? You won't feel it anyway!" That has to go down as one of *the* most embarrassing nights of my life, but hey, I'm glad it cheered you up.'

Davina was glad her da's jacket collar was pulled up and he had his cap down. She wasn't sure he'd approve of his sons' bawdy conversation, had he actually heard any of it. As it was, he was on a mission, oblivious to what was going on behind him. All he could see was the bar up ahead. Davina smiled, and walked into the pub with her da, believing everything would be just fine.

'I'll get the seats!' shouted Da. He greeted the other eight people sitting at the bar – 'How's it going?' – but never stopped. Just like in the house, Da had his favourite seat, and hell mend anyone that sat in it.

'He's a tight old cunt,' said Joshua. 'Maybe I'd be better off if he didn't speak to me again. What you having, Davina?' Joshua's demeanour was a lot more relaxed than before, and it filtered through to Davina and Hector.

'A pint of lager and lime please.' Davina turned back around in her seat to find her da scowling at her.

'Women don't drink pints,' he barked.

'And how many women have you bought a drink for lately?' asked Hector, sitting down beside them. 'In fact, when was the last time you bought a drink full stop?'

'You don't ask your da out for a drink and expect him to pay.'

'We never mentioned drink,' Hector corrected him. 'You did. We were happy just to go for a walk.'

'Shut your face, you moany shite. Next you'll be saying you're not paying for a game of pool.' Da linked his fingers together and cracked his knuckles as Joshua sat the tray of drinks on the table. 'Have you got any coins on you for the table, Joshua? I'll show you all why they call me Black Ball Brown.' Da's jacket and jumper were off and he was rolling up his shirt sleeves before he'd even taken the first sip of his pint.

'Bullshitter Brown, more like,' Hector whispered.

Davina sprayed the table with a mouthful of lager. *Arse*. 'Do you have to wait till I'm drinking to be funny?' She wiped the lager off her chin and got a cloth from the barman.

Time passed quickly. As usual, the banter between them was great. Someone once accused the Browns of having their own humour that only they understood. They were right. Watching her brothers take on Da and Lazy-Eyed Laidlaw, a close friend of their parents with the unfortunate ability of being able to look both east and west at the same time, at doubles, had Davina remembering something Hamish and Isobel had said and a wave of inspiration washed over her. Why was it, she thought with a stupid drunken grin, that all your best ideas come when you've been drinking? She pulled out her phone and texted Gavin.

'Christ's sake, Lazy, what eye were you using for that shot? I'd be as well partnering The Wean.' Da was in good form. He had a good rapport with everybody in the pub.

'What are you on about?' said Lazy. 'I only missed that by a midge's pube.'

'Hey, watch your language, my daughter's here.' Da was serious.

'Sorry, Davina.' Lazy raised an apologetic hand.

'You're okay, Mr Laidlaw. I've heard worse. Does Mrs Laidlaw not come out any more?'

'No,' said Lazy. 'Apparently I look at other women all the time.' There weren't many people left in the pub by now, but it was in uproar.

Hector had been mid-shot and his laughter had caused him to miss a sitter. 'Shit!'

'Okay, Black Ball Brown!' Lazy winked at a smirking Hector and Joshua. 'My work here is done. You clear up, I'm away home.' Da's face had a slight red tinge to it. Obviously he hadn't meant anyone else to hear his bullshitting. Putting on his jacket and swallowing the dregs of his half, Lazy-Eyed Laidlaw waved without looking back and left the pub. Da cleared up easily. Apart from the Browns and one random punter, the place was empty. Back in his favourite chair, with six black 'n' tans down his neck and numerous pools wins under his belt, Da looked quite pleased with himself.

'Strike while the iron's hot.' Joshua lifted his pint and downed what was left. He took a deep breath. 'Da, I've something I need to tell you.' Taking a couple more breaths, his eyes darted between his older siblings.

'Out with it, son,' said Da. 'You can tell your old da anything.' He put his arm around Joshua's shoulder and pulled him towards his good ear. Joshua took one last deep breath, which Davina and Hector took with him.

'I'm gay.' Joshua was a lot more composed this time around, almost matter of fact.

'Say that again.' Da's grip on Joshua tightened and he pulled his son towards him, his face hard and serious, and surprisingly sober. Davina and Hector grimaced at each other. *Oh shit.*

'I'm gay, Da . . .' The silence was long and awkward, and he had to break it himself. 'Look, Da, I never asked for this, never wanted this, but it's just the way it is. It took me years to get to grips with it, but I'm not ashamed. Do I wish it hadn't happened? Of course I do. It's not been easy for me, but I'm happy now and I'd like you to be happy for me too.'

Da pulled away from Joshua, stood up, not looking at anyone, rolled down his sleeves, buttoned them and, without a word, lifted his jumper and coat and left the pub.

Three set of eyes watched him go.

'Well, that went better than I thought it would,' said Joshua, his tone flat, his disappointment obvious. 'At least he never hit me. Are we going home?'

121

'I'll catch up with him,' said Davina. 'I'm staying there tonight.' *This'll be a laugh and a half.* Putting on her coat, she rubbed her brother's arm. 'It'll be fine, Joshua.'

Joshua smiled weakly. 'Thanks, Davina, but I'm past caring what anyone thinks now. He can like it or lump it, as long as Ma doesn't get it in the neck from him.' The mood was really sombre now. 'I'll phone her and give her a heads-up before he gets in.'

'Good idea. I'll see you on Saturday.'

She caught up with her da outside their house. Neither of them spoke as they entered. Da headed straight for his bedroom, followed by an anxious looking Ma. Davina brushed her teeth and went to the bed she was to share with Lucy. She could hear her parents talking, mostly Ma, but their voices weren't raised. Unable to sleep, she got up and was making herself a cup of tea in the kitchen when Ma came in. Davina could tell she'd been crying. They fixed two cups and took them to the table in the living room. Sitting across from each other, Davina broke the silence. 'How's Da? How are you?'

Ma shuddered and breathed in deeply. 'He's hurt, disappointed and confused. Truth be told, I'm a bit confused too. How long have you known?'

'We've known for a while, Ma, but it wasn't easy for him to tell us either. We knew something was up. He wasn't as easy going as he used to be. He was quieter, more withdrawn. Me and Hector wouldn't let it drop. Next thing we know he's joining the army and we hardly saw him. Turns out he did that rather than tell us he was gay. Thing was, though, once he joined up, he loved it. Up until Iraq, when he came out.' She gave a small laugh. 'Well, he literally came out. Never spoke of what he'd seen, just that he'd seen enough. And that life was too short to live a lie. Don't be disappointed, Ma. He needs us behind him.'

'Aw, Davina,' said Ma. 'I'm only upset he never came to me. He's still my wee boy. The torment he must've gone through all his life! Why did I not notice? I could've helped him.' Her face contorted with anguish. 'I should've been there for him.' Davina walked round the table and wrapped her arms around her ma.

'You *were* there for him! You were always there, and still are, for all of us. I suppose he just didn't know what was going on and was confused, but he's told us now and we can deal with it as long as you and Da are okay with it, and with each other. He doesn't want us all to be at each other's throats over this.'

'He would never say it, but your da loves and cares for the lot of you just as much as I do.' *Right then.* 'He'll be fine, just give him time.' *I hope you're right, Ma.* 'Now, come on, you're working tomorrow.' They both stood and cuddled for a while before pulling apart. Walking to the door, Ma looked over her shoulder. 'I've never really understood what it is you do at those fancy-schmancy places, but whatever it is, it can't be wrong. You've never looked better. Night, pal.'

'Night, Ma.' As she headed back to her room, Davina knew hell would freeze over before she would divulge to Ma the secret she'd been living with; the one that had her looking so good.

Breakfast with the four kids was the usual rabble, all of them vying to be fed first: toast and cereal, eaten as fast as it was sat down, with milk being passed and spilt all over the table. Having volunteered for nursery duty, Davina helped The Wean with her coat, then put on her own. Schoolbags were grabbed, dollies and footballs lifted, as the five of them headed out to school and nursery. The three boys shouted a hasty 'Bye!', then went their separate ways.

Holding hands, Davina and The Wean sang 'Let's Go Fly a Kite' from *Mary Poppins* as they half-skipped, half-walked down the street. Memories soon transported Davina back to a less carefree childhood, and the taunts and snubs from so-called classmates quickly returned. Looking back, Davina could relate to Joshua not telling anyone of his torment. The bullying she'd suffered at school had been horrendous, but she'd never let on to her family just how bad things were. Even now, she struggled to comprehend why she hadn't. Ma would have been so incensed. Both her brothers, she was sure, would have been dispatched to deal with her tormentors, both male and female.

Turning the corner into her old school, where the nursery was now held as well, everything looked so tiny. Davina towered above the railing that had seemed so intimidating to her when she was little. She could step over the hopscotch drawn on the ground with almost one step. As they walked into the cloakroom before the nursery proper, she imagined this must have been how Gulliver had felt waking up in Lilliput. She smiled ironically. For once in her life, she wasn't self-conscious about feeling massive at school. She helped The Wean off with her coat and let her find her peg. She was glad she'd done this. She signed the attendance sheet, kissed her sister, and turned to leave.

'Are you coming back for me, Davina?' A hopeful smile covered The Wean's wee face, and her tiny hand grabbed the tips of Davina's fingers. Davina had plans for later on, but didn't want to disappoint her sister.

'I will if I can,' she said. 'But if not, we'll definitely play dollies on Saturday. How's that?' The Wean wrapped her arms around Davina's leg.

'Okay, Davina. You're the best.' The Wean smiled, turned, and skipped happily into the nursery.

Walking back out the school gates, Davina was suddenly frozen to the spot.

'Davina Brown!' the woman before her blurted.

In the blink of an eye, Davina was nine years old again, sitting by herself on the entrance step to the school door, trying to look as small as possible. Being aged nine and seven stone meant that was no mean feat. "It's just puppy fat" Ma would say, annoyed whenever Davina mentioned it. Most kids loved playtime, but Davina dreaded it. While everyone else had a single sandwich for a playpiece, Davina would have three, with pieces on jam being her favourite. "No wean of mine will go hungry" was Ma's mantra. Davina was usually full after one and a half pieces, and would have great intentions of putting the rest in the bucket – but the mere thought of it would make her ill, and not just because she hated waste, or because, according to Ma, "There are starving weans in Africa that would be glad of that." No, her reasons were purely for self-preservation. Eating all her pieces meant she wouldn't need to cross the playground to the bin, which in turn meant she wouldn't draw any unnecessary attention to herself.

No matter how far away her tormentors were, the minute she stood up, they seemed to be beamed right in front of her like something out of *Star Trek*. And from her shoes, to her size, to her hair, to her eye colour, even to the jam on her piece, you name it, as far as Davina was concerned, everything about her was plain wrong in the eyes of her so-called classmates. Sometimes she would've been just as well walking to the bin. With no-one else to torture, Jennifer Caldwell and her cronies sought her out anyway:

'David Brown, why are you wearing a skirt?'

'Dafty Brown, my mum says if I eat too many sweeties, I'll end up like you.'

Not content with just name-calling, they'd lull her into a false sense of security, telling her they were sorry for calling her names and did she want to play hide and seek with them? Jennifer Caldwell would take her to her special hidey-hole and leave her there for the whole of the playtime. When the bell rang and she left the hidey-hole and walked back around the playground, Jennifer and co would be playing ropes, beds, or balls against the wall. They'd catch sight of her and point and laugh and sing. 'Davina, Davina, has anybody seen her?'

Aware now that people were having to walk around her to get out the school gates, Davina still couldn't move. She closed her eyes, took a huge breath, then turned tentatively around to face her childhood bully, Jennifer Caldwell, who, to Davina's surprise, cuddled her.

'My God, look at you! You look amazing! What have you been up to? Do you still stay here? Were you dropping the weans off? I haven't seen you in years!' The barrage of questions seemed fragmented, yet relentless. Watching this unkempt, unwashed, toothless, anxious skeleton in front of her, Davina couldn't help but laugh. Jennifer smiled nervously, scratching her pin cushion of an arm. 'What's so funny?' she asked. How often Davina had wished she'd had the knowledge she had now, back when she was younger. This rancid, pathetic excuse for a human being wouldn't have dared pick on her, or anyone else for that matter. Davina almost felt sorry for her. Almost! Her face contorted into a snarl.

'You! You're what's funny. You made my life *hell*. And everybody else's at school you decided not to like.' The shock in her tormentor's face spurred Davina on. *Worthless junkie bitch*. The bile and hatred rose in her throat, yet she couldn't quite bring herself to vent any of it. Remembering a spoof sketch she'd seen of someone getting a makeover on Lorraine Kelly's TV show, Davina put on her best Dundee accent, moved nose-to-nose with the skeleton, and grinned. 'You look like shite,' she said. And with that, she about-turned and headed home.

She'd run the scenario of meeting Jennifer again umpteen times in her head. It had inevitably always involved rolling about on the ground, fists and hair flying, with Davina walking away triumphant, and people slapping her on the back saying, "Well done, she's been asking for that for years." Right at this moment, though, she didn't feel very triumphant. In fact, as she made her way back to her parents' house, she felt shite.

With the surface wiped and cleared of the earlier mess, the three adults had replaced the kids at the breakfast table. Both men, having been fed, had their heads in a newspaper each. Ma was staring into space, humming along to The Jam on the radio. Davina joined them at the table, poured a hot cup of tea from the pot, and dipped cold toast into it. Bliss. She couldn't get the image of Jennifer Caldwell out of her head. The atmosphere at the table was more relaxed than she'd expected. The men discussed the state of Scottish football, while the women discussed the state of Jennifer Caldwell.

'She's wasted on drugs, that one,' said Ma. 'I'm glad you didn't hang about with her at school! She has three weans, but two are in foster homes.' *How the mighty fall.*

'Her and I moved in different circles at school,' said Davina.

'Is that a fancy way to say you didn't get on?' Ma smiled and started tidying the table. Davina helped her, then made her bed, blethering with Granda till after lunch. Making her excuses, she left with the knowledge that she'd soon be under a scintillating shower at The Admiral Hotel, and then later on, she thought with a disparaging image, under her next encounter, Brian Hunter.

Once she was in the comfort of her car, she pulled out her mobile to call Hector. Her stomach dropped when she noticed a message from Gavin. She vaguely remembered sending him a text last night. Cringing, she opened his message.

> It was good hearing from you but unfortunately I won't be in Glasgow this weekend.

What the hell had she texted him? Scrolling back, she read the text she'd sent him back to herself. *Why is it all your worst ideas come when you're drunk?*

> Hi Gav,

'Gav!' she repeated. 'How embarrassing. You never called him that.'

> going for a drink on Satday a-noon with some friends if you fancy it.

'Oh my God, what was I thinking?' She banged her head on her steering wheel. 'Arse.' Straightening up, she noticed Nosey Parker, their long-time neighbour, watching her curiously. *That'll give you something to talk about when you're sparring with your man tonight.*

No longer in the mood to talk, she texted Hector instead, informing him that the fallout from Joshua's disclosure hadn't been too bad. She headed to the hotel, embarrassed and annoyed with herself. She never let things get personal with her clients and she'd only acted with the best of intentions. Being under the influence of several lagers, and mindful of what Hamish and Isobel had said, her brain had gone into Dr Pepper mode i.e. what's the worst that can happen? *Has there ever been a recorded incident in history of someone dying of embarrassment?* She'd need to explain herself to Gavin and hope he would take it the right way.

CHAPTER 7

BROWN SAUCE

Davina parked her car beneath The Admiral Hotel in Glasgow then checked in. Knowing she had a few hours before seeing her next client, she decided to treat herself to the amazing massage service they had here.

The massage, followed by an awesome shower, worked wonders. She felt more relaxed than she had in ages. In the early stages of her new-found profession, she'd avoided any assignations in her home town, but after her transformation from frumpy tomboy to slender-ish sex machine, she'd stopped worrying about it. After all, why would someone that comes from Glasgow be staying in a hotel in Glasgow? She'd reassured herself of this countless times. Sitting on top of her bed wrapped from head to toe in a luxurious bathrobe, glass of wine in hand, she phoned Hamish. After three rings she hung up. *What are you doing, Brown? He obviously needs space; needs time to think. It's only been a week. He'll text you when he's ready.*

Her phone was vibrating next to her. Hamish's name flashed up. 'Shit-shit-shit! Be normal, be normal.' A deep breath was followed by a quick slurp of wine. 'Hello, stranger,' she managed. 'How's things?' *God, why was this suddenly so awkward?*

'I'm good, thanks. You?' He sounded like she felt. *Bad idea, Brown.*

130

'Sorry, I shouldn't have phoned . . . Text me sometime . . . if you want, that is . . .' *Smooth, Brown, super-smooth.*

'I've missed you, Davina . . . Missed our wee talks.' The silence was unbearable. There had never been this tension between them before, creating this dull feeling in her chest. She wanted things back the way they'd been, the way they always had been: fun and relaxed. *Tell him you've missed him as well.* She let out a huge sigh.

'Hamish . . .'

He cut her off before she could finish. 'I'm in London until next Wednesday. Could we meet then, talk face to face, instead of this awkward shite?' He sounded more like himself now, but there was still a touch of uncertainty in his voice.

'I'll get my secretary to call yours and make the arrangements, Mr Hamilton,' she replied, trying to lighten the mood.

'I'll be making my own arrangements from now on, Miss Brown. My secretary left. I asked her to come in to my office and take down some briefs and the next thing I know I'm getting done for sexual harassment.' The old Hamish was back.

'You've got a one track mind, Mr Hamilton.' She was speaking through laughter now, but wasn't sure if it was because she found him funny or just because she was relieved.

'No, if I had a one track mind I'd have suggested nipple to nipple, not face to face.'

'The one thing usually leads to the other with you.' She felt a familiar tingle in her groin and wished he was there with her.

'Only with the right company.' His voice was low and seductive now, all traces of awkwardness gone. 'I need to go. Something's come up that I'll need to thrash out.' She could almost hear his smile.

'Bye, Hamish. Perv.'

'Bye. And Davina?' He was serious again.

'Yes.' Her face was beaming.

'Thanks for phoning.' He hung up before she could respond. Davina sat staring at her mobile for an age after that. Yes, she'd really missed him. Suddenly the thought of a night being berated and rogered by Brian Hunter, owner of Trash for Cash, one of Scotland's largest recycling firms, didn't seem so daunting.

Brian Hunter was in his early 60s and as rotund as he was tall. The little hair he had left was sheared to a gauge two length. This quiet, unassuming, cheerful, and happily married businessman had a deviant side to him, however, which apparently Mrs Hunter was either totally against or totally oblivious to. Either way, Davina was the woman who accompanied him when he was splurging out on his workforce. She was feeling particularly uncomfortable tonight, not because of the knowing leers she knew she'd be on the receiving end of from their fellow diners, but from the so-called underwear that was ripping her in two. Not to mention the vibrating egg inside her. Normally she found this fun and erotic, but with Brian in charge of the remote control it was neither. Every time he made it buzz she was expected to shoot him one of her more lustful looks, when in actual fact she just wanted to shoot him full stop.

The leather concoction he insisted she wore under the flimsy thigh-length orange dress with matching lipstick was just as irritating. She stepped into it, with the narrowest strap she'd ever seen cutting her fandango in two. The equally thin waistband, if you could call it that, had straps attached at either side that crisscrossed her chest and fastened at the back of her neck. The only underwear she was wearing, to speak of, were black fishnet hold-ups that just reached her dress and no more. Her heeled black leather boots came up above her knees the way he liked them. Although her body was toned more than it had ever been, and she now described herself as being curvaceous instead of fat, the fact that she had no bra on was glaringly obvious. Her dress, which crisscrossed beneath her chest, did nothing to disguise this. Brian had chosen her attire for tonight, as he often did. The only saving grace was that they never danced at these functions. Having barely anything to drink, she could wait until they were back in his room to pee, if he allowed it. This meant the only time she'd need to stand up and let her chest fight the laws of gravity was when they left the table.

They got ready in their separate rooms and met in the bar where his workforce was taking full advantage of the free bar he had generously laid on for them. It seemed to her that the entire assembly stopped talking as she approached the beaming Brian. His eyes undressed her with every step she took, something she knew he would never literally do.

'Katy, you look ravishing.' He stood up and leaned in as she gave him a slight cuddle. She air-kissed both his cheeks, using their closeness to discretely place the vibrating egg controller in his jacket pocket.

'As do you, Brian,' she lied. He was already sweating profusely and his round face was bright red, his tie loosened around his neck. The maître d' informed everyone in the bar that they were to be seated. Leading her by the elbow, Brian walked Davina into the dining room. She jumped slightly and let out a little 'oh' as the egg inside her suddenly vibrated. Some of the other guests looked at her quizzically. Most, thankfully, were oblivious to what had just happened. *Here we go.*

'Just checking,' he sneered.

Davina was suddenly reminded of the *French and Saunders* 'What happened to Baby Jane?' sketch, where, parodying the film *Misery*, Dawn French smacks Jennifer Saunders' paralysed legs with a sledgehammer, then in a drunken slur says "Jusht checking." *What I'd give for a sledgehammer right now.* Despite her discomfort, she managed a wee laugh to herself.

The meal passed without incident. The one thing in life that Brian Hunter will not be distracted from, she'd learnt, is his food. However, she was becoming more and more uneasy with the man seated next to her. He'd introduced himself earlier, but she hadn't liked the look of him, so hadn't paid any attention to what he'd said his name was. When he shook her hand, she was disgusted by how clammy it was, and had to stop herself from flinching. With most of the complementary wine at the table down his neck, he was now almost sitting on Davina's knee. Dessert was long finished and the band had started.

'I know your face,' he said. She could feel his spittle in her ear. She wouldn't have long to wait before Brian excused them both, so she tried to be nice.

'I doubt that very much,' she replied. He was practically nose-to-nose with her now. Apparently his morning mouth smell followed him all through the day. She reached into her bag for a packet of mints.

'You look a bit like this fat girl I was at school with,' he said. 'Except you're nicer looking and not as fat. And her name wasn't . . .' – he had one of her business cards in his hand. *Shit, how did he get hold of one of them?* – 'Katy Miller. But I'm fucked if I can remember what it was.'

134

Although she liked Brian Hunter as a person, she didn't enjoy wearing his choice of clothing, or what they did in the privacy of his hotel suites. The extra money he gave her to indulge him helped her get over those hurdles immensely. This, though, was something else entirely. This was her worse nightmare come true. Being recognised doing this was huge. The sudden panic she felt was threatening to overpower her. Fuck's sake. She almost jumped out of her seat. She'd forgotten all about the egg inside her. The sudden jolt took her completely by surprise. Clammy-palms was staring at her as if she was a nutter. Remembering where she was, she composed herself.

'Wind,' she whispered to Clammy-palms. His expression didn't change. Smoothly, she turned to Brian. Every pair of eyes at the table seemed to be on her. *Ground, just open up and swallow me whole, please.* With as much willpower as she could muster, and keeping her irritation in check, she looked at Brian from under her eyelashes with a wicked smile. 'Thank you' she mouthed to him. His own mouth curled up in the sleaziest smirk she'd ever seen. 'You know what that does to me,' she whispered in his ear, trying to sound sexy. As her lips accidentally brushed against his skin, he pulled back from her as though she'd just accosted him, or she was something he'd just trodden in. He wiped his ear with his napkin, turned his back on her, and started up a conversation with the woman next to him. *Shit! Forgot I was with Mr Hygiene himself. No touching him. No skin to skin. And definitely no looking at him during sex. Which was impossible anyway, unless I've got eyes in the back of my head.*

'Sorry, Brian.' This was spoken louder so she didn't have to risk getting too close again.

'It's okay.' He sounded okay, but it was hard to tell as he hadn't turned around. *Piss off, ya moody git.* She jumped again, but not so high this time. The clammy hand on her shoulder made her wince. The sleazeball had moved even closer to her.

'Trouble in paradise?' he sneered. *Remember your manners, Davina.* She mustered up a smile from somewhere. Reading the place tag in front of him, she vaguely remembered someone at her school called Mark Jones, but he'd been older than Hector and she couldn't remember what he looked like.

'So, Katy Miller!' He pushed even further in to her. 'How does a guy like me meet up with a woman like you?' His slavery smile was making her queasy. She pulled her shoulders back, composed herself, and put a bit of space between them. *Manners, Davina, manners.*

'Mark, is it?' She pretended to read his place tag for the first time. 'I'm sure there's someone out there just waiting for you to speak to them. In fact, there's a table over there' – she pointed in the same direction as the band – 'that's all women.' She planted her "now piss off" smile on her face. One of his clammy hands was on hers and the other was rifling about in his trouser pocket. He pulled out some five pound notes.

'I'm not under any illusions here,' he said. 'We both know what you are.' He was sneering at her now. 'My money's just as good as his.' He nodded at his boss. 'And I bet I'm a better fuck.' He straightened up in his seat, looking very pleased with himself. 'But it's up to you who you go upstairs with. You're under no pressure, doll.' The smug grin on his face had her raging. *Fuck the manners, Davina.* She gave him one of her sweetest smiles as they both leaned into each other. When her mouth was next to his ear, she spat her words at him.

'Under no fucking pressure, doll? I would need to be under fucking anesthetic to sleep with you . . . doll!'

Unsteadily, he pushed himself up from his seat. 'Fucking whore. Who are you to talk to me like that?'

For a big man, Brian moved very swiftly, forcing himself between Clammy-hands and Davina. 'That's enough, Jones!' he roared. Even Davina was surprised at the intimidating tone in Brian's voice. For all of his quirks, he was normally a softly-spoken man. Mark lifted his glass, flashed Davina a look that turned her blood cold, opened his mouth to say something, looked at Brian and thought better of it, then headed over to the table of women next to the band, holding court.

Assisting a slightly shaken Davina to her feet, Brian excused them from the rest of the company.

They entered his room without having spoken a word, neither in the lift nor corridor. He hadn't even bothered to give her a buzz below. Once inside, Brian went straight to the bathroom. Davina knew he'd be a wee while. He liked to wash and dry his hands three times, vigorously, regardless of what he'd done in there. *Great, now what? Do I go to my room and not get paid 'for services rendered'? No way. Get paid from the time you started getting ready until now. After all, you've earned it.* With an uneasy feeling in her gut, she slouched in one of the seats. *Oh my God, Brown, when did the money start coming before your pride? Who are you kidding? You leave your pride at the door every time you enter someone else's hotel room, and every time you let a stranger touch, poke or do whatever the hell else they want to you. Where's the pride in wearing this ridiculous get-up just so you can have money in the bank?* Her eyes nipped, and for the first time since she'd met Hamish and entered this lifestyle, she was ashamed of herself. *Clammy-hands is right, plain and simple. You are a whore.* She stood up and strode to the

137

door. *Enough is enough.* Reaching for the handle, she was stopped in her tracks by an elongated buzz in her nether regions. She turned to face a butt-naked, very aroused Brian. *Wow, was I off the mark with your mood.* His rotund body was glistening with sweat, and his dick and his hands were sheathed in latex. That was all he wore, except for the huge grin on his face. The sensation between her legs was becoming annoying just as it stopped.

'Where do you think you're going?' He sat the control on the table in the middle of the room. *Shit, could you not have washed your hands just once more? I'd have been out of here and out of this sordid world. Right, Davina, this is the last time you take one for the team. You're retiring to Barbados after this.* Smiling with forced, pretend seductiveness, she sauntered over to him.

'I didn't think the door had closed properly.' She stopped right in front of him, glanced down at the hand vigorously rubbing his rock-hard dick, then looked back up at his face. She never touched him with her hands. Never had. He was always in control.

'Bedroom.' His voice was rough and harsh. She walked in front of him and felt the buzz start up again. She noted the baby oil on the side of the bed and knew exactly where he wanted her.

'Undress!' She pulled her dress slowly over her head.

'Squeeze your tits!' Avoiding eye contact, something he strictly forbade when they were in his room, she gently fondled herself.

'Enough!' he hissed, eyeing her up and down. 'Just leave the hold-ups and boots on and assume the position.' *Thank God. My fandango couldn't take much more of that contraption.* Spreading her legs as far as was comfortable, Davina bent the top half of her body over the bed with her arse in the air. Brian handed her the egg control and stood behind her. He squirted some oil onto her arse cheeks and massaged her lightly, both hands working in unison, gradually getting rougher, until he was grabbing and pinching her skin.

'Very nice.' *OMG, a compliment. Be still my beating heart.* Perversely, she was actually enjoying this; enjoying the fact that it would be her last time with someone who paid to be with her. Without warning, he pushed two fingers into her star anise. The violent intrusion had her catching her breath. Recovering quickly, she squirmed against them. She was aware he was pleasuring the two of them at the same time, as was his wont. With both hands now, he separated her bum cheeks to a point verging on uncomfortable, and thrust himself into her. The fullness she felt with both him and the egg inside her was immense and she had to steady herself on the bed. Holding her hips with his gloved hands, he really started to move.

'Push the fucking button.' He sounded like a man out of control. She did as he ordered and his breathing grew quicker and quicker, the sensation clearly mind-blowing. *Here we go, Davina. Think happy thoughts.*

'Fucking bitch! Fucking whore! Useless cunt!' With each new thrust came a new expletive. She'd never enjoyed these encounters, choosing to mentally work on her shopping list while he got his jollies. Today, however, having decided that this was the last time she would ever be doing this – doing *him* – she was relaxed and about to explode. Her orgasm took over at the same time as his. With one final thrust, he threw his head back and shouted, reminding her, weirdly, of Mel Gibson. 'Baaaaaastard!'

With her face pushed firmly into the quilt, she laughed at her very own William Wallace moment. 'Freedom!' she shouted, but it was muffled by the quilt, like she knew it would be. He had already recovered from their tryst and was heading to the bathroom. Davina slipped the dress back on, minus the so-called underwear. Her room was two floors down and the shower was calling her. She lifted her remote control and leather thingy and entered the living room. The noise from the bathroom stopped and Brian came back out, wrapped now in a fluffy white bathrobe, hands clasped behind his back. He was rocking back and forth on his heels, looking everywhere but at her.

'So . . . how's things, Katy? Been up to anything exciting? How's the family?' It never ceased to amaze her that this man was the same arrogant, self-centered, bad-mouthed arsehole that had just fucked her. He was normal now, almost apologetic in his demeanour. They knew practically nothing about each other apart from the fact that she came from a big family and he was married to the loveliest, most innocent woman ever, and that they lived blissfully happy somewhere in the Borders. Small-talk had become one of their things to ease his embarrassment.

'I'm great, thanks.' Then she grinned, mainly to herself. 'Thinking of going to Barbados, actually.' *In fact, I thought of it just before your alter ego stopped me leaving.*

'Oh, you should definitely go. Took the wife there for our honeymoon. She loved it.' His face turned bright red and he cleared his throat. 'Well, it was good seeing you again, Katy.' He removed a thick envelope from the drawer and approached her awkwardly with it at arms-length. Taking it from him, she grabbed him in a huge embrace, feeling his whole body tense up. She even kissed him on the cheek. *What the hell, it's been an experience knowing you, Mr Hunter. And your money has gone a long way to pay for the lifestyle I now know and love.*

There was utter disgust on his face as she pulled away. *Right then, you hypocrite. After what you've just done to me, not to mention called me, you can look at me as if I'm something you just stood on in the street?* He was at the bathroom door before she was at the main one.

'Thanks for everything,' she said. 'It's been surreal.' The last thing she saw before she left her old life for good was the perplexed expression on Brian Hunter's face. *Fuck it.*

Stripping off in her room, she tossed the leather thingy and horrendous orange dress into the bin. She decided to keep the egg in as a treat until after her shower. Well, she was celebrating after all.

Later, sitting on her plush hotel bed, naked apart for the towel wrapped around her wet hair, Davina massaged moisturiser onto her face and took stock of her current situation. She was 30 years old, still single – *yeah right, you've more men in your life than women* – and a home and property owner. Her financial adviser, Douglas Bruce, who she'd met through one of her clients, Andrew Collins, a part-time MP, was pleased with her investments, despite the state of the economy.

With each positive thought, she felt less and less ashamed and more and more proud of herself and her achievements. There was no doubt her run-in with the clammy-handed Mark Jones had upset and riled her though. The fact that she didn't stand on street corners, caked in make-up with half her body on show – *heaven forbid* – didn't make her any less a prostitute. The luxury and comfort in which she plied her trade meant she'd never thought of it like that. Until tonight. She refused to let a slimy, sleazy prick like him make her feel dirty. The money and security it brought with it made her happy. *Very* happy.

What had made her even happier, though, was the fact that all her clients had enjoyed the time they spent with her. Each of them, over the past eight years, had been with her at least three times. For the majority, it was a lot more often than that. To her, at least, that proved they must have liked her. Not all the men she'd encountered had been gentlemen. Apart from Brian, however, none of them had insulted her or made her feel cheap. *One look at her bank balance would prove she was anything but.* Most of her encounters had ended with mutual pleasure and respect. Never again would she put herself in a situation where any man thought he could speak to her like dirt or make her feel the way Mark Jones had. The thought of him actually recognising her filled her with dread, sending a shiver down her spine.

Davina knew her weight loss didn't have her looking like Victoria Beckham, but then again she'd never want to be that thin. But it definitely had changed her appearance. Added to the fact that she could now afford to go to top boutiques to get a makeover before meeting her clients meant that even her own mother would struggle to recognise her most of the time. Tonight, however, wasn't one of those nights. Her client had chosen her outfit and make-up and she'd done her hair herself. Yes, looking back, she'd been careless, and it could have all ended in tears. Although she wouldn't change her new life for the world, enough was enough. Surely she was financially secure by now and could take a further interest in some of the businesses she'd invested in. She could take her younger siblings to Disneyland, or maybe treat Marge to a well-deserved holiday, as long as it wasn't to bloody Benidorm. Marge loved the fact that Benidorm was full of British people and pubs, and saw it as Blackpool in the sun. Davina hated it for the exact same reason. She suddenly sat up and clicked her fingers.

'Barbados!' *Now that would be worth a visit. I could have a break from all the men in my life.* Locating her phone, she texted her financial adviser. It was half past 12 now, but she couldn't wait. Knowing Douglas Bruce turned his work phone off at six, there was little chance she'd wake him up. Tomorrow was Saturday so she probably wouldn't hear from him for a couple of days, but that didn't matter. She'd got the ball rolling. This was definitely happening. She brushed her teeth and emptied her bladder, and felt a lot happier than she had earlier. Loads of ideas ran through her head as she drifted off to sleep and, for the first time in what felt like forever, none of them involved a man.

Sleeping late had never been Davina's forte, but she lay in bed as long as she could, savouring the warmth and the quiet, before showering and brushing her teeth. 'That's better,' she said to herself. *We're good to go, Brown.* With a genuine smile of contentment, she winked at herself in the mirror and broke into the opening lines of Black Eyed Peas' 'I Gotta Feeling'. Struggling with the tuning a little, but not in the least bit bothered, she crossed the room to the phone and called downstairs, ordering two poached eggs, toast, and a pot of tea. She was already dressed and packed, her belly rumbling, when there was a knock at the door.

'Room service,' said a bright, friendly voice.

Opening the door, Davina was greeted with the widest smile and the whitest teeth she'd ever seen. The handsome young man looked good enough to eat. *Never mind the eggs, Davina, treat yourself to one last tumble.* She took the tray and discreetly slipped him a fiver, her smile matching his. 'Thank you.'

'No,' replied the young man, 'thank *you*.' He turned and Davina watched his tight wee arse disappear down the corridor into the lift. *Tasty*.

Davina set the tray on the bed. She wasn't in the same league as her clients, the ones who could afford suites with separate eating areas, but it didn't matter. The sight of that tight wee arse had more than made up for the lack of a table. She tucked into her breakfast, saucy thoughts making her smile. *You can still window shop, Brown*.

CHAPTER 8

BROWN SAUCE

Davina had arranged to get ready and stay the night at Grace's, so after checking out, she headed straight to her friend's flat. Grace opened the door in her onesie, brushing her teeth and looking like she'd been dragged through a hedge backwards. Onesie. Davina shivered. The word was right up there with *girly* and *pressie* for getting on her tits. Recovering quickly, she flashed Grace her best smile.

'Did you have the hairdresser in through the night? You look amazing.'

'Shut it and put the kettle on, I'll be five minutes.' Grace padded back down the hall to the bathroom, scratching her arse. *Charming.* Having made both of them a cup of tea, Davina sat on the couch waiting for Grace to return, the excitement building inside her. When Grace finally did reappear, she looked exactly the same as when she'd opened the door. Davina shook her head in amazement. Oblivious to her friend's reaction, Grace plonked herself down beside her.

'So how was Mr Tourette's last night?' She blew across the top of her tea.

'I'm fed up telling you he doesn't have bloody Tourette's,' said Davina. 'At least people who do have a reason for their bad language.' She laughed and gave Grace a playful push.

'Whatever, slut, whore, trollop, cocksucker.'

'He's never called me a cocksucker,' Davina stated, mock-serious.

'How would you know? You're too busy making up your shopping list while he's getting his kicks, ya bastard.' Davina's sides were getting sore now. Grace was the only person she knew who could take a serious subject and turn it into the funniest thing you ever heard.

Once the laughter had subsided, they got down to the serious job of getting ready for their night out. Barbara Bryceland was back singing at Merchant Pride, and they couldn't miss it. In-between showering, blow-drying then straightening their hair, and putting on make-up, Davina told Grace all about her plan to retire from the "hospitality" business. Maybe the two of them could even have a wee holiday together, before working out what to do with all this free time Davina had coming up.

'How about instead of a high class escort you become a high class Madame?' Grace pouted and threw her long auburn hair back seductively. She winked at Davina. 'I could be first on your books.'

'No,' said Davina, keeping as straight a face as possible and being as serious as she could. 'If I was to do that I'd only take on young, good-looking women.' She zipped up her knee-length black boots over her tight black jeans and admired herself in the full-length mirror. 'What do you think?'

Grace glowered at her with feigned annoyance. 'I think you're a cheeky, cock-sucking slut, whore, trollop, if I'm being honest.' She turned away. 'I wouldn't like that line of work anyway. You've got to be a bit of a slapper to sleep with millions of men. And, more to the point, you'll need to wear TENA pants all the time now. Your fanny muscles, not to put too fine a point on it, are

146

well and truly fucked.' Ignoring Davina's shocked expression, she craned her neck to look in the mirror over her shoulder. 'Do these jeans make my arse look big?' she asked.

'No,' replied Davina. 'The fact you've got a big arse makes your arse look big!' She grabbed her lime cardigan off the bed and stormed out the room, trying hard not to laugh.

'Uh-oh, someone got out the wrong bed today!' shouted Grace. She checked her make-up one last time. 'There's wine chilling in the fridge, Davina. Can you pour me a glass?' She walked backwards into the living room, her brows furrowed. 'No, seriously, Davina, is my arse huge in these? It's alright for you, you're becoming celibate through choice. Some of us don't have that luxury.' *Celibate, my arse.*

Davina shook her head. 'Your arse looks fine.' Logan's ditty from the other morning played in her subconscious. A smile spread across her face. She wished her friend could find someone special like she had. Her plan from the other night sprang into her head. She handed Grace her wine.

'How would you feel about a blind date? Well, it wouldn't be a blind date as such, I've told you quite a lot about him, so you'd have an unfair advantage.' She took a sip from her own glass and watched Grace's face change from absolute shock to contemplation, and then uncertainty.

'Who?' Grace asked. Her mind was obviously working overtime and Davina toyed with the idea of naming one of her less desirable clients, but decided against it.

'Gavin. Gavin Anderson. He's a really lovely guy. You'd like him, Grace.' Grace held her chin, deep in thought, then looked Davina straight in the eye.

'You've not shagged him, have you?' This was more of a statement than a question.

'No, I haven't. Do you have to be so crude? Not everyone I've had dealings with wanted sex.' For some reason it was important for Davina to defend Gavin.

'Calm down, Davina, I'm only asking. Would it not freak you out to sleep with someone I'd slept with?'

'Sleep with! You've not even met him yet. But as Christian Grey would say, "Good point, well made." He really is nice, and I think the two of you would hit it off.' Grace's face had a faraway, dreamy look about it.

'Now, if it were Christian Grey you were setting me up with,' she said, 'that would be a no-brainer. But Gavin . . .' She paused. 'I'm not so sure.'

'What's not to be sure about?' asked Davina. 'Christian Grey is the figment of someone's fantastic imagination. Gavin is real flesh and blood and he's a gentleman.'

They sat in silence drinking their wine. Checking her watch, Davina realised it was already 25 past one and Grace hadn't even had breakfast. She sat her glass on the table and stood up. 'Come on. You don't have to decide right now. We've a whole afternoon session in front of us and you're rubbish drinking on an empty head.'

'Cheeky bitch.' Grace downed her wine and grimaced. 'Need to remember wine's not like shots.' She stood in front of Davina and cuddled her with an extra strong squeeze. 'Thanks, Davina. You really are a great pal. Let's do it. If you say Gavin's worth a try, who am I to disagree?' *Yeah right, Annie Lennox.*

'Great,' said Davina. 'It's a pisser he said he was too busy to come tonight, but I'll phone him on Monday.' Grace's expression suddenly had Davina pulling back. 'What? Have you changed your mind already?'

'No!' said Grace. 'I just can't believe you'd try and organise all this without speaking to me first.' Davina walked past her into the bathroom, not sure why Grace was so annoyed. 'I'm trying to help you out here!' she shouted through the half-open door. 'Phone us a taxi while I pee.'

The discussion/argument carried on throughout the whole of the taxi ride and right through lunch. Grace talked herself in and out of the idea 100 times. The upshot was that Davina was to phone Gavin on Monday and find out if he was interested. Feeling the effects of two more glasses of wine, and with Grace at the toilet, she sent Gavin a text. Why did all her best ideas come when she was drinking?

They were meeting everyone else in Merchant Pride at half past three. With so much wine sloshing around inside them, they decided walking would do them the world of good.

Linked arm-in-arm, they talked and laughed all the way along to the Merchant City, reaching the pub a good half hour early. Although it had a dance-floor, the pub's décor was old-fashioned and dark, giving it a rustic, traditional feel that contributed to its charm and popularity. When they walked through the door, it was already busy, the seating areas cramped. Davina was surprised to see her brothers had already arrived. Luckily, they'd managed to bag a table for seven, right next to the dance-floor. There were two men sitting with them. One of them Davina recognised right away, even though his muscular back was to them. Well, she *should* recognise it. She'd clawed, scratched and held on to it in the throes of passion often enough! Hector was sitting to his left. Joshua was sitting opposite them with a guy she'd never seen before, who was also muscular and good-looking.

Joshua nodded to indicate to the rest of them that Davina and Grace had arrived. She watched her brother, who looked slightly uneasy, take a deep breath, rub his hands down his thighs, and stand to greet them, the other men following suit.

'Hi, Davina. Hi, Grace. This is Craig Wallace, my partner.' Davina's eyes almost popped out of her head. *A bit of a warning would have been nice.* Shaking Craig's outstretched hand, Davina liked him straight away. His smile was warm and genuine, and his teeth were perfect.

'Nice to meet you, Davina,' said Craig. 'I've heard a lot about you.'

'Lucky you.' Davina threw both her brothers a questioning look. 'It's really nice to meet you too.' While Grace was being introduced, Davina was treated to a kiss on the cheek from Logan. Her insides flipped.

'Hi, Davina,' he said. 'Long time no see.' Now positioned with his back to her brothers, he stood close to her and brushed against her breasts. His arrogant, smug look told her it was no accident, and the flutter in her groin made her catch her breath slightly. She narrowed her eyes at him. *So that's the game, is it?*

'You're looking good, Logan,' said Davina, loud enough for everyone to hear. 'Been on the sunbeds again?'

'Sunbeds?' Hector said, eyeing Logan sceptically. 'Bloody told us you were in Saudi Arabia.'

'I was in Saudi. Sunbeds are for poofs.' Logan squeezed his eyes shut tight. Then, opening them gingerly, he faced Joshua and Craig. 'Sorry! Fuck! Sorry, I can't believe I just said that.' He was visibly dying, and Grace, not known for her tact, roared with laughter. Davina and Hector had the decency to at least try to hold theirs in. Craig slapped him hard on the shoulder and Logan stumbled forwards slightly.

'Can't argue with that, Logan. Us gays like our tans.' He sat down and everyone else followed his lead.

'Very smooth,' Davina whispered into Logan's ear, making sure her tongue made contact.

He shook his head in embarrassment. 'I can't believe I just said that. I don't even talk like that normally.'

'So it must be this place that brings out your bitch . . . eh, I mean *butch* side?' Davina smirked.

'Yes . . . No! Shut up, stop putting words in my mouth.' His face flushed. The Browns were loving his discomfort.

'Dig a hole,' Hector laughed, playfully punching him on the arm.

Grace stood up. 'Right, even though I love watching handsome men squirm, I need a drink,' she said. 'Logan, will I get you a double? Or maybe a cocktail with an umbrella and cherry?'

'Very funny,' he replied. 'Just a pint, thanks.'

Grace looked over at Davina. 'Davina, can you give me a hand?' The two women took everyone's orders and went to the bar. Having finally been served, they leaned on the counter and looked back at the table.

'I take it you didn't know Joshua's boyfriend was coming,' said Grace,

'Coming? I didn't even know he had one. They kept that quiet.' Davina's eyes were fixed on Logan. *A wee text would have been nice, McIntyre.*

Grace sighed. 'How come the good looking ones are all bloody gay?' She followed Davina's gaze. 'Well, nearly all of them. I thought you said he was away for a month? You should have seen your face when we walked in.'

151

'I know,' said Davina. 'I almost had a heart attack. Why didn't he text or phone to say he'd be here?' She leant in and whispered in Grace's ear. 'See, I told you we were just fuck buddies!' She hoped her disappointment wasn't too evident.

'Maybe you're right,' said Grace. 'But I wish I had your worries. Luscious Logan or Handsome Hamish . . . decisions decisions. Why not have both? Oh! That's right, you have been. Lucky slut, whore, trollop.' Davina gave her a dig in the ribs. Laughing, they turned back to the bar. Their drinks had already been placed on a tray and the barmaid was staring at Grace with her mouth wide open. Davina lifted the tray and nodded in Grace's direction.

'Tourette's.'

Davina walked away, and was still laughing when she got back to the table.

'What's so funny?' Hector was smiling up at her.

'Aw, you had to be there.'

She sat back down between Logan and Hector. Quizzing Craig across the table, she discovered that he and Joshua had known each other in the army, but had only hooked up eight months ago. His family, which consisted of his parents, a younger sister and a sister two years older, had known for years that he was gay and were fine with it. They all lived in Edinburgh, as did he.

'He seems very nice,' said Davina, as soon as Craig went to the toilet.

Joshua grinned. 'Thanks, Davina,' he said, relieved. 'Glad you like him. That means a lot.'

The pub was rowdy and heaving now. Standing room only. Hector tapped Davina's hand and nodded discretely to the side of her, two tables along. Desperate Dan's doppelganger was wearing a skirt and a nice yellow twin set, set off lovely with his five o'clock shadow. His companion, his sister, rocked the whole spiked hair, shirt and dungarees look. In fact, if she'd brought a metal bucket to finish the ensemble, she could've given one of the many standing punters a seat.

'Didn't you have a shirt like that, Davina?' asked Hector. *Shit! So I did.*

'Shut it,' she said. Logan laughed.

'Did you not have that haircut as well?' *You would bloody remember that.* Not to be left out, Joshua and Grace joined in, everyone around the table now laughing with and at Davina. No-one noticed Marge come in.

'Hi guys, what's so funny?' With a few drinks in them all now, Marge was greeted like a long-lost friend. Her make-up was minimal and her blouse only had one button undone, but even Davina had to admit she looked great. Joshua patted the seat next to him.

'I've kept you a seat, Marge. We were just reminding Davina of her fashion faux pas when she was young.'

'We all had a few of them, Joshua,' said Marge. 'Mind they suede trousers you had?' She slapped her head with the palm of her hand. 'We should've known back then you were as gay as a gay thing.' Joshua's mouth fell open, but no words came out. 'Is there another seat?' asked Marge. 'Robert's paying the taxi.' *Oh, good!* Davina raised her eyes at Hector in a *told you so* look. He half-smiled, half-grimaced in return.

'Hi, everyone.' Robert was standing behind Marge. Craig returned from the toilet and introductions were made. There wasn't a spare seat in the place so they bunched in together, all squashed round the table. Davina's irritation was forgotten, as the communal crush now meant she was practically sitting on Logan's knee. Another round was bought just as Barbara Bryceland

153

came on. As usual, she was amazing, and soon had the crowd singing and dancing both on the dance-floor and between the tables. Taking full advantage of their closeness, Davina and Logan exchanged the occasional fleeting touch and whispered innuendo, and sang to one another meaningfully. Oblivious to everyone else around them, and with the deadly combination of alcohol and flirting slowly taking over, Davina could feel herself becoming hot and bothered. Probably in the nick of time, Grace grabbed her hand and pulled her away from a smoldering Logan.

'Toilet!' she bellowed in her friend's ear. Before Davina had a chance to say no, they were maneuvering through the throng of punters. With there only being three stalls and the place being rammed, there was a queue for the toilets. Girls were singing, shouting, and touching up their make-up. A couple of them Davina thought should be in the men's toilet.

'What are you playing at, Davina?' demanded Grace. 'I know there's a lot of weird and wonderful things go on in this place at the best of times, but I don't think the management, far less your family, would thank you for a live sex show!'

'What are you talking about?' Davina's confusion was genuine.

'You and Mr Fuck Buddy out there!' Grace yelled.

A couple of heads turned in their direction. Grace glowered at them then pulled Davina into an empty cubicle. It was a tight squeeze. Grace plonked herself on the toilet seat and started to pee. 'Christ, Davina, you looked like you were going to swallow him whole any minute.' She grinned, mid-flow. 'Not that I blame you, he's sex on legs.'

It was now Davina's turn to pee. They squeezed around each other awkwardly, swapping places. Unsteadily, Davina pulled down her jeans and pants. 'I thought we were being discrete,' she said. 'I think we've shown great restraint, given the circumstances. I really, really love him, Grace. I know I've always loved him, but now I know I'm *in* love with him.' Her smile was splitting her face in two as she stumbled back to her feet and sorted herself. Grace gave her a huge hug.

'Holy crap, Davina. When did you decide that?' She was genuinely excited for her friend.

'Right now!' Davina blurted out. A sharp bang on the door interrupted their laughter.

'Some of us are bursting out here!' The shrill voice reminded them where they were. They squeezed back out and apologised to the owner of the shrill voice, who pushed urgently past them into the cubicle.

'What are you going to do now?' asked Grace. They were facing each other in the mirror, washing their hands. Shrugging, but still smiling, Davina dried her hands and reapplied her lipstick. When she finally did reply, her voice took on a dreamy, drunken tone.

'I'm going to go out there and suck the face of him, then I think it's time I told him how much I love him. Don't you?'

'Yeah, right,' said Grace. 'You're asking me! The only thing I love is chocolate . . . oh, and wine. Personally, I don't think you should suck anything in front of your brothers. I also think that whatever you're going to say to him you should say it when you're both sober. That way you'll remember what you said *and* his reaction.' Grace took Davina's hand. 'Come on.'

Even drunk, Davina knew her friend made sense. 'Okay,' she said, and let herself be led.

They made their way back through the throng of bodies to their table. The intro to Lady Gaga's 'Edge of Glory' was playing. Improvising, Davina sang her own version into Grace's ear. 'There ain't no reason me and Logan shouldn't be shagging tonight, yeah baby.'

Grace shook her head and laughed. 'What happened to being celibate?'

'I never said that,' protested Davina. 'You did. And anyway, when it comes to Logan I never sell a bit, I just give him it.' She laughed loudly at her own bad joke. *Oh shit, I'm drunk.* She turned in the opposite direction, made her way to the bar and bought herself a bottle of water. *Don't want to make a complete arse of yourself, Brown.* With her eyes fixed firmly on Logan, she headed back to the table. *Yip, McIntyre, I'm in love with you, you lucky man.* Just as she sat down next to him, Barbara Bryceland started singing Eliza Doolittle's 'Skinny Jeans'. Davina stopped, instantly transported back to the shower she'd shared with Hamish not that long ago. A pang of guilt ran through her. *Sorry, Hamish.*

'Penny for your thoughts?' said Logan. 'As if I didn't know already, you dirty midden.' Smelling his aftershave, Davina could have jumped Logan's bones right there and then.

'Nosey. Take me home and I'll tell you,' she said directly into his ear. A look of panic ran across Logan's face.

'I would if I could,' he said, 'but I'd be hung, drawn, and quartered by your brothers if I did that.' Davina sighed. Even she couldn't argue with that kind of logic.

The rest of the day passed in a blur of music, dancing, laughter and teasing. Everyone, even Marge and Robert, were enjoying themselves. Three bottles of water later, Davina was feeling less drunk but definitely not sober.

Barbara was finished by then, so most of the punters had left. The disco afterwards was slightly quieter. Nobody had to shout so much to be heard. Joshua and Craig had excused themselves and left, a little worse for wear. Grace had dragged Robert up to dance, and Hector and Logan were having a fly drink at the bar, which left Davina and Marge alone at the table.

'How's things with you, Marge?' asked Davina.

'Really brilliant, Davina. This was a great idea. Robert thinks Barbara's a great singer.' *Good old Robert. I bet Babs would feel a lot better if she knew that.* As enthusiastic as her sister sounded, Davina thought she seemed a little apprehensive. Buoyed by the alcohol and her new found insight into love, she took Marge's hand.

'Is everything okay with Robert?'

Marge pulled her hand away and shook her head. 'Every time, Davina! Every time! What is it with you and Robert? Can't you just be happy for me?' The annoyance in her voice surprised Davina.

'That's what I want *you* to be,' she said.

'For the hundredth time,' said Marge through gritted teeth, 'I am fucking happy. If you don't believe me, that's your problem, not mine.' There was venom in her reply, and it stung Davina. *Where did that come from?* Pulling back slightly, but staying resolute, she took a deep breath. *Here goes.*

'You never look happy.' She nodded towards the dance floor. 'He's always telling you what you can and can't wear, where you can and can't go. You never go anywhere without him. He's a control freak.'

'You don't know what you're talking about, Davina. He's the best thing that's ever happened to me.' This was the most serious Davina had ever seen her sister. Marge bent right in and continued. 'Don't take this the wrong way, Davina, but I think I've got more experience with men than you. You're 30 years old and, as far as I've seen, you've never had a boyfriend, far less been in love, so don't pretend you know anything about it. I swear, Davina, if you ever say anything else about Robert, I'll never speak to you again.' Marge stood up and glowered down at a gobsmacked Davina. 'Robert, are we heading?' she shouted over to the dance-floor. 'I've had enough.' She bent over and whispered in Davina's ear. 'And I'm not talking about drink.'

A relieved Robert practically ran off the dance-floor. He and Grace had been the only two left dancing and he'd been looking for any excuse to escape that particular horror. He helped Marge on with her coat and then pulled his own on, waving over at Hector and Logan at the bar.

'Great day, Davina!' he shouted. 'We need to do it again soon. Grace, thanks for the dance lesson. Hope I didn't break any of your toes!' He grimaced and Grace laughed. Davina's blood boiled. *Don't laugh with him, you're on my side.*

As Marge and Robert left, Marge gave Davina a parting kiss on the cheek. 'I mean it, Davina,' she said. 'You don't know half the shit I put up with before I met Robert.' *What the hell does that mean?* 'I love him and he loves me.' Shocked by her sister's words, Davina numbly watched them leave. Grace swayed slightly beside her.

'You should see your face, it's a picture. Are you wanting another drink?' Still perplexed by what Marge had said, Davina was speechless. Impatient, Grace walked over to the bar, letting Logan drop into the seat next to Davina.

'What a great day,' he said. 'But this drinking through the day malarkey's not good for you. It's only nine

158

o'clock and I'm jiggered. Where you staying tonight?' *The shit SHE put up with? What the hell?* 'Are you even listening to me, Davina?' Logan's hand touched Davina's, surprising her. She looked up at him, her smile genuine and automatic.

'Sorry, what were you saying?' *Oh, I know what love feels like alright, Marge.*

'Where are you staying tonight?'

'I was staying at Grace's, but if you've a better offer, I'm open to persuasion.'

'It's up to you, but we'll need to get rid of Hector.' *Not exactly a glowing invitation for mind-blowing sex, McIntyre.* He'd no sooner said this than they were joined by Hector and Grace.

'We're going to see if we can get a seat in the restaurant next door,' announced Hector. 'I'm starving. You coming?'

'Where the hell do you put it, Hector?' asked Logan, struggling to keep his eyes open. 'We had a massive lunch earlier. I'm alright, thanks.'

Hector turned his attention to his sister. 'What about you, Davina?' Despite being a good foot and a half taller than Grace, he was using her to hold himself up.

'I'm okay too. Grace, are you needing the toilet before we go?' Taking her cue, Grace escaped from under Hector and followed Davina to the toilet.

'So what's the plan?' Davina asked.

'Well,' said Grace, 'I thought if I took Hector next door, then love's young dream, i.e. you two, could bugger off into the moonlight and hey nonie nonie, Bob's your Uncle Jimmy Durante. But looking at the pair of you, I don't think there'll be much nonie nonie going on tonight at all. Is everything okay?'

'You might be pissed,' replied Davina, 'but you never miss a thing.' Putting on her sincerest voice, she cuddled her best friend tight. 'You know, Grace, you're a right nosey bastard!' Both them laughed and cuddled tighter still. 'That's a great plan though,' she said. 'You go for dinner with Hector and I'll take sleeping beauty home. I'll pop around some time tomorrow if that's okay.' The bathroom was all theirs, so they headed to separate cubicles this time.

'Only come around if you've something juicy to pass on, slut, whore and trollop,' Grace said.

'That barmaid's face was a picture earlier on with you,' Davina replied, laughing again.

'I know. Every time she served me today I should have said "fucking slut" and handed her the list. That would've been hilarious.' They laughed even harder. Just as they were leaving the toilet, the barmaid came in. Tactful as ever, Grace burst out laughing again, even louder this time. Davina had to push her out the door to avoid a fight.

'It's part of her condition,' she explained. 'Sorry!'

Still laughing, they rushed to the table, grabbed their coats and ushered the men out the door.

CHAPTER 9

BROWN SAUCE

Logan was asleep and snoring by the time the taxi pulled up outside his place. Davina had to nudge him a couple of times to wake him, before shoving a tenner through the glass partition at the impatient driver.

The hallway in Logan's flat was only ten feet long, with a door on either side. One led to the bathroom, the other to a dark, fusty cupboard. The end of the hall opened out into the living room. It took all of Davina's strength to keep Logan upright until they reached it. Despite not being the biggest of guys, the L-shaped settee groaned as he slumped into it and instantly fell back asleep, a fug of alcohol surrounding him. Davina took his socks and shoes off and unbuckled his belt, tugging off his trousers. She found a tartan blanket in the bedroom and threw it over him.

After making herself a milky coffee with sugar, her preferred drink when drunk, she sat next to the gently snoring love of her life. His soft looks made him appear years younger than he actually was. His barely parted lips were crying out for her to kiss them, so she did just that. She could have sucked the face off him and he'd have been none the wiser.

Looking around his flat, it dawned on her that most of their liaisons had taken place at her bungalow. For all his flat was well decorated, it wasn't very homely. It was carpeted all the way through in the same design: thick, dark green Axminster with cream flecks. The cream chairs and settee set it off well, but with no ornaments, pictures or any personal belongings other than a TV, Xbox, computer and Sky box – if you could call them personal – the flat had a lonely feel about it. It wasn't quite as tidy as her brothers' place, but almost. Then again, Logan didn't seem to have that many possessions to clutter the place up with. A cup and saucer with toast crumbs on it sat on the living room floor beside the couch.

The musky kitchen, just off the living room, had an opened cereal box and tub of butter lying on one of the cream-speckled worktops. Some cutlery and a bowl were in the basin. All the appliances, except the oven, were integrated in the same dark oak panelling as the units. The floor was covered with wooden tile effect vinyl. The bathroom off the hall was fitted with a shower, but only had the bare essentials in it. The cupboard across from it housed his hoover, iron, and ironing board.

'Yip, Davina,' she muttered, 'I think we'll move into the bungalow together. This place doesn't feel quite right . . . Okay, calm down,' she chided herself. *You've never even been out for a meal with him, so why the hell are you thinking about moving in together?* With the comatose Logan oblivious to their future living plans, and feeling a bit bored, Davina decided to tidy up. She washed the small amount of dishes in the sink, then tidied away the breakfast things. Putting the butter back in the fridge, she noticed a tube of Collagen Cream in the milk shelf. *How vain, McIntyre.* She poured herself a glass of water, lifted her bag, and went to bed.

At silly o'clock in the morning, she was woken by Logan cuddling into her.

'Bugger off,' she said. 'Your feet are Baltic.' She tried escaping to the edge of the bed, but he just followed her.

'Well, it was you who took my socks off and left me out there all night,' he said. 'You could have at least put me to bed.' His rough chin was scratching her neck, causing goose pimples to pop up all over her body. She wasn't sure if it was with the cold or the horny sensation that had suddenly hit her. She could smell the toothpaste on his breath and smiled to herself. *You're learning.* When his feet and legs had sufficiently heated up and his cuddles had loosened, Davina freed herself, went to the toilet, did her business, and gave her own teeth a quick brush.

'Do you want a cuppa?' She slipped on his slippers and housecoat and headed for the door.

'Please. And two painkillers. I think somebody put alcohol in my drink yesterday.' It sounded painful for him to even say that. 'They're in a box under the sink.' Davina returned with a full tray. As well as tea and coffee, she'd also made them two slices of toast each, lashings of butter melting off them.

'Room service!' she chirped. 'You'll need to sit up.' She positioned herself on the edge of the bed and waited for him to pull himself up to a sitting position, which he finally – with some effort – managed to do. The tray was balanced on his thighs now, so she crept back under the covers.

'I could get used to this,' he said. *That's the idea.* Even smiling seemed to hurt him. They both took two painkillers with their breakfast and went back to sleep.

It was well after one before they stirred again, and again she was woken by a stiff Logan, rubbing himself against her bum, his hand rubbing between her legs at

163

the front. Shifting her weight to accommodate his hand better, she reached behind her and fondled him lazily.

'I could get used to this!' she laughed, as he disappeared under the duvet, heading south. Gently, he pulled her pants off, kissing his way back up her legs and stomach. He sucked and nipped at her nipple, and his hand started up its sensual torture on her fandango again. He pushed two fingers fully into her. Barely awake, but fully responsive, she pulled his hair and gyrated her hips.

'We need to brush our teeth again!' Her breathing was getting raspy now. Ignoring her, he positioned himself above her. His mouth had her nipples aching with pleasure, his dick was right at her entrance, and they were at the point of no return.

'Well, no kissing then,' she relented. 'Just hurry up and fuck me.' The lust in her voice almost embarrassed her. She didn't care, she needed this too much, wanted it too much. She suddenly realised he'd stopped. He wasn't circling his hips and teasing her, wasn't flicking her nipple with his delectable tongue. *Uh-oh.* She opened an eye tentatively. He was on his hunkers, between her legs, playfully gazing up at her. His smile stopped just short of a laugh and an eyebrow was raised in an amazed gesture. The heat started from her neck and spread at a furious rate.

'No kissing? Just fuck you?' His voice was incredulous. Even his eyes were laughing at her. 'Will I just pay you when you leave?' *Great, you can take the girl out of whoring . . .* Taking advantage of the break in frivolities, Davina squirmed over to the side of the bed, retrieved her bag from the floor and took out her mints, one for each of them. Her embarrassment was calming down now. *Bloody McIntyre.* She turned to see him still smiling and shaking his head at her. They stared at each other whilst chewing. *Time to put that mouth to better use, McIntyre.* With a carnal look, she repositioned herself with him between her legs.

'You're a bit of a conundrum, Miss Brown,' said Logan. His head was slightly tilted and he had a pensive look on his face. 'If your brothers are to be believed, you're the most innocent, pure, trusting, shy, retiring person on the planet. Not to mention very naive when it comes to men. And yet here we are about to go at it like rabbits and you start barking orders at me like you've done this all your life. If the look in your eyes is anything to go by, you're gagging for it as much as me.' He was smirking at her now. He swallowed the remainder of his mint and placed his hands either side of her shoulders. They were almost nose to nose. 'Is there something you'd like to share with the class?' he asked. *Well, actually, I've recently retired from being an escort in order to settle down with you.*

'The only thing I want to share, sir, is your bed for the day.' Swallowing her mint too, Davina pulled Logan's glorious mouth to hers. They kissed at a frantic pace. With one arm under her back he lifted her closer to him, kissing her greedily, as her fingers tweaked and pulled at his nipples. Laying her back on the bed, Logan opened Davina's legs and found her fandango with the tip of his dick. He gazed down at her, unsmiling. Wordlessly, he rammed into her. His roughness made her jolt, and turned her on even more. As though challenging her, he never broke eye contact, his look hotly intense, his thrusts slow, hard and deliberate. Their bodies, slippery with sweat, worked in unison, their breathing heavy and labored, the mints failing to mask the smells of hungover breath and animalistic lust. The drumming in Davina's ear was beginning to give her a sore head. *Not just now.* She quickened things up with her hips and he, in turn, upped his own tempo. Her headache and imminent orgasm were becoming harder to ignore. She screwed her eyes tightly shut and concentrated on the latter. Her climax was building at a furious rate.

'Logan. Logan!' She screamed uninhibitedly as she lost herself in him, wave after wave of orgasm taking her over. Coming back to earth, Logan's pounding matched the pounding of her head. *Jeezo, McIntyre, have you not finished yet?* Teasing his nipple with one hand, she massaged the pounding on the back of her head with the other, her hips grinding mercilessly into his. *Now this is multitasking.* He was really going for it now. The headboard was battering against the wall, doing nothing for her sore head situation.

'I'm . . . I'm . . . aaahhh!' He collapsed on top of her, his breathing as strained as hers. Unceremoniously, he rolled off her.

'I thought I wasn't going to get there,' Logan panted. 'My head's fecking bouncing. Are there any painkillers left?' Despite the pain, Davina couldn't help laughing. Logan turned to her, only one eye open. 'What's so funny? I'm in agony here making sure you enjoyed yourself and all you can do is laugh?' Davina lay with both eyes screwed shut against her own pain. She could barely manage a whisper.

'Enjoy myself?' she muttered. 'Are you kidding me? I feel like the seven dwarfs are mining in my brain.' Logan scrabbled about for the paracetamol box on the tray and took two out for both of them. Davina sat up and found the glass of water she'd brought through the night before.

'Why didn't you say something? I wouldn't have minded.' It was Logan's turn to screw up his eyes in pain.

'Right then!' scoffed Davina. 'The old "I've got a sore head" routine. That would have gone down well, and anyway, according to you, I was gagging for it.' Logan grinned then winced with pain. Davina slipped off the bed and wrapped his robe around her. 'So, rather than upset you, I faked it.' Logan's eyes sprang open, much to his discomfort.

'You're lying.' This was both a statement and a question. Davina shrugged and flounced into the en-suite bathroom.

She peed, brushed her teeth, then turned on the shower. Standing under the cascading warm water helped ease her sore head slightly. She'd only just started washing herself when Logan joined her. He eyed her suspiciously, but said nothing. Their washing took place in silence, broken by the occasional smile. *I've got you thinking, McIntyre.* As she went to step out of the shower, he stopped her and pulled her back under the water, kissing her gently, his tongue running lightly over her lips. Softly, he let her go. *Holy shit, that was nice.* They gazed into each other's eyes for what seemed like an eternity, before he turned the shower off, still looking at her.

'I would've taken that further,' he said, 'but I've got a headache.' *Oooh, touchy-touchy.* He let her step out of the shower. Wrapping herself in one of his huge towels, she lifted his hairbrush and faced him with narrowed eyes.

'That's a shame. I was going to offer you a blow job.' Logan's brows shot up. 'But I know what it's like,' Davina continued, 'pretending to enjoy yourself when you're anything but!' Laughing, she managed to escape before he could grab her. He chased her back into the

167

bedroom, where she gathered up her clothes from the night before.

'Should I even bother with my clothes?' she asked coyly. Logan straightened the quilt, then lay damp and naked on top of it.

'I'm not,' he said, grinning. With a welcoming nod, he patted the space next to him. Davina brushed her damp hair and wrapped a towel around it. Unable and unwilling to deny his request, she lay down next to him. 'My head's still sore,' he moaned. 'Must've been a bad pint.'

'Right then!' Davina sniggered. 'So it was the quality, not the quantity, of lager you drank. That must be the same case for the wine then, cos my head's bouncing just as bad.'

They lay there quietly for ages, drifting in and out of sleep. In-between snoozes, Davina shivered. Logan was snoring softly beside her. Taking advantage of the lull, she padded down the hall to the toilet and relieved herself.

When she got back, Davina took her mobile to bed with her, sneaking it under the quilt. She had a few messages to get through. Douglas Bruce, her financial adviser, had texted the day before to arrange a face-to-face on Wednesday at 12noon, if that was okay. Reading this line made her think of Hamish. *Shit, how am I going to handle him?* She skipped to the next text. Gavin was really pleased to hear from her. *For Christ's sake, Davina, do you never learn? That's it, you're never taking this out with you again when you're drinking.* "Meeting for drinks with you and Grace sounds like a great idea" Gavin had written. He'd get back to her later on in the week to make the arrangements. Next up, Joshua wanted to know – honestly – what she thought of Craig. *That can wait.*

Head's still too delicate to focus on actual writing. Grace was next. She just wanted to know if Davina was getting any or "were you both too drunk?"

It was after six now and her stomach was rumbling. The flat was in darkness and she felt the cold keener now. She walked back to the bathroom and put Logan's robe back on. She knew the fridge was empty, so she checked the cupboard for food. She found some tins of soup, tuna and a mountain of takeaway menus. *He told me he doesn't like tuna. Liar.* She stuffed the takeaway menus into the pocket of the robe, took two steaming cups of coffee back to the bedroom and placed them on the bedside unit in the dark. Gently, she shook Logan awake.

'Hey, babe, what time is it?' He sounded groggy. *Babe! That's progress.*

'About half past six.' She flicked on the bedside lamp and they both blinked in pain. Quickly taking in his surroundings, Logan sat up and composed himself. Davina took her cup with her around the other side of the bed. Logan's dopey-ness made her smile. 'You okay?' she asked.

'I'm not the brightest when I first wake up,' Logan replied. 'All this travelling disorientates me.' He slipped back under the quilt. Throwing the robe onto the bed, Davina joined him.

'I was going to cook us something, but like Old Mother Hubbard, the cupboard is bare . . . That reminds me, I thought you didn't like tuna?' Logan's eyes pulled back in surprise. Davina tilted her head. 'Don't you even know what's in your cupboards?' Smiling at his confusion, she sipped her coffee, waiting for his brain to fire up. Eventually, it did.

'My mum brings me stuff over sometimes when I'm away.' *What, and she forgot you don't like tuna? Poor Mrs*

McIntyre, she must be getting a bit dippy. 'I'm starving!' he said, rubbing his face and yawning.

Not wanting to come over too pushy, Davina didn't say anything.

'What about a carry out?' Logan asked. 'I've got some menus in the cupboard.'

Davina slipped her hand into the pocket of the robe, unsure of what Logan's reaction might be.

'Ta da!' She waved the menus in front of his face. *Don't be annoyed.*

'I take it you're staying for dinner.' Davina's face flushed slightly. *Forever, actually, if you'll have me.*

'Hey, I'm only yanking your chain.' He leaned over and kissed her. 'You know I don't mind.' He placed a hand on his chest and adopted a mocked, shocked tone. 'Oh my God, I kissed you and I haven't brushed my teeth. Does that mean you'll melt or something?' She slapped him hard against the arm.

'Are you ripping the piss?' The two of them laughed.

'Come off it, Davina,' said Logan. 'As idiosyncrasies go, that one is really weird.' He lifted his cup and drank some coffee.

'Try living with it!' replied Davina. 'It can really put a dampener on things if you don't have an understanding partner. It does my head in too.'

Logan turned to her, eyes wide, mouth slightly open. 'So just how many understanding partners are we talking about here?' *Shit, backtrack, backtrack!*

'What I mean,' she explained, 'is that if a partner was to come along, I hope he'd understand.' She lifted up her cup, more to hide her red face than to drink.

'No you didn't.' Logan sat his cup back down. Naked on his hunkers in front of her, his expression was a mix of surprise and intrigue. *Don't do this, Logan.* 'That's not what you said at all, and you know it. I promise I won't tell your brothers.' Even though lying had become a way of life for Davina, she still hated doing it. As usual, though, the alternative didn't bear thinking about.

She took a deep breath, which Logan took with her. This small gesture filled her with hope. *He knows this is difficult for you, Davina.*

'Three,' she said. The surprise on Logan's face was evident. *Did he expect more? Less? Imagine his face if you'd told him the real figure.* The corner of his lip lifted slowly as though something had just occurred to him. This really confused her.

'Go you!' he said. 'You really are a dark horse, Davina.' He got off the bed, rummaged through a drawer, threw her some joggers and a top, then put the same on himself. Then he took the menus and walked out the room. 'Let's get some dinner,' he said over his shoulder. 'Are you staying the night? It's not a problem to me either way.' She couldn't quite read his reaction. She dressed slowly, the whole situation throwing her for a loop. *It's not the most heartfelt invitation I've ever heard, but he isn't exactly rushing me out the door either. And if I'm not mistaken, there was a hint of pride in the fact that I'd slept with three guys. If you'd been honest, Brown, he'd be pinning a medal of honour on your chest.* 'I'd prefer an Indian tonight,' he continued. 'Is that okay with you?' He said this just as she entered the living room wearing his top and only a pair of pants down below. His joggers were a bit snug and her stomach still felt dodgy from the previous day's drinking.

'A man after my own heart,' she said.

He was sitting on the couch with his phone and stood up as she approached. 'Can you get me a Chicken Tikka Madras?' he asked. 'I'm nipping to the shop for more painkillers and some fresh orange. Do you want anything?'

'No, I'm good, thanks,' she replied.

In his absence, she ordered dinner, tidied their clothes from the day before and made the bed. There was something niggling her, but she couldn't quite put her finger on it.

Logan returned just before the takeaway arrived. Davina had opted for a Rogan Josh. A Madras would have been her preferred choice too, but she didn't think her stomach could handle it tonight. She especially didn't want to risk stinking out his flat, so she played it safe.

The meals were dished out, eaten, and then tidied up, all in relative quiet. Glasses of fresh orange were accompanied with more painkillers. The telly was on, but neither of them were particularly watching it. They were both stretched out on Logan's L-shaped settee, opposite each other but facing one another. As usual, the atmosphere between them was relaxed.

'What a waste of a day,' said Logan. 'I forgot going out with you lot involved so much drinking. I've not had a hangover like this in ages.'

'Yeah, right, blame us,' replied Davina. 'I don't remember anyone forcing drink down your throat.'

He looked at her suggestively. 'You know I can't say no to you Browns.' *Is that right, McIntyre?* She inhaled deeply. *Strike while the iron's hot, Davina.*

'Well, in that case,' she said, 'how'd you feel about telling everyone about us?'

He looked at her in amazement. It was his turn to inhale deeply. After a slight pause, he found a reply. 'I thought we were enjoying ourselves the way things were.' *That's not quite the answer I was looking for.*

'I'm not saying I'm not enjoying myself,' she argued. 'I just think it would be nice if we could go to the pictures or for a meal together.' *Why is this so difficult?* 'You know, like a normal couple?' He'd swung his legs over the edge of the couch, and was scratching his head, seemingly lost for something to say. *Shit, shit, shit. Why couldn't you leave things the way they were, Brown? Now you know how Hamish felt.* 'Forget it. Forget I even said it.' She stood up, feeling really awkward now. 'Do you still want me to stay?' He stood up next to her and took her hands in his.

'Of course I do, Davina,' he said. 'You're right, we should do the things you said. It's just . . .' – *there's that pause again* – 'complicated.'

'How's it complicated? If you mean Hector and Joshua, then who cares what they think? I don't interfere in *their* lives.' She was annoyed at his reaction. Trying to read his expression was difficult. He wouldn't make eye contact with her, just kept looking at the floor. Then, like a bolt of lightning, her self-destruct, low-esteem barriers sprang up. She pulled her hands from his. 'You're embarrassed to be seen with me!' Logan's head snapped up in astonishment. The venom in Davina's voice surprised even her. 'Wouldn't want anyone to know you had a thing with Dafty Brown.' Furious and hurt, she headed to the bedroom and picked up her clothes. He was right behind her and grabbed them from her.

'Don't you ever say that again!' It was his turn to be angry. 'You should know by now how fond of you I am.'

'Fond of me? Fucking fond of me? You sound like my granda.' *I was ready to move in with you, you prick.* He was just staring at her, totally flummoxed by her outburst.

'Obviously,' he finally managed, 'you're looking for more from me, and so you should. You're beautiful, clever and brilliant company, not to mention hilarious, and you deserve more.' She was trying to get her clothes back, without success.

'So what is your problem?' she nipped, not surrendering to his attempts at flattery.

Logan sat on the bed and motioned for her to join him. Sitting next to him, she thought about holding his hand, but decided against it. The turmoil in his eyes was obvious and it confused her.

'Davina, my life's . . .' – he shrugged – 'well, it's complicated. I'm overseas more often than not. I can't ask you to wait for me, to always be there if and when I come back. And I couldn't ask you to give up your work and fly here, there and everywhere with me. It's not that glamorous a life living out of a suitcase all the time and waking up struggling to remember what country you're in. You'd get bored stiff.' *Numpty. I'd do all of that at the drop of a hat if you asked me to, and I could never get bored waking up with you.*

'Surely I should be the one to decide what I would and wouldn't put up with,' said Davina. 'You of all people should surely know how . . .' – she made air quotes – '"fond" of you I am.' *Finally, a smile.* 'Things don't have to change that much, just . . . when you're here, we go out as a couple with our friends and family, see how it pans out. I'm not going to drag you down the aisle kicking and screaming. Well, not yet anyway.' Logan's smile suddenly vanished and Davina couldn't help but laugh. She put on her best Liverpudlian accent. 'Calm down, calm down. I'm only joking ye.' Slowly, Logan's smile returned.

'Okay, Davina, you're right,' he agreed. 'I'm only back for two more days then away again, but when I'm back next time, you can buy me dinner. I'm warning you though, I'm not a cheap date.' The hearty laugh she let

174

out took him by surprise. *I don't think we should compare prices.* 'It wasn't that funny, Davina!' *Want a bet?* He turned serious. 'Can you hold off telling everyone for a bit, though? I'd like to be the one to tell Hector and Joshua.'

Davina nodded. 'Okay, if it'll make you feel better. But I don't see what all the fuss is about.'

'They're like family to me,' said Logan. 'I'd hate to fall out with them over this. As the saying goes, bros before hos.' He eyed her warily, gauging her reaction, his relief evident when she threw her head back and let out another laugh. *How right you are, McIntyre.* Composing herself, she stood in front of him, threw her arms around his neck, and looked him dead in the eye.

'So it's a date,' she said, assertively. 'A proper date.' She pushed Logan backwards onto the bed and straddled the top half of his body. They kissed, briefly, before he pushed her away, jumping frantically off the bed and out the room.

'Sorry, Davina!' he shouted. 'That Madras isn't hanging about!'

CHAPTER 10

BROWN SAUCE

After a great night's sleep, and an even better morning's sex, Davina – reluctantly – kissed Logan goodbye. He had a few meetings and phone calls to make, and she had her own things to see to. He would let her know when he was heading back from Saudi and she would then book them a meal, together, in public. Since they were testing new waters on the romantic front, she agreed to keep their relationship to themselves for the time being, just in case getting serious didn't work out.

Deciding she'd seen enough of her family for now, and feeling light-hearted and happier than she had in ages, Davina began the long, three-hour drive home. She had the luxury of being able to leave after ten, so missed the morning rush hour traffic out of Glasgow. As she headed back to Inverness at a leisurely pace, she spilled the beans about her weekend exploits over her hands-free to Grace, who "couldn't be any fecking happier" for her. Apparently Davina "owed her big time" for taking Hector off her hands. When Grace eventually hung up, Davina stuck on her Fairground Attraction CD, wound down the window and sang along to 'Perfect', her voice as high as her spirits.

Back in the comfort of her bungalow, Davina made herself a cup of tea and sat at the kitchen table. She was still feeling pretty pleased with herself for having decided to change vocation, and for working up the courage to suggest to Logan that they take their relationship to the next level. *Yes, life is good.* Smiling, she took her phone from her bag and texted Douglas, telling him that Wednesday at 12 was fine. *Will I drive or take the train? It's a fair trek to Falkirk.*

Next, Joshua was treated to some truthful rave reviews about Craig. He really had impressed her, and he'd fitted into their little group perfectly. Which was more than could be said about Robert. Marge was definitely on her to-do list, but what to do? How the hell was she going to get her on her own and talk things over properly? That wasn't her sister talking the other day.

A-ha! Finding her bag, she took out the business card Marge had given her ages ago and, using her nom de plume, Katy Miller, booked Marge for a half hour waxing and plucking session on Thursday at five. *If things went well they could go for a glass of wine afterwards.* Once it was sent, she noticed she had a text from Hamish and her stomach dipped.

> Are we still ok to meet up on Wednesday and if so what part of the country will you be in? ☺

Shit, shit, buggery shit. Davina checked the phone she used for her clients. There were numerous messages, all requesting the pleasure of her company. They'd need to wait until after her meeting with Douglas. *No point biting the hand that feeds you just yet.*

Her head was all over the place. She'd finally admitted to herself what she'd known for years: that she was in love with Logan. Having had the nerve to tell him, she now wanted more from him. She smiled to herself. How ironic, she thought. They'd been sleeping together for

177

years, and yet here she was all jittery because she'd soon be going for a meal with him.

Her smile faded. She couldn't lie to herself anymore. She had to admit she had strong feelings for Hamish. Although she wasn't *in* love with him, she definitely did love him. In many respects he was the best thing that had ever happened to her, and the thought of severing all ties with him upset her. What else could she do? Could they be just good friends without benefits?

What the hell, Brown? Now you're just being stupid. You knew it couldn't last forever . . . Right, stop this. All your life you've wanted Logan to notice you; to feel the same way about you as you do about him. Finally, you've got the chance of that happening and you're still not happy. What the hell!

She walked into the living room, a cup of tea and her mobile in her hands. Her mood was a lot less buoyant. Texting, and then deleting, every response to Hamish she could think of, she finally gave up. She tossed the phone on the couch next to her and decided she needed time to think.

She changed into her hardly used walking gear and left the bungalow at a blistering pace. The sunshine and tranquil scenery along the River Ness was in complete contrast to her dark, turbulent mood. She was annoyed with everything and everyone. The sun was too hot, the hill-walkers too damn happy. One of her shoes was too tight, the other too loose.

'Aaaaaaaaaaaaaaaahhhhhhh!' she screamed like a banshee. *God, that felt good.* The hill-walkers up ahead turned around and stared. Davina held her hand up, indicating she was fine. She lowered her voice.

'Don't mind me, I'm just having a nervous breakdown. Not sure which man I want to screw for the rest of my life. There's nothing to see here, move along.

You'll probably read about me in tomorrow's *Press and Journal* – "Crazy Woman Screams Herself to Death.'" The hill-walkers turned back, oblivious to Davina's ranting, and carried on with their walk. There was a bench 100 yards or so along the track, and Davina used it to take stock of her current situation. *When did my life become so complicated?* She smiled in spite of herself. *When "fucking Hamish Hamilton" sauntered into it, that's when. Did he have to be so likeable, so damned loveable in fact? No way can you see both them at the same time.* This time she laughed out loud. *Yeah, right, Brown. That's exactly what you've been doing for years! Why are you tormenting yourself like this? You're acting like you're the one calling all the shots. Hamish has probably come to his senses and wants to end things anyway. He doesn't do relationships, remember! He'll find a new companion, though not better looking than you! Logan will fall head over heels in love with you, ask you to marry him, you'll have three gorgeous weans, and everybody'll live happily ever after.* Feeling slightly better after this premonition, she headed back home. The sun was still blazing but it had started to rain lightly. She shivered, feeling the cold.

'Good old Scotland. Four seasons in one day right enough,' she said to thin air, quickening her pace.

The warmth hit her as soon as she opened the door. She took off her jacket and shoes and picked up her mobile. She needed to text Hamish back.

> Will be in Falkirk on Wednesday.
> Got to see a man about a horse.
> Was planning on staying overnight
> in Glasgow then home on Thursday,
> so if you want to leave things until
> Friday I don't mind.

The reply was instantaneous.

> I've always wanted to go on the
> Falkirk Wheel so I'll fly in to
> Edinburgh instead of Aberdeen and
> we could go on it together if you
> fancy it. Can leave any time. When
> are you there?

As part of their training in college, Mrs Butcher had encouraged her students to possess at least a modicum of knowledge about Scottish places of interest, which they could then impart to locals and tourists alike. As she was Mrs Butcher's number one fan, Davina swatted up on everything from historical buildings and landmarks to shopping malls. The information she picked up only added to her love of everything Scottish. Now that Hamish had mentioned the Falkirk Wheel, her brain automatically switched to Davina the receptionist again and explained, in her very own posh voice, that it was one of Scotland's greatest feats of engineering, a rotating boat lift that connected the Forth and Clyde Canal with the Union Canal. However, Davina and boats did not get on. *Surely a canal won't be choppy.*

> Sounds good but can't promise I
> won't get seasick lol. I've a meeting
> at 12 so after 2 probably suits me.

> Ok I'll hold your hair back. Lmao. I'll
> see if I can change my flight X

'Kiss!' Davina practically screamed the word across the empty living room. 'No, no, Hamish! We never end our texts with kisses. Don't start messing with my head again. Blow that for a game of soldiers.' Unsure what to do next, she texted Logan.

> Just wanted to say thanks for the weekend but especially for this morning X

And then as an afterthought:

> I deffo didn't fake that. Lol

She was smiling now. *Yes, everything would work out fine.* Not one for watching TV, she was about to take her iPad from the cupboard when her mobile buzzed again. *Logan.* No. It was Hamish.

> I've managed to change flights and land in Edinburgh at 10.10.

Great, we'll get this sorted once and for all.

The iPad held Davina's attention for a full half hour before her rumbling stomach alerted her to the time. She rummaged in the freezer and found a tub of chilli she'd made. *Ah, brilliant.* She made some mashed sweet potato to go with it.

Conventionality wasn't Davina's strong point. She checked the TV guide for football and found her luck was in. Everton v Tottenham. There was still an hour to wait, though, so she happily passed it playing a game on her mobile.

After the match, she got ready for bed. Lying there, sleep still ahead of her, she realised Logan hadn't texted back. *Must have been too busy . . . Oh no, what if he didn't find your quip about faking it funny? Surely he's not that touchy. He'll know you were joking. Well, nothing you can do about it now, so go to sleep.* With that, she switched the lamp off, which was more than could be said for her brain.

181

She tossed and turned most of the night. At 4.56am, the kettle was boiled. At 5.15am, she returned to the game on her mobile. It was all pointless though. Her concentration levels were zero. Thoughts of Hamish wouldn't leave her alone. What if he was angry with her, shouted at her, called her names or, worse, was really hurt and never wanted to speak to her again? Not a single scenario that played over in her head panned out well.

When she checked the time again, it was 6.03am in the morning and her half-drunk cup of tea was cold. She put the iPad down and switched her phone off. Eventually, she fell asleep. When she finally woke, hours later, it wasn't because she'd had enough sleep, it was because her head was bouncing. Apparently, lying in bed trying to ignore it doesn't really get rid of a sore head. Reluctantly, she got up, put on her slippers, padded to the kitchen and boiled the kettle. It was 12.26pm. Definitely lunchtime. Cheesy beans were the order of the day. Her sore head subsided of its own accord, thankfully, although her mood, despite her being freshly showered and dressed, was sombre. Deciding a distraction was needed, and not exactly caring what kind of mood her da would be in, she collected up her bag and her mobile and headed off to her parents' house.

The drive back to Glasgow was a lot less leisurely. People were either driving too fast or too slow. Even having Elvis on in the background didn't help. Having sat behind Mr "I'll drive in the outside lane at 60mph if I like" for what seemed like a lifetime, something inside Davina snapped and she yelled at the top of her voice.

'Fucking overtake or pull in, prick! Four times I had to sit my test. Now they just let any arsehole drive!' Davina had always vented her disgust for people hiding behind the whole road rage excuse, believing it akin to saying a child had the terrible twos. The minute you put a label on something, apparently it becomes real. Right now, though, she knew that if they were to pull over, the driver in front wouldn't leave without at least a black eye. As she caught her own reflection in the mirror, she barely recognised the hard-faced cow glowering back at her. Weirdly enough, it made her laugh.

Holy shit, Brown, you're in a whore of a mood today. She pulled in to the inside lane, her mood calming in line with her speed. She knew that if Grace was in the car with her, she'd be telling her she was fixating on the other driver's behaviour rather than focusing on what was really bothering her. And Davina knew she'd be right. Smiling ruefully, she turned up her Elvis album and murdered every song on it.

Davina parked outside her parents' house and let out a big sigh. She felt better. Inside, it was as raucous as ever. The three boys had friends over and they all seemed to be talking at once. *Well, you did want a distraction.*

She managed to sneak unseen into the kitchen. Ma was at her usual posting, washing dishes. Silently, Davina sat on the chair next to the small table. 'I see I've missed feeding time at the zoo.'

Ma turned, smiling but surprised. 'To what do we owe the honour of this visit?'

From nowhere, tears bubbled up in Davina's eyes. Then, the floodgates opened. With wet hands, Ma pulled her up from the chair, cuddling and rocking her lovingly. She let Davina get it all out before speaking.

'What's the matter, Davina? Is it man trouble?' *How do you do that?* Davina pulled away from her and unfurled some kitchen roll. *What the hell do I tell her?* She blew her nose and washed her face with cold water. Ma had boiled the kettle and was sorting the cups. Davina managed a smile, and sighed deeply.

'Sit down and tell me all about it, hen,' said Ma, handing Davina a cup of tea and leaning back on the sink. Davina took a deep breath. *Here goes.*

'Well, it's actually *men* trouble,' she said. Ma raised her eyebrows at this, but didn't say a word. 'I've been seeing two men on and off for a while now.'

Ma stared at her, horrified. 'Davina Roseanne Brown, how the hell did that happen? I thought I'd brought you up better than that.' *Shit, shit, buggery shit.* 'Do they know about each other?'

Davina couldn't look at her now. Her whole body felt as if it was burning with embarrassment. 'No, not exactly.'

Ma screwed up her face in disbelief. 'Not exactly? What the hell does that mean? They either do or they don't.' Her voice was filled with anger and hurt, or was it disappointment? Whatever it was, it cut Davina to the quick.

'Forget I said anything.' She stood to leave, but Ma blocked her escape. Tears of shame streamed down Davina's cheeks. *What did you think she'd say? You go, girl, hope they're great in bed?* They stood inches from each other, Ma with her arms crossed over her ample chest, Davina staring at the floor, neither speaking for what felt like an eternity.

'Sit down and start again,' said Ma. *Fuck.* After a few seconds of feeling like a child again, Davina reluctantly did as she was told. Although her ma's tone had softened somewhat, Davina knew she was still disappointed in her. *And she doesn't even know the half of it.*

Ma handed her some more kitchen roll, which Davina used to dry her eyes and blow her nose. *Come on, Davina, pull yourself together. And don't let anything slip or she'll be on you like a flash.* It was an age before she felt composed enough to speak, and when she did, it was with more bravado than she actually felt.

'Both of them work away a lot,' explained Davina, 'so I don't see them that often.' Ma's scowl seemed to ease a little at this, but she didn't say anything. 'I never meant for this to happen.' The lies came easily now. 'It just did. I didn't plan on seeing the two of them at the same time, but you know my record with boyfriends when I was younger wasn't great.' *Fecking non-existent would be more accurate.* This seemed to thaw Ma a little more. 'Then, all of a sudden, they're like buses. Two come along at the same time.' *Wow, was that almost a smile, Ma?* 'I'm only human, Ma. I suppose I was flattered by the attention of two men.' *You'll never go to heaven, Davina Brown.*

Finally, Ma's arms fell from her chest and her whole demeanour changed. 'Sorry, Davina, I shouldn't have jumped to conclusions like that. I should have known something like this would be hard for you to cope with, and here's me treating you like some slapper that's jumping in and out of bed with everybody.' *Holy fuck!* Davina managed a weak smile but her stomach was doing cartwheels. *Well, at least I know how she'd react if she knew the truth.* 'Did you meet them through your hotel work?' *Thank God, an easy question.*

'Yes,' said Davina. 'And I love them both. But I've recently decided I want to get more serious with one of them, and he's agreed, but I don't know what to tell the other one.'

'Why?' Ma's question baffled Davina.

'Why what?'

'If, like you say, you've been with the two of them for ages, why have things changed now? Are you pregnant to

185

one of them?' There was no challenge in the way this was said, but it was now Davina's turn to feel hurt.

'No, I'm not pregnant, Ma.' *That's all I'd need.* 'I've loved him for ages, but only just worked up the courage to do something about it.'

Ma was standing rigidly now. 'So you've just been stringing the other poor bugger along?' *Holy shit, she's raging again.*

'No, not at all. I love him too, Ma, just in a different way. We've been good friends and confidants over the years.'

'Years? So it's strictly platonic between you?' Eyes wide, Davina puffed out her cheeks. 'I'll take that as a no, will I?'

Trying again to ignore the awkwardness, Davina carried on, looking anywhere but at Ma. 'There's never been any expectations on either side.' She sighed. 'It's hard to explain.' Silence fell heavy around them again, Ma being the first to break it.

'I don't understand, Davina. If it's the way you say it is, what's the problem?' The confusion was written all over Ma's face.

Davina's voice shrank. 'I'd hate to lose him as a friend.'

Ma's eyebrows shot up again. 'So really what you're saying is you want to have your cake and eat it?' *Is that really what you want? Who are you kidding, Brown, that's exactly what you want.* Davina was taken aback by her ma's bluntness, but knew she was coming across as a selfish bitch and was too embarrassed to admit it. Ma took a long, slow mouthful of tea. 'Look, Davina, your da might not have been the only man in my life, but he's the one I picked, so it seems to me that if it's hurting you this much, maybe you need to make sure *you've* picked the

186

right man.' Davina managed to meet Ma's gaze and smiled weakly. *Of course I've picked the right man. But you'll never fully understand, Ma, because you don't know the full story, and never will.* Ma crossed the kitchen and treated Davina to one of her rib-crushing cuddles. 'Sorry I've not been much help, Davina. But it seems to me that you need to be honest with yourself.'

The kitchen door was suddenly flung open and the twins burst in with their pals. 'Can we get a drink, Ma? Hi, Davina!' the twins said in perfect stereo.

With their privacy well and truly disrupted, juice was dispersed and the dishes finished. Davina crossed the narrow lobby and joined the kids and Granda at the dining table in the living room, the long narrow room that had three functions: dining area, sitting area and, at nighttime, a sleeping area for Granda. At the moment, it was buzzing with young voices. She had to speak loudly in order to be heard by the solitary figure half-hidden behind a newspaper.

'Hi, Da.'

'Davina,' he said, flatly. This was to be the only thing her da said the whole time she was there. She squeezed her granda's bony shoulders and gave him a peck on the cheek, the familiar smell of his aftershave comforting. The Wean came over and cuddled into her arm, giving Davina one of her famous smiles. Davina took in all the eager faces fixed on Granda.

'So, what's the subject we're discussing tonight?' she asked.

Henry, who Davina liked to think of as the posh one in the family, pushed his glasses up his nose. 'Evolution,' he replied.

Davina glanced over at a chuckling Granda. 'That's a bit serious, is it not?' she asked. 'Is it homework?'

'No, Davina,' said Granda, with a wink. 'We're just having a debate.' Henry and his friend Gordon had clasped their hands, laid them on the table, and were staring right at her. The twins, Derek and Kenneth, who'd apparently been playing football and brought half the park back home with them on their jeans, were sitting with their own friends. They both piped up in unison.

'We're not having a debate, Davina, we're just talking about it!'

'Where do you stand on the subject, Davina?' asked Henry. Davina's eyes flicked between him and her granda, who shrugged, as if to say "What do you say to that?" 'What I mean is,' Henry continued, 'are you with Darwin or God?' *Oh, that's a lot easier to answer. Not.*

Gordon sat up, his posh voice all too evident. 'My father says we're all God's creatures.'

The twins mimicked his stance and, as usual, replied as one. 'Well, our da says we're wee monkeys and when we grow up we'll be big monkeys.' Both nodded their heads at Gordon and folded their arms, smugly.

It was now Henry's turn to get his tuppence-worth in. He sat up straight and cleared his throat. 'I'm confused about this,' he said. 'I believe Darwin was correct. However, if we did evolve from apes, why do apes and monkeys still exist? Why did they cease to evolve?' Davina was smiling wide-eyed at her brother. *Who other than you could have thought of that?*

'Well' said Granda. *Uh-oh, here we go.* 'I don't know if it was your man Darwin or God that was right, but what I can tell you is when I was in the Great War of Africa,' *Oh, good, Africa again!* 'me and my best pal, Tam Colson, were scouts, and we were out patrolling an area before the rest of the squad came through, when, in the middle of nowhere, we found this village. All the people were walking and talking just like us, but foreign talk, mind you. Colson took out his binoculars and lifter them to his face.' Granda slapped the table so hard, even Da jumped. 'Bang! He hit the ground! He'd fainted!'

There was a spontaneous intake of breath around the table. The Wean had gripped Davina's hand and wasn't for letting go.

'Well, I didn't know what was going on,' Granda continued. 'I tried to wake him, but he was out cold, so I took his binoculars from his neck.' Forming circles with his thumb and index finger, Granda lifted them to his face, mimicking binoculars. He scanned the living room as though looking for something. Staring at nothing in particular, his mouth fell open. As did all the kids'. Everyone slowly leaned in. Granda's eyes strained in their sockets. He lowered his make-believe binoculars, rubbed his eyes, and raised them again. Then he lowered them once more and – with a deadly serious look – addressed every expectant face, including Davina's. 'The folk in the village had chimpanzee faces,' he said, and then paused, milking the moment . . . 'They were humonkeys!'

Looking very pleased with himself, Granda sat up, put his unlit pipe in his mouth and gently chewed on the end. Henry closed his eyes and shook his head in embarrassment.

'Come on, Gordon,' he said. 'We'll read in my room.'

The twins and their pals were whispering away to each other.

'There's a boy at school called Frank Grimshaw,' said Kenneth.

'And everyone's always saying he's half monkey,' added Derek.

'Do you think he's from that village?' they asked together, awe and excitement in their voices. *Come on, Granda, answer that one.*

Spluttering with his pipe, Granda turned serious. 'Now, listen lads, you can't go about asking folk if they're humonkeys or not.'

The twins' faces looked fixed in deep concentration. Then, suddenly, they jumped out of their seats and scampered out of the living room, quickly followed by their pals and a tottering Lucy. 'Don't worry, Granda, we'll not!' Kenneth shouted back. 'We'll just ask him if he's from Africa!'

Even Da had a chortle at this, before quickly disguising it as a cough. Granda just shrugged his shoulders, resigned.

With just the two of them at the table, Davina took the opportunity to quiz Granda about the fallout of Joshua coming out. Before answering, Granda checked that Da was still engrossed in his paper, then leaned over the table.

'Me and your ma have talked about it a lot,' he whispered. 'She just wishes he'd told her when he first realised, but she's coming to terms with it now.' He looked at Da and sighed. 'He's another matter altogether. Never talks about it. In fact, he never talks about much at all now. His arse talks about as much as his mouth.'

'And what about you, Granda?' Davina asked. 'How do you feel about it?'

Granda sat up as straight as his old body would let him. 'Nothing surprises me anymore,' he said with uncharacteristic serious. 'I've seen and heard it all, pal. Humonkeys, bloody women Prime Ministers, Women priests; Christ, there's even been a black man in the White House, and I don't mean an ice-cream wafer!'

Not sure if it was because of, or in spite of, the fact that there was no humour meant in this statement, Davina struggled to hold back her laugh. Still straight-faced and very serious, Granda carried on. 'Weans starving, bloody pointless wars going on and on and on . . . Do you think the bampots that were shooting at our Joshua gave a shit if he was gay or not? I mean, it's not like their bullets had gaydar fitted into them, did they? A dead soldier's a dead soldier!' *Gaydar! Where the hell did you pull that from?* Granda raised his voice, obviously for the benefit of Davina's da. 'I love all my grandweans and I'm proud of you all. This is a fine family that any man would want to be part of.'

Da cleared his throat and flicked his newspaper straight, the outward extent of his response to Granda's comments. Davina and Granda looked at each other across the table with lopsided smiles, and shrugged.

CHAPTER 11

BROWN SAUCE

The next morning, after another restless night, Davina helped Ma with breakfast. Granda and Da volunteered for the nursery run. Apparently, there was a big race meeting on and they wanted to get the early odds on a tip they'd been given.

'Bye, Davina!' Granda and The Wean said in unison, leaving her and Ma in the quiet of the kitchen. Ma turned on the sink tap and squeezed in some washing-up liquid.

'How's things with you and Da since Joshua's news?' Davina asked.

Ma sighed, a sure sign that things weren't good. 'He's never mentioned it,' she said, scrubbing at a bowl. 'Won't let me talk about it about either.' She straightened her shoulders, lightening up a little. 'I've spoken to Joshua, though. He says he's got someone and that he's very happy. That's all I'm interested in.' She stopped washing and looked directly at Davina. 'My wean's happiness.' Her undisguised shot hit its mark. Davina walked over and took Ma's wet hands in hers.

'Ma, I know right now my love life's all over the place, but I'm still happy.' The realisation that this statement was the truth alleviated her stress, and a smile broke out over her face. *If things don't work out with either Logan or Hamish, I've still had fantastic experiences with both men, which I'd never have thought possible when I was younger. And, after all,*

192

as Grace so eloquently put it, I could have a different cock-end every weekend. She didn't realise she was laughing until Ma interrupted her thoughts.

'What's so funny?' she asked.

'Nothing, Ma.' Davina's cheeks tinged slightly as Ma went back to her dishes.

'You always were a terrible liar, Davina Brown.' She then looked at her daughter as though seeing her in a different light. 'Or maybe I've been wrong all these years. After all, you've managed to keep two men on the go at the same time without letting anything slip. What else are you not telling us?'

Davina's face turned crimson and she shifted uncomfortably in her seat. *Shite and onions, time for a sharp exit.* 'I'm going to jump in the shower,' she replied, and as she walked out the kitchen, she could have sworn she heard Ma snigger. She just wasn't brave enough to look back.

She showered leisurely – the advantage of having a near-empty house – and dressed in the quiet of Lucy's bedroom. Gathering her things together, she went back into the kitchen. Ma was still there, tidying up.

'Is that you ready for the off, hen?' Another rib-crushing cuddle almost had Davina gasping for air.

'Yip. Thanks for everything, Ma.'

'Any time. I'm here if you ever need me.' She pulled away from her daughter. 'I can't condone what you've been doing, and you do realise somebody's going to get hurt, don't you? . . . I just hope to God that it isn't you.'

Davina's responded with a weak smile and a sigh. They cuddled again at the front door, and then said their goodbyes.

Davina headed up the M80 to Falkirk with a lighter heart, reaching the town in well under an hour. She parked across from Behind the Wall, a well-known Mexican restaurant, and one of Davina's favourites. With half an hour to spare, she popped in for a cup of tea. The décor and staff were as welcoming as she remembered. She checked the menu for her favourite: chilli nachos. She was in luck. *Yes, Davina, if you survive the Falkirk Wheel, the pair of you are definitely coming here for dinner.*

The next stop was her financial adviser. On the short distance to Douglas's office, she checked her phone. There was a message from Hamish:

> Hi D, just boarding will text when I land. X

There's that bloody kiss again. She smiled. It didn't irk her as much this time.

When she got to Douglas's office she switched the phone off and put it back in her bag. Her jacket was removed and hung up by the ever efficient, ever annoying, Miss Wilson. The few times Davina had been here, Susan Wilson had always looked immaculate, her hair and make-up flawless, her teeth shining. This wasn't what got Davina's goat, however. For some reason she always looked down her nose at Davina, the look she'd been subjected to all her life. *I could probably buy and sell you, you stuck-up bitch.*

Trying not to let Miss Wilson get to her, Davina tried to strike up a conversation. 'Some weather we're having.'

No response. Susan Wilson looked Davina up and down, her distaste obvious, her grin – if it could be called that – lopsided. She grudgingly offered Davina all kinds of teas: green, nettle, rosehip, dandelion, and organic Echinacea, whatever the hell that was when it

194

was at home. Davina should have guessed Susan Wilson was a health fanatic.

For no other reason than to watch the obvious discomfort it caused the woman to even speak to Davina, Davina made her repeat a few weird and wonderful flavours back to her, only to refuse them all. In response, Miss Stuck-Up Bitch stomped back to her immaculately set out desk.

But Davina wasn't finished with her yet. She approached the desk, acting as stupid and common as Susan evidently thought her. 'I wouldn't know whether to drink or wash my hands with some of those,' she said, and was rewarded with a look that could have turned milk sour. *Result!* Lifting a perfectly sharpened pencil from its tub, Davina chewed on the end. *Holy shit, if looks could kill.* 'Mind you,' she continued, 'that green tea might have come in handy on Sunday morning. What a hangover!' Susan was raging now. Not only had Davina desecrated one of her beloved, probably never used, pencils, but she was still making small talk with her! Davina shook her head and blew out her cheeks. 'Phew, you know the kind of hangover where you don't know if you need a shit or a haircut?' The stuck-up bitch's mouth fell open.

'Davina Brown, long time no see.' Douglas was standing at the door to his office. 'You look amazing.' Davina raised her eyebrows smugly at Susan. *Get that right up you.* 'Come in, come in.' He stood to the side to let her pass.

'Oh, almost forgot.' She handed back the chewed pencil. 'Here you are, Stephanie.'

Susan held the pencil between two fingers as though it were poisoned. 'Thank you,' she said, through gritted

195

teeth and an agonising smile. 'By the way, my name's Susan.'

Davina slapped a palm to her forehead. 'So it is,' she said. 'I'll need to remember that the next time we have one of our wee chit-chats.' With that, she headed into the office, followed by an oblivious, beaming Douglas.

Douglas Bruce, like most people, was taller than Davina, about 20 years her senior, and had an ex-forces look about him, even though he'd never served in any of them. He obviously spent as much time on his appearance as Miss Stuck-Up Bitch. *I wonder if you frequent the same beautician.* His fingernails were well manicured and his complexion was flawless. There wasn't a facial hair to be seen, except for his symmetrical eyebrows. His slate-grey Armani suit had razor-sharp creases, and his pink shirt and pink striped tie certainly weren't purchased from any high street shop.

'Seen much of Andrew recently?' he asked. Indicating that Davina sit down, he took his own seat behind the well-loved but well-worn mahogany desk.

Andrew Collins had been the client who'd pointed Davina in Douglas's direction. Whilst attending one of her many functions, she'd discretely placed four of Katy Miller's cards on a table occupied by four unaccompanied, well-dressed, well-mannered older men. The next day, she received a phone call from a Mr Andrew Collins and they arranged to meet for drinks in The Waverly Hotel in Edinburgh the following week. Andrew was in his 60s, but didn't look it. He had a slender, almost feminine look and build to him. He wasn't much taller than Davina, and his hair was dark and cropped quite short. Davina couldn't help thinking she'd seen him somewhere before, but chalked it up to one of the many, *many* functions she'd attended previously. They talked about everything and nothing. Davina quickly learnt that Andrew was a lonely widower. His beloved wife, Jessie, had died of cancer a few years ago. He'd also spent a lot of time in London as an MP. At that, the penny dropped. Of course! Davina had seen him on TV and in the newspapers. Andrew's two sons, of whom he was very proud, both lived in London. Both were married and childless.

After they'd met a few times – and shopped, and lunched, and done various other mundane things – they realised they really enjoyed each other's company. Davina felt bad. She felt she was being paid just for giving a nice man someone to talk to. Surely there were cheaper ways to befriend someone?

After one of their enjoyable lunches, he invited her to his house in Troon to discuss taking their friendship further. Distant alarm bells started to ring for Davina. She'd never made house calls before. Still, there was something kind and gentle about this man. She trusted him. When she accepted the invitation, he gave her a piece of paper with his address and directions on it.

'Would you like me to bring anything with me?' she asked, not exactly sure what the meeting would entail. Andrew pursed his lips and narrowed his eyes, giving the question some serious thought. If Davina was being honest, she'd have to admit she was slightly disappointed by his reaction. *This is it. This is where I find out what kind of sick pervy things you're really into.* But his response both surprised and cheered her.

'Like what?' he asked. 'A nice cake for tea?' He searched her face for a clue as to what she could possibly mean. *Seriously? Is this how we're going to play this?*

'Yes, exactly,' she replied. 'Or some nice sandwiches, like the ones we saw in Marks's the other day.'

'Oh no, sweet child,' said Andrew. 'I'm quite handy in the kitchen department.' His beaming smile told Davina that he was very proud of this fact.

A week later she found herself driving through Troon. If Andrew hadn't given her directions, she would have driven past the secluded entrance to his house. Driving upwards on a very long and windy road, she eventually came to a tree-lined gravel drive. This, too, was very long. She was beginning to think she was actually lost, until, taking a sharp left, a massive red sandstone block mansion suddenly came into view.

'Holy shit!' The garden surrounding the house was equally impressive in size. The lawns were immaculate, and looked better than the greens on the golf courses she'd passed on the way. Various hedges were perfectly clipped to form animal shapes, and the vibrant colours of the rose bushes and bedding plants were breathtaking. Unsure where to park – *Let's face it, Davina, it's going to look out of place wherever you park it* – Davina followed the drive to the side of the mansion, then made her way to the front entrance. She was too enthralled with the carvings on the ornate eight-feet high doors to notice the woman watching her from a side window. She was still feeling the smooth intricate carvings when the doors opened. The woman greeting her had to have been Andrew's sister. *You kept her quiet, Collins. It better not be her that's into the kinky stuff.* Her hair was blonde and shoulder length, her eyes the same colour as Andrew's. Unlike him, however, she wore glasses. However, there was something not quite right about her make-up and she exuded a slightly sickly floral scent.

She shook Davina's hand. 'I'm Angela,' she said, her voice unnaturally high. 'So pleased to meet you.' Davina followed Angela through another set of equally

198

impressive doors into a sitting room with a ceiling adorned in cherubs and vines. On the far wall was a gloriously ornate fireplace, while the view of the sea from the floor to ceiling window was breathtaking. Standing there in her linen trousers and flimsy blouse, Davina felt very underdressed. Everywhere she looked there was something else to gawp over.

Angela's unnaturally high voice took on a more realistic, and deeper, tone. 'So, what do you think of my modest home?' Davina turned to answer, and her mouth dropped when the realisation finally hit her.

'Oh my God! Andrew?'

'No, dear,' she replied. 'In these clothes, I'm Angela.' Davina thought she looked a little embarrassed at the revelation. 'What do you think?' Angela asked, the high voice returning, 'Did I pull it off?' *Holy shit, you look better in a dress than I do. Not to mention walking in fecking five-inch heels without faltering.* Davina walked over and took Angela's hands in hers, raising them from her stomach up to shoulder height. She took in the whole ensemble with fresh eyes and beamed.

'You look amazing.' Angela's smile reminded Davina of the girl she once resembled, who finally felt accepted for who she was. Behind Angela's Red or Dead glasses, her eyes had misted over. Davina felt her heartstrings being pulled tight and she almost cried for her new friend. She reached out. Angela was in her arms in seconds. Her cuddle, however, definitely didn't have a feminine feel to it. *You'll have to work on that.* They sat down on the same couch and Angela poured them both tea from a silver teapot, which matched the silver sugar bowl and tongs, all three polished to perfection. Crustless salad sandwiches cut into perfect triangles sat on a china plate. With her attention elsewhere, Davina hadn't even noticed them on the impressive coffee table.

In a shaky voice, Angela told Davina her life story. She'd always wanted to be a woman, and knew she'd been born in the wrong body. Her parents weren't the approachable type, however, especially with something of this magnitude. Being an only son, it was Andrew's duty to produce an heir to carry on the family name. With this hanging over his head, he was forced to find and marry someone of good standing. Jessie Whitehall wasn't who Andrew's parents had in mind, but the shy, unassuming, shrinking violet suited perfectly. Jessie never knew about Angela and, as far as she was concerned, Andrew was the perfect husband.

'I used to help her choose dresses, shoes, jewellery, even make-up,' admitted Angela. 'If only she knew the real reason behind my enthusiasm.' She shuddered. 'Thankfully, she never did.' Davina's heart went out to her. She herself knew only too well what it was like to live a lie. Angela smiled awkwardly at her. 'The reason I got in touch with you is that . . .' She put her cup back in its saucer, gracefully crossed her knees and clasped her dainty hands over them. 'I, Angela, would love to go out in public, but I've never had the nerve. So, I thought I'd get to know you, and if we got on well . . .' – her smile was contagious – 'which, I think we do, then you could escort *me* instead of Andrew.' *Wow! I definitely never saw that one coming.* Davina set her cup down.

'In what capacity do you mean?' Once again Davina had perplexed her. Angela's brows furrowed deeply. Davina carried on. 'Most of the people I escort . . .' – it was her turn to feel awkward now, and she pushed herself as far back on the couch as possible – 'well, they don't just want my company,' she blurted out. 'If you know what I mean.' Her face was crimson. The penny finally dropped for Angela and her eyes widened.

'Heaven forbid!' She seemed genuinely appalled. 'No, nothing like that, sweet child,' she said. 'I'm not that kind of lady. No, I would just like to put on one of my dresses,' she said, flicking her blonde wig behind her ears, 'get you to help me with my make-up, and go for a meal or clothes shopping. Normal things that women do.' *Thank God for that.*

'I think I would quite enjoy Angela's company actually,' said Davina.

'But?'

'But where could we go? I mean, obviously you don't want to be recognised.'

The smile that spread across Angela's face lit up the room. 'If that's the only problem you have with this situation,' she said, 'then we're good to go.'

That had been the start of a very good friendship, and although shopping wasn't one of Davina's favourite pastimes, she endured it for Angela's sake. And after a while, Angela even ventured out without her. When they did meet up, Davina would no longer take money from her. It didn't feel right. They really did get on well and, if she was honest, she actually felt sorry for her. Life hadn't exactly dealt Davina the best of hands but Angela's, by comparison, was 100 times worse. And because Angela was vehemently opposed to not paying for Davina's services, she introduced Davina to her family's financial adviser, Douglas Bruce. It was Angela's way of repaying her.

Now, sitting in Douglas's office, with hopes of retiring at the ripe old age of 30, she was very happy that Angela had chosen this particular method of repayment. Davina knew that no financial adviser with Douglas's pedigree would have given her a second glance. Angela – or, to be more realistic, Angela's money – obviously carried a lot of weight.

'Yes,' said Davina, answering Douglas's question, 'I was with Andrew two weeks ago.'

He smiled at her. 'Well, I don't know what you've done to him, but he's a new man since he met you.' *Not quite, he's a new woman.* Davina returned the smile but said nothing.

Douglas looked down at the paperwork in front of him. He had his businessman head on now. 'I've been trying to pin you down for a couple of weeks,' he said, mildly rebuking her. 'You're a hard woman to get a hold of.' *Oh shit. What was so important he'd wanted to speak to me? Don't tell me I've got to keep going at this for another eight years.*

'I've not ignored that many of your texts, have I?' she asked. She was nervous now, and her words came out in a rush. 'And anyway, every time we meet I just tell you to do what you want. I don't have a clue how investments work. As long as I'm not bankrupt, I'm happy.' She gulped for breath. 'I'm not, am I?' *I'm glad I didn't eat before I came here. I think I'm going to throw up.*

'Calm down, Davina.' Douglas smiled and pressed the intercom. 'Susan, could you bring in a glass of water please?' He waited until Miss Wilson had given Davina an icy glass of water, which went very nicely with her even icier stare, before carrying on. 'Are you okay?' Davina nodded and sipped her water. *Just give me the bad news, Doc.*

'No,' said Douglas, 'you're not bankrupt, Davina. Far from it.' She let out the breath she hadn't realised she'd been holding. *Oh, that sounds good.* 'I'm actually glad you finally came in. There's something I wanted to discuss with you in person.' He was serious again. He lifted the top sheet from a pile in front of him and pushed it across the desk. It was a picture of the run-down office block Angela had acquired for her just outside Coatbridge.

'Just a small sign of my enormous gratitude for you,' Angela had gushed when Davina had opposed this act of kindness. 'You've been like the sister I never had.'

'We've been made an offer on one of the properties you're currently renting out,' Douglas continued. 'It's not what you could get if you hang on to it for maybe another three or four years, however they're offering a damn sight more than was initially paid for it. It's not the most desirable building you own, and the current tenant's a pain in the derrière, if you'll excuse my French . . .' – he afforded himself a small smile at his own joke – 'but apparently planning permission has just been passed to build houses on the land surrounding it and a couple of businesses have shown a great deal of interest. So you'd earn a pretty penny on your investment.' *You mean Angela's investment, but we'll not split hairs.* Douglas sat back in his plush leather swivel chair, the only item of furniture in the room that hadn't obviously been there for years. His relaxed smile returned. 'So, what do you think?'

'Well, actually,' said Davina, 'I wanted to speak to you as well.' The fact that Douglas knew how she made her money meant there was no embarrassment between them. She took her time, explaining how she hoped to leave the "hospitality" business and maybe help out with one of the smaller enterprises she was invested in, in order to pay for her early retirement. She had no intention of turning into her father, doing nothing all day but waste money. Douglas sat up straight. His serious face was back.

'Davina, do you realise how much you're worth?'

Davina shrugged her shoulders. 'You mean, like a ball park figure? No, I don't. Obviously, my bank balance is very healthy at the moment, but if I stop putting money in, in a few years it'll all be gone. I just want to know that I'll still get enough back from my investments to stay afloat.'

When Angela had told her about Douglas, she'd pointed out that he was a very shrewd businessman. He was one of the sons in Bruce and Sons, and his own son worked there too. The company had been operating for more than 70 years, and they still plied their trade out of the same modest offices they'd started up in. They were as shrewd with their own money as they were with their clients'.

'You will,' Douglas reassured her. 'As long as you're not planning on drastically changing your spending habits. Like buying an island in the Seychelles.' Davina's brows shot up in excitement. 'That was a joke,' said Douglas. 'You don't have *those* kinds of resources. But I see no reason why you shouldn't live very comfortably with what you have coming in at the moment.' He leaned across his desk and clasped his hands. 'However, things can change dramatically in this current climate, so I do suggest you keep in touch more often and answer my correspondence quicker, so we can assess how things are going.' Davina felt as though she were back at school, being reprimanded by her teacher. Her face coloured slightly.

'Sorry,' she said. 'I just have a lot going on at the moment.'

'Well, apparently that's about to change, Miss Brown, so you've no excuse.' Douglas's voice had softened but his tone was still serious.

Papers were signed, promises not to ignore texts were made, and a very happy Davina said her goodbyes to a smiling Douglas and a frowning, bitch-faced Miss Wilson.

CHAPTER 12

BROWN SAUCE

Once she left Douglas's office, smiling on the inside as well as the outside, Davina checked her mobile. As she knew there would be, there was a message from Hamish.

> Hi I'm in a pub called Behind the Wall. Having a coffee and a quick bite. Let me know when you're out.
> X

Taking a deep breath, Davina pushed the call button.

'Hello, stranger.' Hamish's voice was so warm and welcoming that Davina's anxieties fell away instantly.

'Hi, pal. How's you?'

'I'm great, where are you?' She told him where she was and he told her to stay there; he'd come to her. It was a nice day, and he wanted to show her something a short walk away, in Camelon. After that, they'd move on to the Falkirk Wheel.

She noticed him first. His good looks, formidable size, and bright pink polo top were being rewarded with admiring glances from women he hadn't even noticed. Davina grinned, happy in the knowledge that it was her he was there to see. *You're a selfish cow, Brown. Here you are about to tell him you're in love with another man, but you still want other people to see him with you. Unbelievable.*

When he finally saw her, Hamish beamed with joy and quickened his pace. *Shit, this is going to be hard.* Still smiling, he took her face in his hands and kissed her. Not a normal friendly peck on the cheek, oh no. This was an open-mouthed, tongue-tangling, pants-combusting, full-on kiss. Finally, he let her come up for air.

'Hi.' He was staring right into her soul. His sexy as fuck voice had her feeling things she was hoping not to. *Shit, shit, buggery shit.* She pulled herself back from him, hoping her own voice came across as light and breezy.

'Hi, yourself.' She kept her smile brief. 'So, what is it you wanted to show me?' Her sudden abruptness threw Hamish for a split second, before he took her hand and led her across the road. The feel of his hand in hers felt good and she subconsciously squeezed it tight. As they walked along the busy main road, Davina's head and insides were in turmoil.

'I take it you didn't miss me as much as I missed you?' His frankness caught her off-guard. *Of course I missed you, you idiot.* They carried on in silence. 'I'll take your lack of response as confirmation.' His spirits had obviously been dampened, but only slightly. Their pace never slowed, and it was clear he was excited about something. He eventually broke the awkward silence but avoided making eye contact. 'While I was in London I did a lot of thinking.'

Frightened of what was coming next, Davina tried to cut him off. 'Me too,' she said.

Hamish was insistent. 'Let me finish, Davina, or I might never say this.' *Please don't.* 'I know ours is quite an unconventional relationship,' he continued, 'but a relationship nonetheless. I love your company, your wicked humour, your tenderness, your ability to see the good in everyone. I even love your aversion to being kissed first thing in the morning without brushing our teeth or chewing a mint.' He was laughing at her now and her cheeks flushed. *You need to stop him now, Brown.* Tenderly, he grazed his knuckles across her hot cheek. 'I especially love this about you.' Stopping abruptly, he kissed her. There was less urgency this time, but no less passion. *Don't do this, Hamish.*

'I can't do this, Hami–' He placed a finger over her lips and cut her off.

'Shhh,' he said. 'We're here.' She looked around. They were standing next to a derelict building with traffic on their left. Her annoyance at herself made her almost screech.

'Where?' Unfazed and smiling, Hamish took her hand again and led her towards the derelict building.

'As I was saying, I did a lot – a *lot* – of thinking in London. I handled things in Aberdeen all wrong. Hindsight is a wonderful thing.' His eyes narrowed as he smiled at her. 'Although I am a very gifted man.' *True.* Her eyebrows raised briefly, as did the corners of her mouth.

Hamish shook his head. 'Has anyone ever told you that you have a one track mind, Davina Brown?'

Davina's mouth was now an open smile. 'I never said a word.'

'You never have to,' said Hamish. 'Your pheromones are leaking all over the place. Remember, I've not had sex since we last copulated and your behaviour is making me hard.'

'My behaviour?'

'Anyway,' he smiled, bringing the conversation back on track. 'As I was saying before I was so crudely interrupted, hindsight is one gift I do not possess in my repertoire, so what I want to know is, even though we've been having amazing sex for the past eight years, can we just start again and have a normal relationship?' He let out a deep sigh. *Nooooooo, no, no, no. Why now, Hamish?*

'Hamish, yes, we've had some amazing sex,' said Davina, 'but you were the one who said no strings attached, remember, and that arrangement works for both of us.' She kept her tone as light as she could.

'I know, I know, but I've changed,' he said. 'You've changed me, Davina.' His enthusiasm was back, and he gave her a swift kiss. 'It just seems crazy to me that I know every nook and cranny . . .' He smiled at her slyly. 'Did I say that right? Cranny? . . . of your body, but I don't even know where you stay. I know it's near Inverness, but then again so is Fort William.' He took a deep breath. 'I know you're the second oldest of eight, but I've never met any of your family.' He ran his fingers through his hair nervously. *Shit, what now?* 'I also know it was me who got you into this line of work and I have absolutely no right to ask you to stop.' *Jeezo, Hamish, give me a chance to talk and you'll find out I already have.* 'But if we did this and we both liked it, I would expect you to stop working as an escort. In other words, I want to be the only man in your life.' *Holy shit.* Ignoring Davina's stunned reaction, Hamish spread his hands out and looked up. 'Having said that, though, this is the other love in my life.' He was smiling again, and looked relaxed, as though everything was falling into place for him, whilst everything seemed to be falling apart for her. *Why did you have to waste it, Hamilton? Why did you have to fall for me? Shit, shit, fucking buggery shit.*

Eventually, realising what he'd just said, she followed his gaze upwards. An ancient, though no less impressive looking, round, red-bricked chimney stack towered at

209

least 200 feet above them. Forgetting her turmoil for a minute, Davina's mouth fell open in awe. *How the hell did I miss that?*

'What is this place?' Both their heads were bent all the way back.

'This, Davina, is the old Rosebank Whisky Distillery, home of one of Scotland's tastiest oak-barrelled whiskies.' There was real pride in Hamish's voice. 'It was built in the early 1800s.' He pointed across the busy road, where a red-bricked, historic building stood on the side of a canal, the words Rosebank Beefeater emblazoned across it. 'That was the bonded warehouse over there,' said Hamish. 'The malt was produced here, then transferred over there via a swing bridge.'

Davina found herself enjoying both the break from Hamish professing his love for her and the history lesson. The gusto with which he spoke made her smile.

'You always said you didn't want to bore me with details about your work,' Davina said.

'Not everyone shares my enthusiasm for this stuff,' said Hamish, looking slightly embarrassed. 'And when I get started, especially about a whisky as tasty as this, I tend to bore people, but that's something you'll experience personally.' He took her hand again and led her carefully across the busy road. They walked along the side of the canal, where the Beefeater restaurant was, enjoying the gloriously sunny weather. Hamish looked relaxed and happy. *You can't do this to him today.*

'Where are we going now?' Davina asked.

'The Falkirk Wheel, remember?'

'How could I possibly forget?' Davina said, rolling her eyes.

'You'll love it,' said Hamish. 'And don't worry, I'll be with you all the way.' He winked at her, and they walked on in silence, both lost in their own thoughts.

Davina nodded back in the direction they'd just come. 'So what happened to the distillery?'

'It closed down in 1993. The owners couldn't afford the money required to bring it up to . . .' – *here come those bloody air quotes again* – '"European" standards. Bloody Europeans,' humphed Hamish. 'What do they know about distilling the perfect whisky? There were plans to open a new distillery here in 2008, but the original stills and some other equipment had been stolen.'

'Stolen! That's shocking. That would never happen in Glasgow.' Davina's smirk spoke volumes. Hamish stopped her abruptly and kissed her hard on the lips.

'No, Miss Brown,' he said, looking at her intensely. 'Glaswegians only steal hearts.'

Welling up, Davina held him tight. 'Don't say that, Hamish.'

He squeezed her tightly back, his smile nowhere near as broad as it had been earlier. 'Come on,' he said. 'There's the Wheel.' He pointed above the tree line on the other side of the canal. Way in the distance was a weird looking contraption 'We'll talk after you've thrown up on one of Scotland's biggest feats of engineering.' Davina slapped his chest playfully, glad of the break in tension.

Even though the ache in Davina's stomach never left her, the Falkirk Wheel experience was much better than she expected. Hamish impressed her by explaining more about the difference between Highland and Lowland whiskies, but when he tried to regale her with facts and figures about the Falkirk Wheel, Davina had a few of her own to offer, which seemed to impress and astound him

211

at the same time. She never came close to throwing up, and spent a lot of the time listening and talking to the young children who were also on the trip.

'Do you not just love kids, Hamish?' she asked.

Hamish visibly stiffened on the bench next to her, and then sighed. 'Well, most people in life would love to be a parent, I suppose, but . . . eh . . . I think I'm far too old now.' His response surprised and saddened Davina. She really wanted to say something encouraging back about him making a great da. However, the situation being what it was, she didn't want him getting the wrong idea, so they just sat there in awkward silence till the boat trip was over.

Once back on dry land, they treated themselves to Falkirk Wheel ornaments and Edinburgh rock. Walking out of the visitor centre, Davina took a small piece of the rock from its box and popped it into Hamish's open mouth.

'You know,' he said, crunching down hard, 'I think they even sell this stuff in Blackpool.'

'I know,' said Davina. 'Crazy, isn't it? That's like the Arabs importing sand.' She looked around. 'Where's your car, now that I think about it?'

'It's parked outside that pub you phoned me from, in Falkirk. My plan was, if my stomach was okay after this, which thankfully it is, to treat you to some chilli nachos from there. They're amazing.' Hamish took his phone out his pocket. 'I'll phone us a taxi.'

Davina raised her eyebrows and threw a thumb in the direction of a bus parked nearby. 'Are you allergic to public transport, like?' Not waiting on his answer, she boarded and paid both fares. Hamish only just managed to squeeze into the same seat as her.

'How do you know the nachos are amazing in Behind the Wall?' Davina asked.

Hamish wriggled uncomfortably on the seat. 'Well, as I said, I love the history behind Scottish whisky, and I love visiting distilleries that are closed or still in use, so I find myself in a lot of different places.' He rubbed his firm but generous physique. 'One of my other great passions is food, so I like to try different types of restaurants when I'm on my travels and Mexican food is one of my favourites. It's not easy maintaining this size. Which reminds me, budge over. My arse is hanging off here.' They smiled at each other and Davina did try and budge over a bit. *This is what I'm talking about: some friendly banter. None of your sexually-charged carry-on.* 'It's the same when we're in bed,' he added. The smile fell from Davina's face and she stared out the window. *And there it is.* He held her chin gently, turned her head back to him, and kissed her tenderly. 'Don't worry, Davina,' he said. 'Whatever's bothering you, we'll sort it out.' *I doubt it.*

The silence enveloping them was strained and Davina wasn't sure if the chill was caused by the weather changing or the atmosphere between them. When the bus pulled up outside Asda, they both thanked the driver and got off. Again, Hamish took her hand, and again it felt natural to her. But the knot in her stomach was tightening. *Why did feelings have to complicate things?* They walked the short distance to the restaurant and Hamish pointed to the car park opposite. 'Ah, there's Chitty Chitty Bang Bang there!' he teased.

Davina delivered a swift dig to his ribs before opening the door to Behind the Wall. 'My car's nothing like Chitty Chitty Bang Bang,' she laughed, while Hamish hammed up how much pain he was in from her dig. A few diners and beer-swillers looked over to see what the noise was. 'Over there' Davina said, pointing at an available alcove seat. Hands over their mouths like schoolchildren who had been told to behave, Davina and Hamish made their way over and got themselves settled. They decided to share chilli nachos with extra jalapenos, and a stuffed cannelloni with chips. A young, curvy waitress came over and took their order.

'That was my point,' said Hamish, randomly, once the waitress had gone.

Davina hadn't a clue what he was talking about. 'What point?'

'About your car . . . How would I know if it runs like Chitty Chitty Bang Bang or not? I've never had the pleasure of being inside it.' *If you'd ever been in my car, there would definitely have been some sort of bang bang going on, but now we'll never know.* 'You're having dirty thoughts again, Miss Brown,' he added. *Take that sexy as fuck smile of yours and ram it, Hamilton, we're not doing this.*

'No, smart arse,' she said. 'I was trying to think if you had been in my car.'

'Liar.' Before Davina had a chance to remonstrate further, their drinks arrived.

Davina thought back to when Behind the Wall had an open fire and found herself distracted, transported to the coal, sometimes peat, fire in her bungalow. She and Logan had spent a few romantic nights in front of that fire. After a meal of something she'd cooked or he'd concocted, they sprawled in front of it, chilled wine and glasses at the ready. *Why couldn't you just have asked me out years ago, McIntyre? I wouldn't be in this bloody mess today.*

'A penny for them.' Looking up now at the tender face that belonged to Hamish Hamilton, Davina knew that although it would hurt them both, honesty was the best policy. It was just a question of timing.

214

'Any condiments?' The attractive waitress was back, and smiling. With a nacho already stuffed in her mouth – *God, I'm starving* – Davina could only shake her head.

'No thanks . . .' said Hamish, edging forward to read her name badge. 'Jane.' *Ah, the old Hamilton charm.* Jane's wide grin told Davina that his small gesture was appreciated. 'I have my own homemade Brown Sauce right here,' he added, struggling to hold in a laugh. 'And it's in a handy squeezable container.' He put his arm around Davina's shoulder and squeezed her to him, indicating just what he meant by this. The grin Jane had been wearing was replaced with a dumfounded look. She smiled weakly at them and left. Finally, Hamish could let out his laugh.

Davina straightened up. 'You're a tube. Bloody Brown Sauce. Where did you pull that from?'

'I don't know! But you've got to admit it was a good one.'

'No it wasn't.' She knew by the stupid look on his face that he hadn't finished with his bullshit.

'And besides,' he said, 'the only thing that could make this meal any better is having you with it.'

'Your patter's crap,' said Davina. 'And while we're on the subject of crap patter, does that old reading the name tag cliché still work?'

He playfully bumped shoulders with her. 'If memory serves, it definitely had the desired effect on you.' *Can't argue with that, Brown.*

The rest of the meal was interrupted only by animalistic noises of pleasure emanating from both of them, before the plates were cleared and fresh colas ordered.

Hamish collapsed back onto his seat, closed his eyes, and patted his stomach. 'I'm full to the gunnels.'

'I know what you mean,' Davina agreed. 'I could sleep right now.'

Opening one eye, Hamish looked sideways at her. 'If that's a proposition, you're half an hour too late.'

Davina took a gulp of cola. *Okay, Brown, this has gone on long enough. You need to tell him how you feel.*

'Hamish, I need to tell you something.' As she sat up straight, she had his undivided attention, his playful look replaced with a more sombre one.

'This sounds ominous,' he said.

Keeping her composure, she took his hand in hers. 'You know you're one of the best things that's ever happened to me. I'm so grateful for everything you've taught me and shown me.' *Shit, shit, fucking shit.* 'You're kind, generous, funny, caring, I could go on all day.' She dabbed her eyes with her napkin. He was looking at her with a lost puppy look. 'I really love you, Hamish . . .'

'But?'

'But I'm not *in* love with you.'

He turned to face her front on, clearly driven to persuade her otherwise. 'I get that, Davina,' he said, enthusiastically. 'That's what I've been trying to say all day. If we just spend some time together like a . . .' – *will you stop with the bloody air quotes!* – '"normal couple", we'll get to know each other better, do everyday things together, like, eh, like . . .' As he struggled for words, she struggled to keep her emotions in check, but with both palms facing upwards, he soldiered on. 'Well, like this, or just hanging out together more often.' He was desperate now.

'I can't, Hamish.'

He looked at her, dejected. He let go of her hand and she let go the tears she could no longer control. He stood up. The hurt look etched on his face cut her to her core. 'Let's carry on this discussion in your car,' he said, forlorn.

While Hamish paid the bill, Davina went to the toilet and stared at her pathetic reflection in the mirror. *Smooth, Brown. Really smooth.*

The young waitress, Jane, popped her head around the door. 'Are you okay? Do you need me to get a taxi for you?' she asked.

Davina smiled at her, taking a shaky breath. 'No, I've got my car, thanks,' she managed.

Jane stepped in fully, the toilet door closing softly behind her. 'I can see why you're upset,' she said. 'He's gorgeous, but so are you . . . and there's plenty more fish in the sea. Apparently.'

It took Davina a few seconds to understand what she was getting at. *She thinks he's breaking up with me.* She caught her reflection again. *I wonder what gave her that idea.* She managed a weak smile.

'Apparently!' Davina echoed.

'Well,' Jane continued, 'I got rid of my arsehole boyfriend over two weeks ago and I'm still waiting to catch another one.'

Davina couldn't believe this lovely young girl thought two weeks was a long time between boyfriends. *The fucking hardship.* 'Well, try to be patient,' she consoled the girl. 'I'm sure Mr Right is just around the corner.' Davina pulled some tissues from the dispenser and left. Hamish was waiting for her at the bottom of the stairs. He took her hand and led her outside.

'Bye!' Jane shouted. Davina waved in response, while Hamish – uncharacteristically – scowled without reply.

Davina beeped the car open and got in, but Hamish remained outside. She put the key in the ignition and wound down the passenger side window. 'What are you doing?' she enquired with a shrug.

'I'm only going to the train station,' Hamish replied, not really looking at her. 'It's only two streets away.'

'Shut up and get in,' Davina commanded. 'We need to talk.'

With obvious reluctance, Hamish opened the door and sat in the passenger seat.

'That wasn't very nice of you,' Davina said. 'That wee girl came up to check on me. You could at least have said goodbye.'

'That wee girl,' Hamish raged, 'asked me out and gave me her number while you were upstairs sorting yourself out.' Davina took a sharp intake of breath, so sharp it made her cough. *Fucking bitch.* 'Do you still think I should've been nice to her?'

The anger in Hamish's voice remained, but Davina wondered who it was really aimed at. 'Well, apparently she hasn't had a boyfriend in over two weeks,' she said, cynically. 'She's obviously having withdrawal symptoms.'

'I'm old enough to be her dad.' His voice was incredulous.

'No you're not. You're only 37. She must be at least . . .'

'Nineteen? Exactly. I'm old enough to be her dad.'

'Ew, yuck! Perv!' Davina's attempt at easing the tension failed miserably.

'Can we get out of here please?' Hamish asked. 'In case she gives me her mum's number.'

Pulling out of the car park, Davina realised she didn't know where to go. 'Well, you seem to know this area well, so where do you suggest?' she asked.

'The train station at the bottom of the road,' he barked. *Shit, I know you're hurting, Hamish, but this isn't easy for me either.* He was looking at her as if to say "You got a problem with that?"

'My suitcase is in the left luggage department. I had to leave it somewhere after taking the red-eye to be with you, which obviously I shouldn't have bothered with. What thanks did I get for it? All you've done is call me a perv and, if I'm not mistaken, after me telling you I want to be the only man in your life, you now want me out of it.' He shot her a questioning look. *I don't want you out my life. I just can't sleep with you anymore.* Her non-response only made Hamish angrier. He shook his head. 'Just as I thought.'

Davina drove the exceptionally short journey to the train station and parked. Before the car had stopped completely, Hamish jumped out. Davina checked her reflection in the rearview mirror. *God, you look crap. Right, pull it together, Brown. You knew there was a possibility he wouldn't take this well.* Hamish strode back to her car, flung his suitcase unceremoniously onto the back seat, got back in the front and slammed the door. *Watch my bloody car!* His anger had spilled over onto her now.

'It was hardly the red-eye,' she spat. 'You're lucky if you're in the air for an hour coming from London.'

'It's the red-eye if you've been up for hours thinking how the hell you tell the woman you've been fucking for eight years that–'

'Wow! Calm down. There's no need to talk like that.'

'–you've fallen in love with her!' Hamish finished, as though Davina hadn't spoken. '. . . Where are we going now?' The tension lay heavy between them, and her hackles were up.

'I never asked you to fall in love with me. And I thought *you* were deciding where we were going, Mr I know fucking everywhere!'

He narrowed his eyes and folded his arms across his chest, his teeth clenched. 'My plans were simple, Davina. Meet you in Falkirk, talk about our future, show you the distillery, go on the Falkirk Wheel, and then fuck your brains out. However, you have other plans for us, if I'm not mistaken. So, you tell me, Davina. Where do we go now?' The implication of this statement wasn't lost on her.

'Well, I'm sorry if I've ruined your plans for a . . .' – her face turned into a snarl as she mocked his irritating overuse of air quotes – '"fucking happily ever after", but did it never occur to you that I might have plans of my own?'

'Well, obviously you do, and they don't include me.' He grabbed the door handle and barged out, nearly taking the door off its hinges.

'Watch the fucking car!' shouted Davina. Challenging her with raging eyes, he slammed the door shut behind him. Davina jumped out her own side. Two taxi drivers leaning on their parked cars watched them, fascinated. *Nosey bastards*. Hamish then wrenched the back door of the car open and yanked out his suitcase. 'I'm fucking warning you, Hamish Hamilton.' They glowered at each other across the top of the car. 'Just try it. Just fucking try it.' With as much, if not more, force than before, he slammed the back door shut. Davina then shocked him by running around the front of the car and booting him in the shin.

'Oyah! Bet that hurt!' shouted one of the taxi drivers. Davina gave him the finger.

Shit, shit, fucking shit. With her toes throbbing, Davina hobbled back around the car to the driver's side.

Rubbing his shin, he glared up at her. 'Crazy bitch!' he growled, then stood tall and made air quotes. 'And just

so you know, I fucking hate when people do this shit.'
Leaving Davina gobsmacked, he picked up his suitcase,
turned his back on her and marched over to the only taxi
that still had a driver inside.

'Hey, pal, it's this one!' One of the two nosey drivers
pointed to his own car. Hamish, like Davina before him,
gave the guy the finger. The driver threw his hands up
defensively. 'Suit yourself, big man.'

Hamish threw the suitcase in the back seat, slammed
that door as well, and dropped into the front. The taxi
bounced with the additional weight. He stared out the
window, returning the daggers that Davina was drawing
him until the taxi turned the corner and disappeared out
of sight.

'Hey, darling!' one of the taxi drivers at the rank
shouted. 'If you're not fit to drive, I'll gladly give you a
ride.' Davina heard both drivers laughing, but didn't turn
round. She just got back in her car. Raging, she drove
out of the railway station car park and away.

CHAPTER 13

BROWN SAUCE

After the Hamish episode, Davina was in no mood to face anyone, far less talk to them. With her emotions still raw she decided the best thing to do was head home; her own home; her sanctuary. It was after five when she left Falkirk and the evening traffic did nothing for her agitated mood. One minute she was angry with herself, the next with Hamish. The fact he hadn't given her a chance to speak about, never mind explain, her feelings towards him, really pissed her off. She phoned her ma on the hands-free and told her something had come up at work and that she wouldn't be staying there tonight. It was late when she finally pulled up outside the bungalow. She didn't bother turning the lights on, just left the phone on the kitchen table and headed straight for the bathroom, before crawling into bed. Not having the excuse of driving to hold them back any more, the tears flowed for what felt like most of the night.

The next morning, she awoke to a jackhammer in her head. Gingerly, she put on her slippers, made tea, took two painkillers, and headed back to bed. She slept fitfully for most of the morning and early afternoon. In her semi-conscious, upset state, she was aware that her mobile was begging for attention somewhere in the distance.

'Piss off, whoever you are.'

At 1.34pm, she finally conceded there was no chance of falling back asleep, so grudgingly got up and padded to the bathroom, scratching her arse and farting along the way. She remembered a conversation she'd once had and smiled to herself.

'See, Logan, that's exactly why I bought this place.' Thinking of Logan lifted her mood a little as she brushed her teeth. *Well, it didn't go quite as we hoped with Hamish, but at least it's done. We know where we stand now. Time to move on.* After forcing herself to have a shower, followed by fresh tea and toast, she dressed, finally able to face the world again. Well, through text anyway. Her mood dipped. None of the texts or missed calls were from Hamish, although there was a text from Marge.

What are you up to this weekend?

Well, we had such a great time last week, let's do it again. Not! 'You'll just have to wait, Marge. I'm in no mood to deal with you right now,' she said to her phone screen, which triggered another memory. *Shit-shit-shit.* Flicking through her phone she found the number for the salon Marge worked in. It rang three times before a chirpy voice piped up.

'Venus Ventures, Selena speaking. How may I help you?' *Well, you could start by not being so bloody happy.* Davina cleared her throat and put on her posh telephone voice.

'Hi, my name's Dav–' *Shit-shit-shit!* 'Katy Miller. I have an appointment this afternoon with Marge Brown. Sorry, but I'm not going to make it. I think I must be coming down with something.'

'Katy Miller . . . Katy Miller.' Davina could hear pages being turned as her name was sing-songed over the phone. 'Ah, here we are. Oh, I'm glad you called. We don't have a contact number for you. There must be something in the air. Marge is off sick today as well and we've been trying to cancel or move her appointments.' *Marge having a day off? It must be bad.* Davina's sarcastic mood annoyed her. *It's not Marge's fault.* Selena's false caring voice continued. 'Would you like to make another appointment with someone else while you're on the phone, or do you want to wait until you're feeling better?' *Do they teach you that voice in training? Christ's sake, Brown, give the girl a break. It's not her who's pissed you off.*

'I'll just leave it until Marge is back, if that's okay. She's the one I always use because she's the best person at waxing there. Thanks.' *That should give you something to bitch about.* 'Oh, do you know what's the matter with her?'

'Poor thing's been up all night with the runs, so if you try again next week she should be back.'

'That's what I'll do, thanks. Bye.' Hanging up, Davina tapped her chin thoughtfully with the edge of her mobile. She couldn't exactly phone and ask Marge how she was feeling as she'd want to know how she knew she was ill in the first place. She wasn't in the mood for another argument right now, so she just answered Marge's text instead.

> I'm working in Perth all weekend.
> What about you?

Checking her other texts, she found Gavin had been back in touch.

> I'm available this weekend if you
> and your friend are still up for a drink

'Great! I'm the perfect person to play cupid. Not. And I'm certainly not in the mood to watch two of my favourite people be all lovey-dovey. Blow that for a game of soldiers.'

She called Grace.

'Hi there, pal. What's happening?' Grace's cheery disposition put a genuine smile on Davina's face.

'Not much. Listen, how would you feel about meeting Gavin by yourself this weekend?'

'Are you joking? I can't do that. What if we don't like each other? No, you come with me.' Davina hadn't heard panic in Grace's voice like that for years.

'Calm down. You'll like each other. I wouldn't have suggested you meet up otherwise.'

'How are you not coming? Have you got a hot date?' Davina could practically hear the sneering down the line. *From panicky Grace to nosey Grace in the blink of an eye.*

'Yes, I have. I need to go to Perth tonight and won't be back till Monday. Last minute thing. So, what do you think?' *You'll never get to heaven at this rate, Brown.*

'Well, I suppose if it's okay with Gavin, it's okay with me.' Grace sighed as she said this, but Davina could tell she was actually loving the idea now.

'I'll just phone him and run it by him,' Davina said.

'What! You haven't asked him yet?'

Grace had shouted so loud, Davina had to pull the phone away from her ear. 'Calm down, calm down. I just thought I should ask you first.'

'No, no,' bleated Grace, 'that's not how it works. You ask him first, and if he says no he doesn't want to meet your crazy friend on her own, then your crazy friend doesn't find out he said that! Arse!'

Davina laughed. 'Trust you to think like that. He won't say no. He's really up for meeting you.'

'Liar. And you're one to talk. Surely humping most of Britain's given you some confidence. If he says no, just kid on to me that you couldn't get through to him.' Before she could retaliate, Grace had hung up. A much more relaxed Davina phoned a much calmer Gavin.

With times agreed, and meeting place arranged, Davina hung up with a smug grin on her face. 'My work here is done. Now to sort out my own life!'

It had been four days since she'd seen or spoken to Logan. He still hadn't answered her text. *Surely you're not that busy, McIntyre?* Davina picked up her mobile to check again. There were two missed calls from her ma. 'Whatever it is, it'll need to wait, Ma.' She took a deep breath and texted Logan.

> Hi stranger long time no speak. How's Saudi. I've got some free time on my hands if you fancy a visitor.

Come on, Davina. Think of something witty to say.

> I promise not to get you too drunk if I do come over.

Not quite the side-splitter I had in mind, but then I'm not in the most humorous of moods right now. She pushed the Send button. As she pulled on her walking boots, the phone vibrated on the table. She grabbed it, her stomach like a washing machine on spin. 'Jeezo, that was fast.' She opened his text and grinned.

> Hi Davina, sorry I didn't text earlier. Been too busy. In fact I'm that busy it wouldn't be worth your while coming over. I'm back home in two weeks time. I'll text when I know exact times and dates then we can go on that dinner date.

She read the message twice. *Dinner date.* Placing the mobile in her pocket, she set off for her walk in a far happier frame of mind. *Two weeks. I can do that. I didn't fancy flying on my own anyway.* She reached the bench she'd rested on before, although it seemed to have taken her no time at all to reach it this time. She finally felt ready to face what was surely going to be an inquisition from Ma. She pulled out her mobile and rang her number.

It rang six times. Davina knew the phone at home was within touching distance for Da. Answering phones apparently wasn't in his remit though.

'Hello, Brown residence, Henry speaking.' *How did you end up in a family like ours?*

'Hi, Henry. Is Ma there please?'

'Oh, hello, Davina. One minute. I'll pass you over.' A couple of seconds passed, and then the posh voice of her brother came back on the line. 'Here she is, Davina. It was very nice speaking to you again. Goodbye.' Davina smiled at her brother's formalness, until Ma broke into her thoughts.

'Hiya, Davina, can you make it quick?' she said. 'I've got something on the cooker.'

'Oh, sorry, Ma. I can call back. It's just that I've got two missed calls from you. The reception's dodgy up here sometimes.' *Maybe one day I'll be able to do a full 24 hours without telling a lie.*

'Oh. it's not me who wants you,' she said. 'Just hang on.'

Ma was quickly replaced by a shouting Granda. 'Hello, hen! How's it going?' Davina pulled the phone away from her ear. *Holy shit.*

'You don't have to shout, Granda. I can hear you just fine.'

'Was I shouting? Sorry, hen!' The volume was marginally better now, but Davina still had to hold the receiver a good distance from her ear. 'What it was . . . mind you said about coming up to stay with you for a few days? Did you mean it?' *Now, you would definitely be a distraction.*

A smile broke out on Davina's face. 'Of course I did. When were you thinking?'

'How does this Monday to Friday suit you?' Then, almost as an afterthought, 'I'd have a pal with me, mind.'

'Two handsome men to entertain? How can I say no? Or is it a lady friend you're bringing?' Granda laughed the heartiest of laughs at this.

'Chance would be a fine thing!' he boomed. 'No, it's my pal, Tam. Tam Colson.'

'No problem, Granda.'

'We'll see you on Monday then, hen. Thanks, Davina, you're the best!' And at that, he hung up. Davina cleared out her ear with her index finger, still smiling. *Oh well, looks like Ma didn't want a word after all.*

It was after five now. The chill in the air sped Davina's pace up and she was soon home. As she entered the warm bungalow, she noticed her rosy cheeks in the hall mirror and gave herself a quick wink and click of the tongue.

'That's what being in love will do to you,' she said to her reflection, before heading into the kitchen and putting the kettle on. As the water heated, she tackled the coal fire. It had already been cleaned and set for its next light. Davina struck the extra-long match, hoping it would catch first time. Granda was a master at lighting coal fires even without wood. He'd shown all of them how to twist newspapers so tightly that they'd burn slower, which meant the coal had a better chance of catching light. Davina, at the age of 30, was still mastering the technique. She pulled the fire guard across and left it in the hands of the gods. Deciding against tea, she poured herself a glass of wine, put her Ten Thousand Maniacs CD on, cranked the volume, and then went about making a chorizo and sweet potato risotto.

To her delight, the fire caught hold. She set her touch lamps to their dimmest setting and swapped Ten Thousand Maniacs for Celine Dion, turning the volume down quite a bit. Closing the curtains, she ate her dinner in peace and quiet.

She was tired after dinner, so she wrapped herself in a spare quilt on the couch and fell asleep almost instantly. An hour or so later, she sat bolt upright, her whole body frozen in fear. The music had stopped, but she was sure she'd heard something. Blood was pounding in her ears and her heart was going like the clappers. She stared at the door. There it was again. *Shit, shit, fucking shit*. For all her mind was willing her to get up and see what the noise was, she was rooted to the spot. The fear had paralysed her. Then came the distinct sound of the front door closing.

From under the door, the lobby light was suddenly visible. *Thieves don't turn on lights*. Davina's eyes, the only part of her body she could physically move, scanned the room for an escape route. The door was out of the question, as it led to the lobby and the direction of whoever had broken in. The only other way out the small sitting room was through the large window that took up most of the side wall. Davina had had it fitted to let more light into the room, and since there was no way she would ever get rid of the coal fire, she needed an escape route in case of an emergency. *Move, Brown, fucking move.* She tried to swallow, but her mouth was bone dry. As if in slow motion, the door handle started to turn. Bile rose in Davina's throat. But when she noticed the poker by the fire, her legs regained their power.

She rose quickly and quietly and took the poker from the stand, making her way to the back of the door. Her tightly-gripped weapon shook above her head. She watched as a slender hand slid down the wall, searching for the light switch. Finding it, a finger flicked it on. The fright caused by the tall, slim figure stepping into Davina's hidey-hole made her scream like a lunatic, despite the fact that she had, by now, recognised the intruder. She and her sister shrieked uncontrollably in each other's face until both of them ran out of breath.

'What are you doing here?' they blurted out in unison.

'Fuck's sake, Marge!' said Davina. 'I nearly shat myself.'

'You said you were in Perth all weekend. I thought this place was empty.' Davina shivered. 'Come in,' she said. 'Shut the door.' *Christ, she better not have brought that prick with her.* 'Are you here by yourself?' She tried to sound nonchalant, but failed miserably. Marge hadn't dared come all the way in yet.

'Don't worry, Davina,' said Marge. 'Robert's not with me.' She sounded really sad. Davina lifted the quilt off the couch and sat down. She patted the seat next to her.

'Come in. Tell your big sis all about it.' Marge grinned and walked over to the fire. She removed the fire guard and put a shovel of coal in.

'I always loved the fire up here,' she said. She was still smiling and sounded like her old carefree self. *Well, little sis, I don't know why you're here, but I'm glad you are.*

'I know,' said Davina, 'so did I. That's why I kept it.' Marge put the fire guard back in place and sat down at the opposite end of the couch. She took her shoes and socks off, then swung her bare feet up towards her big sister. Davina swung her own feet towards Marge, then threw the quilt over both of them. After some wriggling, they got settled.

'So, I would ask to what do I owe the pleasure, but since you didn't expect me to be here, obviously it's not me you're here to see.' Marge's expression changed. Her face fell on her chest and she wrung her fingers together. *Shit, not that look. Anything but that look.* Davina smiled mischievously and stuck her big toe as far up Marge's jeans-covered arse as she possibly could. Marge laughed and tried to push it away.

'Stop it, Davina. Any further up and we'll be engaged.' They were both laughing now.

'That's better,' said Davina. 'Now, I take it you wanted to be on your own, but this happens to be my house, you do remember that?' She was teasing the blushing Marge. 'So I'm not going to Perth this weekend. In fact, I'm not going anywhere. You're welcome to stay as long as you want, and when and if you'd like to talk, well . . . I'm a good listener.'

'Thanks, Davina. I'm sorry I didn't ask you before I came up. I just wanted some time to myself. So I flung some clothes in a bag and instead of going to work, here I am.' *Holy shit, me and Logan could've been having sex in here.*

'What would you have done if you'd walked in on me with a man?' Davina asked. Marge let out a hearty laugh and stood up, sliding into Davina's slippers.

'Thanks, Davina. You always cheer me up.' She walked to the door, talking over her shoulder. 'Is there any wine in the house?'

'That's what I'm here for,' said Davina. 'To cheer you up. There's wine in the fridge.'

Clutching a large glass of wine each, the sisters sat on top of the quilt, one of Davina's country CDs providing the background soundtrack.

'God, Davina. That fire's roasting.'

'I know, it's brilliant.'

'Maybe one day you'll get to lie in front of it with some handsome man,' Marge smiled hopefully.

Davina sighed. 'You never know, Marge. Stranger things have happened.'

'Don't be sad, Davina. You'll find somebody. You're still kind of young.' *Gee, thanks for that, Marge. I love you too. Oh, and by the way, I have found someone. He's handsome, witty, and great in bed. In fact, we fought over him when we were young and guess what? It was actually me he fancied.* 'But we're not talking about men the night.'

They made short work of the first bottle of wine and moved swiftly on to the second. Tipsy by now, and holding the bottles up as microphones, they sang 'Stand By Your Man' at the top of their voices, then collapsed, exhausted, onto the couch.

'You can't beat a bit of Tammy Wynette,' Davina said, then burst out laughing.

'What's so funny?' Marge asked, joining in with the laughter despite not knowing what the joke was.

'I was just thinking,' said Davina, 'how many times Hector took the piss out of Da being half deaf with that country and western joke. Mind we'd all be in the living room, with Granda sleeping on the couch. Or so we thought. We'll need to watch what we're saying in front of him, the fly old bugger.'

'I know! Joshua told me what happened.'

'We'd all be in the living room,' Davina continued, 'and Hector would say to Da . . .'

"'How about some cunt from Preston?'" Both girls collapsed in hysterics. 'And Da would say . . .'

"'Great idea, I'll put on your ma's favourite," and he'd pull out Sydney Devine. Then Hector would say, "I didn't know he was from Preston.'" Davina was holding her sides, the laughter causing genuine pain.

Marge jumped up off the couch. 'I'm going to pee myself!' She ran as fast as humanly possible with her legs crossed and only just made it to bathroom in time. When she returned, she was still laughing. 'If I'd known you were going to be here, I'd have worn some TENA pants,' she giggled, sitting back down at the opposite end of the couch.

'But mind the time Da got his own back without even realising it,' said Davina, topping up their glasses. 'Let's face it, just about everybody in Glasgow knows how much our Hector likes his food. Well, mind the day we were all in the living room and his belly was rumbling, and Da got up from his chair and said "Who fancies a wee bit steak and kidney?'" Laughter erupted from both sisters. 'Hector's eyes nearly fell out his head,' Davina continued. '"Great idea, Da," he said, "I'm all for that." Next thing you know, Sydney Devine's blasting out 'Tiny Bubbles', and without a break in his stride, Da says "Yip, you can't beat a bit of Scotland's very own steak and kidney." Hector was raging!'

The laughter continued well into the night. They swapped similar stories until Marge found herself struggling to stay awake, so they called it a night. They had to support each other in a drunken embrace as they headed to bed.

'Thanks, Davina,' said Marge, suddenly serious. 'For letting me stay. I know it's not been great between us lately, but I do love you.'

Davina pulled away from her sister. 'I know that, Marge. And I love you too.'

For no apparent reason, both women began to cry. They held and cuddled each other tightly, staying that way for about ten minutes. When they separated, their smiles were in sharp contrast to their tear-streaked faces. They said good night, kissed each other on the cheek, and went off to their separate rooms.

It was after 11 in the morning when they both surfaced.

'Morning,' they said to each other in unison.

'How did you sleep?' asked Davina. Marge stretched and yawned noisily in front of her. *Even first thing in the morning you look good. Bitch.*

There was still a hint of tiredness in Marge's reply. 'Fine, thanks.'

With perfect synchronicity, they sorted breakfast without a word being spoken. Marge flicked through a glossy magazine she'd brought with her while Davina read the *Press and Journal*, which she still managed to get delivered. When she'd finished with her mag, Marge started to clear the breakfast things away.

'Have you got a dishwasher?' she asked.

Davina didn't lift her head from the paper. 'Yeah, but it's his day off.'

'Oh, very funny, I'll just put them in the sink. I can't be bothered doing them the now.'

'You're joking . . . and you were always so fussy about that kind of thing when we stayed with Ma and Da.' Davina's reply dripped with sarcasm. Marge poked her tongue out and screwed her face up at her sister. Davina smirked. 'And don't bother making faces behind my back!'

234

With all the breakfast dishes washed and put away, Davina treated herself to a fresh cuppa. 'So what are your plans for today?' she asked Marge, her hands wrapped around the ceramic mug.

Marge was full of beans now, having been suitably fed and watered. 'I'm going for a long walk along the river,' she said. 'Clear my head. Do you want to come?'

Seeing Marge like this worked wonders for Davina. 'Okay, but none of that power-walking crap,' she said. 'It's like going a walk with Usain Bolt going out with you.'

Having promised Davina they would walk back at a leisurely pace, as long as they did a power walk to the bench they'd always sat on as kids first, Marge led the way. Halfway there, Davina regretted agreeing to this madness. She was bent over double, gulping for air, the stitch in her side agony. Marge was jogging around her because, apparently, "It's not good for you to let your muscles cool down too much." *What the actual fuck?*

'Come on, Davina,' she urged. 'We're nearly there. You can even see the bench from here.' *You'll be wearing that bench if you don't shut your mouth.* Davina didn't answer. She didn't have the energy. She stood up slowly and rubbed at the pain in her side. The ever-bouncy Marge came over and, thinking she was helping, massaged Davina's side a little over-enthusiastically.

'Christ almighty, Marge! Are you trying to rub a hole in my side?'

'Great,' said Marge. 'You've got your breath back.' And with that, she grabbed Davina's arm and started walking at a relentless pace, coaxing and spurring her sister on until, finally, Davina was allowed to collapse on the bench. Marge took her thick backpack off and handed her sister a cold bottle of water. She took in the glorious landscape and beamed. 'I wish I'd had the money to buy the bungalow. I love it up here.' Davina was three-quarters of the way through the bottle of water. When she took it from her lips, her breathing was heavy.

'You know you can come up any time,' she said. *Maybe you could ask next time though.* 'I know what this place means to all of us. That's partly why I bought it.' Marge came back and joined her on the bench. 'By the way,' Davina said, inquisitively, 'how did you get my keys anyway?'

Embarrassed, Marge stuck her head in the backpack and pretended to look for something.

'I took them out of Ma's house,' she mumbled. 'I know they're only there in case you lose yours, but I was going to leave you a note to say I'd been up. Honest. Like I said, I just wanted to get away to clear my head.' *That's it. I'll need to get a new lock now. That's all I'd need, getting caught in the act with Logan.* The thought of him excited her and made her feel lonely at the same time.

'It would have been nice to have been asked! I wouldn't have minded.'

'I wasn't so sure. The last time we spoke . . . well, let's just say we were both drunk and things got said.' An uncomfortable silence descended. 'I know you don't like Robert very much.' *Understatement of the year.* 'But I've never interfered in your life before.'

Not wanting the relaxed atmosphere between them to disappear completely, Davina took Marge's hand and gave it a squeeze. 'Sorry, Marge. I just think you look miserable all the time now. You hardly wear make-up, you wear tops that are fastened right up to your ears . . .' A little smile crossed Marge's lips. Davina took it as a good sign and carried on. 'And you never phone or text

236

any more. I'm always the one to make contact. You were never like that before. I used to have to make up excuses to get you off the phone.'

Marge smiled resignedly, distracting herself with a couple of stretches, before stuffing her water bottle in her pack and flinging it onto her back. She took Davina by the hand and pulled her off the bench. 'Come on, old one,' she said. 'Before you seize up.' *At least she's still talking to me.*

In silence, they walked slowly, hand-in-hand, back the way they'd come. Without breaking her stride, and looking straight ahead, Marge finally spoke, her voice brittle.

'He scares me sometimes.' Davina's stomach knotted, but she didn't interrupt. 'I never know what I'm going home to.' Smiling, despite what she was feeling inside, Marge carried on. 'Once, I came home from work and he'd made dinner. There was music on and he'd even splashed out on a bottle of wine.' *Be still my beating heart.* Marge's smile faded. 'I had to do the dishes later on, right enough, but it was really nice. Most of the time he's just angry.' She looked horrified as if she'd just said something wrong. 'A lot of the time it's my fault though. I'm that clumsy and stupid.'

It took all of Davina's willpower to stay silent.

'Sometimes I ruin his night,' Marge continued. 'I put the cutlery in the wrong place on the table, or I take the TV remote into the kitchen with me.' She slapped her forehead with the palm of her hand. 'I mean, what kind of idiot does that? No wonder he goes mental and makes me stand in the lobby.'

Enough was enough. Near to exploding, and raging with contempt, Davina pulled her sister around to face her. *The bastard. I'll kill him.* She snarled through gritted teeth. 'He makes you what?'

Marge laughed nervously. 'It's not that bad. I'm not out there very long, and when I apologise for being so daft, he lets me back in the living room and everything's back to normal.'

'Normal! Fucking normal?' Davina couldn't hold back her anger any longer. 'I wouldn't treat a dog like that, never mind a partner. Why would you move in with someone like that?'

Rather than reply, Marge walked on ahead. Davina caught up with her and took her hand again. *Unbelievable. Why would you put up with that shit?*

'You don't understand,' said Marge. 'I love him.'

Davina shook her head in disbelief. 'Don't understand? Too right I don't understand. He's a control freak. How the hell can you love a man that does that to you?'

'You've no idea what it's like being me! Yes, I wore lots of make-up and low tops when I was younger, but that was so people would notice me.' Davina's eyes widened. 'Are you kidding me? Everybody noticed you. I was so jealous of you growing up. You were thin and gorgeous and popular.'

'And thick,' Marge interrupted. 'Not to mention boring. I was jealous of *you*! You could play football, were hilarious and, let's face it, easily the smartest out of all of us. So I just worked with what I had – my looks – and ended up with a reputation for being easy.' She stopped suddenly and faced Davina. 'Which I'm not, by the way, so don't believe everything you hear about me.'

This entire revelation flummoxed Davina. 'Listen, you!' she said, as they continued walking. 'You're not thick and you're not boring, and as for people talking

238

about you, that's just rubbish. I've never heard of anyone bad mouthing you about anything. If I had, I'd have told you and done something about it.'

'Yeah, right,' said Marge. 'You never heard the girls at school singing "Marge Brown, Marge Brown, she always gets her knickers down!"'

Davina was appalled at the thought of her sister being picked on at school. *If that was Jennifer Caldwell, I'll fucking kill the junkie bitch.* There was a rage to Davina's voice now. 'Who said that about you?'

To her surprise, Marge started laughing. 'Why? What are you going to do? Fight them after school?'

'I bloody would have,' replied Davina, annoyed now, 'if you'd told me at the time. Why didn't you?' *Pot, kettle, must be a Brown trait to suffer in silence.*

'Right, Davina. You wouldn't have said boo to a goose back then, never mind fight anybody. And Joshua, he was a moody git in them days.' They looked at each other with knowing smiles. 'But I suppose we know the reason for that now,' said Marge. 'And Hector, well, he had enough problems of his own. All the boys at school wanted to fight the big yin, and I don't mean Billy Connolly.' This made the two of them snigger.

'See, you are funny,' said Davina.

'Around the family I am,' Marge said, 'but nowhere else.'

Davina bumped Marge's shoulder with hers. 'You'll never beat the Brown humour, pal.'

The rest of the way home was spent in silence, both girls in reflective moods. Back inside, with their shoes off and slippers and kettle on, they again worked in unison sorting cups and making sandwiches. Finally seated at the table, Davina couldn't contain herself any longer.

'So where the hell does Robert fit into all of this?'

Marge took a sip of tea, and smiled and sighed at the same time. 'He wasn't like all the other boys I'd been out with. They just wanted in my pants.' She lifted her head from her cup and looked at Davina sheepishly. 'A couple of them even succeeded.' *Holy shit, I wish I could say it was just a couple.* Davina reached over and gave Marge's hand a reassuring squeeze.

'Well,' Marge continued, 'as Ma would say, "You've got to try before you buy." Robert wasn't like that. He was a gentleman. When we were going out, he paid for everything.' Davina's surprised reaction wasn't lost on her sister. 'Mind you, I'm paying it all back now. He thought I was funny and he found me interesting. He encouraged me not to wear so much make-up. Said I didn't need it.' *Okay, I'll give him that.* 'And to show less of my cleavage.' *No, he's not getting that one. If you've got it, flaunt it.* 'He just wanted to spend time with me. Just me.' Davina could see the tears in her sister's eyes. 'That's all I ever wanted, someone to like me for who I was.' Marge tried to sniff back her tears but failed miserably. Davina watched them run down both her cheeks. Marge wiped them away absently, her mind elsewhere. Davina stood up, walked around the table and cuddled her sister's head into her stomach. 'So putting up with his moods seems to be a small price to pay,' whispered Marge. Davina stroked her sister's hair. Her heart was breaking just as much as Marge's, but it was time to put on her big sister cap. *Keep it calm, Davina.*

'Relationships are all about compromising: give and take, getting to know each other's faults, and accepting or dealing with them. They're not about punishing and belittling your partner because they made a mistake or they put the remote control in the wrong place. That isn't right, Marge. You deserve a lot better, and deep down in your heart you know that.' She planted a kiss on her sister's head, then took the kitchen roll from its stand and handed it to Marge. 'Here you go, pal.' Marge wiped her face and nose. 'I'd give you a toilet roll,' said Davina, 'but it's Andrex. You know, with the puppies on them, and they cost an arm and a leg.' Marge smiled up at her. Davina shook her head. 'Unbelievable. Here you are all blubbering, red-eyed, snot running everywhere, and you're still gorgeous. Bitch.'

'I wish.'

Davina removed a notepad and pen from one of the kitchen drawers. She pushed it in front of a now semi-composed, albeit confused, Marge.

'Right,' said Davina. 'I want you to make two lists: one for, one against.' The look on Marge's face told Davina she didn't have a clue what she was on about. 'On one side,' she explained, 'put the things you like about being with Robert, and on the other put the opposite. That way, you can weigh up the reasons for being with him against the reasons for leaving him.'

'I never said I wanted to leave him.' *God, give me strength. You're leaving that prick if it's the last thing you do.*

Davina forced herself to smile and tried to sound impartial. 'Okay, but right now you're not happy and you did come up here to figure things out. You don't have to show me the list if you don't want to, but you do have to write it.' This had been one of Mrs Butcher's strategies when she'd been at college. It helped people decide if they were doing the right course or not. A couple of fellow students, after completing their lists, actually left the Hospitality course. One had gone on to do Media Studies, while the other did Electrical Engineering, which baffled everyone, especially Mrs Butcher.

241

'Right,' said Davina, 'I'm going to clean out the fireplace. You take your time. And be honest. You can fool everyone else in life but you can't fool yourself.' She gave her sister's arm a reassuring squeeze and left the kitchen.

Half an hour later, she'd finished cleaning and resetting the fire. Marge still hadn't emerged from the kitchen. Davina was happy to give her sister the space she obviously needed, and busied herself in her room with her mobile. There were umpteen missed calls from home.

'Don't worry, Granda, I'll look out your fishing gear.' There was also a text from Hamish and Andrew. 'Well, you two can wait.'

She rang Ma. A panicky voice answered before the second ring. 'Hullo?' Davina's stomach hit the floor. *Oh no, what's happened?* 'Hi, Ma, is everything alright?'

'Where the hell have you been? I've been phoning all morning.'

Davina wasn't used to Ma being this angry or upset. 'Sorry, Ma. Our Marge came for a visit last night and we went–'

'Marge is with you?' she interrupted. The relief in her voice was palpable. 'Thank God.'

'Why? What's going on?'

'I've had that Robert here this morning, turning on the waterworks. He said Marge never came home last night, so he took it she'd stayed here, but when he discovered she wasn't here, he went berserk. He's away looking for her right now. I've been worried sick. What's going on, Davina?' *Cheers for the heads-up, Marge.*

Davina had to think fast. 'They had a falling out,' she explained. 'And she fancied a change of scenery, that's

242

all. But she doesn't want him to know where she is. She said she'll phone him after.'

'Well, he won't find out where she is from me.' Ma's tone told Davina that Robert wasn't exactly flavour of the month with her either. 'Let me talk to her.'

Knowing Marge wasn't up to an inquisition from their ma, Davina felt compelled to tell a wee white lie. 'She's having a shower,' she said. 'We're a bit sweaty after our power walk.'

There was an audible giggle on the other end of the line. 'Marge I can believe,' began Ma. 'But *you* power walking? I'd pay to see that.' Davina opened her mouth to defend herself, but Ma wasn't finished. 'Get her to phone me as soon as she gets out, will you?'

'Okay, Ma. No problem.'

They said their goodbyes and hung up.

'I can so power walk,' Davina said to her phone, poking her tongue out. 'I just don't like to.' Just then, Marge knocked on her door.

'Can I come in?' *No you can't. I've just had it in the neck for you.*

'Of course.' Davina sat her mobile down and smiled at her sister. Marge joined her on the bed and leaned her head on Davina's shoulder. A few minutes passed in comfortable silence. With a heavy sigh, Marge finally spoke.

'I don't have much to put on the good side of my list.' She sighed again. Davina felt her sister's body jerk with sobs. She put an arm around her shoulder and pulled her in closer.

'What am I going to do?' Marge implored. The hopelessness in this question pulled at Davina's heartstrings, but she remained strong for her sister. *Shoot the spineless git.* She gently pushed away from her until

243

they were looking into each other's eyes. It wasn't easy, but she managed to muster up a lot more conviction than she actually felt.

'What do you want to do?' she asked, enthusiastically. 'The world's your oyster. You're only 28. You've got your whole life in front of you.' A stark realisation hit her. Not only was this true for Marge, it was true for her as well. 'Oh my God, Marge,' she said. 'I've got it! We'll go into business together!' Marge drew back and looked at Davina as though she'd gone nuts. Excited now, Davina was sitting on her hunkers, talking at 100 miles an hour. 'No, hear me out. I'm bored with what I'm doing, so I've recently been looking for something new to do. With my business skills and your beautician skills, we could open our own wee place.' She remembered the texts in her phone and her eyebrows shot up in the air. 'And I know the very place, if you don't mind working outside of Glasgow.'

Davina's infectious excitement was having the desired effect on Marge. She was down on her hunkers too now, her eyes like dinner plates.

'We could call it M and D's.'

'No we can't,' laughed Davina.

'Why not?' quizzed Marge. 'Do you want your initial first, like?' This was obviously a joke, but it was also a challenge. *There's the wee sister I grew up with.*

'No, you balloon, there's already a theme park called that.'

A glint formed in Marge's eyes. 'That's true, and we wouldn't want anyone turning up expecting a ride.' They both fell back, laughing into the pillows Davina had just fluffed up.

'That would only happen if they'd heard about your reputation,' said Davina, before adding, in a sing-song

244

voice, 'Marge Brown, Marge Brown, she always gets her knickers down!' A grinning Marge pushed her sister onto the floor, where she remained until their laughter dissipated. After a while, Davina caught her breath. 'I'm being serious, Marge. I've got a fair bit of money set aside for a rainy day.'

Marge grabbed Davina's mobile, jumped up onto the bed, and pointed down to her older sister on the floor. 'Well, you're in luck,' she said, 'because . . .' Using the phone as a microphone, Marge started to sing 'It's Raining Men'.

Davina sprang up from the floor. 'Seriously? You'll do it? You'll go into business with me? Hallelujah!'

'Yeeeessssss!' yelled Marge, raising her hands in the air. Davina grabbed onto her and cuddled her tight, as they jumped deliriously around the room in a circle.

Back at the kitchen table, Marge stared at the words she'd written down earlier, her recent euphoria now gone. Davina chose to ignore her sister's sombre mood and yanked a chilled bottle of champagne from her cold front lobby cupboard, or her second fridge as she liked to think of it. She poured them both a drink and sat at the other end of the table. She passed Marge her glass and held the other one in the air, waiting for her sister to clink it and make a toast. It didn't happen. Instead, Marge looked up with sad, weepy eyes.

'What will I say to him?' *Tell him he's the scum of the earth and if he does anything to hurt you again, I'll set Ma on him.* 'He's a good man really.' *Is he fuck. He's a knob.* 'He just gets annoyed sometimes.'

Davina lowered her arm reluctantly and again forced herself to be calm. 'That's no reason or excuse for the way he treats you,' she said. 'Do you want to go back to him?'

Marge shook her head slowly and Davina let out an inward sigh of relief. *Thank God.* 'But I don't want to see him upset.'

Davina remembered her recent run-in with Hamish and let out a deep sigh. 'We don't always get what we want in life,' she said, 'but at the end of the day, we've got to do what's going to make us happy.' She was staring in to space and hadn't noticed Marge lift her glass in the air.

'To M and D's,' toasted Marge. 'Where there's no rides, but plenty of screaming.'

A sudden memory of her first experience of waxing, at Aphrodite's Apex, hit Davina like an articulated lorry. *Maybe we should have a soundproofed room for virgin waxers.*

'Whoever said you were boring and unfunny,' said Davina, 'doesn't know you at all. But our salon is not having a corny name.' The sisters clinked glasses and quickly polished off the bottle.

Marge stayed until Sunday afternoon. They'd gone for another half-power walk, half-saunter in the morning, and were now recovering over lunch. Davina wasn't finding it easy convincing Marge that going into business together would work, or that she could afford to do it. With no capital behind her, Marge didn't feel she was bringing that much to the table, but Davina pointed out that Marge was the one with the salon experience, so it'd be her doing most of the work before and after it opened. Yes, Davina would sit in on interviews if asked, but it was Marge who would have final say over who worked for them. She alone knew what she was looking for regarding the day-to-day running of the place. Davina was strictly the business side only.

By the time she left for Glasgow, with detailed instructions written on a notepad, Marge looked the happiest Davina had seen her in ages. She'd finally accepted that they could actually do this. And so it was a more buoyant, confident Marge heading back to face the wrath of Robert Clarke. She'd promised Davina she wouldn't face him alone. He still scared her. Just to be on the safe side, Davina phoned Hector after Marge had left. Sometimes it helped having a policeman for a brother. Still, she wasn't sure if involving the police made her feel more relieved or more worried.

CHAPTER 14

BROWN SAUCE

Davina sat at the kitchen table and reflected on everything she'd learnt about her sister in the past two days. It had surprised her immensely to discover how insecure about herself Marge was. And the thought of her being bullied at school made Davina's blood boil. *What gives one human being the right to make another's life miserable? What kind of kick do they get from it?* What really got to her, though, was the fact that Robert Clarke, Marge's so-called knight in shining armour, instead of helping her get rid of them, had used her vulnerabilities against her. That was lower than low. She thought about what Marge had said about her brothers too.

It was true Joshua had definitely been moody most of his life, and Hector was always being challenged to a fight because of his height. On the whole, Davina had always thought she and her siblings had had a great childhood, yet when she scratched beneath the surface – outside of the family home, and often inside it too – it had actually been quite sad and hard going.

Why the hell didn't we talk to each other about these things back then? Life would have been so much easier. With all her heart, she wanted more than anything to help her sister get out of her abusive relationship and be the happy-go-lucky girl Davina had always thought she was.

When she was done with her self-reflection, Davina made herself a to-do list and phoned a jubilant Angela. She told her she was hoping to be down her neck of the woods sometime this week, and made plans for them both to go on a shopping spree. Davina also said she had some good news for her that she'd share when they met up. Next she had to deal with Hamish's text.

> I can't believe we parted like that.
> We should talk if and when you're
> ready. I'm really sorry.

In her current state, she wasn't able to think of anything quirky or funny to say, so kept her reply brief.

> Apology accepted.

It was just after two, and raining. Davina lit the coal fire, grabbed the spare quilt and settled down on the couch. Laptop in hand, she searched online for buildings to rent or buy in Troon. Angela had told her that a lot of affluent people stayed down here. At the time, Davina had got the impression that Angela didn't include herself in that bracket. And yet she certainly was. If Marge was to make home visits, Angela would jump at the chance of a professional makeover. If Marge couldn't get her looking like a real woman, no-one could. First, though, Davina needed to tell Marge about her unique friend. Not that it would be a problem. Knowing her sister as she did, she knew Marge would love the challenge. She might have had a setback in her life, but when it came to looking feminine, there was no-one better in Davina's eyes.

She'd already noted down three possible premises when her mobile rang. 'Bollocks, I forgot all about you,' she said to herself. 'Well, it's shit or bust. Please tell me you liked each other. Please-please-please.' She answered the call as upbeat as she could.

'Hi! How did it go?' She needn't have worried. The scream at the other end of the phone went on for ages.

'Oh . . . my . . . God, Davina! He is absolutely amazing. What a day! What a night! What a laugh!' Grace's voice finally calmed to a frenzy.

'I take it it went well then?' Davina smiled. *Looks like my work here is done.*

'Well? Went well? That must be *thee* understatement of the year.' Grace put on her smarmy posh accent. 'Of course, darling. I looked fab–u–lous, and was my usual funny, charming and, need I say, sophisticated self. He, on the other hand, was alright. I might see him again, and I might not.'

Davina laughed hard on the other end, then cleared her throat, pretending to be serious. 'I'll text him and let him down gently for you, shall I?'

'You go anywhere near your phone to text him,' said Grace, the laughter still in her voice, 'and I'll break your fingers. Seriously, Davina, why didn't you introduce me to him years ago?' *Eh, I was trying to make a living.* 'He's amazing. He's gorgeous, funny, clever, sophisticated. Did I mention gorgeous?'

'Alright, alright, I get the idea. Try to remember I have actually spent some time with the guy. It was me that introduced you after all.' Silence from the other end. *Cat got your tongue, Steele?* 'Where did you end up going?' Although she was deliriously happy for her friend, there was more than a tiny bit of her that was jealous. *Get a grip, Brown.*

'Well, we met in Spoons, like what all the posh people of Glasgow do, had a couple there, then went across to the Corinthian. We talked and talked. I felt as if I'd known him for years.'

Davina smiled to herself. She could just picture Gavin struggling to get a word in. 'He is really easy to get along with. I never felt awkward in his company at all.' Davina could have kicked herself for saying this. *Shit-shit-shit.* Luckily, Grace didn't sound as though it bothered her.

'God, Davina, how strange is this? Us talking about being out with the same guy.' There was a moment's silence, before the old gobby Grace made an appearance. 'But I can live with it as long as I know you were never in his pants.'

They continued talking about the God-like Gavin Anderson for another hour. Grace would have gone on all night, but she was due to entertain him in her flat in less than four hours and hadn't even decided what revealing little number she was going to wear yet.

'Just remember to go easy on him.' Davina was 30 percent joking, 70 percent serious.

'Don't worry, Davina,' said Grace. 'I don't intend to scare this one off. I'll phone tomorrow night. I've got a nightmare of a day in front of me tomorrow. Bye.'

'Bye, pal. Tell Gavin I was asking for him.'

Davina returned to the laptop, noting down a few more places of interest. She wasn't sure if Marge would drive every day, get public transport, or mix and match. This would need to be discussed, but she felt strongly about their boutique being in Troon. Davina was happy being left to organise the financial side of things. She knew Marge would be just as busy compiling a list of necessary items they'd need to start off with. Hopefully they'd be able to cash in on someone else's bad luck. This had sounded harsh to Marge when Davina had suggested it.

'It's dog eat dog out there, Marge,' she'd told her sister. 'As long as it looks okay, why shouldn't we buy second-hand?'

Marge had told her that a couple of her workmates were talking about finding somewhere else to work. They weren't happy in the salon. When Davina had pressed her on this, Marge admitted that it was a case of bullying, and that she herself was occasionally on the receiving end. Her boss, Lesley Greene, was a pure bitch who made everyone's life a misery, apparently. Again, Davina struggled with the person her sister had become. *Have I been walking around with blinkers on for years?*

'Why didn't you mention this to any of us?' she'd asked.

'What? And have the Brown clan storm Venus Ventures and save me? Then what? I lose my job and you all go back to normal. Are you trying to tell me you've never put up with crap for the sake of money?' Davina didn't have an answer to that; well . . . not one she was willing to share with her sister.

With a to-do list the length of her arm written out, Davina switched the laptop off and put the quilt away. She spread the remaining embers in the fire around, so they'd burn out quicker, brushed her teeth, did a pee, then double-checked that everything was locked up properly. 'Bloody Marge,' she muttered. 'I nearly shit myself the other night.'

It took ages for her brain to finally switch off. A million and one ideas and plans were swirling through her head. When sleep eventually came, Davina succumbed to it, probably with a little smile on her lips.

She was up early the next day. She was showered, dressed and fed by the back of seven. She tried to find things to do before nine o'clock, the time Douglas Bruce

252

started work. She double-checked the two bedrooms in her extension that she'd made up for Granda and his friend, then wiped down every surface in the kitchen for the umpteenth time. At 8.30am, she went for a walk. Thoughts of starting her own business were suddenly crowded out by thoughts of Hamish. He always told her she could do anything, be anything she wanted. He would've been so pleased for her.

'I wonder what he made of my text yesterday. You should have given it a day or two, Brown; thought about a better answer, and then texted.' She checked her watch: eight minutes past nine. 'Bugger the power walking, Brown. This calls for a sprint!' Her spontaneous plan was both a success and a failure. She reached the bungalow in double quick time, but it took her a good five minutes or so to get her breath back.

Finally, she was on the phone to the ever helpful Susan, who took great pleasure in telling Davina that Douglas wouldn't be available until lunchtime. *Liar, but who can blame her? You really got on her tits the last time you saw her.* Davina turned on the charm and thanked her, telling her to have a nice day, which, in hindsight, was a bit daft. She'd be talking to her later on, after all. Champing at the bit, she decided now was as good a time as any to head into Inverness. There was something she wanted to buy for Granda and his friend, Tam Colson. She'd met Tam a few times at her parents' house and really liked him, even though his patter was just as bad, if not worse, than Granda's. They'd served together as young men in the army and been best friends ever since. Both had been each other's best man at their weddings, but although her Granma had died when she was young, Tam's wife was alive and well.

She found what she was looking for in the third shop she tried, and almost passed out at the price. *If you don't like this, Granda, I'll definitely be acquiring a taste for it.*

There were a couple of salons in town that appeared to cater for everything Davina and Marge were planning to offer, so she popped in and asked the receptionists – all of them heavily made-up – for a price list. One of them had the neck to ask if Davina was looking to get her moustache done. Davina grabbed the price list off her and stepped back outside. 'Cheeky bitch,' she hissed, just out of earshot.

She made two mental notes. First: to make sure that whoever Marge decided to take on as receptionist never asked potential customers about their moustache. It was way too embarrassing. Second: to remember and check that her own moustache didn't resemble a silent movie baddy's.

At half 11, after an exhausting trek around the shops, Davina treated herself to a six-inch sweet onion teriyaki baguette with extra jalapenos. She decided to wait until she got home before eating it, but the smell rising from the passenger seat was sheer torture. *Not one of your better ideas, Brown.*

When she got out the car, she noticed the wind had really picked up. 'You won't be fishing in that, Granda,' she said, and shivered, quickly letting herself into the bungalow. In the kitchen, she switched the kettle on and bit into her sandwich. Bliss. Still chewing, she sauntered into the bedroom and brought out the dominoes. *Just in case, although I don't know why I even bother playing. He usually ends up telling me which dom to play anyway, without even seeing what I've got.*

Patience had never been one of Davina's virtues, so at quarter past twelve, she phoned Douglas's office again.

The ever-efficient Miss Wilson informed her – reluctantly, Davina felt – that Mr Bruce would now be able to take her call. Suddenly, she felt very nervous. Everything that she and Marge had decided hung on the outcome of this one call. *Arse. I should have run it past him before spouting it out to Marge.*

'Davina.' Douglas's cheery voice eased Davina's nerves a little. 'I know I said keep in touch more often, but this is a bit much.' His laugh was an easy one, but it stopped just as abruptly as it had started. Davina could picture him mentally putting on his businessman's cap. 'So . . . what can I do for you this fine day?'

Speaking for a considerable time without interruption, Davina detailed everything from where she wanted to open the business to how many staff Marge thought they'd need to get started. She could hear him typing notes into his computer as she spoke. Relieved she'd got it all out, she took a huge breath. For a couple of seconds, Douglas didn't say anything. *Don't tell me we were cut off and I need to say all that again.*

'Firstly,' said Douglas, finally, 'let me just say that that must be the shortest retirement in history. Now, secondly, if I may get serious for a moment.' *Surely not.* 'There would be places a lot cheaper to buy or rent from than Troon. However, as you so eloquently put it, you do have to speculate to accumulate and Troon does seem to house a better sort of clientele, shall we say. Having recently gone over your file with you, I don't see there being too many problems, but I will have to go over the figures more thoroughly, just to be sure. It may also mean selling some of the property you've invested in. Would that be a problem for you?'

'Not at all. As I said before, I trust you 200 percent. I know you'll be honest with me and keep me on the right path.' Douglas cleared his throat. Davina wondered if she'd embarrassed him with her praise.

'Splendid,' he replied. 'Splendid. Righty-o. I'll be in touch, hopefully within the next two days. Don't panic if it's a bit longer, I'll definitely get back to you.' Douglas's tone told Davina that their conversation had now come to an end.

'Thank you, Douglas. I'll hear from you soon. Bye.'

'Goodbye, Davina.'

The next two days were going to be hell, Davina thought, but at least she had two huge distractions arriving imminently. From the shelter of her car, she watched Granda get off the bus first, followed by the only other person to alight, a man the same height and build as her granda; a man with a soldier's walk: Tam Colson. The wind was intense, and both men had a hand clamped to their skull. It was all they could do to keep their flat caps from flying off into the wilderness.

Davina got out the car and waved them over. Even getting the boot open in this wind was a struggle. She was being blown all over the place. Granda threw his holdall in and gave Davina a cuddle.

'How's my favourite girl?' Davina loved when he called her this.

'I'm great, Granda,' she lied. Tam's suitcase was in the boot too now, and Davina had to use all her strength to close it.

'Hiya, pal,' Tam smiled, giving Davina's arm a gentle squeeze.

'Hiya, Mr Colson. How have you been?'

'Are we going to stand in this wind all day?' Granda grumped, opening the driver's side back door, trying to squeeze himself in.

'Ignore that cranky old sod, he's no manners,' Tam said, shaking his head and winking at Davina whilst fighting against the wind to open the rear passenger door.

It was a short journey to the bungalow. Granda and Tam enthused over the scenery and all the fish that were bound to be in the river, and then hopefully in their bellies.

'God almighty,' said Tam, as they slowed to a halt. 'Your granda said you'd done some work on the place, but this is amazing, Davina. It's as if you've built another house onto the end.'

Having had its kitchen enlarged and two extra en-suite double bedrooms added, the once L-shaped bungalow was now T-shaped.

'Thanks, Mr Colson,' beamed Davina. They got out of the car and walked to the gap in the three-foot-high, dry stone wall that had always surrounded the family bungalow. Before building the extension, Davina had brought in a professional to extend and repair the existing wall. The extension to the house had been built using materials as close to the original as possible. Although it was obvious where the work had been added, Davina was proud of what she'd done. She opened the front door and let the men hang their coats in the front lobby.

'That's a rare heat, hen,' said Granda, following Davina along the lobby. They passed the living room on the left and the now larger kitchen on the right. At the open door to one of the guest bedrooms, Davina stopped and turned, glowing with pride.

'You're in here, Mr Colson.'

Tam walked past her and whistled, impressed. 'My old man was Mr Colson,' he said. 'I'm just Tam.' He sat his

257

battered suitcase on the floor next to the bed and moved over to the large window, taking in the scenery.

'Amazing, isn't it, Tam?' said Granda, standing behind him. 'A room each as well, and no sharing a bed with Lucy or the two wee monkeys for me this time.' Tam had found the Kleenex with aloe vera on the bedside table and was rubbing them between his thumb and index finger, smiling.

'I remember when we used to come up here,' he said. 'There was none of this fancy-shmancy stuff, and we had to go outside for the toilet.'

'So you've been here before Mr–' The look Tam threw her reminded her of the one Hamish had used, when she'd made the same mistake with him. The thought saddened her. *You really should text him.* 'Sorry! Tam.'

'Oh, yes,' Tam replied. 'Many's the time we'd come up here after your ma inherited it.' His eyes took on a faraway look. 'With just a bottle and the scenery for company. Them were the days.' He pulled himself out of his reverie. 'Not like today. You can't move up here for bloody tourists these days. Pain in the arse the lot of them, all coming to try and get a glimpse of Nessie. Little do they know that me and your granda caught her years ago.' Davina rolled her eyes. There wasn't even a hint of pretence in Tam's voice. *Great, it's started already. Bullshitting must have been compulsory at school back in the day.*

'That's right,' added Granda, backing Tam up, 'with just a stick and a bit of string with a worm dangling from the end. She was a fighter though, I'll tell you.'

Davina had heard enough. She left them to settle in and out-bullshit each other. The fire, to her amazement, caught first time again, and she mentally patted herself on the back. *You're getting the hang of this, Brown.*

In the kitchen, she put the kettle on and took three cups down from the cupboard. When Granda and Tam came in, they looked at her strangely.

'Is something the matter, Granda?'

'No, no, you're fine, hen. Just don't bother with tea for us. We were just saying that there'll be no fishing getting done today, so we might as well have a wee dram, if it's all the same to you.'

'Great idea,' said Davina. 'Would you like me to get the doms out?'

Granda and Tam looked at one another, suddenly serious. 'Yes!' they enthused in unison.

'Great,' said Davina to herself as she walked back in to her bedroom. 'A nice wee friendly game of dominoes.'

When she returned to the kitchen, the two men had positioned themselves across from each other at the large, light oak, farmhouse style dining table with ten matching chairs. Davina had loved the atmosphere in her parents' home when family and friends sat around the long oblong dining table that took up most of the living room. The banter and food were never disappointing. When she'd decided to extend the bungalow, she wanted the dining table in the kitchen instead. Her thinking behind this was that, unlike Ma, she would be able to talk to her guests as she prepared and cooked a meal for them.

Three glasses sat on coasters on the table, and a bottle of ten-year-old Glenfiddich, with an accompanying jug of water, sat beside Tam. Both he and Granda had undone the top button of their shirts and rolled their sleeves up to just below the elbows. They were staring at each other across the table, domino gladiators about to do battle.

Davina carefully lay the box of dominoes between them. 'I hope this isn't going to get violent,' she cautioned. Neither man spoke, nor moved. Davina opened one of the lower kitchen cupboards. She was quite excited. She hoped to impress them with her new-found insight into whisky. *God, I hope this is as good as Hamish said.* She straightened back up, hiding what she held in her hands.

'That's a very nice Highland malt you've got there if I'm not very much mistaken,' she said, turning around with a bottle of 12 year-old Rosebank whisky offered out. 'However, I have it from a very good source that this Lowland malt could give it a good run for its money.' Both men's mouths fell open. Eventually, Granda took it gingerly from her and held it like it was the most precious thing he'd ever seen.

'Good grief,' he cooed. 'Where did you get this, lass?' The admiration in his voice was unmistakable. Davina beamed from ear to ear. *Good call, Hamilton.* She removed the three tumblers from the table and pulled out a boxed set of Edinburgh Crystal from the cupboard, a house-warming gift from her parents. "Every Scottish home should have a decent set of whisky tumblers," Da had informed her. She handed the tumblers out and placed the box back in the cupboard. Tam sat his bottle of Glenmorangie on the floor and cleared his throat.

'The old Morangie'll take some beating,' he said, 'but I'll give it a try since you went to all the bother of buying it.'

Granda read the label on the Rosebank without looking up. 'Don't do us any favours,' he said. 'Just you drink your old Morangie and I'll tell you if the Rosebank's as good as we've always thought.' The tip of Granda's tongue moved slowly, achingly, across his lips.

An impatient Tam challenged him. 'Are you going to open it, Brown, or winch it?'

A broad smile crossed Granda's face. 'I was thinking, since you're not too sure about it, I might just take it down the road with me.' Turning, he winked at Davina. 'What do you think, Davina? Would that be alright with you?'

Davina sat down at the top of the table, between the two men. 'Well, to be honest, Granda, my friend talked it up that much I wouldn't mind having a wee taste myself, if it's all the same to you.'

Tam jumped all over this. 'You heard her, Brown, open the damn bottle and give us all a dram.'

Granda snorted, clearly not happy with the state of affairs. He slowly twisted the lid off and inhaled deeply, sucking in the aroma. An appreciative smile told Davina and Tam exactly what he thought. Without uttering a word, he handed the open bottle to his old friend, who sniffed and smiled just as Granda had done.

'You can smell the oak in it,' he said. 'Will I do the honours?' Davina and Granda nodded. Tam poured a half-inch of amber liquid into each tumbler. He then passed round the water jug, which Davina declined.

'I'll try it without water first, thanks, she said.

'Suit yourself, pal,' said Granda. He raised his tumbler. 'Slàinte Mhath!' They clinked their glasses together and all took a sip. Granda and Tam's eyes opened wide in appreciation as they slowly savoured the liquid in their mouths. Davina's face, by contrast, crumpled in disappointment. She'd wanted to like the whisky as much as the men and, if she was honest with herself, as much as Hamish, but she didn't. She decided to try it with some water but the outcome was the same. *How can you drink this stuff? It must be an acquired taste.*

'Whoever your source is,' said Granda, 'tell them from me that they're spot on with their whisky. I've never tasted the likes before.'

'Thanks, Granda. I'll be sure to pass your praise on to him.' *If he ever speaks to me again that is.*

After the whisky – and for the next two hours – came the dominoes. Granda and Tam took it far too seriously for Davina's liking, both of them often getting annoyed with her choice of dom. Completely oblivious to the score, all Davina knew for certain was that she hadn't won a down. Intermittently, she'd check on the fire. She'd swapped her whisky for wine and was now feeling as tipsy as the other two looked. Granda stood up and stretched his legs. 'That seat does nothing for me fur,' he groaned. 'Even my bum's gone to sleep.'

'Fine we know.' Tam winked at Davina. 'We heard it snoring.' Davina almost fell off her chair laughing.

An indignant Granda lifted his tumbler and the bottle of whisky. 'I'm retiring to the sitting room,' he said. Davina and Tam, still laughing, lifted their own drinks and followed him.

The sitting room was lovely and warm. Davina and Granda shared the couch, while Tam settled on an armchair.

'I'll tell you who would appreciate that whisky,' said Tam.

Granda held up the half-empty bottle and chuckled. 'Yeah, cause we're not.'

'Dick Baxter,' Tam continued.

'Dick!' Davina shouted. Tam and Granda looked at each other and shrugged their shoulders.

'He liked his whisky, did old Dick,' said Tam. This time Davina, clearly drunk, laughed out loud.

'Ignore her, Tam,' said Granda, shaking his head at Davina. 'Carry on with what you were saying.' *Laughing at the word dick, Brown. Calm down.*

'It was a shame what happened to him though,' said Tam, pensively.

Davina put on her serious voice, trying to make amends for her earlier indiscretion. 'Did he die?' she asked.

Tam looked at her as if she were nuts. 'No!' he said, 'He didn't die. He came home from the war to a hero's welcome from all his family and friends. They even had a street party for him.'

Davina was confused. 'That doesn't sound like it's a shame for him.'

'Yes,' said Tam, nodding knowingly, 'but it was the *reason* he got a hero's welcome.' He lifted his whisky and settled in his chair. 'When we were fighting in the war, he was just a young lad.'

'We were all young lads, Tam!' Davina thought there was more than a touch of annoyance in Granda's voice.

'I know that, Brown,' Tam retorted, 'but give him his due, Baxter was a bit younger than us.'

'Alright,' said Granda, grudgingly. *Wow. Whoever he is, he seriously pisses you off.*

'Well, anyway,' continued Tam, 'Jawbreaker Johnston, after being moaned at from the rest of the squad . . .' – he motioned with his thumb to himself and Granda – 'including us pair, reluctantly put him on night patrol. The lad was terrified. When his name was shouted out for it, his eyes nearly fell out of his head. But, to give him his due, he never refused . . . not that you could!' Tam broke off from his storytelling to take a drink. Granda and Davina followed suit. Tam smacked his lips and carried on. 'Halfway through the night, you can imagine

263

how he was feeling. Nerves all over the place. The silence gets to you, and any wee noise has you jumping about like a numpty.' He slid forward to the edge of his chair and shook his head. 'Well, did a bloody explosion not go off about half a mile from us. The poor boy was that strung out, he shat himself. Of course, the rest of us were up and running around, getting into position, so there was no way he could keep it a secret.' Tam focused on the flames in the fire. He shook his head again and grimaced, as though reliving the nightmare for the boy. Then he settled back in his seat and took another sip of whisky. A bemused Davina looked from him to her granda, who also seemed to be back in the moment. The suspense was too much for her.

'What's that got to do with a hero's welcome?' she asked.

Right on cue, Tam sat forward in his chair again. 'Well, wee Baxter took some slagging for this.' Tam and Granda shared a knowing glance before Tam continued. 'Give him his due, Jawbreaker, our sarge, did his best to shield the boy, making anyone who gave him a hard time peel potatoes and clean everybody's pots for a week, but the boy was never the same after it. So, he wrote a letter to his mum, telling her he'd shat himself on night patrol and just wanted to come home.' Feeling he had to explain this next part to Davina, Tam's voice took on a condescending tone. 'The army won't send you home just because you've embarrassed yourself.' *Obviously, but what the hell has that to do with him being a hero though?* The wine Davina had consumed earlier was now having a battle royale with her bladder.

'The thing was, though,' Tam went on, 'that when his mum read his letter, she thought it said he'd *shot* himself – and because he wasn't getting home, she'd taken it upon herself to tell anyone that would listen that he'd been injured in the line of duty but was too important to be sent back.'

Davina was laughing so hard she thought her bladder was going to give up the ghost. She jumped from the couch and made it to the toilet just in time. Feeling mightily relieved, she quickly rejoined the men in the living room, where Tam was in the process of topping their drinks up.

'Okay, wait a minute,' Davina said, sitting down and stifling another bout of laughter. 'You're telling me his mum – who thought he'd *shot* himself – managed to get him a hero's welcome?'

'That's right,' said Tam.

Feeling tipsy and a little baffled, Davina took a sip of her drink. 'But didn't she question if he'd done it intentionally or not? I know it didn't actually happen, but surely the only reason someone would shoot themselves would be so they could get discharged early and sent home.'

'I know what you're saying, Davina,' said Tam, 'but his mum wasn't interested in any of that. As far as she was concerned, he was shot in the line of duty, fighting for his country. What was it that Mark Twain character said, Brown?'

'"Never let the truth get in the way of a good story."' Granda raised his glass and winked.

Davina rolled her eyes and laughed at the same time. 'So, what happened next?' she asked.

'Well,' said Tam, matter of factly, 'with there being a street party in his honour, he couldn't very well come out and say "Sorry, everybody, but it turns out my mum got it wrong: I never shot myself, I shat myself." So, from

265

then on, he was known as the best thing that ever came out of Auchtermuchty.'

Davina furrowed her brows. 'But I don't understand why you said it was a shame for him.'

Tam took a deep breath. 'Well, as if he wasn't embarrassed enough, when anybody asked to see his war wound, the only way he'd get away with not showing them was to tell them he'd been shot in the arse. He took some slagging for this of course, but most folk were quite happy to leave it at that. However, his mum being his mum, insisted he show her. After all, as she'd said to him, and I quote . . .' – Tam put on the worst female voice Davina had ever heard – '"It's nothing I haven't seen before."' He cleared his throat and carried on. 'So, that was that, his secret was out! His mum never told a soul though. How could she? It was her mistake after all. But that's not how she saw it. As far as she was concerned, he'd brought shame on the family, and although they lived together for the rest of her life, she barely spoke to him. We visited him a few times and became pretty good friends. He said he was miserable and that living a lie was killing him.' *I can relate to that.* 'He never married and hardly goes out. When he does, he just sits on the bench in the middle of town and watches the world go by. The town'll likely put a plaque on that bench when he dies.'

Davina felt really sad, but her sick sense of humour kicked in. 'Maybe the plaque could read – Here shat Dick Baxter.'

The look both men gave her sent a chill down her spine. Her face turned scarlet. Even her ears were burning. 'That was a bit too far, Davina!' said Granda. He had never been ashamed of her in her life and it hurt to hear him talk like this.

'Sorry, Granda.' Davina climbed off the couch, embarrassed to her very core. 'I'll start the dinner.' She lifted her glass and walked out of the living room. As she closed the door behind her, she leaned against the frame to compose herself. *Shit shit, fucking buggery shit.* A split second later, laughter erupted from the living room and she could easily make out Tam's booming voice.

'That was genius! Here shat Dick Baxter! If they don't put that on the bench, I will. Have you any idea how many potatoes we peeled and how many pots we washed because of him?'

'Fine I know,' said Granda. 'He was always grassing us up to Jawbreaker, but it was worth it.'

Davina's mouth fell open. 'You old buggers,' she whispered to herself as she crept away from the door. *You really had me there. I've a good mind to put jalapenos in your dinner. Or, better still, laxatives!*

Dinner was the lasagne Davina had made the day before. In-between forkfuls, Granda and Tam discussed the fish they were apparently going to catch the next day.

Davina felt the moment needed a little injection of sarcasm. 'As long as you don't catch Nessie again,' she said. 'There's no way I'm gutting her.'

Granda didn't miss a beat. 'Oh, we can't catch her again, she's not there anymore. Once we caught her, we . . .' – he nodded at Tam – 'got on the phone to the Army who, with the assistance of the RAF, airlifted her out of the loch. She was then transported to Area 51.' He winked at Davina and tapped his nose. 'That's in America, you know?' *That's it. You've taken the piss out of me enough for one day.* The alcohol inside Davina gave her a false bravado. *I've never sworn in front of you before, but enough is enough.* She looked him straight in the eyes and feigned interest.

'Were you ever used as an interpreter in the Army, Granda? You know, with you being bilingual?' A perplexed Granda and Tam looked at one another, then back at Davina. 'Because, let's face it,' she said. 'you can talk English and you can definitely talk shite.'

Tam laughed so hard, bits of his dinner flew from his mouth and hit Granda in the chest. 'She got you there, Brown!' he bellowed.

Granda didn't respond. He was too busy picking bits of lasagne off himself. He threw Davina a reproachful look, but eventually a smile crossed his face. He took the sheet of kitchen towel she offered him. 'That she did,' he said.

After dinner, Granda and Tam said good night and thanked Davina again for putting up with them. They all hugged, Davina the meat in the sandwich. Tam gave her an extra tight squeeze. *Christ's sake, you've some strength for a wee old man.*

'But what I'd really like to thank you for,' said Tam, 'is introducing me to that wonderful whisky.' Thoughts of Hamish flooded her brain. *I miss my big pal.* They pulled apart, slowly. Both men looked done in.

'It was my pleasure,' said Davina. 'I'm just glad you liked it.' *At that price, you better have liked it. As Ma would say, "I'm no bloody Carnegie."*

With her lodgers dispatched to their beds, Davina tidied the dinner things away. She knew what her head would be like in the morning, so she forced down two tall glasses of water. In the bathroom, she slipped into something a little comfier: her fleece pajamas. She checked the coal fire was dying out sufficiently, then gave the coals a final rake over, before replacing the fireguard. There was nothing left to do after that except go to bed. It was only 8.22pm, but she felt really tired.

She only lifted her phone up to switch it off, but found herself checking to see if she'd missed any calls or texts. The part of her brain that was supposed to stop her from texting when she was drunk had switched itself off again. She found her conversation with Hamish and clicked on it. With a stupid smile on her face, she started to type.

> Because you gave it such rave reviews I bought a bottle of Rosebank whisky. My granda and his army buddie Tam loved it. In fact I think I've converted them. It was worth every penny to see the pleasure they got from drinking it.
> p.s I really miss my big pal.

She pushed the Send button and threw the phone into the drawer. Then she fell asleep.

She woke at 8.27am, twelve hours later, her head mushy and feeling as rough as a badger's arse. She crossed the room to the en-suite, scratching her arse and farting en-route. She smiled ruefully. *How very lady like, Brown.* She brushed her teeth and assessed her hangover. She'd definitely felt worse, but then she'd definitely felt better. As she approached the kitchen, she could hear the sound of laughter. She entered smiling.

'Morning, troops,' said Davina, brightly. Both men stepped away from the table, clicked their heels together, and saluted her.

'Sarge!' said Granda, followed by the pair of them wincing and rubbing their lower backs from the exertion.

'We're getting a bit old for that, Brown,' said Tam. Davina agreed. Unshaven, she thought they definitely looked more their age now.

269

Granda was standing by the cooker, guarding a pot full of water and a box of eggs. 'We're having boiled eggs if you fancy it.' He turned and pulled open a cupboard drawer, raking through it with both hands.

'No thanks, Granda, I'll just be having fresh orange and two painkillers.'

'Painkillers?' Tam shouted. 'Painkillers? Man up, soldier.' He looked at her seriously. 'There was none of that carry on when we were young, even when we were in the Great War.' *Not the Great War again. I'm not in the mood.* 'And do you know why there wasn't any painkillers in the jungle?' Davina raised an eyebrow up at him. *No, but I'm sure you'll enlighten me.* 'Because the parrotseatthemall.'

Davina smiled and playfully slapped his arm. 'It's too early for that rubbish,' she said, gathering up her fresh orange and the ever-handy paracetamol. She sat at the table beside Tam, who looked over at her knowingly.

'I'm going to give you the three best bits of advice I was ever given,' he said. Davina was immediately sceptical, but said nothing. 'One: Laugh whenever you can. Life's serious enough. Two: Never pass up the chance to go for a pee, especially when you get older. Three: And as far as I'm concerned, this is the most important one: never trust a fart!' His lips formed an O shape and he inhaled, shaking his head. 'Many's a time I've been caught out with that one.'

Davina smiled and shook her head back at him. 'Where the hell do you get them from?' she asked.

'Language, Davina!' came a voice from the other side of the kitchen. Granda was still looking in the drawers.

'What are you looking for, Granda?'

'Do you have an egg timer?' he asked.

'Yeah, but it's his day off.' Davina giggled to herself. *If you can't beat them, join them.*

'Do you have a boy that does that as well?' Tam said. *Don't bite.* Tam carried on regardless. 'There was a boy in our regiment.' He squeezed his eyes shut in concentration. 'What was his name, Brown?' *What's the matter? Can you not think up a stupid name fast enough yourself?*

A veteran of not missing a beat, Granda quickly supplied the answer. 'Hogg,' he said.

'That was it,' said Tam. 'Hold-your-breath-Hogg.' Tam looked pleased with himself. 'The second the bubbles started rising in the pot, he'd hold his breath. We'd all stare at him,' he added, wide-eyed. 'Some of us even tried to hold our own breath as well, but nobody could match him.' He slapped the table and Davina jumped. 'The second – and I mean the *exact* second – he breathed out, the pot was taken off the fire. The eggs were done to perfection.' Tam closed his thumb and index finger together, kissed them, then pulled them away from his lips with a smack. 'Mwah!'

Davina rose from the table, once again nonplussed by the men's banter. 'It's definitely too early for this,' she muttered, and headed off to her room. She returned with the bedside clock in her hand.

'There you go, Granda,' she said, handing it over. 'There's a second hand on this.' She helped him with the teas and Tam's coffee and took them over to the table. She didn't realise that Tam hadn't finished with his story.

'It was a hell of a way for Hogg to die though.' *Really? We're still at this?* 'We'd survived poison darts, booby traps, poisoned streams, and God knows what else.' Davina's head was better than it was, but she still wasn't in the mood for more bullshit. *Here we go again.*

'Don't forget the humonkeys,' she said. Granda spun around and looked at her incredulously. Tam shook his head at his former comrade.

'That was classified, Brown.'

Davina looked from one straight-faced man to the other. *Shocking.* Granda sat his and Tam's plates on the table. Both men peeled and then sliced their perfectly cooked eggs.

'Ahhhh, who needs Hold-your-breath-Hogg when we've got you, Brown,' said Tam. *Don't ask, just don't ask . . . Oh, to hell with it!*

'So, how did Mr Hogg die?' Davina enquired.

Tam took a second or two and then sighed. 'Well, since you're so interested.' He sat his cutlery down. 'He'd not been back on leave that long, and he was down the street getting some shopping for his mum, when he got killed crossing the road.' *Holy shit.*

Davina flopped back in her chair. 'My God, that's terrible.' Her morbid side was screaming at her and she was trying to look and sound mournful. It wasn't quite working. 'Was it a bus or a car that killed him? Or a lorry?'

'Neither. It was a piano.' *Well, you did ask, Brown.*

'A piano!'

Tam carried on as though Davina hadn't spoken. 'In those days, you couldn't afford to pay folk to help you move house. Even if it took you 100 trips, back and forth, your belongings were shoved in a wheelbarrow or strapped to the top of your car.'

'That's if you could afford one,' added Granda.

'Well, anyway, Hold-your-breath-Hogg wasn't paying attention and stepped out onto the road. The car wasn't going that fast. The driver saw Hogg in plenty of time and hit the brakes, but whoever tied the piano to the roof hadn't done a particularly good job. It came flying off and whacked Hogg on the head.' He slapped the table hard again. 'That was him, brown bread.'

With his story and breakfast finished, Tam sat back in his seat and folded his arms.

'Yip,' threw in Granda, 'but he got a *grand* send-off.' *A grand send off? Are you shitting me? And I'm supposed to take you seriously?* Davina scanned their faces for any sign of a smile or a smirk, but found none. She ran her tongue around the inside of her mouth to prevent herself from swearing, then walked out the kitchen. Just outside the door, she stopped and listened.

'What the hell's a humonkey, Brown?' asked Tam.

'I'll tell you after,' said Granda.

Davina carried on to her room and closed the door quietly behind her. *What a pair they are.*

After changing into her walking gear, Davina picked up her phone and headed out the door. Granda loomed up behind her.

'Going out, hen?' he asked. 'Will you be long? Just me and Tam were hoping for a lift to Raigmore Hospital. We were going to fish in the river, but with you mentioning Nessie, we've decided to try the loch. The bus leaves there at six minutes past 12.'

Davina checked her watch. 'It's only just ten,' she said. 'I'll make it a quick walk to clear my head.' She kissed her granda's cheek and headed out.

'You always were my favourite!' Granda shouted after her.

She looked back over her shoulder. His old eyes were twinkling at her. 'I'll be back soon, Granda,' she smiled.

She set off at a fairly brisk jaunt. Her mobile told her there was still no word from Douglas, but she did have two missed calls, one from Grace and one from Marge.

There was also a text from Hamish. Thankfully, her stomach didn't lurch this time. *Priorities, Brown.* She slowed down and called Marge.

'Hi, Davina.' Her sister sounded terrible.

'No point asking how things went then.'

'Well, it started off alright. I stayed at Ma's on Sunday night, but I never told her everything I told you, just that I wanted to leave him. So the tom-tom drums were out in force of course, which meant I didn't have to tell our Hector and Joshua. I phoned Robert on Sunday night and told him it was over. He said it wouldn't be over until he said so.' Davina heard a massive sigh on the other end of the phone and really felt for her sister. 'So, after my work yesterday, me, Hector, and Joshua went to get my things from his flat. He asked if we could talk in private, but I didn't want to. With Hector and Joshua there, he never said anything, but I could tell he was raging. I couldn't find all my things, but I got most of them. I don't know what he did with the rest, and I don't care, he can keep them. Hector told him if he comes near me again, it'll be a police matter. Then we left.' *I hope Joshua gave him a black eye.*

'That doesn't sound too bad, Marge. I thought he would have been a lot worse. What did Joshua do?'

'He never did anything. Hector told him if anything happened he'd get in trouble at work.' It was Davina's turn to sigh. *Bummer. I bet our Joshua was champing at the bit to smack him one.*

'That's true. So why do you sound so fed up? You got your stuff and you got him out of your life.' Another huge sigh came down the line.

'Well,' said Marge, 'when I went into work this morning, everything was fine. I'd half expected him to be there, so I arranged to pick up one of the girls on the way. At half ten Lesley, my boss, shouted me into the office. Apparently, she'd received a phone call from a man who said I was touching him up when I was supposed to be giving him a wax.' Davina let out a half-laugh.

'It's not funny, Davina. Apparently his pal then phoned and said I'd done the same to him, so she's suspended me without pay until she investigates it.'

'She's an arsehole, Marge! Did you tell her it was Robert just trying to get back at you?'

'No. I don't want everybody knowing my business. I just told her she's a cranky bitch that nobody likes and that she couldn't run a bath, never mind a business.' Another sigh. Davina could imagine Marge shaking her head, remonstrating with herself. 'Then I told her she could stick her job up her big fat arse.'

Davina burst out laughing. 'Good for you, Marge! You weren't happy there anyway. And another thing, if she believes you of all people would touch somebody up while giving them a back, sack and crack, well, she doesn't deserve you.'

Marge laughed, but quickly turned serious again. 'I know that, Davina, but what if we don't get the go-ahead to start our own business? Nobody's going to take me on after that carry on!'

The concern in Marge's voice only made Davina even more determined. 'Listen to me, Marge,' she said. 'We'll be in business together one way or another. If it means opening somewhere cheaper than Troon, well, so be it, but it's going to happen, do you hear me? Think about it this way: you've got more time on your hands now to make that list of things we'll need, and to work out how many staff are going to make things work.' The enthusiasm in her own voice had Davina walking a mile a minute in her head.

Marge's response bristled with excitement. 'You're right, Davina. I've already made some notes, so I'll get back to it and we'll talk later.'

'Okay, pal. I need to go as well.' She was just about to hang up when she heard Marge shout her name down the phone.

'Hello? You still there, Marge?'

Davina could hear the smile in Marge's voice. 'I just wanted to say thanks, Davina. For everything. I love you. Bye.'

Davina was touched by the sincerity in her words. 'No probs, Marge,' she said. 'Anytime. And I love you too, pal. Bye just now.'

Granda and Tam had refused a lift straight to Loch Ness, so she'd dropped them off at the bus stop with enough sandwiches to last all day and a flask of tea each.

'What's the point in having a bus pass if you don't use it?' Tam had asked. 'There's not much us old ones get from the government, so you're bloody right we'll take all that's going.'

Davina had watched them struggle to get in her car with all their paraphernalia. *God knows what they'll be like getting on and off the bus.*

Now, sitting at her kitchen table with a cup of tea, she was reading Hamish's reply to her text for the second time.

> I'm glad your granda and his friend liked the Rosebank. The price is irrelevant when it's for a thing of beauty. P.s I really miss my wee pal too and I don't mean the butt plug.

> But now that I've written that I
> realise that's a lie, I miss him too. ☺

What am I supposed to say to that? Her emotions were all over the place. On the one hand, she really missed the closeness they'd shared, but on the other, she didn't trust herself to talk to him, either face to face or on the phone. She wasn't 100 percent sure she wouldn't start crying. She really missed him. Just the sight of his name on her phone had made the butterflies in her stomach twitch. *That's only natural, Davina. You haven't had sex since Logan went back to Saudi. And that was . . .* She closed one eye and did a mental calculation.

'My God, eight days. Eight days without sex.'

Memories of her last tryst with Logan came flooding back . . .

He'd woken her, standing by the side of the bed, bollock naked, evidently pleased to see her. He had a loaded toothbrush in one hand, a jug of water in the other, and a sexy as hell grin on his face. Sitting up, pushed against the pillows, she watched him run his perfect tongue across his perfect gleaming teeth. She took the toothbrush from him, thanking him with a firm squeeze of his dick. Trying to brush her teeth and pleasure him at the same time made her smile. *This is like trying to rub your belly and pat your head at the same time. Impossible!* Logan sat the jug on the bedside table. Still rubbing his impressive shaft, she crawled over to him, her head level with his crotch. Her mouth now wanted in on the action. She ran her tongue around his crown, teasing him. The guttural noises he made told her everything she needed to know. He pulled her deeper onto him, her tongue and lips working him relentlessly. Without warning, he pulled out of her. She looked up. He had a strange, almost shameful look on his face. She

277

was about to ask if he was okay when he bent over and kissed her so softly and passionately that her concerns disappeared without another thought. He pulled her up and off the bed and they stood, barely moving, pressed naked together. Their kisses grew fiercer, his tongue invaded her mouth, and she sucked on it just as she had with his dick. His hands were kneading and nipping her breasts, while hers were squeezing his arse cheeks, pulling him against her, their breathing ragged. Birling her around, he bent her over the bed. She used her hands to support herself and pushed backwards into him. He held her by the hips, prising her legs apart with his own. She could feel the crown of his dick probing her wetness. In one swift movement, he pulled her back on to him, slamming into her at the same time. The force of his actions had her whimpering in both pain and delicious pleasure. Slowly, he pulled out almost all the way and then slammed back inside her. Her whole body cried out for him to quicken. As one of Logan's hands held her hip, the other pleasured her from the front, his technique vigorous but spot on.

'Oh my God, Logan! . . . Faster . . . Faster!'

Her pleas fell on deaf ears as he continued at his leisurely pace, pounding her relentlessly from behind. Finally, he removed his hand from her clitoris and grabbed both her hips. He picked up the pace. The ferocity of his thrusts had her impressive breasts swinging like pendulums. An orgasm rippled through her and she bent further into the bed, her screams muffled by the quilt. She was suddenly aware that Logan had collapsed, spent, on top of her. With one arm under her stomach, his chest was heaving on her back. Gratified by their exertions, they lay like that until their breathing returned to normal. Eventually, he rolled over beside her, his right arm still beneath her. He gazed up at the ceiling, his left arm slung over his eyes.

'Why didn't we do this years ago?' he asked, his tone surprisingly sombre.

Davina smiled at the memory, feeling horny as hell. *Maybe we could give one of our wee toys a go tonight, Brown.* Her ringing phone pulled her back from her reverie. Douglas, her financial adviser, had some good news for her. She was good to go! He gave her a figure to work with and suggested she take out a 12-month lease on a place, with the option to buy it outright when, or if, the business took off properly. That way they had a get out plan if things didn't go as they hoped. Coming off the phone elated, she immediately phoned Marge and arranged to pick her up in Glasgow the following day and then head down to Troon together. Next, she phoned Angela, letting her know they'd be in her neck of the woods the next day. Angela excitedly insisted they both have lunch at her house. With everything settled, and her choice of property having dwindled to four places, Davina printed off the locations and poured herself a fresh cup of tea.

It was just after six in the evening when a beaming Granda and Tam burst through the front door, their booming voices filled with laughter and excitement. Their eyes danced as they handed Davina their fastened cool-box. She took it by the handle and carried it to the kitchen table, where she unhooked the clasps.

'I take it you caught something then?' She felt as excited as the two men looked. She opened up the box. Three large brown trout stared out at her. 'Jeezo,' she said, 'they're huge.'

Granda and Tam peeled off their fishing gear and talked over each other, vying for Davina's attention with their tales of not only the ones they'd managed to catch, but also the humungous ones that – apparently – had gotten away. They did manage to agree, however, that it had been a joint effort catching the three that they had. No longer as strong as they'd once been, it had taken a combined effort to reel and net the fish in. They carried their squabbling over into the front lobby press, where they ditched their equipment, pushing one another like schoolboys and debating over something that could never be proven or, more to the point, disproven. Back in the kitchen, the kettle boiled.

'I think this calls for something a bit stronger than tea,' said Granda, rubbing his hands together as he entered. 'Where's that nice wee dram you got us?' *Shameful.*

Sorting the fish was practically a military operation. First they had to be gutted and scaled, a job in itself. Two of them were then left out to be cooked, while the other one went in the fridge. The two to be cooked went in the oven with a generous dollop of butter, salt, pepper, and slices of lemon. It took a bit of convincing for Davina to be allowed to tart up the fish with herbs. Granda and Tam initially objected to the use of tarragon, but Davina promised them they were in for a real treat. And so it was with some trepidation that she placed the cooked fish, with warm sliced crusty bread, on the table. Both men, grudgingly, and much to Davina's relief, agreed that it tasted nice.

Most of the meal involved the over-telling of the men's adventure at Loch Ness, and short work was made of the remaining Rosebank whisky. Pretty soon they'd moved on to the Glenfiddich. Davina passed on the offer of 'another of Scotland's finest drams'. She said she had a big day tomorrow and wanted a clear head for it.

Washing up the dinner things, she told them they'd be on their own all day.

'And remember,' she said over her shoulder, 'you've not to invite any wild women or throw any wild parties.'

'Now she tells us,' grunted Granda, slightly glassy-eyed with drink and still on a high from the day's excursion. He winked over at Tam. 'If I'd known we were getting the place to ourselves tomorrow, I would've asked those women that were on the bus to come over.'

With arrangements made with Marge for the next day, Davina got ready for bed. She walked along to the living room to say goodnight to Granda and Tam, but both men were sound asleep in their chairs. Davina took the good crystal glasses from their hands, spread the ashes around in the fire, replaced the fireguard, then threw blankets over the twin snorers. She gave both of them a gentle kiss on the forehead and returned to her room.

Her mobile notified her that a couple of former clients were requesting the pleasure of her company. Grinning contentedly, she let them know she'd no longer be available to them. One of them wished her well and thanked her for her companionship over the years. The other simply asked if she could recommend someone else to take her place. Both responses made Davina smile. This was another one of those things that reminded her of Hamish, and again her stomach dipped in response to how much she missed her confidante. *One day we'll get past this weird shit and talk like we used to, Hamilton.*

CHAPTER 15

BROWN SAUCE

Davina wasn't sure if she'd be back before Granda and Tam left on Friday. If not, they were to pop the keys through the letterbox when they left. Granda told her not to worry; her beloved bungalow was in capable hands. Well, his were capable at least. He couldn't speak for Tam's.

She drove to Glasgow, said hello to her family, then picked up Marge. To her surprise and delight, she discovered Marge had been taken over by a very competent, very experienced businesswoman. Her insistence that they start with at least one Nail Technician had Davina stifling a laugh. *What next? Fecking Hair Engineers?* Apparently, Marge already had someone interested in hiring a nail bar with them. She said that, if possible, seven hairdressers would be a good start, but she'd like to add to that as the business grew. Two hairdressers also wanted to hire chairs from them depending on the rates.

Marge and her friend, Amber, a no-nonsense, fully-qualified beautician from Venus Ventures, would need a room each. Marge would be a lot happier though, she told Davina, if somehow they could open with at least three qualified beauticians in place. This prompted Davina to recall the receptionist she'd spoken to in Inverness. She told Marge that whoever they hired to man reception should be well-versed in what was and wasn't acceptable to say to prospective clients. Marge had also comprised a list of essentials they'd need to open with, and another list of things they could acquire if and when they were needed.

An impressed, and very happy, Davina was looking at her sister through different eyes. There was no sign of the naive, scatterbrained girl she'd grown up with. Instead, she was articulate both with her words and her ideas. It seemed to Davina that this was what Marge had been waiting for all her life. Once her sister had stopped for air, Davina broached the subject of Angela. Marge didn't so much as raise a beautifully-shaped eyebrow at this revelation. Davina also explained that she was hoping house calls would be something they could look into. That way, the shy, elderly and infirm could also be on their books.

Pulling up outside the impressive stately home, Marge was quiet for the first time since they'd left Glasgow. It was an incredible looking building. They were greeted at the door by a happy and colourful Angela, dressed in a pink, flowery dress with matching shoes and lipstick. She air-kissed them both dramatically and immediately led Marge by the arm into the house.

'Your sister didn't do you justice, Marge,' she said. 'You're absolutely gorgeous!'

Behind them, Davina smiled and shook her head. 'Calm down, Angela,' she said. 'Granted she'll do a turn, but that's about all.' An open-mouthed Marge was too busy trying to take in her surroundings to notice what had been said. Angela led them into the sitting room and took a seat, motioning for Davina and Marge to do the same. Davina sat opposite her on the other couch. Marge did one last sweep of the impressive room with her doe eyes, wiped down her trousers, and sat next to Angela, caressing the coffee table that divided them from Davina.

'Oh my God, Angela,' she enthused. 'This place is amazing. You have a beautiful home.'

'Thank you, Marge,' said Angela, in response not just to her comments on the house, but also her acknowledgement of her identity. 'But it is just a house, with only me residing here. I no longer look at it as being a home.' Her lips were curved in a smile, but her eyes betrayed how sad she really felt. Marge took her hand and gave it a gentle squeeze. Davina noticed that her sister's eyes had misted over and wondered if she was thinking the same as her . . . *Yes, we Browns all get on each other's nerves from time to time, but we wouldn't be without each other for the world.*

Angela coughed, breaking up the solemn mood. 'So,' she continued, 'tell me all about this grand plan of yours.'

That was all that was needed to set Marge off. Davina sat back and watched as her sister effortlessly slid back into her businesswoman role. Angela lifted a notepad and pen from the telephone desk and took the occasional note. She never interrupted, and her expression never changed. She was totally focused on Marge.

When Marge finally paused for breath, Davina showed Angela the locations of the buildings that fell into their price range and fitted their size requirements. Angela put them in order, starting with the one she thought would be the most prosperous i.e. the one in the most respectable part of town with the heaviest footfall. Then there were the areas to avoid, the less visited areas and rougher communities. Angela asked if they'd be interested in a silent partner; she'd be only too happy to be part of this venture. She wasn't averse to a no strings attached loan either. The idea of home visits, however, excited her the most, as long as it was Marge who would, personally, be seeing to her needs. The fact they were also taking the elderly and infirm into consideration impressed her greatly. When Jessie had become bedridden, Andrew had struggled to find someone willing to do her nails, eyebrows and make-up. This had upset Jessie far more than the chemo treatment. Marge, angry at this revelation, assured Angela that no-one would be overlooked by any salon run by her. Davina insisted, though, that it would be her who would be going shopping with Angela, when she was able. Marge would likely be too busy with clients to do that.

Angela left them to make some tea. Marge took advantage of her absence to tell Davina that the financial side of things was down to her. It was therefore her decision what to do about Angela's offer. When Angela returned bearing a tray of tea and sandwiches, she sat down beside Marge. 'So,' she asked, 'what do we do next?'

Davina lifted up a sandwich. 'We'll check the places out in the order you put them and hopefully we'll find one we like. Then we'll just need to look into getting it fitted out and decorated.' She took a bite and talked around the cold ham as best she could. 'There's plenty second-hand equipment on sale on the Internet. Marge has made a list of must-have items to get us up and running . . .' – she swallowed – 'and both of us now have the time to trawl the net for the best bargains.' She picked up her tea and took a sip.

Angela raised her eyebrows. 'Why will you need to get second-hand things?'

Davina sat her tea back down. *Be honest, Brown. This is you and Marge's dream, a chance to prove yourselves.* 'It's not that I'm not grateful for your offer, Angela,' she said, not breaking eye contact.

'But?' said Angela.

Davina smiled, grateful for her easy response. 'But . . . we feel quite strongly about doing this ourselves, to start with at least. Not through misguided pride or pigheadedness, but because we would really like to try and do this on our own. Give our family something they can look up to us for. Show the people back home just what we're made of.'

Angela looked at Davina with something akin to pride in her eyes. 'Hear, hear,' she said, and stood up. She lifted her cup in a toast. 'To Brown's Body Boutique.' Davina and Marge looked at each other in astonishment. They hadn't thought of that. Automatically, they repeated it together.

'Brown's Body Boutique.' All three took a sip of tea in celebration.

'Promise me, though,' Angela pressed, 'if you do get into any difficulties, financial or otherwise, you'll come to me.'

Davina placed her cup down and walked around the table, pulled Angela gently to her feet, and hugged her tight. With everything that had happened recently, Davina found herself suddenly feeling very emotional.

'We both know I wouldn't be in a position to even contemplate opening my own business if it wasn't for you,' she said. 'If you hadn't coaxed Douglas into taking me on as one of his clients, and then buying that property for me, I'd probably have dwindled my money away by now.' She squeezed Angela even tighter. 'You have my word that if we ever need a back-up plan . . .' –

eyes stinging, Davina pulled away from Angela and took a deep breath – 'you'll be the first to know.'

Wiping away Davina's tears with a thumb, Andrew appeared for a moment, albeit only vocally. 'My sweet child, what I gave you were mere material things.' The softest of kisses was placed on Davina's cheek. 'What you gave me was so much more. Finally, I can be the person I've always wanted to be.' With glazed eyes, Andrew took a huge intake of breath, the emotion of the moment clearly having an impact, and then continued. 'I could give you all my worldly possessions and it still wouldn't express the gratitude I feel towards you.' They hugged, tenderly, stroking each other's backs in reciprocation. A few deep breaths each later, they parted and straightened up.

Marge looked positively perplexed. Angela returned and cleared her throat, back in charge of the situation. 'Righty-o,' she said, her voice rising. 'Let's take this business to the next level.' She lifted up the tray of half-eaten sandwiches and half-drunk tea. 'We'll all pop into your car . . . and case the joint in question,' she said with a snigger, and then headed back to the kitchen.

With Angela out of the room, Marge turned to Davina, curiosity making her fidgety. *Here comes the Spanish Inquisition.*

'You never did tell me how you met Angela,' she said. 'Or was it Andrew you met first?' Her immaculate eyebrows were raised as high as they would go.

Davina smiled at the open door Angela had just walked through, then turned to her sister. 'It's a long story, and one that's too personal to share.'

Marge's eyes narrowed and she grinned. 'Okay, sis, but you know where I am if you ever want to share.'

Davina's phone buzzed with a message. Logan. She caught her breath.

I'll be flying in to Aberdeen early on Saturday morning let me know if were still on for that meal. X

Oh, we're on alright, McIntyre.

'Well,' said Marge, peering over the top of Davina's mobile. 'Whoever that is, they've got you all hot and bothered.'

Davina pulled the phone in to her chest. She could feel the heat of embarrassment on her face and the heat of arousal between her legs. Slowly, the smile on her lips grew, splitting her face with happiness.

'That's for me to know and you to find out,' she grinned. 'Come on, let's case the joint in question.'

The joint in question was in a suitable location, so Davina and Marge arranged a viewing for the following day. Much to Angela's delight, both girls spent the night with her. The viewing itself went well. It was generally agreed that the space was more than adequate for their needs. It had been empty for about a month and paperwork was already in place with the seller's lawyers. Davina passed Douglas's firm's address on to the estate agent. Douglas's lawyer would check the contract over, then all that would be needed were Davina and Marge's signatures.

The upshot was they could have the keys to their own salon as early as the middle of the following week, which was astonishing. But they couldn't afford to rest on their laurels. Davina and Marge set up office in Angela's spacious sitting room. Davina would sort out the building work and décor. And she was in luck. The builders that had worked on her bungalow were available after Monday. Marge would acquire as much good quality second-hand equipment as she could lay her hands on. If all went according to plan, they could be open in as little as three weeks.

From start to finish, all the work was done in a matter of months, and the girls thanked an emotional Angela for her hospitality before heading back to Glasgow. The whole of the drive back was spent brainstorming about their opening day: special offers, money off vouchers for return visits, glasses of champagne, free canapés, etc etc.

They were still buzzing with excitement when they burst through the door of their parents' house. Gathering everyone to the dinner table, except Da, who chose to stay seated in his chair, the girls gushed about their new joint venture. The twins, being typical boys, showed a slight interest, then headed back to their Xbox. Henry asked if they'd have a chain of shops. Lucy wanted to know when she could come and work for them. Ma asked about the financial side of things, why they had decided to open in Troon, and what would be the outcome if things didn't work out. There was no negativity in her questions, just natural parental concern. Davina answered all her questions to the best of her ability. Then her sister interjected.

'Don't worry, Ma,' she said. 'We're going to make this work. And if it doesn't,' she added, matter of factly, 'our Davina knows this really lovely millionaire who'll help out. Isn't that right, Davina?' *Oh shit. Cheers, Marge.* Ma looked just as astonished as Davina at Marge's announcement. Da coughed and rumpled his paper but never uttered a word. Marge was oblivious to all of this and blithely carried on. 'She's a lovely woman. You'll need to meet her, Ma.' *Very good, Marge. I can see it now. Ma, Da, this is Angela, sometimes Andrew, who I met when I worked as an escort.* Henry and Lucy, predictably, hit her with a barrage of questions about knowing a millionaire. Ma had a questioning sneer on her face, seemingly enjoying Davina's discomfort.

Nervously, Davina changed the subject. 'I think a celebration's in order. Who fancies a drink?'

Ma leaned over the table and whispered that Da hadn't been out or had a drink since his talk with Joshua.

'We could go to the corner shop and bring some drink back,' Davina whispered back to her.

Ma shook her head and turned her attention to Marge, aware of the influence she had over him. 'Go and see if you can talk your da into going out for a pint. He's starting to get on my nerves with all his moods.' She lowered her voice further still. 'His arse talks about as much as his mouth. Trying to have a conversation with him lately is like trying to get blood from a stone. Tell him it's quiz night, he likes that.'

Marge smiled, then sidled over to Da to work her magic. Five minutes later, they were ready to leave. Marge excused herself and went to the toilet before they left.

'Are you sure you don't want us to have a drink here with you, Ma?' Davina asked. She knew Ma wasn't much of a drinker, but really wanted her to share in their excitement.

'You're alright, Davina,' said Ma. 'I'll be quite happy getting the weans to bed and sitting with my feet up watching the telly in peace.' She inclined her head towards Da and whispered again. 'It'll be good for him to get out.' *I'm sure it's not killed him staying out the pub for a wee while.* Ma smiled knowingly at Davina. 'Have a drink for me when you're out. It might loosen your tongue – and when you get back, you can tell me all about your millionaire friend.' Davina's face flushed. *I'll kill you, Marge.*

'There's nothing to tell, Ma.'

'You always were a terrible liar, Davina Brown,' Ma beamed.

Marge walked in front, arm in arm with Da, both of them talking about the new salon. Davina felt slightly resentful that he never showed this much enthusiasm when they'd been talking about it in the house. The fact she knew there was a special bond between Marge and Da did little to appease her.

Up ahead, the twins were passing a football back and forth along the street. Davina hadn't wanted any of the weans to miss out on the celebrations, so she'd asked the three boys if they wanted to come with them. She'd buy them sweets and juice from the corner shop to take back and share with Lucy. No sooner were the words out her mouth than they were ready. Henry had taken Davina's hand and she shared Granda's story about Nessie being in Area 51 with him. Henry rubbed his chin thoughtfully.

'I don't believe for one minute,' he said in his posh voice, 'that Granda and his pal Tam actually caught her. I do, however, believe she existed and the likelihood of her being in Area 51 isn't that much of a stretch of one's imagination. That is one place that is definitely on my to-do list when I'm older.'

Outside the pub, Da took money from Marge for the first round. Well, it was her who'd talked him in to coming out in the first place, as he so eloquently put it. The rest of them entered the corner shop at the end of the street. The advertising board outside puzzled Davina, and she made a mental note to ask her sister what it meant when they came back out. Two carrier bags of tooth-decaying rubbish later, the three brothers hugged and thanked Davina, then ran home.

Davina pointed to the advertising board declaring GET YOUR FRESHLY LAID EGGS HERE and asked Marge why somebody had scored out EGGS and added ASSISTANT. Marge took Davina's arm as they headed to the pub.

'Well,' explained Marge, 'it turns out Mr Duncan, who owns the shop, has been having an affair with his assistant. Every day, they lock the shop for about half an hour, go through the back and do their thing. Apparently, just the other day, they each thought the other had locked the door and a customer caught them in the act.'

Davina's jaw dropped. 'I can't believe that! Mr Duncan? He's a nice old man.'

Marge just raised her eyebrows and smiled.

'So why is the sign still there?' Davina asked.

'Yeah, right!' said Marge. 'Have you seen his assistant? She's half his age and stunning looking.' Her face was a picture of sheer disgust. 'He probably wants everybody in town to know. Dirty old men like him would normally have to pay somebody like her to sleep with them. I can tell you right now, I wouldn't sleep with any man I didn't love. Not for all the tea in China.' *How about a beauty salon in Troon?*

'Maybe she loves him,' said Davina.

'Yeah, and maybe Da will put his hand in his pocket tonight!' Marge laughed, pulling Davina into the pub.

As she entered, Davina picked up a pen and paper for the quiz from the bar. There was a nice wee crowd in and the atmosphere was friendly as usual. Da was already sat in his usual seat. Halfway through their first drink, his demeanour changed drastically. Davina followed his line of vision and clocked her brothers coming in. *Oh, great.* She quickly downed the remainder of her drink. Ever the optimist, Marge waved them over. Hector and Joshua looked down at Da in surprise and took their seats in silence. *Marge must have texted them from the bathroom at home. Great idea, Marge. NOT.* The quiz started. The atmosphere surrounding them was tense, to say the least, and Marge seemed the only one oblivious to it. In-between questions, she gushed about the salon to their proud, but clearly agitated, brothers.

The rest of the night passed in the same vein. As the others argued over the answers, Da drank in complete silence. Basically, he was being his usual awkward and stubborn self. The quiz finished and a hubbub of conversation rang around the pub. Marge looked from Da to Joshua and cleared her throat.

'Right, you two,' she said. 'This has gone on long enough. It's about time you started talking again.' Her half-hearted smile told Davina she wasn't completely immune to the awkward atmosphere, despite her earlier behaviour. Without a word, Da stood up and pulled his jacket from off the back of his chair. Joshua, facing him across the table, did likewise. They glowered at one another with something akin to loathing. The other three were holding their breath, waiting for one of them to make the first move. The rest of the pub was oblivious to the scene unfolding in the corner. Hector tried to rebalance the delicate situation by clapping his hands together.

'Righto. I'll get another drink in. What are you having, Da?' All eyes landed on Da. *Come on, Da. For once in your life, be a proper parent.* Slowly, Da's burning gaze left Joshua and found Hector, his voice a low, menacing growl.

'I'm not drinking with the likes of that,' he said, nodding towards Joshua and then turning to leave.

'Come on, Da,' Hector reasoned, 'you can't say that! He's still your son.'

'Don't you tell me how to talk to my own flesh and blood,' he snarled.

Joshua, with a rage in his eyes Davina had never seen before, grabbed Da's arm. Da looked at Joshua's hand as if he'd been infected by the plague. He yanked it away and sneered at his son. 'Don't ever touch me again.' *Don't do this, Da.* Joshua didn't flinch. Davina watched his hand clench into a fist and his arm slide back down his side. He kept eye contact with Da, his voice quiet but firm.

'If you leave it like this, Da, we're finished. I'm not chasing after you looking for acceptance all my life.' He straightened up to his full height, chest pushed out. 'Regardless of how you feel, I'm still your son. So . . . what do you say? What's it going to be, Da?' Joshua unfurled his clenched fist and held his hand out in front of him, waiting for it to be shook.

Da bent over the table, barely two inches separating him and his son. 'I'd have rather you came home in a body bag,' he spat, 'than came home gay.' He pushed the table over with both hands, spilling drinks everywhere. It took every last ounce of Davina and Hector's strength to stop Joshua from retaliating. Without looking back, Da made his way through the now bewildered crowd. Joshua was like a man possessed, wriggling beneath Davina and Hector's arms, champing at the bit to get to their da. *Holy shit, did Da really just say that?*

'Fuck you, Da!' he shouted. 'Fuuuuck yooou!' The venom with which this was bawled silenced the entire pub.

Having calmed Joshua down a bit, and tidied the mess around them, the four siblings walked back to Hector and Joshua's flat in stunned silence, each lost in their own thoughts and feelings. Tears ran down Marge's face and she gingerly reached for Joshua's hand. Smiling reassuringly, he took it. Back in the flat, the ramifications of the night's events hit home. No longer willing, or able, to hold their tongues, all four of them vented their anger and disappointment towards their da. A despondent Marge mostly cried. She'd taken it upon herself to arrange for them all to be in the pub at the same time, thinking everything would work out okay, and so felt entirely responsible for the outcome, despite her three siblings' reassurances to the contrary.

It was decided that the girls would sleep in Hector's bed, with Hector relegated to the couch, but they were all still up talking at one in the morning, when an exhausted and resigned Joshua finally announced he wasn't wasting another breath on his da.

'We could sit here all night saying the same things over and over,' he argued. 'It doesn't change a thing. I'm gay and he'll never accept it. Shit happens. It's not as if we were that close anyway, but I had hoped for Ma's sake that we could at least be civil to each other.' He shrugged his shoulders. 'That's obviously not going to happen though, so we need to move on. I'll talk to Ma in a couple of days. Everything'll be fine.' He kissed his sisters. 'Sorry for the way things went the night. We were supposed to be celebrating you going into business together.' His first genuine smile of the night made a surprise appearance. 'I'm really happy for both of you; this time next year, you'll be millionaires!' With that, he said goodnight and went to bed. Marge followed him out.

Once the door was closed, Hector leaned over. 'Can you believe Da actually came away with that?' he half-whispered, half-growled. 'Okay, be angry. Be disappointed. But to say he'd rather he'd came home in a fucking body bag than be gay! For fuck's sake, Davina! *I* wanted to kill him, never mind Joshua. There's no coming back from this.' He shook his head. 'No way. And Christ knows what Ma will say or do.' Davina felt exactly the same. She knew they were all hurting right now but felt something had to be done to at least try and keep the family together, for the sake of the younger siblings if nothing else. *Here goes nothing.*

'I know,' she said. 'I was thinking the same thing myself, but if it came down to taking sides, I think she would be on Joshua's.' Hector looked pensive. Tentatively, Davina continued. 'In fact,' she added, 'I'd go so far as to say this could split her and Da up.'

Hector sighed. 'I'm not so sure which side she'd be on. I'm not going to lie to you, Davina. I can't understand why she's put up with him and his attitude all these years. He's a lazy, selfish bastard. Half of me wishes I'd just let Joshua kick the shit out of him. Fuck, I might have had a dig myself. Sometimes, though, I feel like giving Ma a shake. She can't see past him.'

'I know what you mean, but if we tell her, she'll feel she has to make a choice. It would be a nightmare for her. And what about the weans? They'd be caught slap bang in the middle of this mess.'

Hector was dumbfounded. 'Are you saying he should get away with this?'

Davina shook her head. 'All I'm saying is . . . does Ma really need to know exactly what was said? I mean, what would it accomplish?' Hector sat back on the couch and sighed. Davina was right. Sometimes ignorance really is bliss.

They held another pow-wow in the morning and agreed it would be best to keep quiet about the previous night's horrendous episode. Afterwards, Davina decided against going back to her parents' house, for obvious reasons. She drove home to the bungalow in a bittersweet mood. Desperate to talk to someone, she called Grace. The happiness in the voice that answered could have melted the coldest of hearts.

'Hi, Davina. I can't talk long; I'm leaving for work soon.'

Davina smiled. 'Jeezo,' she said. 'You sound deliriously happy for someone going to their work.'

'Oh my God,' Grace bleated. 'I think I'm in love. I know I hardly know Gavin, but he's amazing! We talk and text each other all the time.'

'Alright, Grace, calm down' Davina cautioned, surprised by her revelation. 'You've only known him a week. I know he's a great guy, but I wouldn't like to see you get hurt.'

'I know that!' said Grace. 'But it just feels . . .' – she struggled to find the right words – 'I don't know,' she said. 'It just does.' Her voice took on a dreamy resonance. 'You know, like when you've got a night out coming up and you know exactly what you want to wear but you can't find it in any shop. Then just when you're about to give up and settle for something else, you see what you've been looking for all along and you think – I don't even need to try you on, I just know you're going to fit.'

Davina couldn't help but smile. 'Grace Steele, you've got it bad!'

'I know, and I love it . . . whatever it is.' They both laughed.

'Well, enough about you,' said Davina. 'Let me tell you all about my week.'

Davina managed to convey everything about her, Marge, the business, Da, Joshua, Hector and Logan all in the few minutes Grace allowed her. They agreed to at least try and meet up sometime before the grand opening, when they could catch up properly, unless of course it coincided with Grace meeting up with Gavin, in which case, she assured Davina, her arse was grass. Davina assured her the same rule applied to her and Logan.

CHAPTER 16

BROWN SAUCE

Granda and Tam's holdalls were sitting in the lobby as she entered the bungalow. Following the voices, she found them at the kitchen table. 'Hiya, troops,' she said.

'Hiya, Davina,' they replied, not quite in tandem, but close enough.

The huge bunch of flowers in the sink were to thank her for her hospitality. Ditto the oblong-shaped bottle of gin on the table. Davina smiled to herself. *Hospitality's my forte.* She found two vases in the cupboard and set about arranging the flowers. *This, on the other hand, is definitely not your forte, Brown.* She returned to the table. Lifting the bottle of gin, she read the label.

'I've never heard of The Botanist gin before.'

'My wife drinks nothing else,' said Tam. 'There's a bottle of elderflower cordial and soda water in your fridge to go with it. I hope you like it as much as she does. Mind and go easy with the cordial though.'

'You didn't need to go to all that trouble,' said Davina. 'I've hardly done anything for you.' She kissed Tam gently on the cheek.

After loading the holdalls into the boot of the car and setting off for the bus stop, Granda and Tam told Davina what they'd been up to in her absence, and she gushed about opening a salon with Marge. She decided against telling them what had happened between Da and Joshua. By then it was time to drop them off anyway.

As Granda unloaded their holdalls, Tam gave Davina an affectionate cuddle. His eyes were smiling. 'It was great to see you again,' he said. 'Thanks very much for putting up with us.' He shot Granda a quick glance and whispered into Davina's ear. 'I know he can talk some rubbish now and again, but he's a good man. There's a lot of us who wouldn't have made it back from the war if it wasn't for him.' *Wow, what the hell does that mean?* He gave her shoulders a final squeeze and kissed her on the forehead. Granda stepped around from the back of the car and caught the puzzled look on Davina's face.

'What did he say to you?' Tam stood behind him tapping his nose with his index finger and one eye shut. Davina let the moment go and, smiling widely, gave her granda a kiss and a cuddle. 'He said the next time he comes, it'll be for a fortnight.' She stepped back in mock horror. 'I'm not sure I could take you for that long though, I'd end up in the loony bin.'

'Being brought up in the Brown household was just like the loony bin,' said Granda. 'Thanks for everything, Davina. You know you're my favourite.' He kissed her cheek and winked at her before turning away.

As she drove back to the bungalow, Davina couldn't get Tam's parting statement out of her head. She couldn't recall Granda having a serious conversation about serving in the Army, ever! To think that he played a part in saving anyone's life and never spoke about it totally flummoxed her. Back home, she stripped the guests' beds. 'Keeping secrets must be a Brown trait,' she muttered to herself.

Whilst changing the bedding, she deliberated over telling Hamish her good news. After all, if it hadn't been

300

for his intervention, not to mention his belief in her, she wouldn't be half the person she was today. She decided she still wanted him as a friend and confidante. With her feet tucked under her on the couch, and half a bottle of Pinot Grigio beside her for courage, she tapped out a text. *Keep it light, Brown. No need to touch on the fact that he mentioned the butt plug.*

> Hi pal, that's my granda and his pal just left. I think they really enjoyed themselves here. Me and Marge, my sister, have decide to go in to business together. We're opening a beauty salon in Troon. Hopefully in the next three or four weeks. I never got a chance to tell you I've retired from the escorting business the last time we met. But sitting around doing nothing all day didn't appeal to me and Marge was in need of a change of scenery so as Spock would say it was the logical thing to do.

She didn't know what else to say so pushed the Send button. Ten minutes later there was still no reply. She pulled out her iPad and checked out colour themes for the new salon. Marge had insisted that in no way was it to be painted aqua with white clinical floors. Apparently, the salon she'd worked in before had had that theme. After what felt like an eternity, and now armed with a list she'd narrowed down to ten colours and ten shades, she switched the iPad off. Lifting up the bottle of wine, she was surprised to find it almost empty. *I'm guessing that's why I'm feeling quite tipsy.* She hadn't eaten all day, so headed into the kitchen to make herself something. Her mobile buzzed on the couch. She rushed back and read the caller ID. Hamish. Her stomach twisted with excitement. When she answered, her slight intoxication made her greeting sound *very* enthusiastic.

'Hello, you!'

'Hello yourself.' In contrast to her own, Hamish's voice was a little tense. 'Listen, Davina. I really need to apologise for my behaviour last week. There was no excuse for it other than the fact that my ego was a bit bruised.' A wave of melancholy washed over Davina and tears stung the back of her eyes. 'I wouldn't hurt you for the world,' Hamish continued. 'You know that. But me and rejection, we don't get on so well. Having said that, I would really like us to stay friends, if you think that could work?' Davina sat at the table with the kitchen roll. She could no longer hold back the floodgates. 'Oh my God, are you crying, Davina?' The anguish in Hamish's voice was unbearable. Agonising, wordless seconds passed between them. 'I'm sorry, Davina,' he said. 'I shouldn't have phoned.'

Davina sensed he was about to hang up. 'Don't go, Hamish! I've . . . I've really missed you.' She poured herself a glass of water and took a gulp. 'I tried to explain when we met up what I was hoping to do with my life, but you never gave me a chance.' She heard Hamish draw in a deep breath. 'I would never intentionally hurt you either,' she pleaded. 'I meant what I said. I owe you so much and I do love you. I'd love us to be friends again. This awkwardness is killing me.' The sigh of relief she heard on the other end brought a smile to her face.

They talked for almost an hour. During the call, Davina's phone bleeped to alert her to a text, but she ignored it. She wanted to know what Gavin had to say about Grace but, unfortunately, Hamish couldn't give her any juicy tidbits as Gavin was impossible to reach lately. This, at least, made Davina hopeful for her friend. At the end of the call, they promised not to leave it so long before speaking again and left everything on a high note. After they'd hung up, Davina read the text. It was from Logan.

> I'll be in Inverness at 9.15 in the morning let me know if you can pick me up from the train station.

There was also a text from Douglas, letting her know that he'd received the paperwork from the estate agents. Both texts had Davina extremely excited. *Things are looking up, Brown.*

The following day, Davina woke feeling like a great weight had been lifted from her shoulders. Knowing Logan would be arriving soon made her feel even lighter, not to mention horny. She hoped to jump Logan's bones the minute he got here. With that in mind, she decided against suspenders and a Basque, opting instead for her red baby doll set. *Easy access, Brown. The man might be too tired to arse about with all that palaver.* She held the items of seduction up in front of her and looked at herself in the mirror. She'd let her hair dry naturally after the shower. It was her belief that its natural kink somehow made it look shaggy and sexy. She grinned in anticipation. *Hurry up and get here, Logan!*

Once she arrived at the train station car park, she used her rearview mirror to check herself out, scrunching her hair up a little more. As she pouted at her reflection, she mentally congratulated herself. Her decision to wear the baby doll set under her jeans and T-shirt was a stroke of genius. So what if her chest was almost sitting on her knees and the skimpy knickers she had on were trying to have anal sex with her? Logan was worth it. She was too busy checking herself out to notice he'd already arrived and was outside the car. He opened the back door and tossed his suitcase inside, before falling into the passenger seat beside her. After a quick kiss, he slumped back in his chair, yawned, and closed his eyes.

'What a flight,' he sighed.

As she pulled out of the station, Davina was more than a little miffed. Logan was quiet all the way back. He still had his eyes closed, but she couldn't tell if he was sleeping or not. *Fuck's sake, McIntyre. When I said I wanted us to act like a normal couple, I didn't mean my ma and da.* She parked outside the bungalow and sat admiring him for a few seconds, before giving him a gentle nudge. She then got out the car and took his suitcase from the back seat. Logan was out by now too, stretching at the side of the car. Sleepily, he looked her up and down. Furrows formed on his brow.

'Did you sleep in, Davina?' He walked to the front door. 'You should've said. I could've got a taxi over.' He had his back to her, otherwise he'd have seen her jaw drop and her face change colour. *Cheers, McIntyre.* Once inside, he headed to the en suite bathroom. Davina waited by the bedroom door, feeling a lot less sexy and a lot less sure of herself. She decided against stripping down to her underwear and lying seductively on the bed. Logan reappeared, naked apart from his flatteringly fitted boxers. He pulled the quilt down and collapsed onto the bed. 'What time's the meal booked for?' He yawned. *Shit, shit, buggery shit. The only thing you had to do and you forgot! Think, Brown, think.*

'I didn't book it in case you were too tired. Thought we could do it tomorrow if that was better for you.'

Barely awake, he turned away from her and pulled the quilt over his shoulder. 'Aw, cheers, Davina. You're a legend.' A few seconds later he was fast asleep and Davina was left feeling sexually frustrated and rejected.

With her earlier euphoria gone, she changed into her walking gear and headed out. Her unsatisfied state had her feeling cranky, which made her walk faster than normal. She tried to assess what had just happened and realised she didn't have a clue how she felt. Her thoughts and feelings were all over the place. On the one hand, this was exactly what she'd pressed Logan for: a normal, everyday relationship; a chance to get to know all aspects of each other, and to share non-sexual endeavours. This, however, was too normal too quickly for her liking. She wanted him to have missed her as much as she'd missed him; to want – no, to *need* – to fuck her brains out because of the time they'd spent apart, regardless of how tired he was. Was she being selfish? Did, as Ma had suggested, she want her cake and to eat it too?

'Too fucking right I do!' she declared in a righteous tone. Luckily, there was no-one within earshot. 'I'm a hot-bloodied woman with needs,' she added, 'and you're going to fulfil them, Logan McIntyre, regardless of how fecking tired you are. And . . . you'll enjoy doing it, even if it kills you!' Fired up now, she headed home in double-quick time, a woman on a mission.

Forty minutes later, freshly showered, red baby doll outfit on (minus panties), vibrating penis ring and vibrator in hand, Davina gently forced Logan from his side and onto his back. He was still snoring lightly. She sat the toys down on the floor and crawled under the bottom of the quilt, reaching for the waistband of Logan's boxers. Gently, she slid them off, causing him to stir slightly. Spreading his legs with her elbows, she placed a soft kiss on his soft dick.

I don't know who's going to enjoy this the most, McIntyre. She slipped back out from under the quilt, retrieved her goodies from the floor, then returned to the sexy world beneath the quilt, scaling Logan's still sleeping body once more. She'd chosen the quietest vibrator she had but it still sounded too loud to her. She was really enjoying herself, but what she was looking forward to more was Logan's expression when he realised what was happening to him. Teasing his soft tip with her tongue, she used the vibrator on his balls. Coming to, he squirmed as a sensual sigh escaped his lips. The effect was instant. His dick now stood proud and erect, ready for the cock ring. Davina moistened him with slow, deliberate licks while teasing him with the vibrator. His sigh was overtaken by a series of soft moans. She pulled the thin elastic membrane of the ring apart to form a larger circle, then slipped it over the tip of his dick, right down to the base of his solid shaft. Then she switched it on. The vibrator, having done its job, was discarded on the bed somewhere. With her man ready, albeit unwittingly, for action, Davina took him fully in her mouth. She stroked and sucked him until, finally, he reached down and tousled her hair. Aware that he was now fully awake, Davina kissed her way up his chest, straddling his slender stomach. She smiled down at her sleepy lover.

'Hi,' he yawned, loudly. 'Have I been sleeping all night?'

'No, I just thought it was time he was up.' Davina licked her lips, winked at him, then went to work on his nipples, gently nipping and flicking them with her tongue. Logan reached to the bedside table, popped one of Davina's mints into his mouth and gently pulled her up to his smiling face. The lust in his eyes matched hers. The kiss, when it finally came, started at a sleepy pace.

As Logan became more and more awake, his kisses became more and more intense. Tongues licked, probed, and cajoled each other. Their hands, lazy at first, caressing and stroking, were now scratching, nipping and kneading. Logan's voice was gruff with sexual need.

'I don't know what you've got on me down there, Davina, but if you don't fuck me soon, you'll miss all the action.' Davina needed no encouragement. She slipped down his body and straddled him with her knees at his sides. Sitting upright, she slowly began sliding back and forth along his length, relishing the feel of him and the vibrating cock ring. A sensation of complete and utter fullness took over her as she gazed at the man she loved; the man she planned to share the rest of her life with. *God, I love you, McIntyre.*

Logan's voice and looks were smouldering. 'Any slower, Davina,' he said, 'and I'll fall back asleep.' *I very much doubt that.* Davina placed her hands either side of his head and lowered her mouth to his ear. Maintaining the same pace, she nipped and sucked at his lobe.

'We both know you're not going back to sleep with that throbbing hard-on,' she said. 'You're gagging for this as much as me.' She straightened up and grinned down at him, ardently. With a wicked glint in his eyes, Logan smiled and rolled them over so he was on top. 'Fuck this,' he said.

They were laughing now as he picked up the momentum. Lost in each other, their laughter stopped as their breathing became one. The harshness of his quickened thrusts were painfully sweet. Their eyes never left each other. Davina's knuckles were white, clutching the sheet tight. The animalistic noises coming from Logan's throat tipped Davina over the edge and she screamed mindlessly as wave after wave of orgasm convulsed her whole body. Exhausted and spent, their bodies went limp. Logan managed to find the energy to push himself off Davina's tingling body and collapsed in a heap next to her, their post-sex scents hugely comforting.

'Can I go back to sleep now?' he said, half laughing, half panting.

'Fuck! You can go back to Saudi Arabia for all I care,' Davina replied, with playful dismissal.

Logan's chest was heaving as he attempted to get his breath back. 'So it's only my body you're after?' he wheezed.

Davina smiled contentedly. 'No, but it'll do for starters.'

Later, Davina watched Logan sleep for a while. His handsome face would occasionally crease in a frown before relaxing again. Davina mimicked his expression, then smiled to herself. *How can you look so good even when you're looking so serious?* She stroked his hair and remembered the first time she'd watched him sleep, after they'd made love that very first time:

It had been just over a year ago, and they'd been playing pool in The Black Bull, her brothers in the corner, deep in conversation, leaving Logan to her. His jeans clung to his tight arse and her eyes took in every contour each time he bent to take a shot. Christ, it was tighter than a tow rope. He was taking ages with one particular shot and she dragged her eyes away from his arse to see what the holdup could be. Of course, Logan had been watching her watching him, or his arse to be precise. Still bent over the pool table, he leisurely stroked his arse and looked straight at her, an arrogant leer on his lips and both eyebrows raised.

'Is there something on my jeans, Davina?' he asked.

Davina was back in the moment. With the most ridiculous smile ever on her burning face, she raised her own eyebrows back at him.

'No,' she said. 'I thought there was, but on closer inspection . . .' – bravely, she took a step closer to him and cocked her head to the side – 'you're good to go.'

Over the years, Logan had often caught a mortified Davina ogling him and had either smiled kindly or winked at her, but that night there was definitely something different going on.

'Well . . .' Logan straightened, slowly rubbing his hand up and down his pool cue. His piercing blue-green eyes challenged Davina. 'Maybe an even closer inspection is required.'

For a split second, she was oblivious to the crowd in the bar. Visions of them on the pool table going at it good style flooded her brain. A glimpse of the tip of his tongue licking his bottom lip had her throwing all her inhibitions out the window. Not caring one iota if her brothers, or anyone else for that matter, didn't approve, she strode purposely towards him.

Suddenly, she was in his arms and very wet, just not in the way she'd hoped. She took a sharp intake of breath, aware of the ice cold drink that had just been spilt down her back, as Lazy-Eyed Laidlaw tried to push past her.

'Christ's sake, Lazy,' said Logan, steadying Davina with his firm grip. 'Watch where you're going.' He tried, unsuccessfully, to hide his laugh at the sight of a soaking wet Davina.

'Shorry, shun,' an inebriated Lazy replied, 'it's this fecking eye. It'sh got a mind of it'sh own.'

Cheers, laughter, and recriminations flew around the pub. Davina pulled at the back of her top and shook off the remaining drink, never looking away from the sexiest eyes she'd ever known. 'I'll need to whip your arse later,' she said. 'At pool, that is.'

Logan's eyes widened and she knew her comment had hit its mark. She turned back towards her brothers, but only a few steps in, Logan took her arm and guided her there himself.

'Hey, lads,' he said. 'Davina's soaking here.' She turned to look at him. The sultry gaze that passed between them made her crotch tingle. 'I'll get her home, okay?'

Davina's brothers barely lifted their heads in acknowledgement before returning to their conversation. As Logan led Davina out the door, he pulled out his phone and ordered a taxi.

'I don't need a taxi,' Davina objected. 'My folks just live down the road, remember?'

Logan scanned the street. It was empty. He led Davina the short distance to the alleyway at the end of the pub. They were barely in it before he'd pushed her against the wall and covered her with needy, hungry kisses. Her hands were all over him, his arse as firm as it had looked. She pulled him tighter into her and could feel his erection against her own excitement.

'I don't think your ma and da should see what I want to do to you,' he moaned.

Once back at his flat by the Clyde, they were like a couple of sex-starved teenagers. They stumbled along the hall, kissing, touching and laughing as they pulled off each other's clothes. They passed through the living room without stopping, finally falling into Logan's adjoining bedroom. They were both naked by now.

With impatient fingers, Davina investigated the hair on Logan's chest. His stomach was the six-pack version she'd always envisaged. Sucking in her own stomach did nothing to hide the fact that she was, as the fashion industry liked to put it, a fuller figured size 14. She let her breath back out. For once in her life, she didn't care what she looked like. She was about to be fucked by the man of her very wet dreams. Logan walked across to the window and closed the blinds.

'Oh my God,' gasped Davina. 'You'll get locked up for indecent exposure.'

'Yeah, right, Davina. We're three stories up.' His gaze headed south. 'And I'm not exactly hung like a horse.'

She took his hand and pulled him to her. 'You'll do for me, big boy.'

Entangled on the bed, they were all arms, legs, hands and mouths. Davina was like a kid in a sweet shop. Having stared through the window for years, she now had permission to go inside and take whatever she wanted. Logan was positioned above her, nipping, biting and sucking her breasts. Resting on his knees, he reached over and took a condom out his drawer. His surprise was evident when Davina, smiling, took it from him.

'Do you have any sexually transmitted diseases, Mr McIntyre?'

'No I bloody don't!'

Davina threw the condom away. 'Well, we won't be needing that then.' Obviously, in her profession, condoms were a way of life. Logan McIntyre, however, was one experience where no jacket was required. Anyway, he didn't have time to object. She'd already forced him onto his back and all the way into her.

'Aahh!' The sensation caught her breath. As she smiled into his beautiful face, she couldn't remember ever wanting something so much in her life. With a slow purposeful pace, she began sliding up and down him, exploring the delicate yet muscular chest that had been inaccessible for so many years. The sensation between her legs increased tenfold. With his hands on her hips, he quickened his pace, the two of them working in perfect harmony. The quickened pace was her undoing.

'Oh my God, oh my God!' she shouted as she dug her nails into his perfect chest.

Her orgasm hit her with such a rush of pleasure, she could no longer move. He kept thrusting in and out, pushing her well and truly over the edge. When she opened her eyes and met his gaze, it was with a slight embarrassment that he had seen her so open, so unashamedly wanton. His reassuring smile melted away all her temporary inhibitions. Bending over, she kissed him with all the longing she'd ever had. Again, his hands were dictating her movements, and again they'd quickened it. His face contorted, his breathing now shallow and labored. The effect she was having on him was blowing her mind. She could feel another orgasm build inside her but couldn't focus on that right now. She was on a mission. With all the strength she could muster, she tried to ignore the ripples that were rising in her. Then, gripping her hips, Logan called out her name in a husky moan.

'Davina!'

She could no longer disregard the onset of her second orgasm. Screaming his name with what little breath she had left, she collapsed, panting on top of him, both their chests heaving. She knew with all her heart that she could lie there forever.

Logan lifted up her head and grinned at her. 'Well, that was definitely worth the wait.' Before she could comprehend what he'd said, he kissed her deeply again.

Once they'd caught their breath, they moved under the quilt, facing one another. The mood between them was relaxed and easy in the aftermath of their quick romp. They laughed, talked, and laughed some more, sharing childhood memories, regrets, and dreams. Through sheer grit and determination, both were doing very well for themselves now, Davina in the hospitality business (well, she was very hospitable to her clients), and Logan in the oil business, jetting here and there, rubbing shoulders with people who made ridiculous amounts of money, as did he. He regaled her with tales of foreign countries and posh hotels that she should visit. He spoke of the vehemence with which her brothers had prevented anyone they thought unworthy, which apparently meant every boy in Glasgow, from approaching either her or Marge. He stroked the hair from her face and kissed her.

'That's the reason I've never asked you out,' he said.

This totally mystified Davina. 'Surely you mean Marge?' she said. 'You were always hanging on her every word.'

Logan laughed so much, he made himself cough. 'Are you kidding me? I know she's your sister, Davina, but she's not the sharpest tool in the box. No offence.' He screwed up his face. 'Did you seriously think I fancied Marge?'

'I seriously thought everyone fancied Marge,' said Davina matter of factly and without a hint of malice.

'Well, not me,' said Logan. 'For all that I liked her, there was only one of the Brown girls I fancied.'

'So my keepy-uppy skills paid off then?'

Logan pulled her hand under the quilt and folded it around his dick. His eyes were smouldering. 'They sure did.'

After making love again, Logan drifted off to sleep, snoring gently beside a delirious Davina. Leaning on her elbow, and staring at the serene face she'd dreamed of kissing all her life, it was as though she was basking in her own private glory. Her heart felt like it could burst out her chest any minute. She took in every crease, every hair of his well-manicured eyebrows, and even a small scar under his chin that she'd never noticed before. Taking this opportunity to admire his well-toned, albeit thin, torso, she lifted the quilt covering his bottom half. She smiled down at his now limp dick. She stroked his torso from navel to flat, dark nipples. Without opening his eyes, he grabbed her hand.

'See anything you like?' he asked.

She hid her embarrassment by cuddling into his chest. She loved him and hoped this was just the beginning of things to come. 'Too right I have,' she replied.

Back in the present, Davina kissed Logan's forehead as another frown tarnished his brow, then she left him in peace. Marge called to tell her about the bargains she'd spotted for the salon on the internet. If they got the go-ahead, she could have them in plenty of time for opening. They agreed on a cream and light blue colour scheme. Marge had used her contacts in the business to good use, and was meeting with four possible candidates for the salon on Monday.

Davina suggested they go shopping for some accessories with Angela later. Marge loved the idea and said she would phone her and make the arrangements. Davina then texted both her brothers to check they were doing okay after the altercation with Da. Joshua was absolutely fine with it. Apparently, once he'd decided to tell everyone he was gay, he'd made three lists in his head: those who would be fine with it, those who wouldn't, and those he wasn't sure of. Da had been on the list of those who wouldn't be fine with it. Davina found this disheartening and sad. Hector, on the other hand, was still seething. He couldn't believe Da would turn on his own flesh and blood like that. If she was being honest, Davina hadn't given much thought to Da's reaction. As long as Ma was onside, she wasn't too worried.

She cooked Logan his favourite meal, fish and chips with mushy peas, and woke him at nine o'clock. They shared a bottle of wine, made love again, and slept until 20 past eight on Sunday morning. After an early stroll along the river bank, they had a leisurely breakfast and read the papers. Logan let slip that he hadn't had a wee Sunday drinking session in ages, so they showered, dressed, then headed out to find a pub with the afternoon football on. Steak pie and chips with a pint wasn't quite the romantic meal Davina had in mind for this weekend, but she was still absolutely loving it. When the waitress asked if they'd like any condiments to go with their meals, Davina, overdosing on happiness, bumped shoulders with Logan.

'No, he's got his own Brown sauce right here.' The waitress and Logan looked at her as though she had horns. She felt her face turn scarlet.

'I don't like brown sauce, Davina,' said Logan. 'I thought you knew that.' He turned his attention to the waitress. 'I'd like some French Mustard, please, if you've got any?' *Bloody arsehole, Brown. He's got his own Brown sauce here. What were you thinking, you numpty?*

Two games of football and several pints of lager later, they decided to head home, practically falling into the bungalow. Davina, although drunk, still had her sensible head on. She opted for the quilt on the couch instead of lighting the coal fire. Logan gave her a can of lager from the fridge and settled at the other end of the couch with one of his own. Davina put on a CD of Neil Diamond's *All-Time Greatest Hits* and they both sang along with drunken gusto. Neither of them remembered much after that.

Davina woke first. She'd fallen asleep on the couch and her neck was agony. It was nothing compared to the pounding in her head, though. She sat up delicately. Looking across at the sleeping Logan brought a huge smile to her face, which itself brought about a huge banging in the front of her brain.

Gingerly, she made her way to the kitchen and put the kettle on. She was staring out the window daydreaming when Logan cuddled her from behind, making her jump. With his chin in the curve of her neck, he rocked her gently. She smiled blissfully and leaned her head into his.

'Morning, alky.' His gruff voice told her he was probably feeling as bad as her.

'Who are you calling alky?' she replied, pulling back from his pungent breath. 'If memory serves, you were the one that wanted to stay and have one last drink.' She turned to face him, still in his embrace. 'And may I add, Mr McIntyre, that you were the one that got us a drink when we came home.' One side of his lips curled up. *God, you're sexy as hell. But there's no way we're having sex with these hangovers.*

'If that's the way you want to remember it,' he conceded, 'I'm too much of a gentleman to say otherwise.'

She pushed away from him and got another mug out the cupboard. They both really needed a cuppa. As Davina fixed the drinks, Logan retrieved some paracetamol from the cupboard.

'A gentleman,' began Davina, 'knowing his girlfriend . . .' – *Oops, did I say girlfriend?* There was no holding back the smile that had taken over her face – 'was under the weather, would have brought her a cuppa in bed.' She turned with a cup in each hand. Logan raised his eyebrows.

'Let me get this straight,' he said. 'Just because we had some mind-blowing sex, went to the pub, watched some football, had the best steak pie I've had in years, and got drunk . . . which, may I say, has given me a stinker of a hangover . . . all of that means you think you're my girlfriend?'

Davina's face was crimson. *Holy shit, McIntyre. Will you ever stop having this effect on me?* She inhaled deeply through her nose and straightened her shoulders, before walking past him back towards the bedroom. *Go for it, Brown.* She managed to keep the laughter out of her voice as he followed her in.

'Did you really think the sex was mind-blowing?' she asked. 'To be honest, having not seen each other for ages, I expected better.' Her face had calmed marginally, and they were facing each other across the bed now. She placed the cups down on the bedside cabinet and carried on. 'Therefore, I put it to you, Logan McIntyre, that only a girlfriend would put up with such disappointment in the bedroom department. Otherwise I would have told you to piss off afterwards.' Now stripped down to his boxers, Logan pulled back the quilt and climbed into bed. She knew he was trying to keep a straight face, but his businesslike voice was very convincing.

'If memory serves, Miss Brown, the last time we were together, you told me you'd faked your orgasm.' *Shit, I forgot about that.* 'Now you inform me after my last effort that you expected better.' She joined him in bed, stripped to her pants. She handed him his tea and he handed her two painkillers. 'Therefore,' he continued, 'I put it to you, Miss Brown . . . why would a woman with such obvious high standards for her sex partners want someone as bad at it as me for a boyfriend?' His whole demeanour seemed to mock her. *a) I'm joking, McIntyre. You're fucking amazing in bed. And b), even if you were shite in bed, it wouldn't matter. I'm in love with you. Always have been, always will be.* Her face was absolutely burning now.

'Shut up and drink your tea,' she said. Logan laughed raucously.

They slept on and off until after midday. Logan, still in just his boxers, brought her breakfast in bed: tea and toast with spreading cheese. He got her to sit up before placing the tray on her lap.

'Shahia Tayebah,' he said, bowing, trying out his Arabic, albeit with a strong Glaswegian accent. 'Enjoy!'

Davina had a gleam in her eyes and a permanent smile on her face. 'Why, Mr McIntyre!' she said. 'I didn't know you were such a cunning linguist.' The look of surprise on his face as she said this had her blushing again.

'Now that's one sex act I've never had any complaints about,' he grinned. And after breakfast, as though it were needed, he proved his point, giving her two toe-curling orgasms with just his thumb and tongue. He had pressed to give her a third but, as embarrassing as it was for her to admit, her bladder had other ideas. She'd struggled to enjoy herself at first as she watched his head bob about in her crotch. She'd never kidded herself that she was the only woman he'd ever slept with. Men as good looking as Logan, in her eyes anyway, had women throwing themselves at them all the time. However, hearing him say he'd never had any complaints for his oral sex abilities had dampened her ardour somewhat. She eventually managed to overcome this by berating herself for being jealous of women she'd never meet, and ones she now knew he'd never see again. Finally, she let her body give in to the amazing sensation he was bestowing upon her.

CHAPTER 17

BROWN SAUCE

The next two days together were bliss. Spending quality time with Logan had surpassed all Davina's expectations. They'd laughed, shopped, laughed, went for meals, laughed, made love, laughed, watched telly, and laughed some more. Davina had never had a happier time in her life. The paperwork for the new shop had been signed by her and Marge and sent back to the estate agents. The builders would be arriving on Thursday to have a look at what was needing to be done, and then hopefully give them a price for the work and an opening date.

Marge had acquired a receptionist called Amanda who, as Marge put it, was "A bit up herself, but really good at her job." A shy, but apparently brilliant, nail technician called Pauline had also been brought on board, as well as three hairdressers called Frances, Emma and Marion. Marge had let Davina know that Emma and Marion were a couple, just to avoid any potential faux pas when they eventually met. She'd discussed the staffing situation with Angela and they'd agreed that all of the above, plus Marge and Amber, the other fully-qualified beautician, were enough to open up with. Realistically, though, Marge would still prefer another four hairdressers in place before then.

Davina was chuffed that her sister and Angela were getting on so well, and certainly didn't mind them discussing the venture without her. She was in no way surprised by Marge's confidence, believing that her sister had, deep down, always been this self-assured. However, the fact she'd gone about recruiting people and buying the items required to get set up in the first place so expeditiously had Davina stupefied. Normally her sister was dithery and air-headed. *No offence, Marge.*

Marge admitted to Davina that her new-found inner strength was helped by having had a raging Robert on the phone telling her she was useless, thick, not all that good looking, nothing without him, and that she'd soon come running back with her tail between her legs. She'd pointed out that he was the one that had had to belittle her in order to feel like a big man. She'd never waste her time with anyone who treated her like that ever again. And, just for his information, she let him know he was shit in bed and that she'd faked most of her orgasms. Imagining that conversation had Davina laughing heartily and hoping that would be the last they heard of Robert Clarke.

Although she didn't want her time with Logan to come to an end, ever, Davina knew it had to. She had to be in Troon the next day to meet up with the builders. Logan, smiling, said he'd taken up enough of her time already – *as if!* – and that he'd get a train to Glasgow later that day. He also let her know he'd be in Scotland for the foreseeable future, but that he'd be working all over the place. If he didn't see her before the opening of the salon, he'd do everything in his power to be there on the day. In a deadpan voice, he asked her for the salon's number. He wanted to book Marge out for a back, sack and crack. Having spent the best part of three days under and above his naked body, Davina knew he was joking. He barely had any hair anywhere on his body. However, it didn't stop the green-eyed monster from rearing its ugly head. Not for the first time, Davina hated herself for feeling like this.

Plans for the refurbishment of the salon had been passed and the work started. As planned, Davina, Marge and Angela went shopping for the accessories that would make the place welcoming and relaxing. Angela offered to pay for it all and wouldn't take no for an answer. As expected, no expense was spared.

Angela had her secretary discretely let slip that MP Andrew Collins would be opening the much needed new beauty salon, Brown's Body Boutique, in Troon. Although he'd been a widower for a few years now, a couple of the red-topped tabloids hinted that perhaps he was getting over his wife's death by getting under one of the Brown sisters. After all, why else would such a successful Member of Parliament be advocating such a down-market business? Davina and Marge were both outraged and ecstatic that they'd been mentioned in the papers in this way. For her part, Angela had no qualms at all about being linked to the girls in such a salacious way. The more the media speculated about which Brown girl he was sleeping with, the further they were from finding out the truth.

Things were rapidly falling into place. Under Davina's instructions, Marge arranged a dinner with the newly acquired staff. And so TGI Friday's in Glasgow was booked for the following Wednesday, nine days before the salon opened. Davina saw this as a chance for everyone to get to know one another before they started working together. In her eyes, a happy workplace meant happy workers which, in turn, meant happy customers. Marge then arranged for flyers to be printed and plans were made for Davina and her to head to Troon on the

Monday before they opened to hand them out. With adverts already in the Troon Times, Ayr Advertiser and the Ayrshire Post, Amanda, the self-assured receptionist, would start work straight away, manning the phone on her makeshift reception desk on a building site that was quickly turning into an impressive-looking salon.

Seated at their table in TGI's, all eight women were excited about the up and coming opening. Apart from Davina, not one of them was over a size twelve. Each was lovely in their own way, but the whole group, as an ensemble, looked amazing. *You picked the wrong profession, Brown. Skinny bitches.* After the meal, with the aid of several bottles of wine and God knows how many shots, the new employees felt relaxed enough to speak freely to their new employers about their hopes for the salon, and about their family and love lives. Some even talked about their lack of a sex life.

Davina smiled. The night had gone better than she'd imagined. The thought of eight women, some meeting for the first time, talking about working together, had made her stomach do cartwheels. Marge had been correct in her assessment of Amanda, the 21-year-old receptionist; she was most definitely up herself. At not much more than five feet, with long blonde hair that sat perfectly and fell all the way down to her waist, there was no denying she was good looking, but she certainly knew it. Davina wasn't sure if she would hit it off with her, but Marge had great faith in her and that was good enough for Davina. For the time being anyway.

Frances, the straight-faced, sexy-looking hairdresser, was hilarious. Davina guessed she was around 26. She was well over six feet tall, but then again she was wearing ridiculously high-heeled boots. She had dark brown hair with various different bright colours through it and although she really suited it, Davina couldn't make up her mind whether she liked it or not. She did, however, like it when Amanda, at one point, had once again turned the conversation back to herself, only to be told in no uncertain terms by Frances that there was no 'I' in team but there was a 'u' in suck. This had the whole table in an uproar, except Amanda of course, who picked up her phone and muttered 'whatever' under her breath. Even Pauline, the shy, ginger-haired, nail technician was crying with laughter. She had had quite a lot of wine though. Davina knew straight away she was going to like her. Her whole body language reminded Davina of her younger self.

Emma and Marion, the gay hairdressers, were nothing like Davina had imagined. Stereotypically, she'd imagined one of them to be butch, tattooed, and maybe pierced a few times, while the other she imagined would look submissive. She couldn't have been more wrong. Both were a perfect ten, their complexions immaculate, torsos well-toned, make-up flawless and nails manicured impeccably. *Fuckers.* It was also glaringly apparent that they were comfortable in their relationship. They badgered each other constantly and smiled with a certain understanding that only close lovers share.

Davina had toyed with the idea of some girl-on-girl action before as, according to Grace, all women do at some point in their lives. Of the two, she figured that Marion, the tall, dark-haired, dark-eyed one was more her type than Emma, who was shorter, blonde and blue-eyed. Amber, the other qualified beautician, was slightly taller than Amanda and also had long blonde hair. Her model-esque appearance was wasted by the serious frown that all too often crossed her face. She seldom interjected in the conversation, but when she did, her observations were clever rather than humorous. Davina knew they'd get on well. At the end of the night, as they left the restaurant, the new employees kissed and thanked their new employers for both the meal and their jobs. Davina and Marge assured them it was their pleasure.

Angela had been thrilled about the upcoming opening of the salon, so much so that she suggested Davina and Marge stay with her the whole of the week running up to it, rather than commuting back and forth every day. Both sisters gladly took her up on her offer. They spent every possible hour that week cleaning, organising and decorating the now painted salon. They made sure no stone was left unturned, even hiring a small local firm of caterers for the big day. And there was no worry about customers either. According to Amanda, the phone had been ringing constantly for days. Everything was ready.

With the smell of fresh paint still in the air, Brown's Body Boutique opened its doors on the first Saturday in May at nine o'clock on the dot. In attendance were Andrew Collins MP, armed with a pair of hairdressing scissors, and a couple of reporters from the local newspapers. Andrew made a lovely speech in his well-fitted Armani suit before cutting in half the oversized blue and cream bow covering the front door. The first person to enter, beaming with pride and with her shoulders pulled back, was Ma Brown, followed by the rest of the family . . . well, everyone except Da.

It wasn't long before the whole place was buzzing. Admittedly, most people were there just for a nosey, lured in by the prospect of free booze and nibbles. Not that that bothered Davina. It was a case of the more the merrier as far as she was concerned. As she watched Amanda handle the crowd, she questioned her initial impression of the girl. Yes, she was most definitely full of herself, but when it came to work, she positively excelled, answering phone and in-person queries with good manners and patience. Ma was in her element, Davina noticed, being treated to a perm by Frances. Even Lucy was being spoilt. Ma had agreed she could have her nails shaped and painted, albeit under the watchful eye of her granda. Henry even let Emma trim half an inch off his hair. As for the twins, they were getting identical tramlines in the shape of saltires from Marion. Hector and Joshua, however, had declined any special treatment, but took full advantage of the free food and drink on offer.

Halfway through the day, the place filled with the smells of hairspray, nail polish and coffee, there were still a number of people coming and going. An ecstatic Ma, flanked by Hector and Joshua, pulled Davina and Marge to one side to let them know how very proud of them she was. She'd always known they would do well in life. When Da was feeling up to it, she added, she'd bring him for a haircut. She also insisted, with a sceptical look aimed mainly at Davina, that one day soon they'd need to tell her how two girls from Glasgow, a millionaire and an MP had become bedfellows. She clearly thought the MP and the millionaire were different people. Just at that, Andrew approached, looking immaculate in his three-piece navy blue pinstripe suit with salmon-coloured shirt and matching tie and kerchief. He shook Ma's hand enthusiastically.

'You must be Mrs. Brown, and these your boys,' he gushed, nodding towards Joshua and Hector. Everyone laughed.

'Yes,' said Marge, nudging a red-faced Joshua, 'and just like the ones on the telly, we've got a gay as well.' Ma shook her head in embarrassment, then smiled at Andrew. 'Helen,' she said. 'Just call me Helen. Mrs Brown was my mother-in-law, bless her soul.'

'Well,' said Andrew, beaming from ear to ear, 'it's very nice to meet you, Helen. You must be ever so proud of your daughters.'

'Oh, I'm proud of all my weans, Andrew.' At six foot two, Ma was a good foot taller than Andrew, so she had to bend down a bit to ask a more personal question. 'But tell me,' she said. 'How is it that somebody like you knows this pair?'

Andrew never missed a beat. 'Myself and the sweet Davina here have the same financial adviser,' he replied.

With a fly wink and a smile aimed at Davina and Marge, Andrew said his goodbyes and left. The exchange had left Ma more bemused than anything else and there was a definite look of skepticism in her eyes. Suddenly, as though a bolt of lightning had hit her, she straightened up to her full height, took Davina's arm, and led her to a quiet corner. Birling on her heels, she pulled Davina round to face her. The look she gave Davina turned her cold.

'Is he one of the men you were telling me about?' she asked. It took Davina a couple of seconds to realise she meant the conversation they'd had about Logan and Hamish. Before she could answer, Ma threw another question at her. 'Is he your sugar daddy? Do you sleep with him and he takes care of you, and that's why you can't decide who to pick?' *Holy shit, Ma, how did you come up with that?*

Davina looked her straight in the eye. 'No,' she said, 'he isn't one of the men I told you about, and I can categorically state that I have not – and never will – sleep with Andrew for money.'

'I'm really sorry, Davina,' Ma said, genuine with her apology. 'It just that it doesn't make any sense to me how you can afford all this, and how you can be pals with an MP and a millionaire. I just put two and two together and came up with five. That was a terrible thing to say to you. Can you ever forgive me?' Her face was crumpled with embarrassment.

Davina really wanted to tell her ma that Andrew was also the millionaire, but that would mean breaking his confidence. She felt bad about it, but definitely couldn't tell Ma just how close to the mark she was.

'There's nothing to forgive, Ma. I'm glad you never went home thinking that.'

'That's true,' Ma smiled. 'Can you imagine your da's face if I told him that not only did we have a gay in the family, but one of his daughters was selling her body as well?' Ma threw her head back and laughed. *Fuuuuuuuck!* Davina's own laugh, by comparison, was a lot more nervous. It wasn't long after this conversation that the Brown clan headed home, much to Davina's relief.

Davina knew absolutely nothing about the beauty side of the business, so was more than happy staying in the background and people-watching. Staff and customers alike seemed to be really enjoying themselves. As her eyes made another sweep of the salon, Davina's breath caught in her throat. Logan was standing by the door. It wasn't his sudden appearance that had caused her to react, it was the fact that he was holding the door open for Hamish! *Shit, shit, buggery shit.*

Both men, ignorant of what they each meant to Davina, smiled courteously at one another but never spoke. They were now standing side-by-side just inside the door. Davina was rooted to the spot and could only watch as both men, having looked around the salon, spotted her at the exact same time. Bizarrely, they approached her as one. Davina's eyes were the only part of her body that could move, so frozen was the rest of her body. As she glanced between both men, she felt her stomach once more in turmoil. *Fuck. Not here, not today. NOT EVER. Just keep smiling.* Both men stopped in front of her. Logan held her by the elbow and kissed her on the cheek.

'This place looks amazing, Davina, and all your girls are gorgeous.' Davina's mouth was hanging open and she had no idea what was going to come out of it.

'Logan!' Marge had suddenly appeared by their side. She kissed Logan's cheek. 'What brings you here?' she asked excitedly, before leaning in closer. 'Surely you're not needing any work done. You're gorgeous just the way you are.' She straightened back up. 'You can't improve on perfection, can you, Davina?' She bumped shoulders with Davina to reiterate her point. *Too true, Marge, and he's all mine.* Davina could see Hamish's eyes boring into hers. *Holy shit, what's eating you, Hamilton?* She squeezed his hand gently and pulled him into the conversation.

'Marge, Logan . . .' – she felt a little nervous and found herself breathing deeply through her nose – 'I'd like you to meet a very good friend of mine.' All three smiled at one another. 'Hamish, this is my sister and business partner, Marge.' Marge devoured Hamish with her eyes. Ever the gentleman, he pretended not to notice. Marge was practically drooling as Hamish offered her his hand.

'Hi, I'm Hamish,' he said, shaking Marge's hand. 'Davina's told me so much about you.' From nowhere, the Marge from Davina's childhood appeared, straightening her shoulders, pushing her small breasts forward slightly and flicking her hair back. She gently shook Hamish's hand, looked him straight in the eye, and put on her poshest voice.

'Well, she's never mentioned you.' Marge slowly looked up and down Hamish's impressive body. 'I would definitely have remembered her telling me about you.' As she watched the scene unfold, Davina knew she had no right to be jealous, yet that was exactly how she felt. *No way, Marge, not this one. He might be free game, but not to you.* She had to bring this obvious flirting to an end. *Here goes, Brown.* She took Logan by the hand and beamed with love and pride.

'And this . . .' she began, but before she had the chance to finish, Logan pulled his hand from hers and shook Hamish's.

'I'm Logan, an old friend of the family.' If Mike Tyson had caught Davina with a body blow at that moment, it wouldn't have had the same impact as this statement. *FUCK YOU, McIntyre!* She scowled at him in disbelief. Logan, sensing the tension, took hold of Marge's hand.

'Come on, Marge,' he said. 'You can show me the rest of the place.' As Marge made to lead Logan away, he took a step towards Davina and whispered in her ear. 'Sorry, I'll make it up to you, I promise.' He smiled an apologetic, sexy-as-fuck smile, winked at her, and then let Marge lead him away. Her heart skipped a beat. *How do you do that, McIntyre?* 'Nice meeting you, Hamish!' Logan shouted back over his shoulder.

Hamish was looking at Davina intensely, but before he had the chance to interrogate her, they were joined by the beautician, Amber. She was slightly more subtle in her appreciation of Hamish's looks and physique than Marge, but it was no less obvious she was attracted to

330

him too. With an outstretched hand, she introduced herself gracefully.

'Hi, I'm Amber.'

Hamish shook her hand and smiled. 'Does that mean any second now you'll be green and we'll be good to go?'

'Well, I'm game if you are,' Amber replied. Davina was starting to feel uncomfortable at the sexual way they were looking at each other. *Fuck's sake. Why don't you just do him on your table right now and get it over with? Slut.* Davina sighed loudly and frowned at Amber.

'First our Marge is all over him like a rash,' she said, 'and now you. Have you been on the free booze?'

Slowly, almost leisurely, Amber dragged her eyes from Hamish to Davina. 'You were the one that pressed upon us the importance of being friendly to the customers,' she said with a shrug.

Davina liked Amber, but today, with both the main players in her love life in her salon at the same time, she had no appetite for humour. She didn't want to come across as flustered or affected by their open flirtation, so she smiled widely and said, 'Well, might I suggest you try to entice Mr Hamilton here with a back, sack and crack wax once I've finished speaking to him?'

Hamish's face fell. 'Woah-woah-woah,' he said. 'I never said anything about wanting any of that.'

Amber tilted her head to the side and smiled at him. 'I'll go easy on you.' As she walked towards the reception desk, she turned and gave him a sultry look. 'Since you're obviously a wax virgin.' *Jeezo, did I accidentally open a brothel?*

Davina had never seen Hamish stuck for words before. She followed his gaze. He was watching Amber walk away. Davina wasn't sure she liked that. At all.

She sorted them tea and coffee and led Hamish to the back office. It was quite cramped, but adequate enough for their needs. On blue checkered linoleum, there was a small table with a chair at either side. A computer, filing cabinet and photocopier filled the rest of the space. The tightness of the room intensified the smell of the gloss paint and made Davina feel light-headed, but she needed to speak with Hamish privately. She sat the drinks down and he held her in a tight embrace. They stood like that for an age, not speaking, just cuddling. *Why does this have to feel so comfortable with you, Hamilton?* Being taller than her, his head was resting on top of hers.

'I'm really sorry for the way I behaved in Falkirk, Davina,' he said. 'I'm glad we've sorted things out. I really have missed you.' He let her go and sat down to drink his coffee. *What! No kiss? Jeezo, Brown, the green-eyed monster has seriously messed with your head. Never mind, there'll be plenty of kissing later with Logan.* She sat opposite him and lifted her tea.

'What are you smiling at?' he asked.

'Was I smiling?' she said, her face flushed. 'I didn't realise.'

'I know that look, Davina. It's your fuck-me-fuck-me look.' *Great! Now he thinks you want to fuck him. Good going, Brown.* Hamish's eyes darkened as he drank his coffee, watching her over the rim of his cup. 'You know, like the one you gave what's his name?' His voice was harsh but controlled. 'Logan, was it? Just before he stopped you telling everyone he's doing you.' *Shit, shit, buggery shit.* Neither of them spoke, nor broke eye contact. Davina's face heated even more. 'So you don't deny you're fucking him?' Hamish's tone was scathing.

Davina pushed herself deeper into her chair. She knew he was really angry, but there was no way she was just going to sit there and let him berate what she had with Logan. 'No, Hamish,' she said. 'I make love with Logan. It was you I fucked.'

'You sure did, Davina,' he replied. 'You sure did.' Davina pushed up from her seat and scraped it across the floor, ready to let rip. Hamish held his hands up in front of his chest in apology, closing his eyes as though he were in pain.

'Sorry, Davina. Sorry. I can't believe I'm being an arsehole again.' He opened his eyes and lowered his hands. 'It's just that this isn't easy for me.' *Easy for you? Easy for you? Do you think I'm enjoying the awkwardness the two of you being in my salon at the same time is causing?*

'Well, maybe you should have just sent a card instead of coming here.' She fell back heavily into her seat.

Hamish breathed out. 'I came here to tell you how proud I am of you and to congratulate you on your new venture. No way would I have just sent a card. I always knew you'd do something with your life. You're too astute and talented not to.' He was smiling at her warmly now.

'Thanks, Hamish,' she said, her mood thawed. 'You always did believe in me and that helped me immensely. I'm eternally grateful for everything you've ever done for me. I will always cherish our friendship. However, I'm not going to be your emotional punchbag every time we meet. It's not fair.'

Hamish grimaced and he dropped his eyes. Twice he raised them again and started to speak, and twice he stopped himself. Davina felt powerless to help. *Jeezo, Hamilton, you're breaking my heart here.* She reached across the table and took his hand, giving it a reassuring squeeze.

333

'I won't lie to you, Davina,' he said, finally. 'I never have.' He knew he'd have to finish what he started. 'I came here today with an ulterior motive. I've been offered a position in America.' Davina gasped. Hamish smiled weakly. 'I'd hoped to somehow convince you I was worth taking a chance on. Depending on your decision, we could have made a go of it here or over there.' Davina opened her mouth to speak, but Hamish held up a hand. 'Let me finish.' His voice had a bitter edge to it now. 'Seeing the way you looked at . . . him.' He tilted his head to the door, unwilling to give Logan his name. Davina knew this was tearing him apart and there was no holding back her tears. 'That made me realise I'm not the one for you and, as painful as it is for me, I do want you to be happy in life and in love.' His own eyes were moist now. 'However, I can't handle seeing you with another man. I want to rip his fucking head off and I don't even know him.' This mountain of a man looked broken as he rubbed his face with his shovel-sized hands. 'Us being just friends isn't working for me right now. I don't know how I'll feel in the future.' He shrugged. 'Maybe I'll get my head around it eventually, but right now I need some distance to get over us.'

Davina's tears were so constant now, they were dripping off her chin onto the table. 'I'm so sorry, Hamish. I didn't mean to hurt you. I just . . .' *Fell in love with another man.*

'I know, Davina. I know.' His resigned tone and half-hearted, lopsided smile broke Davina's heart. She rushed around the table and held him fiercely. Sobs wracked their bodies. They were still wrapped together when, following a weak knock, the door opened.

'Davina, are you in here?' Logan stepped into the room. What he saw had him quickly backing out again. 'Sorry, sorry,' he mumbled. Hamish pulled himself away from Davina and kissed her on the lips. Looking her in the eye, he addressed Logan.

'You're okay, pal. We're finished.' With a squeeze of her hands and one final weak smile, Hamish walked out the room and out of Davina's life.

CHAPTER 18

BROWN SAUCE

Two months later, Davina had thrown herself into her work. Well, as much as was possible. As she didn't have any skills in the beauty business, she concentrated fully on the financial side of things. Douglas was always on hand to help out if and when required, for which Davina had expressed her eternal gratitude. For the most part, though, she handled the work with a business-like authority that surprised even her. She also worked on ways to attract new customers, placing ads in all the local rags and spending much of her downtime handing out flyers in Prestwick, Ayr, Kilmarnock and all the smaller places in-between, come rain or shine. Guilt at feeling less productive than the rest of the staff even took her from Troon to Glasgow and Ayr by train, alternating the journeys for a whole week, and handing out flyers to anyone and everyone. It earned her the nickname The Flyer Scotsman from her staff. Of course, she had to make sure the train conductors never caught her as she left the flyers placed strategically throughout the carriages.

On one such escapade, a female conductor, who was inspecting tickets, had lifted a flyer from a table across the aisle from Davina. She scrunched it up and glowered at Davina with barely masked contempt. 'If I find the person responsible for all these bits of paper,' she said, 'they'll be reported.'

Davina shook her head. 'I know,' she said. 'Every time I get on the train lately, they're here. But, having said that, I must admit their prices are pretty reasonable. And I've heard they're very good, especially at doing your nails.'

The conductor narrowed her eyes and made to walk away. 'I'll shove the lot of them up your arse, hen,' she muttered, her timing perfect, ensuring she was still in earshot but eye contact had been broken.

Davina laughed to herself, not just because it was obvious the conductor knew fine who the flyer culprit was, but also because her reaction stirred up a memory Davina had long since forgotten:

The Brown clan had once decided to spend the weekend up at their holiday home, the bungalow. At the time, the family consisted of Granda, Da, Ma and the four oldest kids, all primary school age. Lazy-Eyed Laidlaw, Da's best pal, had asked Da to watch his racing whippet, Blue Boy, that same weekend. Everything including the kitchen sink had been packed and everyone was ready and waiting at the bus stop. When the bus pulled up, the conductor, Ina McLaren, sporting an eight-inch-high blonde bouffant and 40DD breasts, stepped off to let everyone on. There was a no-nonsense air about Ina. She'd always had an eye for the men and she winked at a beaming Granda as he boarded. The four kids rushed on and made for the empty back seat. Ma got on, but hadn't walked very far when Ina's indignation overtook her.

'You're not bringing that fleabag on my bus!' she boomed.

Da tried to push past her, flustered and embarrassed that a woman had the nerve to speak to him like that. 'He's not a fleabag,' he said, 'and yes I am bringing him on your bus!'

Ina straightened her shoulders and crossed her arms over her plentiful breasts, blocking the doorway. 'The regulations,' she informed Da in an official and firm tone, 'clearly state that no livestock, including pigs, sheep, cats and fleabags are permitted to travel on any company vehicle.'

Da's blood was boiling now. He knew everyone on the bus was waiting on his reaction. 'Well, in that case,' he snarled through gritted teeth, 'you can stick your bus up your arse.'

Ina didn't miss a beat. 'Well,' she smiled, sarcastically, 'if you could stick that fleabag up *your* arse, I could let you on the bus and save us all a bit of time and trouble.'

A fuming Da roared up the bus. 'Browns, off!'

Ma was halfway down the bus and didn't move. She just cleared her throat and spoke calmly. 'Kids, stay where you are. I've not gone to all the bother of getting us all ready just to walk to the bus stop and then back home.' She nodded to Da, who was still standing outside on the pavement. 'We'll see you Monday morning.' Then she turned and walked to the back of the bus. Ina wiggled her arse at the gobsmacked Da, got back on the bus and blew him a kiss.

Davina's smile fell away as one memory replaced another: Da's outburst in the pub. There was a huge rift in the Brown clan now. Nothing had changed at home. Da had refused to accept that he was well out of order disowning Joshua, and Joshua, for his part, was adamant he'd never speak to Da again. Ma knew something was wrong but no-one would enlighten her. It was for her own good. The other three adults caught up in the stramash were on Joshua's side and hardly visited their parents' house now. Davina and a guilt-ridden Marge often spoke about this. Davina's take on the matter was that some things in life were unfixable, and even the Browns could have a serious falling out and never resolve their differences. This scenario totally flummoxed Marge and saddened them both. *As a great man once said, "Life is like a box of chocolates." But sometimes you end up with a shit one.*

The girls in the salon were getting on really well, which Davina had to admit surprised her. Her experience with women up to that point had been one of bitchiness and hurt. The home appointments had taken off amazingly. A local old people's home booked Amber, the beautician, for the whole day, once a month. The other girls each had their regulars and were adding to them every week. Davina and Marge had decided that on the last Wednesday of each month, they'd close at three so they could treat the girls to an early dinner. As most of the girls travelled to and from work by train, there were always at least a couple of bottles of wine consumed. The camaraderie and banter between them all was great. Life in the salon was great.

Davina had given up on texting Hamish. She hadn't seen him since he'd left the salon that day. The one and only text she'd received was short and sweet.

> Hi D just a wee text to let you know I took the job in America. I've been here for two weeks now. The locals are friendly but they all think I'm Irish. I hope you're happy and things are still going well for you. Love always, Hamish. XXX

She'd tried to reply to this a couple of times. The hollow feeling in her chest was taking its time to dissipate.

'How cruel life can be,' she'd said to Grace over a glass of wine one night. 'I waited all my life for someone special to come along, then two come along at once. What a pisser.'

Grace, not known for her tact or diplomacy, told her she was a selfish cow and should be happy with her lot. After all, Logan wasn't that bad a catch.

Davina punched her on the arm. 'He's the catch of the century,' she said. 'I just miss my pal, that's all.'

Logan, much to Davina's surprise, had never mentioned the incident in the salon with Hamish. He'd been abroad twice in the past two months. Each time he returned saw them, for the most part, joined at the sweaty hips. They walked along the River Ness so often they were actually on first name terms with a few hill-walkers. The family still didn't know about her and Logan, although they'd been out a couple of times with Grace and Gavin. Gavin had assured both women that Logan would never find out from him that he'd even known Davina before Grace, let alone hired her as an escort. Davina didn't question his discretion one bit.

It was apparent to Davina that Grace and Gavin had taken their relationship to the next level. They literally couldn't get enough of each other. She was as equally ecstatic for Gavin as she was for her best friend. The change in both of them was amazing. Gavin was much more relaxed within himself and had even put on a little weight. Grace was more confident and, if Davina was correct, thinner.

'Either you've taken up hill-walking,' she joked, squeezing Grace by the waist, 'or you and Gavin are going at it like rabbits.' She remembered the wee white lie she'd used to explain her own weight loss to her family.

'Rabbits! Dogs! Kangaroos! You name the mammal, we've done it!' Grace replied with a huge, smarmy grin on her face.

Davina was rarely needed in the salon. That was fine with her. It enabled her to live a more leisurely life, like returning Angela's hospitality by inviting her up to the bungalow. When Davina collected her from the station, she noticed that Angela didn't seem her usual bubbly self, but chose not to probe any further. They shared a quiet night together in front of the coal fire listening to Ella Fitzgerald – Jessie's favourite singer, according to Angela – and went to bed relatively early. The next morning, at 8.43am precisely, it was Andrew, not Angela, who walked into the kitchen for breakfast. To say Davina was surprised would be an understatement. He wore teal chinos and a silvery-grey polo shirt. She had hardly ever seen him dressed casually. His sombre mood this morning had her worried.

'What do you want for breakfast, Ang . . . rew?' *Shit*.

'Just a cup of tea please,' he said. 'I'm not really hungry.'

Davina took two mugs from the cupboard and half-filled the huge teapot she used when the whole clan descended on her. 'Is everything alright, Andrew?' she asked, sitting across from him at the table.

Andrew's reply was halting, his voice deep and shaky. 'Today, the sixth of June, is the day the sunlight left my world.' His eyes misted. Davina offered up an understanding smile and was rewarded with a reassuring squeeze of her hand. 'I'm sorry,' said Andrew. 'I'm being

341

a silly old man. It's just that I still miss her. She really was my rock.'

Davina had never met Jessie but she felt as though she knew her. No matter where they were, Andrew would always mention her in conversation. He'd point out dresses she'd have loved to have worn, jewellery she'd have found enchanting but would never have let him pay such an extravagant price for, restaurant food she'd probably have ordered even though she would have been appalled at the prices, and people on TV she liked or couldn't abide. Yes, Davina knew a lot about the late Mrs Jessie Collins, and not for the first time wondered if the quiet unassuming rock in Andrew's life had been totally oblivious to his little quirk.

Davina squeezed Andrew's hand. 'Well, I'm sure wherever she is, she's looking down on you right now and saying, "When he gets up here, I'll be having a word with him. He looks better than me in some of those dresses!"'

'Either that or her and my parents will have disowned me.' Andrew's smile told Davina everything she needed to know.

'I doubt that very much,' she said. 'But seriously, if you're not in the mood to go shopping, we don't have to.'

'What, and miss the chance to see the beautiful city of Inverness? I don't think so.' He took a sip of tea. 'However, out of respect for Jessie, I shall be going shopping as Andrew.'

Once out, Davina used the opportunity to pick up some summer clothes: bright, bold, colourful dresses, sarongs, bikinis, and anything else she cared to buy. She'd decided the next time Logan went abroad, she was going with him. This long-distance relationship just

342

wasn't working for her. After three hours of shopping, Andrew insisted on buying her lunch. They decided on Italian food. Little Italy was a quaint, cosy restaurant with red and white checkered table covers, bustling with happy patrons. The nice weather had brought shoppers out in their droves.

'My Jessie would have loved this place,' smiled Andrew, leading Davina to an intimate table for two in the corner. Just then, Davina's mobile rang. It was Logan.

'I'll be back in a minute,' she said. 'I need to take this. Order for me, please. I trust your judgment.' Davina walked back outside, beaming. Logan had been back in Britain for three days but, because of work commitments, they hadn't managed to meet up yet. She walked a few steps away from the entrance.

'Hi!' his enthusiastic voice greeted her. 'Guess what?'

'What?'

'I'm on my way back home. I should be there at eight if you're free to come and have your wicked way with me. And here's the best part: I'll be back for at least another month.'

Davina was mentally packing a bag as he spoke. 'Shit!' she said.

'Shit what?' His enthusiasm waivered. 'I thought you'd be pleased.'

'I am,' she said, 'but I have a friend staying with me.'

'Who?' *Shit, shit, buggery shit.* Having seen Hamish's jealous side, Davina wasn't keen on telling Logan she had a man staying with her. She chewed her bottom lip, deliberating. *Fuck!*

'You don't know her,' she said. 'Her name's Angela. I know her through work.' *Well, that's true.*

'Bugger. How long is she staying?'

'I'm not sure. We haven't really decided what we're doing yet.' *Shit.*

'Oh well, that'll be that then. I'll just have to enjoy my body without you.'

Davina's insides clenched. 'Lucky you.' She was elated and despondent at the same time. She might not be able to see him during the next two days, but after that she'd have him all to herself for a whole month. Her lips curved in a lecherous grin.

Logan's enthusiasm returned. 'I've got an idea,' he said. 'Why don't I phone you when I get home and we could have phone sex? I've never done that before. Have you?' *Yes, with an ignoramus that swore, farted and belched every minute of it.*

'No, but I'm game if you are. Wear something sexy like your Calvin Klein boxers.'

'Eh, am I not supposed to say "wear something sexy" to you?'

'Eh, I think you'll find that's a bit sexist.'

'Okay, if you say so! I'll phone you later. Love you, bye!' He hung up.

'Wow-wow-wow!' Davina exclaimed. 'Love you?' Her stomach was doing loop-de-loops. She was gazing, unseeing and stupefied, at pedestrians milling past her. 'Oh my God, Logan McIntyre just said "Love you!" To me! Hoaaaaaly shit!' She slapped her hand to her mouth and quickly looked around to see if anyone was in earshot. Clutching her phone to her chest, she tried to calm her breathing. When a hand patted her on the shoulder, she almost jumped out her skin.

'Miss?' an Italian accent enquired. 'Is everything okay? Your friend is worried about you.' Davina turned to see the caring young face behind the voice.

'I couldn't be better,' she replied automatically. Given the crack in her throat, she very much doubted that the young girl believed her. Still dazed, she followed the girl back into the bustling restaurant. 'Sorry, sorry,' she said to Andrew when she got to the table. 'I didn't realise I was away that long.'

'Is everything alright, Davina?' *Alright? Alright! No, everything isn't alright. It's fecking amazing!*

She thought her smile was going to split her face in two. 'Everything's great, thank you. It's just great.'

They ate their starters in relative silence, both lost in their own thoughts. A guitarist with a voice to die for walked between the tables, serenading the diners in Italian. Davina poured them both a fresh glass of ice-cold water. She hated herself for wanting to be with Logan rather than Andrew.

'My mushrooms were amazing,' she said. 'Good choice. How were your snails?'

'They were absolutely lovely, my dear. I did offer you one.'

'I know,' said Davina. 'Maybe if I hadn't seen them and didn't know what they were I would've tried them. To be honest, though, I just didn't like the look of them.'

The waiter brought their main meals over. 'Sea bass?'

Andrew indicated to Davina. 'That's there, thank you.'

The waiter placed the fish in front of Davina and set the other plate in front of Andrew. Both the sea bass and the carbonara looked amazing. The crooner was singing an Italian ballad now, 'Santa Lucia'. Davina had heard the song before. Although it was very beautiful, she'd always found it sad. She was about to take another forkful of food when she suddenly stopped. Andrew's shoulders were slumped forward and tears were falling from his immeasurably sad eyes. Davina dropped her fork noisily on her plate and reached for his hands. *Shit.*

'Sorry, Davina,' wept Andrew, nodding in the singer's direction, 'that was one of Jessie's favourite songs.' He stood and walked to the toilet. The crooner approached their table and smiled apologetically. When Andrew returned, they were treated to 'That's Amore'. The crooner winked at Davina knowingly. *Right then, a bit of Dean Martin fixes everything. Not.* Andrew sang along to the song quietly. No way. Davina wasn't fooled by Andrew's smile, but she went along with the charade and joined in at the bits she knew, namely the chorus. The crooner raised his eyebrows, as though to say 'I told you so', before crossing to another table. *Okay, maybe Dean worked a wee bit, smart arse.* With their table now quieter, they finished their plates, declining dessert or coffee. As they walked back to the car, arm-in-arm, they were again lost in their own thoughts.

'Davina,' Andrew eventually said, 'would you mind awfully if I went home?'

Davina pressed her car fob. 'That's where we're going, Andrew,' she said, puzzled.

Andrew looked at her across the top of the car. 'No,' he said sadly, 'I mean *my* home, in Troon.' *Oh my God, I could go and see Logan!* She opened her car door angrily, ashamed of herself. *You selfish bitch. This man has given you more than you could ever thank him for. Here he is, falling apart in front of you, on the saddest day of his life, and all you can think of is yourself.*

Sitting inside, she squeezed Andrew's hand. 'Why would you want to go home?' she asked. 'You haven't even seen Nessie yet.' She started the car and pulled out of the car park. 'Mind you,' she added, 'if my granda's to be believed, she's not there anymore anyway. She's in

Area 51, in America.' For the first time since picking him up at the station, Andrew laughed.

'Was that your grandfather who was at the opening of your boutique?'

'The very one.'

'I can't believe a clever man like him would come away with something like that.' *Wow, a clever man like that!* Davina's eyes flicked between the road and Andrew.

'Are you sure we're talking about the same person?' she snort-laughed.

'Absolutely. The things that man knows about politics puts even me to shame.'

'Seriously? My granda? No way.'

The rest of the drive back to the bungalow was spent talking about the enigma that was Davina's granda. She'd have been lying if she said she wasn't proud of the impression he'd made on Andrew, but his knowledge of how the cogs of Parliament turned had her gobsmacked. Yes, he had shared tidbits of knowledge here and there with all of them over the years, but you could never sit him down and have a serious conversation with him about anything.

At home, sitting at the table with a hot cuppa, Davina tried in vain to talk Andrew out of going back to Troon.

'Well, since I can't convince you to stay,' she conceded, 'and it's a glorious day, why don't I drive you back to Glasgow via Loch Ness and I can visit my family? Kill two birds with one stone.' *I have no intention of seeing my family, I'm just going to have my wicked way with the man that apparently loves me.* Davina felt as though she could explode with happiness.

Andrew looked at her sceptically. 'Isn't that a bit like driving to London via Wales?' he asked.

347

Davina shrugged. 'The scenery makes it worthwhile,' she replied, still smiling. 'And besides, it'll save you being alone on the train.' *And Logan won't be home for another six hours at least.*

Andrew stood up. 'Whatever would I have done if I'd never met you, sweet child?' He kissed her on the cheek and went to his room to pack.

The drive around the loch was more leisurely than Davina had anticipated; every man and his dog had had the same idea. But it didn't matter. The scenery here really was spectacular. Andrew used the time to open his heart about how bad he'd felt tricking Jessie into marrying – she thought – an honest and trustworthy gentleman. Every now and then, his voice would crack with emotion and he'd have to wipe his eyes. For the first few years, he said, he felt their marriage was a sham, until they'd had their two sons. Then things changed. *He* changed.

Knowing deep down what he was, he had never wanted to get married, let alone have children. He didn't want to risk anyone else being hurt if his sordid little secret got out. But then the strangest thing happened: he fell head over heels in love with the woman he'd initially only thought of as the mother of his children. He loved the self-assured woman she'd become since having their sons; loved how she'd brought them up to be the fine gentlemen they were today; loved, yet felt horrid, when she told him how proud of him she was. Their lives together, as lovers, soul mates, and parents had been blissful, so why couldn't he bring himself to tell the one person in life he loved with all his heart what kind of a man he really was?

He stared out the window, wiping away his tears. Davina wanted nothing more than to stop the car and take this lovely, warm-hearted, generous, hurting man in her arms and give him a great big cuddle, but there was nowhere to pull over. Every scenic layby was filled with parked cars and campers. They drove for miles in silence until they reached Fort Augustus. Andrew may not have needed a cuddle anymore, but he was definitely in need of a decent cup of tea.

Armed with a lidded plastic cup of hot, steaming tea and a fresh muffin, they squeezed through a throng of tourists to the mesh sculpture of Nessie. It was an amazing sight. A plethora of plants grew up around the realistic body all the way to its neck. Davina whistled, impressed.

'I'm going to build one of those in my garden,' she said.

'I just wonder how much of the taxpayers' good money was spent on such a thing.' Andrew had his political head on.

'Well, whatever it cost,' Davina said, nudging Andrew's shoulder, 'look at the people it's attracting. As the saying goes, you've got to speculate to accumulate.'

'Hear, hear.' Andrew raised his tea in a toast. 'And if it helps the local economy, then who am I to grumble about a few thousand pounds?'

Davina wasn't sure if the look he shot her was a condescending one or not, but she bumped her tea with his anyway. 'Hear, hear.'

After a trip each to the toilet, they were back at the car, Andrew hunting out his Ella Fitzgerald CD from the boot. When they'd first listened to it together, Davina had been surprised to discover that she already knew quite a few of the songs, mainly as cover versions. Now, hearing it a second time as they headed towards Glasgow, she happily sang along to most of them, exchanging whoops and choruses with a smiling Andrew in the passenger seat.

When they walked into Glasgow Central, it was almost quarter to nine at night. They scanned the information boards for trains going to Troon.

'If I have to wait over an hour,' said Andrew, 'I'll just pop in a hackney carriage.' Davina, straining her neck looking up at the big board, couldn't help but smile at his choice of words. *Or you could just slum it like the rest of us and get a taxi.*

'No need,' she said, pointing upwards. 'There's a train at nine o'clock. Gets you into Troon at just before 20 to ten.'

He followed her gaze. 'Splendid.'

Andrew sat his small suitcase down and took Davina's hands in his. 'As usual, you have been a godsend, sweet child. I should pay you as my therapist. I truly feel a great weight has been lifted off my shoulders having spoken to you.' Davina dropped his hands and gave him a cuddle like the ones her ma gives her, the ones that fix everything. Then she pulled back and looked him in the eye.

'Well, in that case,' she said, 'my fee is for you to stop beating yourself up about things you can never change. From what you've told me, rather than grieving for Jessie, you've torn yourself apart with guilt. So here's what I suggest you do: buy some flowers, take them to her grave, and tell her everything you told me. And if you're struck by lightning after you've finished telling her, you'll know she's mad. If not, you're in the clear.' His smile, then his laughter, spoke volumes. He pecked her on the cheek. 'I truly love you.' *Wow, two men in one day telling me they love me. Must be something in the air.*

'And I you,' she said. 'Now hurry up or you'll be getting a hackney cab and ending up in London.'

Andrew lifted his suitcase and walked away. 'Goodbye, my sweet child.'

Driving in Glasgow wasn't one of Davina's favourite things in life. Even this late at night, the roads were heaving with drivers in a rush to get nowhere fast. The only thought keeping her calm(ish) was that in 15 minutes or so, she'd be with Logan, the man who, only eight hours and 43 minutes ago, had rocked her world by saying he loved her.

'Maybe it was a slip of the tongue,' she said to herself. 'Maybe he won't know what to say to you if you just turn up on his doorstep unannounced wearing this stupid grin that won't leave your stupid face.' She looked at herself in the rearview mirror. 'Yip, that's the stupid grin I'm talking about.' She parked outside his flat. The black car nearby told her he was home. *Why haven't you phoned yet, McIntyre?*

Up ahead, a young couple she recognised from Logan's building were lugging armfuls of bags from the boot of their car. Davina knew she'd lose the element of surprise if she buzzed Logan on the intercom, so she grabbed her own bag of goodies and her handbag from the back seat and caught up with the couple. 'Well, in for a penny,' she muttered. As the couple approached the front door, Davina rummaged in her handbag pretending to look for her keys. The couple unlocked the door and held it open for her.

'Thanks,' she said. Once inside, she climbed nervously to the third floor. Halfway up, her mobile rang. Her hands were shaking so much she almost dropped it. Her panic ebbed slightly when Logan's name flashed on the screen. *This was such a bad idea.* She sat on the empty stairwell staring at the screen and took a deep breath before answering.

'Hi.'

'Hi, you.' Logan's sexy tone melted her concerns immediately. 'Are you alone?' *Shit, phone sex!* Suddenly very conscious of her surroundings, she started climbing the stairs again. When she was sure she was alone, she quietly purred down the phone.

'Yes. Are you wearing your Calvin Klein's?'

'Wow, you don't hang about, do you?'

Davina's cheeks burned, but her stupid grin had returned, as had her courage. 'I'll take that as a yes, shall I?' She was outside his door now. 'What colour?'

'Black.'

'Naughty boy. You know what they do to me. I'm wet already.' She rang his doorbell.

'Fuck.'

'What's the matter, big boy?' Her voice, still low, oozed sex. 'Am I going too fast for you?' She could hear him, both on the phone and through the door, scrambling about. She rang the doorbell again.

'Fuck! No, there's somebody at the door,' he said.

Davina struggled not to laugh, but kept the thickness in her voice. 'You better answer it. It could be the police.'

'The police! Why the hell would the police be at my door?'

'Well, it is criminal how good you look in just your boxers.' She could hear him approach the door.

'Very funny. Hang on just now.' He opened the door, half-pulling on a t-shirt. When he clocked Davina, his eyes bulged and his mouth fell.

'Hi,' smiled Davina. 'I'm PC Wet Knickers. I'm here to take down your briefs.'

352

It was Logan's turn to grin stupidly. He quickly pulled Davina inside and closed the door behind her. 'You bitch. I had to run around and find something to throw on.' His eyes narrowed. 'You enjoyed that, didn't you?' Davina was laughing. This had definitely been one of her better ideas.

'Maybe a little bit,' she said. He kissed her and led her to the couch. Davina dropped both her bags en-route and slipped her shoes off. Sprawled on top of her, Logan beamed down.

'So, you lied to me about having a friend with you.' *Shit. Think, Brown.*

'No,' she said, 'but a family matter came up and she had to go back to Troon, so I thought I'd surprise you. I hope you don't mind.'

'Why would I mind?' He nipped her lobe with his teeth, his breath heavy in her ear. 'Although I do think you have a future in phone sex, as long as it's just me you call.'

She pulled his face back down to hers and kissed him hard. *You have no worries there, McIntyre.* 'So what does a girl have to do to get a drink around here?' she asked.

Logan pushed up with his hands, leering at her. 'Oh, I'm sure I could think of something.'

Davina lowered her hand to his crotch, squeezing and stroking him through his joggers. 'Oh, I'm sure you could, Mr McIntyre,' she said, 'but it's thirsty work all this phone sex.'

Logan stood up grudgingly, helping Davina to her feet. 'If it's a drink the lady wants,' he said, 'then a drink she shall have.' He sauntered into the kitchen. Davina lifted her bags and followed him. He took two bottles of lager out the fridge, opened them, and handed her one. She sat her handbag on the worktop but kept a hold of the carrier bag she'd brought with her. Taking the bottle from him, she locked eyes and clinked hers with his. *Christ's sake, McIntyre, it really is criminal how good you look.* Logan lowered the bottle from his smiling lips. 'You want to do dirty things to me, don't you?'

She stepped closer to him and licked his wet lips. 'Always, Logan. Always.'

Logan pulled her hard into his body. 'Well,' he said, firmly, 'what the fuck are we waiting for?'

His kiss was hard and hungry. Her mouth and body melted into him. *Not yet, Brown, not yet.* Reluctantly, she pushed back from him, lifted her bag, and nodded to it. 'I think it's time I slipped into something a little less . . .'

Logan looked down at the bag in her hand. A sensual smile crept onto his face. 'A little less what?'

Davina downed the rest of her beer, bit and sucked on his bottom lip, and then walked out the kitchen, winking at him over her shoulder. 'Just a little . . . less.'

In Logan's en-suite bathroom, Davina changed into her over-priced lime green and orange bikini. The material barely covered her dignity, never mind her ample frame. She didn't care. There was only one man's opinion that mattered to her.

Logan was sitting on the couch with a fresh bottle of beer in his hand when he caught sight of her in the doorway. She had on a pair of black suede Mary Jane platform sandals, one hand stretched up to the top of the door frame joining the bedroom and the living room, one knee raised against the door jamb. It was one sexy-as-hell seductive pose and she knew it. Logan sat his beer on the carpet and stood slowly, scorching her body with an appreciative leer. His tongue ran eagerly between his lips. He drew closer. *Thank God! I can't hold my belly in much longer*. He lifted her arm and turned her around full circle.

'That's a nyshe little nothing you're almosht wearing, Mish Brown,' he crooned in his best Sean Connery voice. His eyes were sparkling with mischief. The majority of her voluptuous breasts were squeezing out the sides of the tiny triangles, her nipples on full alert. The material, or lack thereof, at her crotch, made her very grateful she'd taken Amber up on her offer of a Brazilian before she'd gone shopping with Andrew. The swift slap Logan delivered to her bum reminded her there was just as little material at the rear. The whole ensemble was having more than the desired effect, however, if the front of Logan's joggers were anything to go by.

'Is there a reason for this amazing floor show?' he asked, sliding two fingers under the triangles at her breasts. Any more and the bikini would have struggled to cope. Scissoring her nipples between his fingers, he licked all the way up her cleavage to her throat. Davina grabbed his hair, forcing his head back to her breast.

'I'm hoping to go abroad with my boyfriend, so I treated myself to some skimpy outfits.'

Logan's zealousness wavered briefly. *Shit.* 'Lucky boyfriend,' he stated.

Davina let out the breath she didn't even know she'd been holding. 'Well, I think so.'

He lifted his gaze to hers. His eyes had never looked so inviting. 'So does he,' said Logan.

The desire between them was palpable. Passionate, breathless kisses took them back into the bedroom. Logan dropped Davina onto the bed and leaned over her, intent written all over his face. Then, suddenly, he stopped, frozen. The shock on his face made Davina wary.

'What's the matter?' she asked.

Logan held his hand up and looked to the door, listening intently. 'Shh,' he said. With his crotch right in front of her, it was hard for Davina to ignore the fact that whatever had gotten his attention had definitely cooled his ardour.

'Hello?' shouted a cheery, thick Latin American voice from the hall. 'Anyone home?' Davina jumped up and stared at the bedroom door. 'Oh my God, Logan,' she said, almost inaudibly, 'someone's in your flat. I thought you locked the door.'

Logan hadn't budged. It looked like he'd stopped breathing. *Holy shit, you're scared shitless.* Whoever was outside the door wasn't going to catch her naked, thought Davina, so she tip-toed slowly back to the safety of the en-suite. She'd barely taken a couple of steps when her heart froze.

'Logan, babe, are you here?' The Latino voice sounded anxious. Davina turned to look at Logan. His eyes were closed and his face creased in anguish. Bile rose in Davina's throat. She couldn't move. She couldn't speak. Her self-destructive low self-esteem barriers were in overdrive. Somehow, she found the use of her legs again and, shaking, – *don't throw up, Brown, don't throw up* – she made her way to the bathroom. Logan attempted a half-hearted grab for her hand, but the tortured look in Davina's eyes stopped him in his tracks. *You utter cunt.*

Silently, she closed the bathroom door behind her and scuffed over to the mirror. Tears streamed down her face. Her hair hadn't been brushed from this morning and her tits were trying to escape from her bikini. *Of course he has someone else! Look at you, you're like mutton dressed as lamb!* Legs like jelly, she grabbed a bath towel from the side of the bath and sat on the toilet, her whole body wracked with pain, wounded animal noises slipping from her. She felt like someone had punched her in the guts and ripped out her insides. Time passed without meaning. She didn't know how long she'd been in there, but one thing was sure: she couldn't stay hidden forever.

'Come on, Brown,' she said to herself. 'Time to go home.'

As she found the energy to get to her feet and get dressed, she heard raised voices coming from the living room. She caught some Spanish amongst the English. Or was it Portuguese? She couldn't make out what was being said, nor did she care. Once dressed, she ventured out into the bedroom where, against her better judgement, she found herself crossing to the door.

Through the crack, she saw her worse nightmare come true. Sitting on the couch next to Logan was a tall, stunning, caramel-skinned, dark-haired, Latino model. Normally Davina would have loved the fact that the model was a lot fatter than she was, but, if her guestimation was correct, that would no longer be the case in a couple of months.

CHAPTER 19

BROWN SAUCE

Human nature being what it is, Davina couldn't help eavesdropping on Logan and his Latino lover before making her presence known. Logan was raging that she'd risked flying to Scotland so close to her delivery date. They'd agreed he'd fly back in plenty of time for the birth. Davina watched her sidle up closer to Logan on the settee and implore him, in her sexy Latino voice, not to be angry with her. She was lonely, and she missed her 'amante escocés'. *Whatever the fuck that is.* She kissed him on the mouth and he let her, briefly.

Davina had seen and heard enough. *So that's why I was getting a month of your precious time. Wanker.* The hurt and pain inside her was now replaced by blind fury. She knew her handbag was in the kitchen and her shoes at the side of the couch, but . . . *Come on, you can do this, Brown.* Taking a huge breath, and pulling her shoulders back, Davina swung the door open and, with all the grace she could muster, sauntered into the living room. Logan didn't look at her, but his lover got the fright of her life, jumping up and clutching her swollen belly. Her eyes were wide with disbelief. She could only watch as Davina slipped on her shoes and walked past them into the kitchen. As she left the living room, Davina heard her shout something in Spanish.

Logan responded angrily with a single word. 'Limpiador!'

In her best English accent, the pregnant hottie spat back. 'What is your cleaner doing here at this time?'

'Fucking cleaner?' Davina stopped in her tracks, turned on her heels, and walked over to the couch. *Oh no you fucking didn't, McIntyre.* Logan's back was to her. She placed her hands on his shoulders and felt him almost leap out his seat. Squeezing as painfully as she could, she stared the pregnant bitch in the eye calmly.

'Yes, I've been cleaning his dick with my tongue for years,' she said seductively. Logan's whole body slumped forward. The pregnant bitch's mouth fell open, but she quickly composed herself again. Then, at the top of her voice, she spat something foreign at both of them, her arms flailing wildly. Logan buried his head in his hands as she slapped and punched him, while Davina made a sharp exit.

Once inside the car, the heaving mess she'd turned into had her whole body in agony. She felt physically incapable of breathing and thought she might die there and then. At one point, she actually wished she *would* die there and then. She even thought about jumping in the Clyde. *Maybe you could jump in with your new sexy bikini on.* She laughed, but there was no pleasure in it, only despair.

It took the best part of the next hour to stop crying and berating herself for being so stupid. A lot of things fell into place now, a lot of things she didn't want to fall into place, the most obvious being not going public with their relationship.

'Oh my God, you can't tell the family about this,' she muttered to her reflection. Then there was the fact that he'd never taken her, or even invited her, over to Saudi Arabia. Was he even bloody there when he said he was?

The tuna in his cupboard and the Collagen cream in his fridge had to belong to Miss fucking-look-at-me-I'm gorgeous-and-pregnant-with-Logan's-wean.

'That's if she's the only one he's screwing behind your back.' Saying this out loud made the reality of the whole sordid situation hit home even harder, bringing fresh hurt and disbelief. He was going to be a dad while sleeping with and – if he was to be believed – falling in love with her. The notion that Logan could be just like the countless men she'd encountered in her profession sickened her to the core. He wasn't that guy! Couldn't be that guy. He was sweet, gentle, kind, considerate, warm, funny, lovable, and . . . well, he was just Logan.

Never before had she given a second thought to the vast amount of women left at home while their men fucked her every which way they fancied and loved it. Never once had she witnessed any form of regret or embarrassment on the men's faces afterwards either. Opening her car door, just in time, she threw up on the tarmac. She was just as bad, just as guilty, as all of them. Now that the shoe was on the other foot, she felt such a hypocrite having the nerve to feel as hurt and used as she did. How would the countless women whose men she'd fucked for money feel if they caught their men with their trousers down, so to speak? And how would they feel about her?

Her head was mush for the whole of the long drive back to the bungalow. The one thought she couldn't get out of her head was that, like Andrew, on this day, the sixth of the sixth, her whole life had just collapsed.

Two days later, Logan sent her a text.

> Dear Davina. I don't know where to start. I know this will be difficult for you to read but believe me when I

say it's just as difficult for me to write. You probably think I'm a heartless, spineless bastard and you have every right. But please please believe me when I say it was never my intention to hurt you. I didn't lie when I told you my life was complicated. I just didn't have the balls to tell you how. I met Pilar two years ago and you could say we have the same arrangement as us. We meet up whenever my work takes me to Spain. She was as devastated as me when she found out she was pregnant. Her religion meant there was no way she would ever have an abortion, I told her I wanted to be a part of my child's life but that didn't mean marriage. Her family have near enough disowned her and I feel terrible about that too. Whenever I came back to you and Scotland there was no pressure, it was great, and I could pretend my life was fine. When you first started talking about getting serious I wanted that so badly but Pilar was already five months pregnant and bitching at me every opportunity she had for being away as often as I was. I wanted to tell you about her and vice versa but bottled out every time. I hoped you'd get fed up with me saying no to telling everyone about us and do what I didn't have the guts to do, break up with me. After Pilar threatened to disappear with my child if I carry on seeing you, we've decided to move in together. I told her there was no need for her threats, you'd never take me back now anyway. Unlike her, you have too much self-respect for that. I have defended you to hell and back again to her. I know that's scant consolation but I hold you in the highest regard. You really are a remarkable woman. Working your way through the ranks of the hotel business and now owning your own home and business. You always were the strongest of the Brown clan, that's why I know in my heart of hearts you'll get over me long before I will get over you. My biggest regret in life will always be that I never plucked up the courage to ask you out when we were younger. Who knows where we would be now. I will always love you, Davina. Love always, Logan. P.S. Try not to hate me too much.

The day she read this, Davina had only gotten out of bed for the toilet. The heartache seemed never-ending. She believed every word he wrote, but knew that it changed nothing. He had used and deceived her in the worst possible way and it hurt like hell. They would never, could never, be together again. Her being the reason for a couple splitting up would have shattered her, but to be the person responsible for splitting a family up? No way. That would kill her. She hadn't yet responded to his text and wasn't sure she ever would. For the next week she did nothing, spoke to no-one, choosing only texts to communicate by. She fobbed Marge off with a story about having laryngitis and feeling shit. Being so wrapped up in the salon and having just started another hairdresser, Marge had barely noticed she wasn't there. She told Davina to take as long as she needed to get better.

Grace was not so easily deceived and, if truth be told, Davina was glad about that. She really needed someone to talk to. The weekend after the worst night of her life, Grace stayed at the bungalow with her. Armed with a glass of Sancerre each, they settled on Davina's couch on the Friday night. Davina hadn't let Grace read the text from Logan, it was too personal, but she gave her a brief summary of it, during which she made short work of the kitchen roll beside her. Grace was her usual tactful self. It was obvious that it pained her to see Davina in such a mess, but she couldn't stand the thought of Logan, or Fuck Face as she now referred to him, getting on with his life while Davina sat here on her own, totally miserable.

'What's the difference between a lying, cheating, two-faced bastard and a bucket of shit?' she asked. 'The bucket.' There was no humour in this. 'You need to forget about Fuck Face, Davina. He's not worth it.'

'But I love him, Grace,' Davina stammered. 'I really love him.'

Grace moved along the couch and pulled Davina's head to her chest. She stroked her friend's hair and sighed. 'I know you do . . . I know you do. But you'll bounce back from this. I know you. You're a lot stronger than you give yourself credit for. At least Fuck Face was right about that. Wank!'

'It doesn't help you calling him names and having a go at him all the time, Grace.' Davina's rebuke was partly muffled by Grace's ample boobs.

'I suppose you're right,' Grace conceded, 'but hell will freeze over before I say anything nice about Fuck Face ever again. Fuck! Even I fancied him at one point. The bastard!'

Davina smiled despite herself. She knew Grace would be hurting as well and she loved her for that. She straightened up and wiped her face. 'You never told me you fancied him.'

Grace shrugged her shoulders. 'I'm only human, and he did have a certain attraction. But let's face it, he was never going to end up on the cover of FHM.' Grace was enjoying herself now, if the cheeky look on her face was anything to go by. 'Plus, I didn't want to say anything when you were with him . . .'

Davina half-scowled, half-smiled at her friend. 'But?'

'But,' Grace echoed, 'compared to Gavin, he didn't look that big in the trouser department.'

Davina's mouth fell open and her first laugh in ages fell out. Whether it was just nerves, she wasn't sure, but the laughter felt good. 'Oh my God, you checked out his package.'

Grace frowned at her in surprise. 'Doesn't everyone?'

'No they bloody don't! And FYI, he might not have been hung like the proverbial horse but he was still a great ride, if you'll pardon the pun.'

'Yeah, but you were the one wearing blinkers.' *Fuck! Don't hold back, Grace.* Fresh tears formed in Davina's eyes. 'Sorry, Davina. You know me, I'm an arsehole,' Grace said, consoling her with a cuddle. 'I can't help myself sometimes.'

They sat that way for ages, Grace gently rocking Davina as she continued to grieve. Eventually, Davina pulled away from Grace's welcoming bosom, blowing her nose like a snorting pig. Then she stood up and sighed, exhausted. 'I'm going to bed,' she said.

Grace pulled herself up off the settee and rubbed Davina's arms affectionately, a faraway look in her eyes.

'What are you thinking about?' Davina asked. 'And please don't say Fuck Face.'

A coy smile crossed Grace's face. 'Do you know who fills a pair of jeans well?' she said with a nudge and a wink. 'If you get my drift.'

'Seriously! Are you still going on about that? I would have thought you were too loved up with Gavin to notice any other man, never mind his lunchbox.'

Grace linked her arm with Davina's and led her out the living room. 'Your Hector,' she said.

Davina pushed Grace away from her, disgusted. 'Ew, yuck! That's my brother you're talking about. I can't believe you just said that. Right! Enough about bloody men and how well-endowed they are! You're supposed to be cheering me up.' Despite herself, Davina started laughing, then stopped abruptly. *Holy shit.* 'Did you two hook up that Saturday after we'd been to Merchant Pride and I went home with–' Her sentence stopped like someone had pressed mute, but she didn't have time to dwell on her anguish. Grace carried on walking to her bedroom, talking over her shoulder.

'Well, if you were disgusted to hear how well-endowed your brother is, you'll certainly not want to know how great he is in the sack. And besides, not all of us kiss and tell.'

Davina, as shocked as she was at this revelation, was grudgingly thankful for it. As she lay in bed, her thoughts – for the first time in what felt like a lifetime – weren't monopolised by Logan bloody McIntyre, and she drifted off to sleep a lot quicker than she had all week.

She slept until 9.46 the next morning, waking to the faint smell of fried meat. She felt well and truly rested, if not any better emotionally. Her bedroom door was thrown open by a fully-dressed Grace, carrying a tray with a breakfast that could choke a horse, a full carrier bag hanging from her wrist.

'Come on, sleeping beauty. Rise and shine,' she chirped.

Davina sat up, stretched, yawned, then rubbed her face, looking between the tray and the bag. 'What's all this?' she asked. 'You're supposed to be the guest, remember.' She got out of bed and headed for the bathroom.

'Where are you going? I've got an idea I think you'll like,' said Grace.

'I need to pee and brush my teeth,' Davina replied, disappearing into the bathroom.

When she returned, the pillows on her bed had been propped up against the headboard. Grace sat against them with a full Scottish fried breakfast balanced on her knees. Davina's was on the tray by the side of her bed. *Jeezo, Steele, I'll never eat all that.*

It took a lot of coaxing from an annoyed Grace, but Davina eventually managed to eat about half the plateful prepared for her. Grace got her to promise to eat more at lunchtime. With breakfast over, attention now turned to the carrier bag. Grace lifted it up and emptied its contents out onto the bed. Images of glorious white sandy beaches with glorious cloudless blue skies covered Davina's quilt.

'So what do you think?' Grace was looking at Davina hopefully. 'A wee bit of sand, sea and surf is just what the doctor ordered. The world's your oyster.'

A smile spread across Davina's face. 'Where did you get these?'

'Early bird catches the worm,' said Grace. 'I've been awake most of the night thinking about you and what would cheer you up, so when I got out of bed I headed into town, bought breakfast, and was the first person in the travel agents.'

Tears of gratitude filled Davina's eyes and they embraced wordlessly.

'I know this won't fix everything you've been through,' Grace mumbled through her own tears, 'but I hate seeing you like this, Davina. You deserve better. You deserve to be happy, and when was the last time you had a holiday?' *Now you're asking.* They separated and wiped their tears away. 'Will you at least have a look at them and think about it?' Davina nodded. 'There's just one thing,' Grace added. 'I won't be able to go with you. I'm using all my holidays up to go on a cruise with Gavin. I was going to tell you sooner, but with everything that's happened, it just didn't feel right.' *I'd be shit company anyway.*

Davina squeezed Grace's hands, genuinely happy for her. 'You lucky bitch.'

They scooped all the brochures up and took them through to the kitchen table. Over a fresh cup of tea, Grace gushed about her up-and-coming Mediterranean cruise with the best thing since sliced bread, Gavin Anderson. As they talked, they jotted down places that looked good on a notepad, to hell with the cost.

'Well, you're a business owner now,' said Grace. 'And besides, that's what our plastic friends are for. God knows you've earned it, Davina. All the shit you've endured, and I don't just mean from Fuck Face.' She held up an open hand. 'I don't want to hear you defend him. Ever. You've worked hard to get where you are today, even if most of the time you've been lying down on the job.'

'Smart arse,' grinned Davina.

Grace ignored her and carried on her argument in favour of a holiday. 'Your face has lit up since we started looking at these brochures. And you've stopped blubbering. Imagine what you'd be like if you were actually there!' She pointed at a random beach on a random page. Her words had stirred something distant in Davina.

'Everywhere does look amazing,' she smiled.

Once Davina had decided on Barbados, they cut out numerous pictures of hotels and stuck them up in multiple places throughout the bungalow. Davina couldn't even pee without seeing sun-kissed white beaches with inviting loungers all along them.

***

In time, Davina got back into work mode, carrying out most of her responsibilities from home – and eventually, she took the train down to Troon. Her thoughts were still all over the place and she didn't want to risk driving while her concentration was elsewhere. The salon hadn't collapsed in her absence. In fact, quite the opposite. The place was buzzing from morning to night. All the staff were pleased to see her and only Amanda the receptionist remarked on how gaunt she looked. Marge insisted that they could cope if and when Davina decided to go on holiday, conceding that she could definitely be doing with a touch of sun.

It was only natural that she arrange a lunch with Angela, who was delighted to accept. When she told her she was thinking of going to Barbados, Angela smiled wistfully. Andrew had taken Jessie to Discovery Bay Resort on St James's Beach, before the onslaught of her illness.

'It's a very peaceful, relaxing place,' she said. 'And if you don't mind me saying, dear, that's exactly what you look like you need.'

She was right. Davina was tired and listless most of the time lately. Some well-deserved R & R might just be in order.

She put the holiday idea on the back burner for a few weeks after that, but had her mind well and truly made up for her when Hector called. She'd been watching telly with the cosy coal fire on and a half-eaten bowl of spaghetti next to her when his name flashed up on her phone. Unwanted and unsolicited images of him and Grace together sprang into her mind. *Thanks, Grace.* Shrugging them off, she stuck on a smile.

'Hello, stranger. How's your promotion to Detective Inspector going?'

Hector laughed. 'I find out in a couple of weeks if I've got it or not, but that's not why I'm phoning.' There was real excitement in his voice, which made Davina smile, even on the inside. This was so un-Hector like. 'Are you sitting down?' he asked.

'Yes, I'm sitting down,' she laughed, curious as to what was going on.

'You'll never believe who showed up at the flat with a wee baby boy.' The laughter stopped, her stomach hit the floor, and what little dinner she'd eaten suddenly threatened to come back up. 'Logan McIntyre!'

Silence . . .

'Are you still there, Davina?' Hector said. 'Did you hear what I said?'

Swallowing hard, she managed to answer, doing her best to hide her shaky voice. 'Yes, I heard you.'

'Fly bugger. He never even mentioned he had a girlfriend, never mind that she was pregnant.' Davina muffled her sobs while her brother gushed on. 'But then again, knowing him, he's probably got a girl in every country he goes to. Uncle Hector, he said, then handed me this wee bundle. It was amazing. You'll be Auntie Davina, won't –'

She hung up on him mid-sentence and turned the mobile off. All the pain and anguish came flooding back. Just as she was starting to get back some semblance of a life, the turmoil returned.

She sobbed intermittently throughout the night, but the next morning she made herself get up and go for one of Marge's power walks. The air was crisp and the river bank empty, so there was no-one to witness the crazy, sometimes crying, sometimes laughing, loony walking at 100 miles an hour. In an unsteady, emotional voice she rebuked herself.

'Of course she's had the baby. It's not like she's an elephant and was going to be pregnant for two years. I fucking wish. No point dwelling on this. He's a da now, end of.' She carried on with her walk, determined not to become upset. 'Time to get on with your life. He's in the past now. It's the future you need to focus on. Life's too short to be miserable all the time and, as Mrs Butcher said, this isn't a dress rehearsal.'

Once back in the comfort of her kitchen, she texted Hector and lied that the battery had ran out on her phone the night before and that she was really shocked and pleased for Logan. Then she sent the hardest text of her life to Logan himself.

Hector told me you're a da. I hope the baby's fine and healthy. I've always believed hate is such a strong emotion and attitude, if you give it head space it can destroy the person inside. For this reason and this reason only, I don't hate you but it's taking so much of my resolve I'm exhausted. How could you do that to me. I read a quote once, it said "Forgiveness is a reflection of loving yourself enough to move on." Personally I think that philosopher must've been stoned. Right now I feel I'll never forgive you and I'm a million miles from loving myself for letting you fool me into loving you. Having said that, I will move on and get over you. Feel free never to get in touch with me again. Davina.

The tears had threatened as she wrote this, but she was determined to move on with her life. So. when she finally sent it and lifted her eyes from the screen and the first thing she saw was the brochure page stuck to the fridge, her mind was made up.

CHAPTER 20

BROWN SAUCE

Lying by the main pool of the Discovery Bay Resort in Barbados, a thinner Davina spread lotion on her stomach. She had to admit that she still wasn't happy with her physique. She could feel the ridge of each rib and it repulsed her. *Can't bloody win with you, Brown.* Despite that, she was relaxed for the first time in what felt like forever. The ache inside her had dulled, although she doubted it would ever heal completely.

Gazing lazily across the water, Davina watched as a couple of young, burly, well-tanned men threw a screaming bikini-clad, caramel-skinned girl into the pool. As she emerged from the sudden chill of the water, her shocked, breathless expression reminded Davina of the Latino hottie, who turned out to be Spanish, in Logan's flat when Davina had finally emerged from his bedroom.

From Davina's room in the resort, the view and scenery were as stunning as they'd been in the brochure. The sky was the deepest shade of blue she'd ever seen and the sand was so white and clean, she didn't mind burning the soles of her feet on the short steps to the sea, which was as clear as crystal and filled with fish of mesmerising colours.

As she drowsed peacefully on one of the loungers by the pool, she was suddenly aware that the sun had disappeared. *Clouds in Barbados? No way.* She opened her eyes slowly and was surprised to see a man hovering above her, blocking out the sun. She blinked and squinted, trying to make out who it was, but it wasn't until he sat in the lounger next to her that she could make out his face. Staring into the most welcoming green eyes she'd ever seen, her jaw dropped. He leaned towards her, speaking in a soft, unsure voice.

'Davina Brown, is it?' She watched, speechless, as he nervously offered out a hand for her to shake. 'Hi, I'm fucking Hamish Hamilton. Pleased to meet you.'

There was a glint in Hamish's eyes, and as he took Davina's hand in his, they both burst out laughing. *Cheers, Grace.*

ACKNOWLEDGMENTS

To Tony and Cameron for always believing in me.

To Gordon Robertson, my literary Mr Miyagi. Thanks so much for your guidance and support, and the belief you showed in my story from the get go. Davina and I are eternally grateful.

To my editor, Dickson Telfer, for your relentless attention to detail. You've taught me so much about writing a book and so much more about the word 'huge'.

To Kellie McCann for having the confidence in my book to recommend I pitch it to Mr Razur Cuts himself, Derek Steel.

To Razur Cuts Books for taking me on and giving *Brown Sauce* the chance I always hoped for.

Born in Manchester in 1967, but having lived in Camelon, Falkirk for most of her life, Pauline Lagan is the second youngest of seven siblings, all of whom have the ability to see the funny side of life, regardless of the circumstances.

Known for telling elaborate, entertaining stories, Pauline decided she'd give writing a novel a bash. *Brown Sauce* was the result.

She lives in Camelon with her long-term partner, Tony, with whom she has one son, Cameron.

BOOKS

razurcuts.com

@razurcutsmag
@PLaganAuthor